Julia James lives in [...] verdant countryside [...] She also loves the M[...] and history, with its s[...] groves, ancient ruins [...] seas. 'The perfect setting for romance!' she says. 'Rivalled only by the lush tropical heat of the Caribbean—palms swaying by a silver sand beach lapped by turquoise water... What more could lovers want?'

Robyn Donald lives in Northland, New Zealand, in a rural landscape bordered by the sea and formed by ancient volcanoes. An avid reader, she discovered romance novels when pregnant with her second child and decided to try her hand at writing one. Ten years later, after abandoning more manuscripts than she cares to remember, her patient husband suggested she actually finish one and send it away. To her utter astonishment and joy it was accepted—with revisions, of course. Since then she's completed another eighty-six, and is thrilled at the thought of some day achieving a century.

THE GREEK'S SECRET SON

JULIA JAMES

CLAIMED BY HER BILLIONAIRE PROTECTOR

ROBYN DONALD

MILLS & BOON

First Published in Great Britain 2018
by Mills & Boon, an imprint of HarperCollins*Publishers*
1 London Bridge Street, London, SE1 9GF

The Greek's Secret Son © 2018 by Julia James

Claimed by Her Billionaire Protector © 2018 by Robyn Donald Kingston

ISBN: 978-0-263-93525-7

MIX
Paper from
responsible sources
FSC C007454

This book is produced from independently certified FSC™ paper
to ensure responsible forest management.
For more information visit www.harpercollins.co.uk/green.

Printed and bound in Spain
by CPI, Barcelona

THE GREEK'S
SECRET SON

JULIA JAMES

To all care-workers everywhere.
How grateful we are to them.
Thank you to you all.

CHAPTER ONE

A FINE DRIZZLE was threatening. Low cloud loured over the country churchyard and the wintry air was damp and chill as Christine stood beside the freshly dug grave. Grief tore at her for the kindly man who had come to her rescue when the one man on earth she'd most craved had been lost to her. But now Vasilis Kyrgiakis was gone, his heart having finally failed as it had long threatened to do. Turning her from wife to widow.

The word tolled in her mind as she stood, head bowed, a lonely figure. Everyone had been very kind to her for Vasilis had been well regarded, even though she was aware that it had been cause for comment that she had been so much younger than her middle-aged husband. But since the most prominent family in the neighbourhood, the Barcourts, had accepted their Greek-born neighbour and his young wife, so had everyone else.

For her part, Christine had been fiercely loyal—grateful—to her husband, even at this final office for him, and felt her eyes misting with tears as the vicar spoke the words of the committal and the coffin was lowered slowly into the grave.

'We therefore commit his body to the ground, earth to earth, ashes to ashes, dust to dust, in sure and certain hope of the Resurrection…'

The vicar gave his final blessing and then he was guiding her away, with the soft thud of earth falling on wood behind her.

Eyes blurred, she felt herself stumble suddenly, lifting her head to steady herself. Her gaze darted outwards, to the lychgate across the churchyard, where so lately her husband's body had rested before its slow procession from the hearse beyond into the church.

And she froze, with a sense of arctic chill.

A car had drawn up beside the hearse—black, too, with dark-tinted windows. And standing beside it, his suit as black as the hearse, his figure tall, unmoving, was a man she knew well. A man she had not seen for five long years.

The last man in the world she wanted to see again.

Anatole stood motionless, watching the scene play out in the churchyard. Emotions churned within him, but his gaze was fixed only on the slight, slender figure, all in black, standing beside the priest in his long white robe at the open grave of his uncle. The uncle he had not seen—had refused to see—since the unbelievable folly of his marriage.

Anger stabbed at him.

At himself.

At the woman who had trapped his vulnerable uncle into marrying her.

He still did not know how, and it had been *his* fault that she had done so.

I did not see what ambition I was engendering.

It was an ambition that had spawned her own attempt to trap him—when thwarted, she had catastrophically turned on his hapless uncle. The uncle who—a life-long bachelor, a mild-mannered scholar, with none of the wary suspicions that Anatole himself had cultivated throughout his life—had proved an easy target for her.

His gaze rested on her now, as she became aware of his presence. Her expression showed naked shock. Then, with an abrupt movement, he wheeled about, threw himself inside his car and, with a spray of gravel, pulled away, accelerating down the quiet country lane.

Emotion churned again, plunging him back into the past.

Five long years ago…

* * *

Anatole drummed his fingers frustratedly on the dashboard. The London rush-hour traffic was gridlocked and had come to a halt, even in this side street. But it was not just the traffic jam that was putting him in a bad mood. It was the prospect of the evening ahead.

With Romola.

His obsidian-dark eyes glinted with unsuppressed annoyance and his sculpted mouth tightened. She was eyeing him up as marriage material. *That* was precisely what he did not welcome.

Marriage was the last thing he wanted! Not for him—no, thank you!

His eyes clouded as he thought of the jangled, tangled mess that was his own parents' lives. Both his parents had married multiple times, and he had been born only seven months after their wedding—evidence they'd both been unfaithful to their previous spouses. Nor had they been faithful to each other, and his mother had walked out when he was eleven.

Both were now remarried—yet again. He'd stopped counting or caring. He'd known all along that providing their only child with a stable family was unimportant to them. Now, in his twenties, his sole purpose, or so it seemed, was to keep the Kyrgiakis coffers filled to the brim in order to fund their lavish lifestyles and expensive divorces.

With his first class degree in economics from a top university, his MBA from a world-famous business school and his keen commercial brain, this was a task that Anatole could perform more than adequately, and he knew he benefitted from it as well. Work hard, play hard—that was the motto he lived by—and he kept the toxic ties of marriage far, far away from him.

His frown deepened and his thoughts of Romola darkened. He'd hoped that her high-flying City career would stop her from having ambitions to marry him, yet here she was, like all the tedious others, thinking to make herself Mrs Anatole Kyrgiakis.

Exasperation filled him.

Why do they always want to marry me?

It was such a damn nuisance…

A dozen vehicles ahead of him he saw the traffic light turn to green. A moment later the chain of traffic was lurching forward and his foot depressed the accelerator.

And at exactly that moment a woman stepped right in front of his car…

Tia's eyes were hazed with unshed tears, her thoughts full of poor Mr Rodgers. She'd been with her ill, elderly client to the end—which had come that morning. His death had brought back all the memories of her own mother's passing, less than two years ago, when her failing hold on life had finally been severed.

Now, though, as she trudged along, lugging her ancient unwieldy suitcase, she knew she had to get to her agency before it closed for the day. She needed to be despatched to her next assignment, for as a live-in carer she had no home of her own.

She would need to cross the street to reach the agency, which was down another side street across the main road, and with the traffic so jammed from the roadworks further ahead she realised she might as well cross here. Other people were darting through the stationary traffic, which was only moving in fits and starts.

Hefting her heavy suitcase with a sudden impulse, she stepped off the pavement…

With a reaction speed he had not known he possessed, Anatole slammed down on the brake, urgently sounding his horn.

But for all his prompt action he heard the sickening thud of his car bumper impacting on something solid. Saw the woman crumple in front of his eyes.

With an oath, he hit the hazard lights then leapt from the car, stomach churning. There on the road was the woman, sunk to her knees, one hand gripping a suitcase that was all but under his bumper. The suitcase had split open, its locks crushed, and Anatole could see clothes spilling out.

The woman lifted her head, stared blankly at Anatole, apparently unaware of the danger she'd been in.

Furious words burst from him. 'What the hell did you think you were doing? Are you a complete idiot, stepping out like that?'

Relief that the only casualty seemed to be the suitcase had flooded through Anatole, making him yell. But the woman who clearly had some kind of death wish was perfectly all right—except that as he finished yelling the blank look vanished into a storm of weeping.

Instantly his anger deflated, and he hunkered down beside the sobbing woman.

'Are you OK?' he asked.

His voice wasn't angry now, but his only answer was a renewed burst of sobbing.

Obviously not, he answered his own question.

With a heavy sigh he took the disgorged clothes, stuffed them randomly back into the suitcase, and made a futile attempt to close the lid. Then he took her arm.

'Let's get you back on the pavement safely,' he said.

He started to draw her upright. Her face lifted. Tears were pouring in an avalanche down her cheeks, and broken, breathless sobs came from her throat. But Anatole was not paying attention to her emotional outburst. As he stood her up on her feet, his brain, as if after a slow motion delay, registered two things.

The woman was younger than he'd first thought. And even weeping she was breathtakingly, jaw-droppingly lovely.

Blonde, heart-shaped face, blue-eyes, rosebud mouth...

He felt something plummet inside him, then ascend, taking shape, rearranging everything. His expression changed.

'You're all right,' he heard himself say. His voice was much gentler, with no more anger in it. 'It was a narrow escape, but you made it.'

'I'm so sorry!' The words stuttered from her as she heaved in breath chokily.

Anatole shook his head, negating her apology. 'It's all right. No harm done. Except to your suitcase.'

As she took in its broken state her face crumpled in distress. With sudden decision Anatole hefted the suitcase into the boot of his car, opened the passenger door.

'I'll drive you to wherever you're going. In you get,' he instructed, all too conscious of the traffic building up behind him, horns tooting noisily.

He propelled her into the car, despite her stammering protest. Throwing himself into his driver's seat, he turned off the hazard lights and gunned the engine.

Absently, he found himself wondering if he would have gone to so much personal inconvenience as he was now had the person who'd stepped right out in front of his car not been the breathtakingly lovely blonde that she was...

'It's no problem,' he said. 'Now, where to?'

She stared blankly. 'Um...' She cast her eyes frantically through the windscreen. 'That side street down there.'

Anatole moved off. The traffic was still crawling, and he threw his glance at his unexpected passenger. She was sniffing, wiping at her cheeks with her fingers. As the traffic halted at a red light Anatole reached for the neatly folded clean handkerchief in his jacket pocket and turned to mop at her face himself. Then he drew back, job done.

Her eyes were like saucers, widening to plates as she looked back at him. And the expression in them suddenly stilled him completely.

Slowly, very slowly, he smiled...

Tia was staring. Gawping. Her heart was thudding like a hammer, and her throat was tight from the storm of weeping triggered by the man whose car she had so blindly, stupidly, stepped in front of when he had laid into her for her carelessness. But it had been building since the grim, sad ordeal of watching an elderly, mortally ill man take his leave of life, reminding her so much of the tearing grief she'd felt at her mother's death.

Now something else was overpowering her. Her eyes were distended, and she was unable to stop staring. Staring at the man who had just mopped her face and was now sitting back in his seat, watching her staring at him with wide eyes filled with wonder...

She gulped silently, still staring disbelievingly, and words tumbled silently, chaotically in her head.

Black hair, like sable, and a face as if...as if it was carved... Eyes like dark chocolate and smoky long, long lashes. Cheekbones a mile high... And his mouth...quirking at the corner like that. I can feel my stomach hollowing out, and I don't know where to look, but I just want to go on gazing at him, because he looks exactly as if he's stepped right out of one of my daydreams... The most incredible man I've ever seen in my life...

Because how could it be otherwise? How could she possibly, in her restricted, constricted life, during which she had done nothing and seen nothing, ever have encountered a man like this?

Of course she hadn't! She'd spent her teenage years looking after her mother, and her days now were spent in caring for the sick and the elderly. There had never been opportunity or time for romantic adventures, for boyfriends, fashion, excitement. Her only romances had been in her head—woven out of time spent staring out of windows, sitting by bedsides, attending to all the chores and tasks that live-in carers had to undertake.

Except that here—right now, right here—was a man

who could have sprung right out of her romantic fantasies…everything she had ever daydreamed about.

Tall, dark and impossibly handsome.

And he was here—right *here*—beside her. A daydream made real.

She gulped again. His smile deepened, indenting around his sculpted mouth, making a wash of weakness go through her again, deeper still.

'Better?' he murmured.

Silently, she nodded, still unable to tear her gaze away. Just wanting to go on gazing and gazing at him.

Then, abruptly, she became hideously aware that although *he* looked exactly as if he'd stepped out of one of her torrid daydreams—a fantasy made wondrously, amazingly real—*she* was looking no such thing. In fact the complete, mortifying opposite.

Burningly, she was brutally aware of how she must look to him—the very last image a man like him should see in any daydream, made real or not. Red eyes, snuffling nose, tear runnels down her cheeks, hair all mussed and not a scrap of make-up. Oh, yes—and she was wearing ancient jeans and a bobbled, battered jumper that hung on her body like a rag. What a disaster…

As the traffic light changed to green Anatole turned into the side street she'd indicated. 'Where now?' he asked.

It came to him that he was hoping it was some way yet. Then he crushed the thought. Picking up stray females off the street—literally, in this case!—was not a smart idea. Even though…

His glance went to her again. *She really is something to look at! Even with those red eyes and rubbish clothes.*

A thought flashed across his mind. One he didn't want but that was there all the same.

How good could she look?

Immediately he cut the thought.

No—don't ask that. Don't think that. Drive her to her destination, then drive on—back to your own life.

Yes, that was what he *should* do—he knew that perfectly well. But in the meantime he could hardly drive in silence. Besides, he didn't want her bursting into those terrifyingly heavy sobs again.

'I'm sorry you were so upset,' he heard himself saying. 'But I hope it's taught you never, *ever* to step out into traffic.'

'I'm so, *so* sorry,' she said again. Her voice was husky now. 'And I'm so, *so* sorry for…for crying like that. It wasn't you! Well, I mean…not really. Only when you yelled at me—'

'It was shock,' Anatole said. 'I was terrified I'd killed you.' He threw a rueful look at her. 'I didn't mean to make you cry.'

She shook her head. 'It wasn't because of that—not really,' she said again. 'It was because—'

She stopped. All thoughts of daydream heroes vanished as the memory of how she'd spent the night at the bedside of a dying man assailed her again.

'Because…?' Anatole prompted, throwing her another brief glance. He found he liked throwing her glances. But that he would have preferred them not to be brief…

Perhaps they need not be—

She was answering him, cutting across the thought he should not have. Most *definitely* should not have.

'It was because of poor Mr Rodgers!' she said in a rush. 'He died this morning. I was there. I was his care worker. It was so sad. He was very old, but all the same—' She broke off, a catch in her voice. 'It reminded me of when my mother died—'

She broke off again, and Anatole could hear the half-sob in her voice. 'I'm sorry,' he said, because it seemed the only thing to say. 'Was your mother's death recent?'

She shook her head. 'No, it was nearly two years ago,

but it brought it all back. She had MS—all the time I was growing up, really—and after my father was killed I looked after her. That's why I became a care worker. I had the experience, and anyway there wasn't much else I could do, and a live-in post was essential because I don't have a place of my own yet—'

She broke off, suddenly horribly aware that she was saying all these personal things to a complete stranger.

She swallowed. 'I'm just going to my agency's offices now—to get a new assignment, somewhere to go tonight.' Her voice changed. 'That's it—just there!'

She pointed to an unprepossessing office block and Anatole drew up alongside it. She got out, tried the front door. It did not open. He stepped out beside her, seeing the notice that said 'Closed'.

'What now?' he heard himself saying in a tight voice.

Tia turned to stare at him, trying to mask the dismay in her face. 'Oh, I'll find a cheap hotel for tonight. There's probably one close by I can walk to.'

Anatole doubted that—especially with her broken suitcase.

His eyes rested on her. She looked lost and helpless. And very, very lovely.

As before, sudden decision took him. There was a voice in his head telling him he was mad, behaving like an idiot, but he ignored it. Instead, he smiled suddenly.

'I've got a much better idea,' he said. 'Look, you can't move that broken suitcase a metre, let alone trail around looking for a mythical cheap hotel in London! So here's what I propose. Why not stay the night at my flat? I won't be there,' he added immediately, because instantly panic had filled her blue eyes, 'so you'll have the run of it. Then you can buy yourself a new suitcase in the morning and head to your agency.' He smiled. 'How would that be?'

She was staring at him as though she dared not believe

what he was saying. 'Are you sure?' That disbelief was in her voice, but her panic was ebbing away.

'I wouldn't offer otherwise,' Anatole replied.

'It's incredibly kind of you,' she answered, her voice sounding husky, her eyes dropping away from his. 'I'm being a total pain to you—'

'Not at all,' he said. 'So, do you accept?'

He smiled again—the deliberate smile that he used when he wanted people to do what he wanted. It worked this time too. Tremulously she nodded.

Refusing to pay any attention to the voice in his head telling him he was an insane idiot to make such an offer to a complete stranger, however lovely, Anatole helped her back into the car and set off again, heading into Mayfair, where his flat was.

He glanced at her. She was sitting very still, hands in her lap, looking out through the windscreen, not at him. She still looked as if she could not believe this was really happening.

He took the next step in making it real for her. For him as well.

'Maybe we should introduce ourselves properly? I'm Anatole Kyrgiakis.'

It was odd to say his own name, because he usually didn't have to, and certainly when he did he expected his surname, at least, to be recognised instantly. Possibly followed by a quick glance to ascertain that he meant *the* Kyrgiakis family. This time, however, his name drew no reaction other than her turning her head to look at him as he spoke.

'Tia Saunders,' she responded shyly.

'Hello, Tia,' Anatole said in a low voice, with a flickering smile.

He saw a flush of colour in her cheeks, then had to pay attention to the traffic again. He let her be as he drove on, needing to concentrate now and wanting her to feel a little more relaxed about what was happening. But she was still clearly tense as he pulled up outside his elegant Georgian town house and guided her indoors, carrying her broken suitcase.

The greeting from the concierge at the desk in the wide hallway seemed to make her shrink against him, and as they entered his top-floor apartment she gave a gasp.

'I can't stay here!' she exclaimed, dismay in her voice. 'I might mess something up!'

Her eyes raced around, taking in a long white sofa, covered in silk cushions, a thick dove-grey carpet that matched the lavish drapes at the wide windows. It was like something out of a movie—absolutely immaculate and obviously incredibly expensive.

Anatole gave a laugh. 'Just don't spill coffee on anything,' he said.

She shook her head violently. 'Please, don't even *say* that!' she cried, aghast at the very thought.

His expression changed. She seemed genuinely worried. He walked up to her. Found himself taking her hand with his free one even without realising it. Patting it reassuringly.

'Speaking of coffee... I could murder a cup! What about you?'

She nodded, swallowing. 'Th...thank you,' she stammered.

'Good. I'll get the machine going. But let me show you to your room first—and, look, why not take a shower, freshen up? You must have had a gruelling night, from what you've said.'

He relinquished her hand, hefted up the broken suitcase again, mentally deciding he'd get a new one delivered by the concierge within the hour, and carried it through to one of the guest bedrooms.

She followed after him, still glancing about her with an air of combined nervousness and wide-eyed amazement at her surroundings, as if she'd never seen anything like it in her life. Which, he realised, she probably never had.

An unusual sense of satisfaction darted within him. It was a good feeling to give this impoverished, waif-like girl, who'd clearly had a pretty sad time of it—both parents dead and a poorly paid job involving distressing end-of-life care—a brief taste of luxury. He found himself wanting her to enjoy it.

Setting down the suitcase, which immediately sprang open again, he pointed out the en suite bathroom, then with another smile left her to it, heading for the kitchen.

Five minutes later the coffee was brewing and he was sprawled on the sofa, checking his emails—trying very, very hard not to let his mind wander to his unexpected guest taking her shower...

He wondered just how far her charms extended beyond her lovely face. He suspected a lot further. She was slender—he'd seen that instantly—but it hadn't made her flat-chested. No, indeed, Even though she was wearing cheap, unflattering clothes, he'd seen the soft swell of her breasts beneath. And she was petite—much more so than the women he usually selected for himself.

Maybe that was because of his own height—over six foot—or maybe it was because the kind of women he went out with tended to be self-assured, self-confident high-achieving females who were his counterparts in many ways, striding through the world knowing their own worth, very sure of themselves and their attractions.

Women like Romola.

His expression changed. Before Tia had plunged in front of his car he'd made the decision to cut Romola out of his life—so why not do that right now? He'd text her to say he couldn't see her tonight after all, that something had come up, and that it was unlikely he'd be back in London any time soon, Say that perhaps they should both accept their time together had run its course...

With a ruthlessness that he could easily exercise whenever he felt himself targeted by a woman wanting more of him than he cared to give, he sent the text, softening the blow with the despatch of a diamond bracelet as a farewell gift as a sop to Romola's considerable ego. Then, with a sense of relief, he turned his thoughts back to tonight.

A smile started around his mouth, his eyes softening slightly. He'd already played out King Cophetua and the Beggar Maid in offering Tia the run of his flat, so why not go the whole hog and give her an evening she would always remember? Champagne, fine dining—the works!

It was something he'd take a bet that she'd never experienced in her deprived life before.

Of course it went without saying that that would be *all* he'd be offering her. He himself would not be staying here—he'd make his way over to the Mayfair hotel where his father kept a permanent suite. Of course he would.

Anything else was completely out of the question—however lovely she was.

Completely out, he told himself sternly.

CHAPTER TWO

TIA STOOD IN a state of physical bliss as the hot water poured over her body, foaming into rich suds the shampoo and body wash she'd found in the basket of expensive-looking toiletries on the marble-topped vanity unit. Never in her whole life had she had such a lavish, luxurious shower.

By the time she stepped out, her hair wrapped up in a fleecy towel, another huge bath sheet wrapped around her, she felt reborn. She still hadn't really got her head around what was happening because it all just seemed like a fairytale—swept off by a prince who took her breath away.

He's just so gorgeous! So incredibly gorgeous! And he's being so kind! He could just as easily have left me on the pavement with my broken suitcase. Driven away and not cared!

But he hadn't driven away—he'd brought her here, and how could she possibly have said no? In all her confined, unexciting life, dedicated to caring for her poor mother and for others, when had anything like this *ever* happened except in her daydreams?

She lifted her chin, staring at her reflection, resolve in her eyes. Whatever was happening, she was going to seize this moment!

She whirled about, yanking off the turban towel, letting her damp hair tumble down, then rapidly sorting through her clothes, desperate to find something—anything—that was more worthy of the occasion than her ancient jeans and baggy top. Of course she had nothing at all that was remotely suitable, but at least she had something that was an improvement. She might never hope to be able to look like a fairytale princess, but she'd do her damnedest!

As she walked back into that pristine, palatial lounge her eyes went straight to the darkly sprawling figure relaxed on the white sofa. Dear Lord, but he was unutterably gorgeous!

He'd shed his formal business jacket and loosened his tie, undone his top button and turned up his cuffs. And through her veins came that same devastating rush she'd felt before, weakening her limbs, making her dizzy with its impact.

He rose to his feet. 'There you are.' He smiled. 'Come and sit down and have your coffee.'

He nodded to where he'd set out a plate of pastries, extracted from the freezer and microwaved by his own fair hand into tempting, fragrant warmth. Two had already been consumed, but there were plenty left.

'Are you on a diet?' he asked convivially. 'Or can I tempt you?'

Anatole watched with a sense of familiarity as the colour rushed into her face and then out again. Maybe he shouldn't have used the word 'tempt'. He had the damnedest feeling that it wasn't the thought of the pastries that were making her colour up like that.

Snap!

Because if *she* was experiencing temptation, then he knew for sure that he was as well. And with good reason…

She'd changed her clothes and, although they were still clearly cheap and high street, they were a definite improvement. She'd put on a skirt—a floaty cotton one, in Indian print—and topped it with a turquoise tee shirt that gave her a whole lot more figure than the baggy jumper she'd had on previously. On top of that, her freshly washed hair was loose now, still damp, but curling in a tousled mane around her shoulders. The redness had finally gone from her eyes, and her skin was clear and unblemished. Her lips rosy, tender…

Still the ingénue, definitely…but no longer a sad waif.

With an expression of intense self-consciousness on her face, she gingerly sat herself down on the sofa, slanting her slender legs. He saw her hands were shaking slightly as she took the coffee he'd poured with a low murmur of thanks.

She drank it thirstily, hoping it would steady her wildly jangling nerves, and her eyes jumped again to Anatole to drink in the gorgeous reality of his presence. Her eyes met his and she realised he was watching her, a smile playing around his mouth. It was a smile that sent little quivers shimmering through her and made her breath shallow.

'Have a pastry,' he said, pushing the plate towards her.

Their warm, yeasty cinnamon scent caught at her, reminding her that she'd not had a chance to eat all day. She took one, grabbing a thick, richly patterned paper napkin as she did so, terrified of dropping buttery flakes on the pristine upholstery or the carpet.

Anatole watched her polish off the pastry, letting his eyes drift over the sweet perfection of her heart-shaped face, the cerulean eyes, the delicate arch of her brows, the soft curls of her fair hair.

She is breathtakingly lovely—and she is taking my breath away just looking at her…

He glanced at his watch. It was coming up to seven, though the evenings were still light. They could drink champagne on his roof terrace. But first…best to order dinner.

He reached for his laptop, brought up the website for the service he used when dining in, then tilted the screen towards her. 'Take a look,' he invited, 'and see what you'd like for dinner. I'm going to order in.'

Immediately—predictably—she shook her head. 'Oh, no, please—not for me. I'm absolutely fine just eating these pastries.'

'Yes, well, I'm not,' he rejoined affably. 'Come on—take a look. What sort of food do you like best? And do *not*,' he added sternly, 'say pizza! Or Indian. Or Chinese. I'm talking gourmet food here—take your pick.'

Wide-eyed, Tia stared at the long page of menu options on the screen. She couldn't understand most of them. She swallowed.

'Will you let me choose for you?' Anatole asked, realising her dilemma.

She nodded gratefully.

'Anything you're allergic to?' he asked.

She shook her head, but all the same he chose relatively safe options—no shellfish, no nuts. A midnight dash to A&E was *not* the way he wanted this evening to end.

And you're not going to let it end the way you're thinking right now either! his conscience admonished him sternly.

Not even when he was leaning towards her, and she towards him, so they could both read the screen, and he could catch the fresh scent of her body. All he would have to do to touch her would be to lift his hand, let it slide through those softly drying curls, splay his fingers around the nape of her neck and draw that sweet, tender mouth to his...

He straightened abruptly, busying himself with putting the order through, then closing his laptop. Time to fetch the champagne.

He returned a few moments later, with a bottle at the perfect temperature from his thermostatically controlled wine store and two flutes dangling from his hand. He crossed to the picture window, sliding it open.

'Come and see the view,' he said invitingly.

Tia got to her feet, following him out on to a roofline terrace with a stone balustrade along it. She was still in a daze. Was he really intending to have dinner with her?

Drink champagne with her? Her heart was beating faster, she knew, just at the very thought of it.

As she stepped out the warm evening air enveloped her. Sunshine was still catching the tops of the trees visible in the park beyond. Nor was that the only greenery visible—copious large stone pots adorned the terrace, lush with plants, creating a little oasis.

'Oh, it's so lovely!' she exclaimed spontaneously, her face lighting up.

Anatole smiled, feeling a kick go through him at her visible pleasure, at how it made her eyes shine, and set down the champagne and flutes on a little ironwork table flanked by two chairs.

'A private green haven,' he said. 'Cities aren't my favourite places, so when I'm forced to be in them—which is all too often, alas—I like to be as green as I can. It's one of the reasons,' he went on, 'that I like penthouse apartments—they come with roof terraces.'

He paused to open the champagne with a soft pop of the cork, then handed her one of the empty flutes.

'Keep it slightly tilted,' he instructed as he poured it half full, letting the liquid foam, but not too much. Then he filled his own glass and lifted it to her, looking down at her. She really was petite, he found himself thinking again. And for some reason it made him feel…protective.

It was an odd thought. Unfamiliar to him when it came to women.

He smiled down at her. She was gazing up at him, and the expression in her eyes sent that kick through him again. He lifted his glass, indicating that she should do the same, which she did, glancing at the foaming liquid as if she could not believe it was in her hand.

'*Yammas,*' he said.

She looked confused.

'It's *cheers* in Greek,' he elucidated.

'Oh,' she said, '*that's* what you are! I knew you must be foreign, because of your name, but I didn't know what—'

She coloured. Had she sounded rude? She hadn't meant to. London was incredibly multicultural—there had been no reason to say he was 'foreign'. He was probably as British as she was—

'I'm sorry,' she said, looking dismayed. 'I didn't mean to imply—'

'No,' he said, reassuringly. 'I *am* foreign. I'm a Greek national. But I do a lot of work in London because it's a major financial hub. I live in Greece, though.' He smiled again, wanting to set her at her ease. 'Have you ever been to Greece? For a holiday, maybe?'

Tia shook her head. 'We went to Spain when I was little,' she said. 'When my dad was still alive and before mum got MS.' She swallowed, looking away.

'It's good to have memories,' Anatole said quietly. 'Especially of family holidays as a child.'

Yes—it *was* good to have such memories. Except he didn't have any. His school holidays—breaks from boarding at the exclusive international school in Switzerland he'd attended from the age of seven—had been spent either at friends' houses or rattling around the huge Kyrgiakis mansion in Athens, with no one except the servants around.

His parents had been busy with their own more important lives.

When he'd reached his teens he'd taken to spending a few weeks with his uncle—his father's older brother. Vasilis had never been interested in business or finance. He was a scholar, content to bury himself in libraries and museums, using the Kyrgiakis money to fund archaeological research and sponsor the arts. He disapproved of his younger brother's amatory dissoluteness, but never criticised him openly. He was a lifelong bachelor, and Anatole had found him kindly, but remote—though very helpful in coaching him in exam revision and for university entrance.

Anatole had come to value him increasingly for his wise, quiet good sense.

He cleared his thoughts. 'Well, here's to your first trip to Greece—which I'm sure you'll make one day.' He smiled, tilting his glass again at Tia, then taking a mouthful of the softly beading champagne. He watched her do likewise, very tentatively, as if she could not believe she was doing so.

'Is this real champagne?' she asked as she lowered her glass again.

Anatole's mouth twitched. 'Definitely,' he assured her. 'Do you like it?'

And suddenly, out of nowhere, a huge smile split her face, transforming the wary nervousness of her expression. 'It's gorgeous!' she exclaimed.

Just like you are!

Those were the words blazing in her head, as she gazed at the man who was standing there, who had scooped up the crumpled heap she'd made on the road and brought her here, to this beautiful apartment, to drink champagne—the first champagne she'd ever tasted.

Should I pinch myself? Is this real—is this really, really real?

She wanted it to be—oh, how she wanted it to be! But she could scarcely believe it.

Maybe the single mouthful of champagne had made her bold. 'This is so incredibly kind of you!' she said in a rush.

Kind? The word resonated in Anatole's head. *Was* he being kind? He'd told himself he was, but was the truth different?

Am I just being incredibly, recklessly self-indulgent?

He lifted his glass again. Right now he didn't care. His only focus was on this lovely woman—so young, so fresh, so breathtakingly captivating in her simple natural beauty.

She is practising no arts to attract me, making no eyes at me, and she asks nothing of me—

He smiled, his expression softening, a tinge of humour at his mouth. 'Drink up,' he said, 'we've a whole bottle to get through!'

He took another mouthful of the fine vintage, encouraging her to do likewise.

She was looking around her as she sipped, out over the rooftops of the houses nearby. 'It's nice to think,' she heard herself say, 'that even though up here used to be the attics, where the servants lived, they got this view!'

Anatole laughed. 'Well, the attics have certainly gone up in the world since then!' he answered, thinking of the multi-million-pound price tag this apartment had come with. 'And it's good that those days are gone. Any house staff these days get a lot better than attics to live in, and they are very decently paid.'

Probably, he found himself adding silently, *a lot more than you get as a care worker...*

He frowned. Essential though such work was, surely it would be good if she aspired to something more in her life?

'Tell me,' he said, taking some more of his champagne, then topping up both their glasses, 'what do you want to do with your life? I know care work is important, but surely you won't want to do it for ever?'

Even as he asked the question it dawned on him that never in his life had he come across anyone from her background. All the women he knew were either in high-powered careers or trust fund princesses. Completely a different species from this young woman with her sad, impoverished, hard-working life.

Tia bit her lip, feeling awkward suddenly. 'Well, because I was off school a lot, looking after Mum, I never passed my exams, so I can't really go to college. And, though I'm saving from my wages, I can't afford accommodation of my own yet.'

'Have you no family at all to help you?' Anatole frowned.

She shook her head. 'It was just Dad, Mum, and me.'

She looked at him. Nearly a glass down on the champagne and she was definitely feeling bold. This might be a daydream, but she was going to indulge herself to the hilt with it.

'What about you?' she asked. 'Aren't Greek families huge?'

Anatole gave a thin smile. 'Not mine,' he said tersely. 'I'm an only child too.' He looked into his champagne flute. 'My parents are divorced, and both of them are married to other people now. I don't see much of them.'

That was from choice. His and theirs. The only regular Kyrgiakis family gathering was the annual board meeting when all the shareholders gathered—himself, his parents and his uncle, and a few distant cousins as well. All of them looked to him to find out how much more money he'd poured into the family coffers, thanks to his business acumen.

'Oh,' Tia said, sympathetically, 'that's a shame.'

An unwelcome flicker went through her. She didn't want to think that fantasy males like this one could have dysfunctional families like ordinary people. Surely when they lived in fantastic, deluxe places like this, and drank vintage champagne, they couldn't have problems like other people?

Anatole gave another thin smile. 'Not particularly,' he countered. 'I'm used to it.'

Absently, he wondered why he'd talked about his family at all. He never did that with women. He glanced at his watch. They should go indoors. Dinner would be arriving shortly and he didn't want to think about his family—or his lack of any that he bothered about. Even Vasilis, kindly though he was, lived in a world of his own, content with his books and his philanthropic activities in the arts world.

He guided his guest indoors. Dusk was gathering outside and he switched on the terrace lighting, casting low pools of soft light around the greenery, giving it an elvish glow.

Once again, Tia was enchanted. 'Oh, that's so pretty!' she exclaimed, as the effect sprang to life. 'It looks like a fairyland!'

She immediately felt childish saying such a thing, even if it were true, but Anatole laughed, clearly amused.

The house phone rang, alerting him that dinner was on its way up, and five minutes later he and Tia were seated, tucking in to their first course—a delicate white fish terrine.

'This is delicious!' she exclaimed, her face lighting up as she ate.

She said the same thing about the chicken bathed in a creamy sauce, with tiny new potatoes and fresh green beans—simple, but beautifully cooked.

Anatole smiled indulgently. 'Eat up,' he urged.

It was good to see a woman eating with appetite, not picking at her food. Good, too, to see the open pleasure in her face at dining with him, her appreciation of everything. Including the champagne as he topped up her glass yet again.

Careful. He heard the warning voice in his head. *Don't give her more than she can handle.*

Or, indeed, more than he could handle either—not when he still had to get to the hotel for the night. But that wasn't yet, and for now he could continue to enjoy every moment of their evening.

A sense of well-being settled over him. Deliberately, he kept the conversation between them light, doing most of the talking himself, but drawing her out as well, intent on making her feel relaxed and comfortable.

'If you do ever manage to get to Greece for a holiday, what kind of thing would you most like doing? Are you a beach bunny or do you like sightseeing? There's plenty of both across the mainland and the islands. And if you like ancient history there's no better place in the world than Greece, to my mind!' he said lightly.

'I don't really know anything about ancient history,' she answered, colouring slightly.

She felt uncomfortable, being reminded of her lack of education. Such realities got in the way of this wonderful, blissful daydream she was having. This real-life fairytale.

'You've heard of the Parthenon?' Anatole prompted.

A look of confusion passed over Tia's face. 'Um…is it a temple?'

'Yes, the most famous in the world—on the Acropolis in Athens. A lot of tall stone pillars around a rectangular ruin.'

'Oh, yes, I've seen pictures!' she acknowledged, relieved that she'd been right.

'Well, there you are, then.' He smiled, and went on to tell her the kind of information most tourists gathered from a visit to the site, then moved on to the other attractions that his homeland offered.

Whether or not she took it all in, he didn't know. Mostly she just gazed at him, her beautiful blue eyes wide—something he found himself enjoying. Especially when he held her gaze and saw the flush of colour mount in her cheeks, her hand reaching hurriedly for the glass of iced water beside her champagne flute.

As they moved on to the final course—a light-as-air pavlova—he opened a bottle of sweet dessert wine, calculating that she would find it more palatable than port.

Which, indeed, she did, sipping the honeyed liquid with appreciation.

When all the pavlova was gone, Anatole got to his feet. He'd set coffee to brew when he'd fetched the dessert wine, and now he collected it, setting it down on the coffee table by the sofa.

He held his hand out to Tia. 'Come and sit down,' he invited.

She got up from the table, suddenly aware that her head was feeling as if there was a very slight swirl inside it. Just how much of that gorgeous champagne had she drunk? she wondered. It seemed to be fizzing in her veins, making her feel breathless, weightless. As if she were floating in a blissful haze. But she didn't care. How could she? An evening like this—something out of fairyland—would never come again!

With a little contented sigh she sank down on the sofa, the dessert wine glass in her hand, her light cotton skirt billowing around her.

Anatole came and sat down beside her. 'Time to relax,' he said genially, flicking on the TV with a remote.

He hefted his feet up onto the coffee table, disposing of his tie over the back of the sofa. He wanted to be totally comfortable. The mix of champagne and sweet wine was creaming pleasantly in his veins. He hoped it was doing so in Tia, as well, allowing her to enjoy the rest of the evening with him before he took himself off to his hotel.

Idly, he wondered whether he should phone and tell them to expect him, but then he decided not to bother. Instead he amused himself by channel-surfing until he chanced upon a channel that made his unexpected guest exclaim, 'Oh, I *love* this movie!'

It was a rom-com, perfectly watchable, and he was happy to do so. Happy to see Tia curl her bare feet under her skirt on the sofa and lean back into the cushions, her eyes on the screen.

At what point, Anatole wondered as he topped up her glass again, had he moved closer to her? At what point, as he'd stretched and flexed his legs, had he also stretched and flexed his arms, so that one of them was now resting along the back of the sofa, his fingertips grazing the top of her shoulder?

At what point had his fingers started idly playing with the now dry silky-soft pale curls around her neck?

At what point had he accepted that he had no desire—none whatsoever—to go anywhere else tonight?

And all the caution and the warnings sounding in his head, in what remained of his conscience, were falling on ears that were totally, profoundly deaf...

The film came to its sentimental end, with the hero sweeping the heroine up into his arms, lavishing an extravagant kiss upon her upturned face, and the music soared into the credits. A huge sigh of satisfaction was breathed from Tia, and she set down her now empty glass, turning back towards Anatole.

Emotion was coursing through her, mingling with the champagne and with that deliciously sweet wine she'd been drinking, with the gorgeous food she'd eaten—the best she'd ever tasted—all set off by candles and soft music and with her very own prince to keep her company.

It was foaming in her bloodstream, shining from her eyes. The rom-com they'd watched was one of her favourites, sighed over many times, but this—this now, *here*, right now—with her very own gorgeous, incredibly handsome man sitting beside her, oh, so tantalisingly close, was *real*! No fairytale, no fantasy—*real*. She'd never been this physically close to a man before—let alone a man like this! A man who could make fairytales come true...

And she knew how fairytales culminated! With the hero kissing the heroine...

Excitement, wonder—*hope*—filled her, and her eyes were shining like stars as she gazed up into the face of this glorious, gorgeous man who represented to her everything she had ever longed for, dreamt of, yearned for.

The man who was looking down at her, his dark eyes

lustrous, his lashes long and lush, his sculpted mouth so beautiful, so sensual—

She felt a little thrill just thinking of it, her breath catching, her eyes widening as she looked up to his.

Anatole looked down at her, seeing the loveliness of her face, of the loose, long pale hair waving like silk over her slender shoulders, seeing how the sweet mounds of her breasts were pressed against the contours of her cotton tee shirt, how her soft tender lips were parted, how her celestial blue eyes were wide, gazing at him with an expression that told him exactly what she wanted.

For one long, endless moment he stayed motionless, while a million conflicting thoughts battled in his head over what he should do next. What he *should* do versus what he wanted to do.

Yet still he held back, knowing that what he wanted so badly to do he should not. He should instead pull back, make some gesture of withdrawal from her, get up, get to his feet, increase the distance between them. Because if he didn't right now, then—

Her hand lifted, almost quivering, and with trembling fingers she let the delicate tips touch his jaw, feather-light, scarcely making contact, as if she hardly dared believe that this was what she was doing. She said his name. Breathed it. Her eyes were pools of longing. Her lips were parted, eyes half closed now. Waiting—yearning... For him.

And Anatole lost it. Lost all remaining shreds of conscience or consciousness.

He leaned towards her. The hand behind her head grazed her nape, his other hand slid along her cheek, his fingers gentle in her hair, cupping her face. Her eyes were wide, like saucers, and in them starlight shone like beacons, drawing him into her, into doing what she so blazingly wanted him to do.

His eyes washed over her, his pulse quickening. She was so lovely. And she so wanted him to kiss her... He could see it in her eyes, in her parted lips, in the quivering pulse in her delicate white throat.

His lashes swept down over his eyes as his mouth touched hers, soft as velvet, tasting the sweet wine on her lips, the warmth of her mouth as he opened it to his questing silken touch. He heard her give a little moan, deep in her throat, and he felt his own pulse surge, arousal spearing within him.

She was so soft to kiss, and he deepened his kiss automatically, instinctively, his hand sliding down over the curve of her shoulder, turning her towards him as he leant into her, drawing her to him, drawing her across him, so that her hand now braced itself against the hard wall of his chest, so that one slender thigh was against his.

He heard her moan again and it quickened his arousal. He said her name, told her how sweet she was, how very lovely. If he spoke in Greek he didn't realise it—didn't realise anything except that the wine was coursing in his bloodstream, recklessness was heady in his smitten synapses, and in his arms was a woman he desired.

Who desired him.

Because that was what her tender, lissom body was telling him—that was what the sudden engorgement of her breasts was showing him in the cresting of her nipples that were somehow beneath the palm of his hand.

Without realisation, she was winding her hand around his waist. He laid her back across his lap, half supported on his arm as he kissed her still, one hand palming her swelling breast until she moaned, eyes closed, her face filled with an expression of bliss he would have had to be blind not to see. He lifted his mouth from hers, let his eyes feast on her a moment, before his mouth descended yet again to graze on the line of her cheekbones, to nip at the tender lobes of her ears.

He let his hand slip reluctantly from her breast and then slide languorously along her flank to rest on her thigh, to smooth away the light cotton of her skirt until his hand found the bare skin beneath. To stroke and to caress and to hear her moan again, to feel her thigh strain against him—feel, too, his own body surge to full arousal.

Desire flamed in him…strong, impossible to resist…

And yet he *must*. This was too fast, too intense. He was letting his overpowering desire for her carry him away and he must draw back.

Heart pounding, he set her aside.

'Tia—' His voice was broken, his hand raised as if to ward her off. To hold himself back from her.

He saw her face fill with anguish. It caught at him like a blow.

'Don't…don't you want me?' There was dismay in her voice, which was a muted whisper.

He gave a groan. 'Tia—I mustn't. This isn't right. I can't take advantage of you like this!'

Immediately she cried out, 'But you aren't! Oh, please, *please* don't tell me you don't want me! I couldn't bear it!'

Her hand flew to her mouth and her look of anguish intensified. Her breathing was fast and breathless and she felt bereft—lost and abandoned.

He caught her face between his hands. 'Tia—I want you very, very much, but—'

But there's more than one bedroom in this apartment and we have to be in separate bedrooms tonight—we just have to be! Because anything else would be…would be…

Her face had lit like a beacon again. 'Please…*please*!' she begged. Her face worked. 'This whole evening with you has been incredible! Fantastic! Wonderful! And now… with you…it's like nothing I've ever experienced in all my life! You are like no one I've ever met! I'll never meet anyone else like you again, and this…all this…'

She gestured at the room, softly lit with table lamps, at the candles still on the dining table, the empty bottle of champagne, the glow of the lights on the terrace beyond.

'All this will never happen to me again!' She bit her lip, mouth quivering. 'I want this *so* much,' she said huskily, her eyes pleading with him, her hand fastening on his strong arm as if she might draw him back to her again. *'Please,'* she begged again. 'Please don't turn me away—*please*!'

And yet again Anatole lost it.

Unable to resist what he did not want to resist, what he could not bear to resist, he swept her back up to him, his mouth descending to taste again the honeyed sweetness of her mouth which opened to his instantly, eagerly… hungrily.

She wants this—she wants this as much as I do. And, however briefly we have known each other, my desire for her is overpowering. And so is hers for me. And because of that…

Because of that, with a rasp deep in his throat, he hefted to his feet, holding her in his arms, his hand sweeping under her knees to cradle her against him as he carried her away.

Away not to the guest room but to his own master suite, where he ripped back the bedcovers to lay her gently upon cool sheets. She was gazing up at him, blindness in her eyes, her pupils flared, lips bee-stung, breasts straining against the moulding of the cotton tee.

He wanted it gone. Wanted all her clothes gone, and all his—wanted no barriers between himself and this lovely woman he wanted now…*right* now…

CHAPTER THREE

TIA GAZED UP at him—at this incredible, unbearably devastating man—her mind in whiteout. Her body seemed to be on fire, with a soft, velvet flame, glowing with a sensual awareness that was possessing her utterly. She reached her arms up to him, yearning for him, beseeching him to take her back in his arms, to kiss and caress her, to sweep her off into the gorgeous bliss of his touch, his desire for her.

He was stripping off his clothes and she could feel her eyes widen as his shirt revealed the smooth, taut contours of his chest. And then his fingers were at his belt, snaking it free...

She gave a little cry, turning her head into the pillow, suddenly desperately shy. She had never dreamt that a man like this would ever be real in her life, and he was suddenly only too real.

Then she felt the mattress dip, felt his weight coming down beside her, heard him murmur soft words, urgent words, seductive, irresistible...and then his hand was curving her face back towards his, and he was so close to her, so very close, and in his eyes was a light she had never seen in a man's eyes before. She'd never seen a man's eyes so filled with blazing, burning fire...

I can't stop this—I can't stop it—and I don't want to! Oh, I don't want to!

She wanted it to happen, wanted what would happen now—what must happen now—wanted it with all her being, yearned and longed for it. It had come out of nowhere—just as the whole encounter with this amazing, fabulous man had come out of nowhere.

And I can't say no to it. I can't and I don't want to. I want to say yes—only yes....

Her eyes fluttered closed and she felt his mouth feather-light on hers, like swansdown. She felt his hands move to her waist, lift the material of her tee shirt from her, easing it over her head with hardly a pause in his sweet kissing. She felt his hands—warm, strong, skilled—slide around her back, unfasten her bra and slip it from her, discarding it somewhere. She knew not where and she did not care— did not care at all except that now he was doing the same with her skirt, skimming it from her, and then... Oh, then he was easing her panties from her quickening thighs.

He lifted himself from her, one hand splaying into her hair as it spread in tumbling golden curls across the pillow. His eyes burned into hers. 'You are so, so beautiful,' he said. 'So beautiful...'

She could say nothing, could only gaze upwards, hearing her mind echoing his words... *He* was beautiful! He with his sable hair and his sculpted cheekbones, with eyes you could drown in. His hard, lean body that her hands were now lifting themselves to of their own accord.

Her fingertips traced every line, every contour of the smooth, honed muscles. He seemed to shudder and she felt his muscles clench, as if what she was doing was unbearable, and then his mouth descended again.

Hungry...oh, so hungry.

And there was a hunger in her too. A ravening hunger that was as instinctive, as overpowering, as her need to be held and kissed and caressed by this most bliss-fully seductive of men. It was making her body arch to his, the blood rush like a torrent in her veins, drowning her senses, turning her into living flame. Never had she imagined that passion could feel like this! Never had her daydreams known what it was to be like this, in the arms of a man filled with urgent desire.

And she desired him.

She clung to him, not knowing what she was doing, only that it was what she burned to do. Her body arched to his, her thighs parting. She heard him say something but was lost to all coherence.

He seemed to pause, pull away from her, and it was unbearable not to have his warm, strong body over hers. And then, with a rush of relief, she felt him there again, kissing her again, his hands urgent, every muscle in his body tautening. She felt his body ease between hers, felt his hips move against hers, felt—

Pain! A sudden, piercing stab of pain!

She cried out, freezing, and he froze too. He gazed down at her, his eyes blind, then clearing into vision. Words escaped him. He was shocked.

He lifted from her and the pain vanished. Her hands reached for him, her head lifting blindly to catch his mouth again. But he was still withdrawn from her.

'I didn't know—I didn't realise—' The words fell from him. Shocked. Abrupt.

She could only gaze up at him. Devastation was flooding through her.

'Don't you want me?' It was all that was in her head now—the devastation of his rejection before.

'Tia…' He said her name again. 'I didn't realise that I would be the first man for you—'

Her hands pressed into his bare shoulders. 'I *want* you to be! Only you! Please—oh, *please*!'

Conflict seared in him. He burned for her, and yet—

But she was pressing her body against his, crushing her breasts against the wall of his chest. Lifting her hips to his in an age-old invitation of woman to man, to possess and be possessed.

'Please…' she said, her voice a low husk, a plea. 'Please—I want this so much—I want *you* so much.'

Her hand slid around the base of his skull, pressing against it, drawing his head down. She reached up with her mouth, feeling as her lips touched his a relief go through her that sated all her ardent yearning, all her desperate desire.

She opened his mouth under hers and Anatole, with a low, helpless groan, abandoned all his inner conflict, let himself yield to what he so wanted to do…to make her his.

It was morning. The undrawn curtains were letting in the light of dawn. Drowsily, wonderingly, Tia lay in Anatole's arms. There had been no more pain, and he had been as gentle with her as if she were made of porcelain—though the soft tenderness of her body now proclaimed that she was flesh and blood. But there was only a fading ache now, and in the cocoon of his strong arms it mattered not at all.

His arm was beneath her shoulder, her head lax upon it, and she smiled up at him, bemused, enchanted. His dark eyes were moving over her face, his other hand smoothing the tendrils of her silken hair from her cheeks. He was smiling back at her—a smile of intimacy, endearment. It made her feel weak with longing.

Bliss enveloped her, and a wonder so great that she could scarcely dare to believe that it was true, what had happened.

'Do you *have* to return to work?' Anatole was asking her.

She frowned a little, not understanding. 'The agency will open again at nine,' she said.

Anatole shook her head. 'I mean, do you have to take up another position? Are you booked to be a carer for someone else?'

Her frown deepened. She was understanding even less.

He smoothed her silken hair again, his eyes searching her face. 'I don't want you to go,' he said to her. 'I want you to stay with me.'

He watched her expression change. Watched it transform before his very eyes. Saw her cerulean blue eyes widen as she took in the meaning of what he'd said.

His smile deepened. Became assured. 'I have to go to Athens this week. Come with me—'

Come with me.

The words echoed in his head. He was sure of them—absolutely, totally sure. He felt a wash of desire go through him—not for consummation but for continuation.

I don't want to let her go—I want to keep her with me.

The realisation was absolute. The clarity of his desire incontrovertible.

'Do you mean it?'

Her words were so faint he could hardly hear them. But he could hear the emotion in her voice, see how her expression had changed, how her eyes were flaring wide, and in them hope blazed, dimmed only by confusion.

He brushed her parted lips. 'I would not ask you otherwise,' he said, knowing that to be true.

His arm around her tightened. She was so soft in his arms, so tiny, it seemed to him, nestling up against him.

He smiled at her. 'Well?' he asked. 'Will you come with me?'

The shadow of confusion, of fear that she had misunderstood, that he did not really mean what he'd said, vanished. Like the sun coming out, her smile lit up her face.

'Oh, yes! Yes, yes, *yes*!'

He laughed. He had had no fear that she would say no—why should she? The night they had spent together had been wondrous for her—he knew that—and he knew that he had coaxed her unschooled body to an ecstasy that had shocked her with its intensity. Knew that her ardent, bemused gaze in the sweet, exhausted aftermath of his lovemaking betokened just what effect he'd had on her.

And if he wanted proof of that today—well, here it was. She was gazing at him now with a look on her face that spread warmth through his whole being.

He brushed her lips with his again. Felt arousal—drowsy, dormant, but still present—start to stir. He deepened his kiss, using slow, sensuous, feather-light touches to stir within her an answering response. He would need to be gentle—very careful indeed—and take account of the dramatic changes to her body after their first union.

He felt her fingertips steal over his body, exploring... daring...fuelling his arousal with every tentative touch and glide...

With a deep, abiding satisfaction he started to make love to her again.

It was several days before they went to Athens. Days in which Tia knew she had, without the slightest doubt, been transported to a fantasy land.

How could she be anywhere else? She had been transported there by the most gorgeous, the most wonderful, the most shiveringly fabulous man she could ever have imagined! A man who had cast a glittering net of enchantment over her life.

That first morning, after he had made love to her again—and how was it possible for her body to feel what it did? She'd never known, never guessed that it was so—they'd breakfasted out on the little terrace, with the morning sun illuming them.

Then he'd whisked her off to one of the most famous luxury department stores in the world, from which she'd emerged, several hours later, with countless carrier bags of designer clothes and a new hairstyle—barely shorter, but so cunningly cut it had felt feather-light on her head, floating over her shoulders. Her make-up had been applied by an expert, and Anatole had smiled in triumphant satisfaction when he saw her.

I knew she could look fantastic with the right clothes and styling!

His eyes had worked over her openly, and he'd seen the

flush of pleasure in her face. The glow in her eyes. Felt the warmth of it.

I've done the right thing—absolutely the right thing.

The certainty of that had streamed through him. This breathtakingly lovely creature that he'd scooped off the road and taken into his life was exactly right for him.

And so it had proved.

Taking Tia to Athens would only be the first of it.

He'd sorted out a passport for her—or rather, his office had—and they were now flying out…first class obviously.

For the entire flight she sat beside him in a state of stupefied bliss, sipping at her glass of champagne and gazing out through the porthole with a look of enchanted disbelief that this could really be happening to her.

In Athens, his chauffeured car was waiting to take him to his apartment—he did not use the Kyrgiakis mansion, far preferring his own palatial flat, with its stunning views of the Acropolis.

'Didn't I tell you that you should see the Parthenon one day?' he quizzed her smilingly, indicating the famous ruins visible from all around. 'It's not in the best of shape because the Ottomans used it as a gunpowder store, which exploded…' He grimaced. 'But it's being preserved as well as possible.'

'Ottomans?' Tia queried.

'They came out of what is now Turkey and conquered Greece in the fifteenth century—it took us four hundred years to be free.' Anatole explained.

Tia looked at him uncertainly. 'Was that Alexander the Great?' she asked tentatively, knowing that the famous character must come into Greek history somewhere.

Anatole's mouth twitched. 'Out by over two thousand years, I'm afraid. Alexander was before the Romans. Greece only became independent in modern times—during the nineteenth century.' He patted her hand. 'Don't worry about it. There's a huge amount of history in

Greece. You'll get the hang of it eventually. I'll take you to the Parthenon while we're here.'

But in the end he didn't, because instead, business matters having been attended to, he decided to charter a yacht and take her off on an Aegean cruise.

His father had commandeered the Kyrgiakis yacht, but the one upon which he and Tia sailed off into the sunset was every bit as luxurious, and it reduced Tia to open-mouthed, saucer-eyed amazement.

'It's got a *helicopter!*' she breathed. 'And a swimming pool!'

'And another one indoors, in case it ever rains,' Anatole grinned. 'We'll go skinny-dipping in both!'

Colour flushed in her cheeks, and he found it endearing. He found everything about her endearing. Despite the fact that after a fortnight together she was *way* past being the virginal ingénue she'd been that first amazing night together, she was still delightfully shy.

But not so shy that she refused to go for a starlit swim with him—the crew having been ordered to keep well below decks—nor declined to let him make love to her in the water, until she cried out with a smothered cry, her head falling back as he lifted her up onto his waiting body.

For ten days they meandered around the Aegean, calling in at little islands where he and Tia strolled along the waterfront, lunching in harbourside restaurants, or drove inland to picnic beneath olive groves, with the endless hum of the cicadas all about them.

Simple pleasures…and Anatole wondered when he had last done anything so peaceful with any female. Certainly not with any female who was as boundlessly appreciative as Tia was.

She adored everything they did together. Was thrilled by everything—whether it was taking the yacht's sailing dinghy to skim over the azure water to a tiny cove on a half-deserted island, where they lunched on fresh bread and olives and ripest peaches and then made love on the sand, washing off in the waves thereafter, or whether, like today, it was drinking a glass of Kir Royale and watching the sun set over a harbour bar, before returning to the yacht, moored out in the bay, for a five-course gourmet meal served on the upper deck by the soft-footed, incredibly attentive staff aboard, while music played from unseen speakers all around, the yacht moved on the slow swell of the sea and the moon rose out of the iridescent waters.

Tia gazed at Anatole across the damask tablecloth, over the candlelight between them.

'This is the most wonderful holiday I could ever have imagined!' she breathed.

Adoration was obvious in her eyes—for how could it not be? How could she not reveal all that she felt for this wonderful, incredible man who had brought her here? Emotion swelled within her like a billowing wave, almost overpowering her.

Anatole's dark eyes lingered on her lovely face. A warm, honeyed tan had turned her skin to gold, and her hair was even paler now from the sun's rays. He felt desire cream within him. How good she was for him, and how good he felt about her…about having her in his life.

'Tell me,' he said, 'have you ever been to Paris?'

Tia shook her head.

Anatole's smile deepened. 'Well, I have to go there on business. You'll love it!'

It felt good to know that he would be the first man to show her the City of Light. Just as it had felt good to take her on this cruise, to see her enjoy the luxury of his lifestyle. Good to see her eyes widen, her intake of breath—good to bestow his largesse upon her, for she was so appreciative of it.

King Cophetua, indeed.

But he liked the feeling. Liked it a lot. For her sake, obviously, he was finding pleasure in bestowing upon her the luxury and treats that had never come her way in her deprived life. But not just for her sake—he was honest enough to admit that. For himself too. It was very good to feel her ardent, adoring gaze upon him. It made him feel—warm.

Loved.

His mind sheered away from the word, as if hitting a rock in a stream. His expression changed as he negated what he'd just heard in his mind.

I don't want her to love me.

Of course he didn't! Love would be a completely unnecessary complication. They were having an affair, just as he'd had with all the women who had been in his life... in his bed. It would run its course and at some point they would part.

Until then—well, Tia, so unlike any other woman he'd known, was just what he wanted.

His only source of disquiet was that she remained so clearly uncomfortable whenever they were in company, wherever they travelled. He didn't want her feeling out of her depth in the inevitably cosmopolitan, sophisticated and wealthy circles he moved in, and he did his best to make things easier for her, but she was always very quiet.

Thoughts flickered uneasily in his head. Had anyone ever thought to ask the Beggar Maid how she'd felt after King Cophetua had plucked her up into his royal and gilded life?

And yet when they were alone she visibly relaxed, coming out of her shell, talkative and at ease. Happy just to be with him and endlessly appreciative. Endlessly desirous of him.

He was in no hurry, he realised, to part with her.

Will I ever be? he thought. Then he put the question out of his head. Whenever that time came, it was not now, and until it did he would enjoy this affair—enjoy Tia—to the full.

* * *

Tia sat at the vanity unit in the palatial en suite bathroom, gazing at her reflection. She was wearing one of the oh-so-many beautiful dresses Anatole had bought for her over the past months of their relationship. His generosity troubled her, but she had accepted it because she knew she couldn't move in his gilded world in her own inexpensive clothes.

And besides, none of these outfits are really mine! I wouldn't dream of taking them with me when—

Her mind cut out. She didn't want to think about that time. She didn't want it spoiling this wonderful, blissful time with Anatole.

Anatole! His very name brought a flush to her cheeks, a glow to her eyes. How wonderful he was—how kind, how *good* to her! Her heart beat faster every time she thought of him. With every glance she threw at him or he at her, she felt emotion burn in her, coursing through her veins.

She felt her expression change, and even as it did so her gaze became more troubled still, her eyes shadowing.

Be careful! Oh, be careful! There is only one way this affair can end when it does end—like fairy gold turning to dust at dawn! And the end will be bad for you—so, so bad.

But it would be worse—and the shadow in her eyes deepened, a chill icing down her veins—much, much worse, if she let her heart fill with the one emotion that it would be madness to feel for Anatole.

I long for the one thing that would keep me in Anatole's life for ever...

Anatole's mood was tense. They were back in Athens, and the annual Kyrgiakis Corp board meeting was looming. It never put him in a good mood. His parents would pester him for more money—sniping at each other across the table—and only the calming presence of his Uncle Vasilis would be any balm.

Putting in long hours at the Kyrgiakis Corp headquarters, closeted with his finance director going through all the figures and reports before the meeting, meant he'd had little time to devote to Tia lately, but when he did spend time with her he could sense that something was troubling her.

He'd had no time to probe, however—he'd told himself he would get this damn board meeting out of the way and then take her on holiday somewhere. The prospect had cheered him. But not enough to lift the perpetually grim expression on his face as he'd prepared for the coming ordeal.

Now, today, over breakfast, he was running through his head all that had to be in readiness for the meeting that morning,

As well as the official business his family would expect a lavish celebratory lunch, to be held at one of the best hotels in Athens where his father liked to stay. His mother, predictably, never stayed there, but at a rival hotel. They ran up huge bills at both, for they both put their stays on the business account—much to Anatole's irritation.

But his parents had always been a law unto themselves, and since he wanted as little to do with them as possible he tolerated their extravagance, and that of their current respective spouses, with gritted teeth. The only person he actually wanted to see was Vasilis, who'd been preoccupied in Turkey for some time now, helping one of the museums there in salvaging ancient artefacts from the ravages of war in the Middle East.

He'd invited Vasilis to lunch the day after the board meeting, knowing that even though his scholarly uncle would be far too academic for Tia his kindly personality would not be intimidating to her.

He reached for his orange juice and paused. Tia was looking at him, her fingers twisting nervously in the handle of her coffee cup, with an expression on her face he'd never seen before in the many weeks they'd spent together.

'What is it?' he asked.

She didn't answer. Only swallowed. Paled. Her fingers twisted again.

'Tia?' he prompted.

Was there an edge in his voice? He didn't mean there to be, but he had to get on—time was at an absolute premium today, and he needed to eat breakfast and be gone. But maybe his tone *had* been a bit off, impatient, though he hadn't intended it to be, because she went even whiter. Bit her lip.

'Tell me,' he instructed, his eyes levelling on her.

Whatever was troubling her, he would deal with it later. For now he'd just offer some reassuring words—it was all he had time for. He set down his orange juice and waited expectantly. An anguished look filled her eyes and he saw her swallow again, clearly reluctant to speak.

When she did, he knew why. Knew with a cold, icy pool in his stomach.

Her voice was faint, almost a stammer.

'I… I think I may be pregnant…'

CHAPTER FOUR

CHRISTINE CLIMBED OUT of the car. Her legs were shaking. How she'd get indoors she did not know. Mrs Hughes, the housekeeper, was there already, having left the church before the committal, and she welcomed her in with a low, sad voice.

'A beautiful service, Mrs K,' she said kindly.

Christine swallowed. 'Yes, it was. The vicar was very good about allowing him a C of E interment considering he was Greek Orthodox.' She tried to make her voice sound normal and failed.

Mrs Hughes nodded sympathetically. 'Well, I'm sure the Good Lord will be welcoming Mr K, whichever door he's come into heaven through—such a lovely gentleman as he was, your poor husband.'

'Thank you.'

Christine felt her throat tighten, tears threaten. She went into her sitting room, throat aching.

The pale yellow and green trellis-pattern wallpaper was in a style she now knew was *chinoiserie*, just as she now knew the dates of all the antique furniture in the house, who the artists were of the Old Masters that hung on the walls, and the age and subject of the artefacts that Vasilis had so carefully had transferred from Athens to adorn the place he had come to call home, with his new young wife.

This gracious Queen Anne house in the heart of the Sussex countryside. Far away from his old life and far away from the shocked and outraged members of his family. A serene, beautiful house in which to live, quietly and remotely. In which, finally, to die.

Her tears spilled over yet again, and she crossed to the

French window, looking out over the lawn. The gardens were not extensive, but they were very private, edged with greenery. Memory shot through her head of how she'd been so enchanted by the green oasis of Anatole's London roof terrace when he'd switched the lights on, turning it into a fairyland.

She sheared her mind away. What use to think…to remember? Fairyland had turned to fairy dust, and had been blown away in the chill, icy wind of reality. The reality that Anatole had spelt out to her.

'I have no intention of marrying you, Tia. Did you do this to try and get me to marry you?'

A shuddering breath shook her and she forced her shoulders back, forced herself to return to the present. She had not invited anyone back after the funeral—she couldn't face it. All she wanted was solitude.

Yet into her head was forced the image of the grim-faced, dark-suited man standing there, watching her at her husband's grave. Fear bit at her.

Surely he won't come here? Why would he? He's come to see his uncle buried, that's all. He won't sully his shoes by crossing this threshold—not while I'm still here.

But even as she turned from the window there came a knock on the door, and it opened to the housekeeper.

'I'm so sorry to disturb you, Mrs K, but you have a visitor. He says he's Mr K's nephew. I've shown him into the drawing room.'

Ice snaked down Christine's back. For a moment she could not move. Then, with an effort, she nodded.

'Thank you, Mrs Hughes,' she said.

Summoning all her strength, and all her courage, she went to confront the man who had destroyed all her naive and foolish hopes and dreams.

Anatole stood in front of the fireplace, looking around him with a closed, tight expression on his face, taking in the *objets d'art* and his uncle's beloved classical statuary, the Old Masters hanging on the panelled walls.

His mouth twisted. *She's done very well for herself, this woman I picked up from the street—*

Anger stabbed in him. Anger and so much more.

But anger was quite enough. She would be inheriting all Vasilis's share of the Kyrgiakis fortune—a handsome sum indeed. Not bad for a woman who'd once had to take any job she could, however menial and poorly paid, provided it came with accommodation.

Well, this job had certainly come with accommodation!

The twist of his mouth grew harsher. He had found a naïve waif and created a gold-digger...

I gave her a taste for all this. I turned her into this.

Sourness filled his mouth.

There were footsteps beyond the double doors and then they opened. His eyes snapped towards them as she stood there. He felt the blade of a knife stab into him as he looked at her. She was still in the black, tailored couture suit. Her hair was pulled back off her face into a tight chignon—no sign of the soft waves that had once played around her shoulders.

Her face was white. Stark. Still marked by tears shed at the graveside.

Memory flashed into his head of how she'd stood trembling beside the bonnet of his car as she broke down into incoherent sobs when he yelled at her for her stupidity in walking right in front of his car. How appalled he'd been at her reaction...how he'd wanted to stop those tears.

The blade twisted in him...

'What are you doing here?'

Her question was terse, tight-lipped, and she did not advance into the room, only closed the double doors behind her. There was something different about her voice, and it took Anatole a moment to realise that it was not just her blank, hostile tone, but her accent. Her voice was as crisp, as crystalline, as if she had been born to all this.

Her appearance echoed that impression. The severity of the suit, her hairstyle, and the poise with which she held herself, all contributed.

'My uncle is dead. Why else do you think I'm here?' His voice was as terse as hers. It was necessary to be so—it was vital.

Something seemed to pass across her eyes. 'Do you want to see his will? Is that it?'

There was defiance in her voice now—he could hear it.

A cynical cast lit his dark eyes. 'What for? He'll have left you everything, after all.' He paused—a deadly pause. 'Isn't that why you married him?'

It was a rhetorical question, one he already knew the answer to.

She whitened, but did not flinch. 'He left some specific items for you. I'm going to have them couriered to you as soon as I've been granted probate.'

She paused, he could see it, as if gathering strength. Then she spoke again, her chin lifting, defiance in her voice—in her very stance.

'Anatole, why have you come here? What for? I'm sorry if you wanted the funeral to be in Athens. Vasilis specifically did not want that. He wanted to be buried here. He was friends with the vicar—they shared a common love of Aeschylus. The vicar read Greats at Oxford, and he and Vasilis would cap quotations with each other. They liked Pindar too—'

She broke off. Was she *mad*, rabbiting on about Ancient Greek playwrights and poets? What did Anatole care?

He was looking at her strangely, as if what she had said surprised him. She wasn't sure why. Surely he would not be surprised to find that his erudite uncle had enjoyed discussing classical Greek literature with a fellow scholar, even one so far away from Greece?

'The vicar is quite a Philhellene…' she said, her voice trailing off.

She took another breath. Got back to the subject in hand. Tension was hauling at her muscles, as if wires were suspending her.

'Please don't think of…of… I don't know…disinterring his coffin to take it back to Greece. He would not wish for that.'

Anatole gave a quick shake of his head, as if the thought had not occurred to him as he'd stood there, watching the farce playing out in the churchyard—Tia grieving beside the grave of the man she'd inveigled into committing the most outrageous act of folly—marrying her, a woman thirty years his junior.

'So what *are* you doing here?'

Her question came again, and he brought his mind back to it. What was he doing here? To put it into words was impossible. It had been an instinct—overpowering—an automatic decision not even consciously made. To… To what?

'I'm here to pay my respects,' he heard his own voice answer.

He saw her expression change, as if he'd just said something quite unbelievable.

'Well, not to *me*!' There was derision in her voice—but it was not targeted at him, he realised. He frowned, focussing on her face.

He felt his muscles clench. *Thee mou*, how beautiful she was! The natural loveliness that had so enchanted him, captivated him, that had inspired him so impulsively to take her into his life, had matured into true beauty. Beauty that had a haunting quality. A sorrow—

Does she feel sorrow at my uncle's death? Can she really feel that?

No, surely there could be only relief that she was now free of a man thirty years her senior—free to enjoy all the money he had left her. Yet again that spike drove into him. He hated what she had become. What he himself had made her.

'Anatole, I know perfectly well what you think of me, so don't prate hypocrisies to me! Tell me why you're here.' And now he saw her shoulders stiffen, her chin rise defiantly. 'If it's merely to heap abuse on my head for having dared to do what I did, then I will simply send you packing. I'm not answerable to you and nor—' the tenor of her voice changed now, and there was a viciousness in it that was like the edge of a blade '—are you answerable to me, either. As you have already had occasion to point out!'

She took another sharp intake of breath.

'Our lives are separate—you made sure of that. And I… I accepted it. You gave me no choice. I had no claim on you—and you most certainly have no claim on me now, nor *any* say in my decisions. Or those your uncle made either. He married me of his own free will—and if you don't like that…well, get over it!'

If she'd sprouted snakes for hair, like Medusa, Anatole could not have been more shocked by her. Was *this* the Tia he remembered? This aggressive harpy? Lashing out at him, her eyes hard and angry?

Tia saw the shock in his face and could have laughed savagely—but laughing was far beyond her on this most gruelling of days. She could feel her heart-rate going insane and knew that she was in shock, as well as still feeling the emotional battering of losing Vasilis—however long it had been expected—and burying him that very day.

To have in front of her now the one man in the entire world she had dreaded seeing again was unbearable. It was unbearable to look at the man who had once been so dear to her.

She lifted a hand, as if to ward him off. 'Anatole, I don't know why you've come here, and I don't care—we've nothing left to say to each other. Nothing!' She shut her eyes, then opened them again with a heavy breath. 'I'm sure you grieve for your uncle… I know you were fond of him and he of you. He did not seek this breach with you—'

She felt her throat closing again and could not continue. Wanted him only to go.

'What will you do with this place?'

Anatole's voice cut across her aching thoughts.

'I suppose you'll sell up and take yourself off to revel in your ill-gotten inheritance?'

She swallowed. How could it hurt that Anatole spoke to her in such a way? She knew what he thought of her marriage to Vasilis.

'I've no intention of selling up,' she replied coldly, taking protection behind her tone. 'This is my home, with many good memories.'

Something changed in his eyes. 'You'll need to live *respectably* here…' there was warning in his voice '…in this country house idyll in an English village.'

'I shall endeavour to do so.' Christine did not bother to keep the sarcasm out of her voice. Why should she? Anatole was making assumptions about her…as he had done before.

A stab went through her, painful and hurtful, but she ignored it.

Again something flashed in his eyes. 'You're a young woman still, Tia—and now that you have all my uncle's wealth to flaunt you can take your pick of men.' His voice twisted. 'And this time around they won't need to be thirty years older than you. You can choose someone young and handsome, even if they're penniless!'

His tone grew harsher still.

'I'd prefer it if you took yourself off to some flash resort where you can party all night and keep your married name out of the tabloid rags!'

Christine felt her expression harden. Was there any limit to how he was going to insult her? 'I'm in mourning, Anatole. I'm not likely to go off and party with hand-picked gigolos.'

She took another heaving breath, turning around to open the double doors.

'Please leave now, Anatole. We've nothing to say to each other. *Nothing*.'

Pointedly, she waited for him to walk into the wide, parquet-floored hall. There was no sign of Mrs Hughes, and Christine was glad. How much the housekeeper—or anyone else—knew about the Kyrgiakis clan, she didn't know and didn't want to think about. Providing everything was kept civil on the surface, that was all that mattered.

Anatole was simply her late husband's nephew, calling to pay his respects on his uncle's death. No reason for Mrs Hughes to think anything else.

With his long stride Anatole walked past her, and Christine caught the faint scent of his aftershave. Familiar—so very familiar.

Memory rushed through her and she felt her body sway with emotion. For a second it was so overwhelmingly powerful she wanted to catch his hand, throw herself into his arms, and sob. To feel his arms go about her, feel him hold her, cradle her, feel his strong chest support her, feel his closeness, his protection. Sob out her grief for his uncle—her grief for so much more.

But Anatole was gone from her. Separated from her as by a thousand miles, by ten thousand. Separated from her by what she had done—what he had *thought* she had done. There was nothing left to bring them together again—not now. Not ever.

This is the last time I shall set eyes on him. It has to be—because I could not bear to see him again.

There was a tearing pain inside her as these words framed in her head—a pain for all that had been, that had not been, that could never be…

He didn't look at her as he strode past her, as he headed

for the large front door. His face was set, closed. She had seen it like that before, that last terrible day in Athens, and she had never wanted to see him look like that again. Like stone, crushing her pathetic hopes.

A silent cry came from her heart.

And then, from the top of the staircase that swept up from the back of the wide hallway to the upper storey of the house, came another cry. Audible this time.

'Mumma!'

Anatole froze. Not believing what he had heard. Froze with his hand on the handle of the door that would take him from the house, his heart infused with blackness.

Slowly he turned. Saw, as if in slow motion, a middle-aged woman in a nanny's uniform descending the stairs, holding by the hand a young child to stop him rushing down too fast. Saw them reach the foot of the staircase and the tiny figure tear across the hall to Tia. Saw her scoop him up, hug him, and set him down again gently.

'Hello, munchkin. Have you been good for Nanny?'

Tia's voice was warm, affectionate, and something about it caused a sliver of pain in Anatole's breast, penetrating his frozen shock.

'Yes!' the little boy cried. 'We've done painting. Come and see.'

'I will, darling, in a little while,' he heard her answer, with that same softness in her voice—a softness he remembered from long, long ago, that sent another sliver of pain through him.

The child's eyes went past her, becoming aware of someone standing by the front door.

'Hello,' he said in his piping voice.

His bright gaze looked right at Anatole. Clearly interested. Waiting for a response.

But Anatole could make none. Could only go on standing there, frozen, as knowledge forced itself into his head like a power hose being turned on.

Theos—she has a son.

He dragged his eyes from the child—the sable-haired, dark-eyed child—to the woman who was the boy's mother. Shock was in his eyes still. Shock, and more than shock. An emotion that seemed to well up out of a place so deep within him he did not know it was there. He could give it no name.

'I didn't know—' His voice broke off.

Did her hand tighten on the child's? He could see her face take on an expression of reserve, completely at odds with the warmth of a moment again when she'd been hugging her child.

'Why should you?' she returned coolly. Her chin lifted slightly. 'This is Nicky.' Her eyes dropped to her son. 'Nicky, this is your—'

She stopped. For a second it seemed to Anatole that a kind of paralysis had come over her face.

It was he who filled the gap. Working out just what his relationship was to the little boy. 'Your cousin,' he said.

Nicky cast him an even more interested look. 'Have you come to play with me?' he asked.

Immediately both his nanny and his mother intervened.

'Now, Nicky, not *everyone* who comes here comes to play with you,' his nanny said, her reproof very mild and given as if it were a routine reminder.

'Munchkin, no—your…your cousin is here because of poor Pappou—'

The moment she spoke Christine wished desperately that she hadn't. But she was in no state to think straight. It was taking every ounce of what little remaining strength she had just to remain where she was, to cope with this nightmare scenario playing out, helpless to stop it. Helpless to do anything but hang on in there until finally—

dear God, *finally*—the front door closed behind Anatole and she could collapse.

'Pappou?'

The single word from Anatole was like a bullet. A bullet right through her. She stared, aghast at what she'd said.

Grandfather.

She could only stare blindly at Anatole. She had to explain, to make sense of what she'd said—what she'd called Vasilis.

But she was spared the ordeal. At her words Nicky's little face had crumpled, and she realised with a knife in her heart that she had made an even worse mistake than saying what she had in front of Anatole.

'Where is he? I want him—I *want* him! I want Pappou!'

She dropped to her knees beside him, hugging him as he sobbed, giving him what comfort she could, reminding him of how Pappou had been so ill, and was now in heaven, where he was well again, where they would see him again one day.

Then, suddenly there was someone else hunkering down beside her and Nicky. Someone resting his hand on Nicky's heaving shoulder.

Anatole spoke, his voice a mix of gentleness and kindness, completely different from any tone she'd heard from him so far in this nightmare encounter. 'Did you say that you've been doing some painting with Nanny?'

Christine felt Nicky turn in her arms, look at the man kneeling down so close. She saw her son nod, his face still crumpled with tears.

'Well,' said Anatole, in the same tone of voice but now with a note of encouragement in it, 'why don't you paint a picture especially for...for Pappou?'

He said the word hesitantly, but said it all the same. His tone of voice changed again, and now there was something new in it.

'When I was little, I can remember I painted a picture for…for Pappou. I painted a train. It was a bright red train. With blue wheels. You could paint one too, if you like, and then he would have one from both of us. How would that be?'

Christine saw her son gaze at Anatole. Her throat felt very tight. As tight as if wire had been wrapped around it—barbed wire that drew blood.

'Can my train be blue?' Nicky asked.

Anatole nodded. 'Of course it can. It can be blue with red wheels.'

Nicky's face lit up, his tears gone now. He looked across to his nanny, standing there, ready to intervene if that were needed. Now it was.

'What a good idea!' she said enthusiastically. 'Shall we go and do it now?'

She held out her hand and Nicky disengaged himself from his mother, trotting up to his nanny and taking her hand. He turned back to Christine. 'Nanny and me are going to paint a picture for Pappou,' he informed her.

Christine gave a watery smile. 'That's a lovely idea, darling,' she said.

'Will you show it to me when you've done it?' It was Anatole who'd spoken, rising to his feet, looking across at the little boy.

Nicky nodded, then tugged on his nanny's hand, and the two of them made their journey back up the stairs, with Nicky talking away animatedly.

Christine watched them go. Her heart was hammering in her chest, so loudly she was sure it must be audible. A feeling of faintness swept over her as she stood up.

Did she sway? She didn't know—knew only that a hand had seized her upper arm, was steadying her. A hand that was like a vice.

Had Anatole done that only to stop her fainting? Or for another reason?

She jerked herself free, stepped back sharply. To have him so close—so close to Nicky...

He spoke, his voice low, so as not to be within earshot of the nanny, but his tone was vehement.

'I had no idea—*none*!'

Christine trembled, but her voice was cool. 'Like I said, why should you? If Vasilis chose not to tell you, *I* was hardly likely to!'

Anatole's dark eyes burned into hers. She felt faintness drumming at her again. Such dark eyes...

So like Nicky.

No—she must not think that. Vasilis's eyes had been dark as well, typically Greek. And brown was genetically dominant over her own blue eyes. Of course Nicky would have the dark eyes of his father's family.

'Why does the boy call my uncle *pappou*?' The demand was terse—requiring an answer.

She took a careful breath. 'Vasilis thought it...wiser,' she said. Her mouth snapped closed. She did not want to talk about it, discuss it, have it questioned or challenged.

But Anatole was not to be silenced. 'Why?' he said bluntly.

His eyes seemed to be burning into hers. She rubbed a hand over her forehead. A great weariness was descending on her after the strain of the last grim months—Vasilis's final illness, the awfulness of the last fortnight since he'd died, and now, the day of her husband's burial, the nightmare eruption into her life of the man who had caused her marriage to Vasilis.

'Vasilis knew his heart was weak. That it would give out while Nicky was still young. So he said...' Her voice wavered and she took another difficult breath, not wanting to look at Anatole but knowing she *must* say what she had to. 'He said it would be...kinder for Nicky to grow up calling him his grandfather.'

She had to fight to keep her lips from trembling, her

eyes from filling with tears. Her hands clenched each other, nails digging into her palms.

'He said Nicky would miss him less when the time came, feel less deprived than if he'd thought of him as his father.'

Anatole was silent but his thoughts were hectic, heaving. And as troubled as a stormy night. Emotion writhed within him. Memory slashed across his synapses. He could hear Tia's voice—his own.

'I have no intention of being a father—so do not even think of forcing my hand!'

Christine looked at him, her expression veiled. Seeing his—guessing what he was remembering.

'Given what has happened,' she said quietly, 'Vasilis made the right decision. Nicky will have only dim memories of him as he grows, but they will be very fond ones and I will always honour Vasilis's memory to him.'

She swallowed, then said what she must.

'Thank you for suggesting he paint Vasilis a picture. It was a very good idea—it diverted him perfectly.'

'I can remember—just—painting the picture for my uncle that I told Nicky about. He'd come to visit and I was excited. He always brought me a present and paid attention to me. Spent time with me. Later I realised he'd come to talk to my father, to tell him that, for my sake, my father should…mend his ways.' His mouth twisted. 'He had a wasted journey. My father was incapable of mending his ways.'

He frowned, as if he had said too much. He took a ragged breath, shook his head as if to clear it of memories that had no purpose any more.

Then he let his eyes rest on Tia.

'We need to talk,' he said.

CHAPTER FIVE

CHRISTINE SAT ON the chintz-covered sofa, tension racking her still as Mrs Hughes set out a tray of coffee on the ormolu table at her side. Her throat was parched and she was desperate for a shot of caffeine—anything to restore her drained energy levels.

In her head, memory cut like a knife.

'I could murder a cup of coffee.'

Anatole had said that the very first afternoon he'd picked her up off the street where she'd fallen in front of his car and brought her back to his flat. Was he remembering it too? She didn't know. His expression was closed.

As her eyes flickered over him she felt emotion churn in her stomach. His physical impact on her was overpowering. As immediate and overwhelming as it had been the very first time she'd set eyes on him. The five years since she had last set eyes on him vanished.

Panic beat in her again.

I've got to make him go away. I've got to—

'You realise that this changes everything—the fact that Vasilis has a son?'

She started, staring at Anatole. 'Why?' she said blankly.

He lifted an impatient hand, a coffee cup in it, before drinking. 'Don't be obtuse,' he said. 'That is, don't be stupid—'

'I know what obtuse means!' she heard herself snap at him.

He paused, rested his eyes on her. He said nothing, but she could see that her sharp tone had taken him by surprise. He wasn't used to her talking to him like that. Wasn't used to hostility from her.

'It changes nothing that he has a son.' Her voice trembled on the final word. Had Anatole noticed the tremor? She hoped not.

'Of course it does!' he replied.

He finished his coffee, roughly set the cup back on the tray. He was on the sofa opposite her, but he was still too close. His eyes flickered over her for a moment, but his expression was still veiled.

'I will not have Nicky punished for what you did.' He spoke quietly, but there was an intensity in his voice that was like a chill down her spine, 'I will not have him exiled from his family just because of you. He needs his family.'

Her coffee cup rattled on its saucer as her hand trembled. 'He *has* a family—*I* am his family!'

Anatole's hand slashed down. 'So am I! And he cannot be raised estranged from his kin.' He took a heavy breath. 'Whatever you have done, Tia, the boy must not pay for it. I want—'

Something snapped inside her. 'What *you* want, Anatole, is irrelevant! *I* am Nicky's mother. I have sole charge of him, sole guardianship. *I*—not you, and not anyone else in the entire world—get to say any single thing about how he grows up, and in whose company, or any other detail of his life. *Do you understand me?*'

She saw his face whiten around his mouth. Again, it was as if she had sprouted snakes for hair.

Stiffly, he answered her. 'I understand that you have been under considerable strain. That whatever your…your feelings you have had to cope with Vasilis's final illness and his death. His funeral today. You are clearly under stress.'

He got to his feet.

How tall he seemed, towering over her as she sat, her legs too weak, suddenly, to support her in standing up to face him.

He looked at her gravely, his face still shuttered.

'It has been a difficult day,' he said, his voice tight. 'I will take my leave now…let you recover. But…'

He paused, then resumed, never taking from her his dark, heavy gaze that pressed like weights on raw flesh.

'But this cannot be the end of the matter. You *must* understand that, Tia. You must accept it.'

She pushed herself to her feet. 'And *you*, Anatole, must accept that you have nothing to do with my child. *My* child.'

The emphasis was clear. Bitter. Darkness flashed in her eyes, and she lifted her chin defiantly, said the words burning in her like brands.

'I don't want you coming here again. You've made your opinion of me very, very clear. I don't want you coming near my son—*my* son! He has quite enough to bear, in losing Vasilis, without having your hatred of me to cope with. I won't have you poisoning his ears with what you think of me.'

She took a sharp breath, her eyes like gimlets, spearing him.

'Stay away, Anatole. Just *stay away*!'

She marched to the drawing room doors, yanking them open. Her heart was thumping in her breast, her chest heaving. She had to get him out of her house—right now.

Wordlessly, Anatole strode past her. This time—*dear God*—this time she would get him out of the house.

Only at the front door did he turn. Pause, then speak. 'Tia—'

'That is no longer my name.' Christine's voice was stark, biting across him, her face expressionless. 'I stopped being Tia a long time ago. Vasilis always called me Christine, my given name, not any diminutive. I am Christine. That's who I am—who I always will be.'

There was a choke in her voice as grief threatened her. But grief was not her greatest threat. Her greatest threat was the man it always had been.

Her nails pressed into her palms and she welcomed

the pain. She turned away, leaving him to let himself out, rapid footsteps impelling her towards the door of her sitting room. She gained it, shut the door behind her, leaning against it, feeling faintness threatening. Her eyes were stark and staring. That barbed wire garrotting her throat.

I will never be Tia again. I can never be Tia again.

The barbed wire pressed tighter yet. Now it was drawing blood.

Anatole drove up the motorway, back towards London. He was pushing the speed limit and did not care. He needed to put as much distance as he could between himself and Tia.

Christine.

That was what she called herself now, she'd said. What his uncle had called her. His eyes shifted. He did not want to think about his uncle calling Tia... Christine...anything at all. Having anything to do with her.

Having a child with her.

His mind sheared away. No, he could not think about that—about the creation of a child between Tia and his uncle—his erudite bachelor uncle who'd never had a romance in his life.

And still never had, either—whatever lures Tia had cast over him.

His expression changed. No, that was the wrong way to look at it—they could not have been lures. Vasilis would have been immune to anything so crude.

She would just have come across as helpless and vulnerable. Cast aside by me—

His mind shifted away again. He still did not want to think about it. Didn't want to remember that day five long years ago.

Yet memory came, all the same...

'I... I think I may be pregnant.'

The words fell into the space between them.

Anatole could feel himself freezing, hear himself responding.

'So are you or aren't you?'

That was what he said. A simple question.

He saw, as if from a long way away, her face blanch.

'I'm not sure,' she whispered, expression strained. 'My period is late—'

'How late?' Again, a simple question.

'I… I think it's about a week late. I… I'm not sure. It may be longer.'

Anatole found himself trying to calculate in his head when she'd last been…indisposed. Could not quite place it. But that wasn't relevant. Only one thing mattered now.

His voice seemed to come from a long way away. A long way from where she was sitting, gazing at him, her expression like nothing he had ever seen before. Like nothing he wanted to see.

'You'd better do a test.' The words came out clipped, completely unemotional. 'With luck it's a false alarm.'

Without luck—

His mind sheared away. He would not think about the alternative. But even as he steeled himself he narrowed his eyes, resting them on her face. There was a stricken look on it, but something more, too.

She's hiding something.

Every instinct told him that. She was concealing something, pushing it back inside her, so that he could not tell what it was. But he knew—oh, he knew.

I haven't given her the right answer—the answer she wanted to hear. I've caught her out by not giving her that answer, and she doesn't know how to react now.

He knew what she'd wanted his reaction to be. It was obvious. He was supposed to have reacted very differently from the way he had.

I was supposed to look amazed—thrilled. I was supposed to sweep her up into my arms. Tell her she was the most treasured thing in the universe to me, carrying my oh-so-precious child! I was supposed to tell her that I was thrilled beyond everything—that she'd given me the best gift I could ever have dreamt of!

And then, of course, he was supposed to have gone down on one knee, taken her hand in his, and asked her to marry him.

Because that was what they *all* wanted, didn't they? All the women who passed through his life. They wanted him to marry them.

And he was so tired of it—so bored, so exasperated.

All of them wanted to be Mrs Kyrgiakis. As if there weren't three of them already—his father's current wife and his two exes. Even his mother had coupled her new husband's name to Kyrgiakis, to ensure so she got kudos from the family connection as well as her hand in the Kyrgiakis coffers.

So, no, with quite enough Mrs Kyrgiakises in the world, he did not want another one.

Not another one who had only become one because she was pregnant—the way his mother had become Mrs Kyrgiakis the Second. Giving her the perfect opportunity to dump her unwanted first husband and snap up a second. Not that she'd wanted his father for long, or he her. They'd both got bored and taken lovers, and then another spouse each. Creating yet another Mrs Kyrgiakis.

And so the circus had gone on.

I will not perpetuate it.

Not willingly. *Never* willingly—

His eyes rested on Tia, his expression veiled. She was looking pale and nervous. He reached out a hand as if to touch her cheek, reassure her. Then he pulled back. What reassurance could he give her? He didn't want to marry her. That would hardly reassure her, would it?

'Did you do it deliberately? Take a chance that you might get pregnant?'

The words were out of his mouth before he could stop them. He heard her gasp, saw her face blanch again. As if he had slapped her.

But he could not unsay them—un-ask the question he'd pushed at her.

'Well?' he persisted.

His eyes were still resting on her, no expression in them, because he did not want to let his feelings show. He needed to keep them banked down, suppressed.

He saw her swallow, shake her head.

'Well, that's something,' he breathed. 'So, how did it happen? How is it even a possibility?'

She'd been on the Pill for months now. Ever since he'd made the decision to keep her in his life. So what had gone wrong?

He saw her drop her eyes, her face convulse. 'It was when we went to San Francisco. The changing time zones muddled me.'

He gave a heavy sigh. He should have checked—made sure she hadn't got 'muddled'.

'Well, hopefully it hasn't screwed things up completely.'

Her expression changed. Anxiety visible. But there was another emotion too. One he could not name. Did not want to.

'Would it?' Her voice was thin, as if stretched too far. Her eyes were searching his. '*Would* it screw things up completely?'

He turned away. Reached for his briefcase. It was going to be a long, draining day—getting through the annual board meeting, seeing his parents again, watching them pointedly ignore each other, pointedly show demonstrations of affection to their current new spouses, glaring testimony to the shallow fickleness of their emotions, constantly imagining themselves in love, rushing into yet another reckless, ill-considered marriage.

No wonder he didn't want to marry—didn't want to

be cornered into marrying by any woman prepared to do anything to get his ring on her finger. Including getting herself pregnant.

I didn't think Tia was like that. I thought what we had suited her, just like it suited me. I thought that she was fond of me, as I am of her—but there's nothing about love. Nothing about marriage. And, dear God, nothing about babies!

But it looked as if he'd been wrong—

He didn't answer her. Couldn't answer her. Instead he simply glanced at his watch—he was running late already.

He looked back at her as he headed for the door, not meeting her eyes. 'I'll have a pregnancy testing kit delivered,' he said—and was gone.

There was a tight wire around his throat. He felt its pressure for the rest of the day. All through the gruelling board meeting—his parents behaving just as he'd known they would, constantly pressing for yet more profits to be distributed to them. And after the meeting was the even more gruelling ordeal of an endlessly long lunch that went on all afternoon.

'You seem distracted, Anatole. Is everything all right?'

This was his Uncle Vasilis, taking the opportunity to draw him aside after the formal meal had finally finished and everyone was milling about, lighting up cigars, drinking vintage port and brandy.

'Call me old-fashioned,' Vasilis said, 'but when a young man is distracted it is usually by a woman.'

He paused again, his eyes studying Anatole even though Anatole had immediately, instinctively, blanked his expression. But it did not silence his uncle.

'You know,' Vasilis continued, 'I would so like you to fall in love and marry—make a *happy* marriage! Yes, I know you are sceptical, and I can understand why—but do not judge the world by your parents. They constantly imagine themselves in love with yet another object of their desire. Making a mess of their lives, being careless of everyone else's. Including,' he added, his eyes not shifting from Anatole's face, 'yours.'

Anatole's mouth tightened. *Making a mess of their lives...* Was that what *he* was going to do too? Had he already done it? Was he simply waiting to find out whether it was so?

Does she have the results already? Does she know if she's messed up my life—and I hers?

But a darker question was already lurking beneath those questions. Would being pregnant by him mess up Tia's life or achieve a dream for her? Attain her goal—her ambition.

Have I given her a taste for the life I lead, so that now she wants to keep it for herself, for ever?

Having a Kyrgiakis child would achieve that for her. A Kyrgiakis child would achieve a Kyrgiakis husband. Access to the Kyrgiakis coffers. To the lavish Kyrgiakis lifestyle.

'Anatole?'

His uncle's voice penetrated his circling thoughts, his turbid emotions. But he could not cope with an inquisition now, so he only gave a brief smile and asked his uncle about his latest philanthropic endeavour.

Vasilis responded easily enough, but Anatole was aware of concern in his uncle's eyes, a sense that he was being studied, worried over. He blanked it, just as he was blanking the question that had been knifing in his head all day. Did Tia have her results, and—dear God—what were they?

He wanted to phone her, but dreaded it too. So much hung in the balance—his whole future depended on Tia's answer.

As everyone finally dispersed from the hotel—Vasilis departing with a smile and saying he was looking forward to accepting his nephew's lunch invitation the next day, an invitation Anatole now wished he'd never made—he found that he actually welcomed his father catching him by the arm and telling him, in a petulant undertone, that thanks to the booming profits Anatole had just announced his latest wife had suddenly decided to divorce him.

'You've made me too rich!' he accused his son ill-temperedly. 'So now I need you to find a way to make sure she gets as little as possible.'

He dragged Anatole off to a bar, pouring into his son's ears a self-pitying moan about greedy ex-wives, and how hard done by he was by them all, while he proceeded to work his way through a bottle of whisky.

Eventually Anatole returned him to his hotel room and left him. Finally heading back to his apartment, he felt his heart start to hammer. He could postpone finding out Tia's results no longer.

Yet when he reached his apartment, close to midnight, Tia was asleep. He did not disturb her. Could not. Of the pregnancy test kit there was no sign, and he had no wish to search for it in the bathroom, to see the result—to know what his future would be. Not now, not yet...

With that wire tightening around his throat, he stood gazing down at her. She looked so small in the huge king-sized bed. Emotions flitted across the surface of her mind. Emotions he had never had cause to feel before. Thoughts he had never had to think before.

Is she carrying my child? Does it grow within her body?

Those emotions flickered again, like currents of electricity, static that could not flow, meeting resistance somewhere in the nerve fibres of his brain.

Yet he could feel the impulse to let it flow, connect, let it overcome him—so that almost, almost he stripped off his clothes to lie own with her, take her into his arms, not to make love to her, but to hold her slender, petite body, to slide his hand across her abdomen where, right now, secret and safe, their baby might be taking hold of life. To hold them both, close and cherishing…

He stepped away. He must not let himself succumb. Must do what he was doing now—walking away, taking himself off to another bedroom, sleeping there the night, his dreams troubled and troubling.

He woke the next morning to see Tia standing in the doorway, her body silhouetted in her nightgown by the morning sun.

'I'm not pregnant,' she said to him. 'I've just got my period.' There was no emotion in her voice. Nor in her face.

Then she turned and left.

Anatole lay motionless, his open eyes staring at the ceiling, where sunlight played around the light socket. It was very strange. Her announcement should have brought relief. Should have made everything well between them.

Yet it had ended everything.

CHAPTER SIX

CHRISTINE SAT AT the desk in Vasilis's study. She could feel
the echo of him here still—here where he had spent so
much of his time—and found comfort in it.

The weeks since his death had turned into months.
Slow, painful, difficult months of getting used to a house
empty of his quiet presence. It had been difficult for her,
difficult for Nicky. Tears and tantrums had been frequent
as the little boy had slowly, unwillingly come to terms
with the loss of his beloved *pappou*.

Pappou—the word stabbed into Christine's head, and
again she heard Anatole's shock. Her mind closed, automatically warding off the memory of that nightmare encounter with the man she had fled. Who had not wanted
her as she had wanted him. Who thought of her as nothing more than a cheap adventuress…a gold-digger who
had married his uncle for the wealth he could bestow
upon her.

Pain hacked at her at the thought of how badly Anatole regarded her. How much he seemed to hate her now.

She had been right to send him packing. Anything else
would have been unbearable! Unthinkable. Yet even as
she felt that resolve she felt another emotion too. Powerful—painful. Nicky had done the painting of a train for
his *pappou* and he wanted to know when his 'big cousin'
was going to come and see it.

She had given evasive answers—he lived in Greece,
Pappou's homeland, and he was very busy, working very
hard.

After a while Nicky had stopped asking, but every now
and then he would still say 'I *want* to see him again! Why

can't I see him again? I painted the picture! I want to show it to him!' And then he'd become tearful and difficult.

Guilt stabbed at Christine. Her son was going through so much now. And he always would. He would be growing up without Vasilis in his life, without the man he thought of as his grandfather.

Growing up without a father—

Her mind sheared away. What use was it to think of that? *None.* Instead, she took a breath, focussing her attention on what she needed to do right now.

Probate had finally been completed—a lengthy task, given that Vasilis's estate was large, his will complex, and it had involved the setting up of both a family trust and a philanthropic foundation to carry on his work.

It was the latter that preoccupied her now. At the end of the week she was going to have to perform her first duty as Vasilis's widow—to represent him at the opening of an exhibition of Greek art and antiquities at a prestigious London museum. Though she had always accompanied him to the events he'd sponsored, this was the first time she would be alone. It was a daunting prospect, but she was resolved to perform to the best of her ability. She owed it to Vasilis to do so.

Now, in preparation, she bowed her head to read through the correspondence and the detailed notes from the curator, to make sure she knew what she must know in time for the event.

This is for Vasilis. For him who gave me so much!

It was a fraction of what she owed him—the man who had rescued her when her life had been at its lowest, most desolate ebb.

Anatole was in a business meeting, but his mind was not on the involved mesh of investments, profits and tax exposure that was its subject. Instead he was focussed mentally on the request he had received that morning from his uncle's lawyers in London. They wanted him to contact them. Probate, apparently, had now been completed.

His mouth thinned. So now he would find out just how rich Vasilis's young widow would be. Just how much she had profited from marrying his middle-aged uncle. Oh, she had done very well indeed out of convincing him to marry her. To rescue her from Anatole, the man who had lifted her—literally—off the street!

I thought she was so devoted to me. But all along it was just the lifestyle I gave her. She couldn't wait to ensure it for herself by getting Vasilis's wedding ring on her finger after I'd made it clear to her that any hope she might have had of letting herself get pregnant to get me to marry her was out of the question.

That old familiar stab came again. It was anger—of *course* it was anger! What else could it be? It was anger that he felt when he thought about Tia abandoning him to snap up his uncle. Only anger.

Restlessly, Anatole shifted in his seat, impatient for the meeting to be done. Yet when he finally was free to get back to his office, to phone London, he knew he was reluctant to do so.

Did he really want to stir up in himself again those mixed emotions that his uncle's death had caused? That his rash visit to England on the day of the funeral had plunged him into? Shouldn't he just leave things be? He could not alter his uncle's will—if his widow had all Vasilis's money to splurge, so what? Why should he care?

Except that—

Except that it is not just about Tia, is it? Or about you. There's someone else to think about.

Vasilis's son. Nicky. The little boy he'd known nothing about—never guessed existed.

That scene burned in his head again—himself hunkering down to offer solace to the heartbroken child. Emotion thrust inside him, but a new one now—one that seemed to pierce more deeply than the thought that the woman he had once romanced, made love to, taken into his life, had abandoned him. It was a piercing that came from the sobs of a bereft child, that made him want to comfort him, console him.

He stared sightlessly across his office. Where did that emotion come from? *Never* had he thought about children—except negatively. Oh, not because he disliked them, but because they had nothing to do with him. Could never have anything to do with him. What he'd said to Tia, that grim day when she'd thought she was pregnant, was as true now as it had been then.

And yet—

What instinct had made him seek to comfort the little boy? To divert him, bring a smile to his face, light up his eyes?

It's because he's Vasilis's son. Because he has no one else to look out for him now. Only a mother who married his father just to endow herself with a wealthy lifestyle she could never have aspired to otherwise.

His expression changed. Turned steely. He had told Tia that Nicky's existence changed everything but she had rejected what he'd said. Sent him from her house. Banned him from making any contact with Nicky. His eyes darkened. Well, that was not going to happen. *Someone* had to look out for Vasilis's child, and now that his widow had a free rein with her late husband's wealth she could do anything she wanted with it! What security would there be for Vasilis's son when his mother was an ambitious, luxury-loving gold-digger?

The phone on his desk sounded, indicating the call to London was ready for him. Grim-faced, he picked it up. Whatever he had to do, he would ensure that his vulnerable young cousin was not left to the mercy of his despised mother.

I'll fight her for justice for her son—for Vasilis's son.

Yet when he slowly hung up the phone, some ten minutes later, his expression was different. Very different. He called through to his secretary.

'Book me on the next flight to London.'

Christine sat back in the car that was taking her up to London for the evening. Her nerves were jittery, and not just because she would be representing Vasilis at the exhibition's opening. It was also because this would be the first time she'd been to London since he'd died—and London held memories that were of more than her husband.

She felt her mind shear away. No, she must not think—must not remember how she had met Anatole, how he had swept her into his life, how she had fallen head over heels for a man who had been to her eyes like a prince out of a fairytale!

But he hadn't been a prince after all. He'd been an ordinary person, however rich and gilded his existence, and he'd had no desire for her to be a permanent part of his life. No desire at all for a baby…a child.

It was Vasilis who'd wanted that. Had wanted the child who'd given him a joy that, as Christine sadly knew, he'd never thought to have.

The knowledge comforted her.

However much he gave me—immense though that was, and eternally grateful though I am—I know that I gave him Nicky to love...

Now she was all Nicky had.

Her nerves jangled again. She must not think of Anatole, must only be grateful that he'd accepted her dismissal. Had made no further attempt to get in touch. Make contact with Nicky.

Her mouth set. Eyes stark.

His knowing of Nicky's existence doesn't change anything. And I won't—I won't!—have anyone near Nicky who thinks so ill of me, poisoning my son's mind against me...

For the remainder of the journey she forced herself to focus only on the evening's event.

Later, when the moment came, she felt a sudden tightening of her throat as she was introduced as Mrs Vasilis Kyrgiakis, then she took a measured breath and began her short, carefully written speech. She said how pleased her husband had been to support this important exhibition of Hellenistic art and artefacts, so expertly curated by the museum—giving a smiling nod to the director, Dr Lanchester—and then diverted a little on descriptions of some of the key exhibits, before concluding with a reassurance that despite Vasilis Kyrgiakis's untimely death his work was being entrusted to a foundation specifically set up for that purpose.

After handing over to Dr Lanchester she stepped away, and as the formal opening was completed started to mingle socially with the invited guests.

Everyone was in evening dress, and although, of course, her dress was black, her state of mourning did not prevent her from accepting a proffered glass of champagne. She sipped it delicately, listening to something the director's wife was saying, and smiling appropriately. She knew both the director and his wife, having dined with them together with Vasilis, before his final illness had taken its fatal grip on him.

She was about to make some remark or other when a voice behind her turned her to stone.

'Won't you introduce me?'

She whipped round, not believing her eyes. But it was impossible to deny who she was seeing.

Anatole.

Anatole in a black tuxedo, like all the other male guests, towering over her.

Shock made faintness drum in her head.

How on earth? What on earth?

He gave a swift, empty smile. 'I felt it my duty to represent the Kyrgiakis family tonight,' he informed her.

If it was meant as a barb, implying that *she* could not possibly do so, she did not let her reaction show. She gave a grave nod.

'I'm sure Vasilis would have appreciated your presence here,' she acknowledged quietly. 'He worked hard to ensure this exhibition would be possible. Many of the artefacts have been rescued from the turmoil in the Middle East, to find safety here, for the time being, until eventually they can be securely returned.'

She indicated with a graceful gesture towards some of the exhibits to which she was referring, but Anatole was not looking. His eyes were only on her. Taking her in. The woman standing there, in a black silk evening gown, with long sleeves and a high-cut neckline, was every inch in mourning, but she was not a woman Anatole recognised.

He'd arrived to see her take centre stage, and had not believed it could be Tia—*Christine*—Vasilis's widow. Poised, elegant, mature—and perfectly capable of addressing a room full of learned dignitaries and opening an exhibition of Hellenistic archaeology.

No, she was definitely not the socially nervous, timid Tia he remembered.

Nor was it the Tia he remembered who was turning now towards the museum's director.

'Dr Lanchester—may I introduce Vasilis's nephew, Anatole Kyrgiakis?'

If there was any tremor in her voice Anatole did not hear it. Her composure was perfect. Only the sudden masking in her eyes as she'd first seen him there had revealed otherwise. And that masking came again as the museum director smiled at Anatole.

'Will you be taking on your uncle's role?' he asked.

'Alas, I will be unable to become as directly involved as he was, but I hope to be one of the trustees of the foundation,' Anatole replied easily. 'Along with, I'm sure, my…' He hesitated slightly, turning to Christine. 'I'm not sure quite what our relationship is,' he said.

Was that another barb? She ignored it, as she had the first. 'I doubt it has a formal designation,' she remarked, with dogged composure. 'And, yes, I shall be one of the foundation's trustees.'

Her mouth tightened. *And no way on earth will I let you be one too!*

The very thought of having to attend trustees' meetings with Anatole there—she felt a cold chill through her. Then he was speaking again. He was smiling a courtesy smile, but she could see the dark glint in his eyes.

'I do hope, then, that you no longer believe Alexander the Great to be contemporary with the Greek War of Independence!' he said lightly.

Did he mean to wound her? If he did, then it only showed how bitter he was towards her.

Before, when she had been Tia—ignorant, uneducated Tia, who'd spent her schooldays nursing her mother—he'd never been anything other than sympathetic towards her in her lack of knowledge of all that he took for granted with his expensive private education.

But he'd meant to wound her now, and she would not let him do so.

So she only smiled in return, not looking at him but at the others. 'Before I married Vasilis,' she explained, 'I was completely ignorant of a great deal of history. But I *do* now know that in the fourth century BC Alexander was pre-dating the Battle of Navarino in 1827 by quite some time!'

Her expression was humorous. It had to be. How else could she deal with this?

'I think—at least, I *hope*!—that now, thanks to Vasilis's tuition, I can recognise the Hellenistic style, at least in obvious examples. Speaking of which…' she turned to the curator of the exhibition and bestowed an optimistic smile upon him '… I wonder if I might impose on you to guide me around the exhibits?'

'I'd be delighted!' he assured her, and to her profound relief she was able to move away.

Nevertheless, as she was conducted around she was burningly conscious of Anatole's presence in all the rooms.

She prayed that she would not have to talk to him again. Why had he turned up? Had he meant it, saying he wanted to be one of the foundation's trustees? What power would she have to prevent him? After all, he was a Kyrgiakis— how could she object?

But perhaps he only said it to get at me. Just like he made that reference to how ignorant I once was…

She felt a little sting inside her. Did he truly hate her so much? Her throat tightened. Of course he did! Hadn't he said it to her face, the day of Vasilis's funeral, calling her such vile names?

But you didn't want me, Anatole—and Vasilis did! So why berate me for accepting what he offered with such kindness, such generosity?

The answer was obvious, of course. Five long years of anger were driving him, and Anatole believed that she had manoeuvred Vasilis into marrying her so that she could enjoy the lavish Kyrgiakis lifestyle he provided. For no other reason.

A great sense of weariness washed over her. The strain of having to represent Vasilis tonight, the poignancy of the occasion and then the shock of Anatole intruding, the barbs he had directed at her—were all overpowering her.

Forcing herself to make some kind of appropriate response to the curator as he introduced each exhibit, she counted the minutes until she could decently call a halt. She had to get away—escape.

Finally, murmuring her excuses—readily accepted,

given her mourning status—she was treading through the empty corridors towards the museum's entrance.

'Leaving so soon?'

The voice behind her on the wide stone staircase echoed in the otherwise deserted building, well away from the exhibition gallery.

This time she was more collected in her reaction. 'Yes,' she said.

'I'll drive you back,'

Anatole's footsteps quickened and he drew level with her. Moved to take her arm. She avoided it, stepping aside.

'Thank you, but my car is waiting.'

Hurriedly, she went out, stepped onto the wide pavement, thankful to see her chauffeured car at the kerbside.

She turned back to Anatole. He seemed taller than ever, more overpowering. She lifted her chin. 'Don't let me keep you, Anatole,' she said.

It was nothing more than an expression, and yet she heard it echo savagely in her head. No, she had not been able to *keep* Anatole, had she?

Because I committed the cardinal sin in his book. The one unforgivable crime.

Her mind sheared away. Why remember the past? It was gone, and gone for ever.

She headed determinedly towards her car, but Anatole was there before her, opening her door. Then, to her consternation, as she got inside as quickly as her long gown permitted Anatole followed.

'I've dismissed my own car. I'll see you to your destination. Where are you staying?'

He realised he had no idea. Had Vasilis acquired a London base? He did not use his father's hotel suite—that he knew.

The suite I never went to that fatal night I took Tia into my arms—into my life.

No, don't remember that night. It was over, gone—nothing was left of that life now.

He heard her give with audible reluctance the name of a hotel. It was a top hotel, but a quiet one—not fashionable. Ideal for his uncle, Anatole acknowledged.

He said as much, and Christine nodded.

'Yes, Vasilis always liked it. Old-fashioned, but peaceful. And it has a lovely roof garden—you'd hardly know you were in London—'

She stopped. Memory sprang, unwanted, of Anatole's verdant roof terrace at his London apartment, of him saying that he did not care for cities.

There was a moment of silence. Was Anatole remembering too?

Well, what if he is? So what?

Defiance filled her, quelling the agitation that had leapt automatically as he'd got into the car. She was sitting as far away as possible, and even knowing the presence of Mr Hughes behind his glass screen was preventing complete privacy with Anatole, her heart was beating hectically. She tried to slow it—she must retain control, composure. She *must*!

I am Vasilis's widow. He can protect me still simply by virtue of that. That is my identity now.

She pulled her mind back—Anatole was speaking.

'I wanted to tell you,' he was saying, his voice stiff, as if the words did not come easily, 'how impressed I was with you tonight. You handled the occasion very well.' He paused. 'You did Vasilis proud.'

Christine's turned her head, her eyes widening. Had Anatole really just said that? Anatole who thought her the lowest of the low?

'I did it for him,' she said quietly, and looked away, out of her window, away from Anatole.

She could feel his presence in the car as something tangible, threatening to overpower her. How many times had she and he driven like this, through the city night? So many nights—so many cities...

It was so long ago—five years ago. A lifetime ago. And I am not the same person—not by any measure. Even my name is different now. I have been a wife, and now I am a widow—I am a mother. And Anatole can mean nothing to me any more. Nothing!

Just as she, in the end, had meant nothing to him.

Memory stabbed at her of how Anatole had sat her down, talked to her, his face tense, the morning she had told him she wasn't pregnant after all.

'Tia—this is something you have to understand. I do not want to marry and I do not want to have children. Not with you—not with anyone. Now, if either or both of those things is something you do want,' he'd continued in the same taut voice, 'then you must accept that it is not going to happen with me. Not *voluntarily.*'

His voice had twisted on that word. He'd been sitting opposite her, leaning forward slightly, his hands hanging loosely between his thighs, an earnest expression on his face as if he were explaining something to someone incapable of understanding.

And that was me—I couldn't understand. So I learned the hard way....

He'd taken a breath, looked her straight in the eyes. 'I like you Tia. You're very sweet, and very lovely, and we've had a really great time together, but...' He'd taken another breath. 'What I will not tolerate is any attempt by you to...to get pregnant and force me to the altar. I won't have that, Tia—I won't have it.'

He'd held her eyes, making her hear what he was telling her.

'So from now on make sure there is no chance of another scare like this one, OK? No more getting "muddled up" over time zones.' And then an edge had come into his voice, and his eyes had had a look of steel in them. 'If that is what really happened.'

He'd got to his feet, his six-foot height dwarfing her seated figure, and she'd looked up at him, her throat tight and painful, her hands twisted in her lap.

'If you want a baby, Tia, accept that it cannot be with me.' His expression had hardened. 'And if it's me you want one with—well, then you had better leave, right away, because it's over between us—*over*.'

He'd left the apartment then, heading to his office, and she'd watched him go. Her vision had grown hazy, and she'd felt feel sobs rising. The moment he'd gone she had rushed into the bathroom, releasing the pent-up tears, hating it that Anatole was being like that—hating it that she'd given him cause.

What she longed for so unbearably was what he did *not* want, and her heart felt as if it was cracking in pieces.

Her red-rimmed eyes had fallen on the little rectangular packet by the basin. It had been delivered the day before but she had dreaded using it. Dreaded finding out. Finding out whether what she had once thought would be a dream come true was instead turning into a nightmare. Was she forcing a child on Anatole—forcing him into a loveless, bitter marriage he did not want to make.

Then her period had arrived after all, making the test unnecessary.

She'd stared at the packet. Fear in her throat.

I've got to be sure—absolutely, totally sure—that I'm not pregnant. Because that's the only way he'll still want me.

She'd shut her eyes. She needed Anatole to want her on any terms at all. *Any* terms.

So she had done the test. Even though she hadn't needed to. Because she hadn't been able to bear not to.

She had done the test…and stared at the little white stick…

* * *

Christine's car was pulling up at the hotel. Anatole leant across, opening her door for her. The brush of his sleeve on her arm made her feel faint, and she had to fight to keep her air of composure, dangerously fragile as it was.

She turned to bid him goodnight. But he was getting out too. Addressing her.

'I need to speak to you.' He glanced at the hotel entrance. 'In private.'

He took her elbow, moved to guide her inside. Unless she wrested herself away from him, made a scene in front of Mr Hughes and the doorman tipping his hat to them, she must comply.

The moment she was indoors, she stepped away.

'Well?' she said, lifting her eyebrows, her expression still unyielding.

His eyes had gone to where a small bar opened up off the lobby, and she walked stiffly to one of the tables, sat herself down. The place was almost empty, and she was glad. She ordered coffee for herself and Anatole did likewise, adding a brandy.

Only when the drinks arrived did he speak. 'I've heard from Vasilis's London solicitors,' he opened.

Christine's eyes went to him. She was burningly conscious of him there—of his tall, effortlessly elegant body, of the achingly familiar scent of his aftershave, of the slight darkening of his jawline at this advanced hour of the evening.

How she had loved to rub her fingers along the roughening edges, feeling passion start to quicken…

Yet again, she hauled her mind away. Anatole's voice was clipped, restrained as he continued. She realised he was tense, and wondered why.

'Now that probate has been granted they have told me the contents of Vasilis's will.' The words came reluctantly from him, his mouth tight. His eyes rested on her face, looking at her blankly. Then his expression changed. 'Why did you let me think you would inherit all my uncle's personal fortune for yourself?'

Christine's eyes widened. 'I didn't,' she said tightly. '*That*, Anatole,' she added, her voice sharp, 'was something you assumed entirely on your own!'

He half lifted his hand—as if her objection were irrelevant. As if there were more he had to say.

'My uncle's wealth has been left entirely in trust for his son—you get only a trivial income for yourself. Everything else belongs to Nicky!'

Her eyes flickered and her chin lifted. 'I wouldn't call my income *trivial*. It's over thirty thousand pounds a year,' she replied.

'Chickenfeed!' he said dismissively.

Her expression tightened. 'To you, yes. To me it's enough to live on if I have to—more than enough. I was penniless when I married Vasilis—as you reminded me. Of *course* everything must go to Nicky. And besides—' she allowed a flash of cynicism to show in her eyes '—as I'm sure you will point out to me, I will continue to reap the benefits of Nicky's inheritance while he's a minor. I get to live in a Queen Anne country house, and I'll have all of Nicky's money to enjoy while he grows up.'

A hand lifted and slashed sideways. 'But you will have no spending money other than your own income.'

Her composure snapped. 'Oh, for heaven's sake, Anatole. What am I going to spend money on? I have enough clothes to last me a lifetime. And I've told you I have no ambition to racket around the world causing scandals, as you so charmingly accused me of wanting to do. I simply want to go on living where I do now—for my sake as much as Nicky's. It's where he's grown up so far, where I have friends and know people who knew Vasilis and liked him, valued him. If I want to take Nicky on holiday, of course funds will be made available to me. I shall want for nothing—though I'm sure you'll be the first to accuse me of the opposite!'

She saw him reach for his brandy, take a hefty mouthful before setting it down on the table with a decisive click.

'I can accuse you of nothing.' He took a breath—a deep, shuddering breath—and focussed his eyes on her. Emotion worked in his face. 'Instead—' He stopped, abruptly. His expression changed. So did his voice. 'Instead,' he repeated, 'I have to apologise. I said things to you that I… that were unfair—'

He broke off again. Reached for his coffee and downed it. Then he was looking at her again. As if she were not the person he had thought her to be.

But she isn't. She's not the avaricious, ambitious gold-digger I thought. It was she who insisted on Vasilis leaving his personal fortune to Nicky, his lawyers told me, with nothing for her apart from that paltry income.

It was not what he'd expected to hear. But because of it…

It changes everything.

It was the same phrase that had burst from him when he'd discovered the existence of Vasilis's son, and now it burned in his head again, bringing to the fore the second thing he had to tell her. The imperative that had been building up in him, fuelled by that strange, compelling emotion that had filled him when he'd crouched down beside the little boy to console and comfort him.

'I would like to see Nicky again—soon.'

Immediately Christine's face was masked.

'He is my blood,' he said tightly. 'He should know me. Even if—' He stopped.

She filled the gap, her face still closed. Her tone was acid. 'Even if *I* am his mother?'

Anatole's brows drew together in a frown. 'I did not mean—' Again he broke off.

He'd just told her he couldn't accuse her of wanting her

husband's fortune—but she'd still persuaded a man thirty years older than her to marry her in order to acquire the lavish lifestyle she could never have achieved otherwise. That alone must condemn her. What other interpretation could there be for what she had done when she had left him to marry his uncle?

Conflict and confusion writhed in him again.

'Yes, you did,' Christine retorted, her tone still acid. 'Anatole, look—try to understand something. *You* may not have wanted to marry me, to have a child with me— but your uncle did. It was his *choice* to marry me. You insult him if you think otherwise and your approval was not necessary.'

She saw his hand clench, emotion flash across his face, but she didn't want to hear any more. She got to her feet, weariness sweeping over her. She longed for Vasilis's protective company, but he was gone. She was alone in the world now. Except for Nicky—her beloved son.

The most precious being in the universe to her.

The very reason she had married.

Anatole watched her walk out—an elegant, graceful woman. A woman he had once held in his arms, known intimately—and yet now she was like a stranger. Even the name she insisted on calling herself emphasised that.

Emotion roiled within him in the confusing mesh that swirled so confusingly in his head, that he could make no sense of.

But there was one thing he *could* make sense of.

Whatever his conflicting thoughts about Tia—or Christine, as she now preferred to be known—and whatever she had done…abandoning him, marrying his uncle, remaking her life as Vasilis's oh-so-young wife…she'd gone up in the world in a way that she could never have imagined possible the day she had trudged down that London street with a heavy suitcase holding all her possessions.

Now she was transformed into a woman who was poised and chicly dressed, who was able—of all things!—to introduce an exhibition of ancient artefacts as if she were perfectly well acquainted with such esoteric knowledge. Yes, whatever she had done in these years when he had never seen her, there was one thing he could make sense of.

Nicky. The little boy who had lost the man he'd thought of as his grandfather—who would now be raised only by his mother, knowing nothing of his paternal background or his heritage.

Anatole's face steeled. Well, he would ensure that did not happen. He owed it to Vasilis—to the little boy himself—to play *some* part in his life at least.

A stab of remorse—even guilt—pierced him. In the five long years since Tia had left him he'd received, from time to time, communications from his uncle. Careful overtures of reconciliation.

He'd ignored them all—blanked them.

But he could not—*would* not—ignore the existence of Vasilis's young son.

I want to see him again!

Resolve filled him. Something about the child called to him.

Again that memory filled his head of how he'd distracted the little boy, talking about painting a picture of a train, just as he himself had once done for his uncle in that long-ago time when it had been he himself who'd been the child without any kind of father figure in his life to take an interest in him. When there had only been occasional visits from Vasilis—never his own father, to whom he had been of no interest at all.

Well, for Nicky it would not be like that.

He'll have me. I'll make sure of it!

And if that meant seeing Tia—Christine—again, well, that was something he would have to endure.

Unease flickered in him. *Can I cope with that? Seeing her in the years to come with Nicky growing up?*

It was a question that, right now, he did not want to think about.

CHAPTER SEVEN

'Mumma, *look*!'

Nicky's excited voice called to her and Christine finished her chat to Nanny Ruth and paid attention to her son.

They were out in the garden now that spring was here, and Nicky was perched on a bench beside a rangy young man who was showing him photos on his mobile phone.

As Nanny Ruth went off to take her well-earned break Christine went and sat herself down too, lifting Nicky onto her lap. 'What have you got there, Giles?' she asked with a smile.

The young man grinned. 'Juno's litter,' he said. 'They arrived last night. I couldn't wait to show Nicky.'

'One of them is going to be mine!' Nicky piped up excitedly. 'You said, Mumma, you *said*!'

'Yes, I did say,' Christine agreed.

She'd talked it through with Giles Barcourt and his parents. They were the village's major landowners from whom Vasilis had bought the former Dower House on the estate. They had always been on very friendly terms, and now, they were recommending to Christine that acquiring a puppy would help Nicky recover from losing his beloved *pappou*. She was in full agreement, seeing just how excited he was at the prospect.

'So,' Giles continued, 'which one shall it be, do you think? It will be a good few weeks before they're ready to leave home, but you can come and visit them to make your final choice.'

He grinned cheerfully at Nicky and Christine, and she smiled warmly back. He was a likeable young man—about her own age, she assumed, with a boyish air about him that she suspected would last all his life. He'd studied agriculture at Cirencester, like so many of his peers, and now ran the family estate along with his father. A born countryman.

'By the way,' he went on, throwing her a cheerful look again, 'Mama—' he always used the old-fashioned moniker in a shamelessly humorous fashion '—would love you to come to dinner next Friday. My sister will be there, with her sproglets and the au pair, so Nicky can join the nursery party. The sproglets are promised one of the pups too, so there'll be a bunfight over choosing. What do you say?'

Christine smiled, knowing the invitation was kindly meant. It would be poignant to be there without Vasilis. But at some point she must start socialising again, and the Barcourts had always been so kind to her. And Nicky would love it.

'That would be lovely—thank you!' she exclaimed, and Giles grinned back even more warmly.

She was aware that he was probably sweet on her—as he might have called it, had any such introspection occurred to him—but he never pushed it.

'Great!' he said. 'I'll let her know.'

He was about to say something else, but at that moment there was the sound of footsteps on the gravel path around the side of the house. She looked up, startled.

A mix of shock and dismay filled her. 'Anatole…' she said faintly.

This time there had not even been any warning from her housekeeper. Anatole must have parked his car, heard voices, and come across the gardens. Now he was striding up to them. Unlike last time he was not in a black business suit, nor in a tuxedo as he had been in London. This time he was wearing jeans, a cashmere sweater and casually styled leather jacket.

He looked…

Devastating.

A thousand memories drummed through her head, swooping like butterflies. Like the butterflies now fluttering inside her stomach as he stood, surveying the group. Her grip was lax suddenly, and she felt Nicky wriggle off her lap.

Excitement blazed from Nicky's face and he rushed up to Anatole. 'You came—you *came*!' he exclaimed. 'I did that painting! I painted it for Pappou, like you said.'

Anatole hunkered down. 'Did you?' He smiled. 'That's great. Will you show it to me later?'

There was something about the ecstatic greeting he was receiving that was sending emotion coursing through him. His grin widened. How could he possibly have stayed away so long when a welcome like this was coming his way?

'Yes!' cried Nicky. 'It's in my playroom.' Then something even more exciting occurred to him. 'Come and see my puppy!'

He caught at Anatole's hand, drew him over to the bench where Giles had got to his feet.

'Puppy?' queried Anatole.

He was focussing on Nicky, but at the same time he was burningly conscious of Tia's presence. Her face was pale, her expression clearly masked. She didn't want him there—it was blaring from her like a beacon—but he didn't care. He wasn't here for *her*, but for Vasilis's son. That was his only concern.

Not the way that her long hair was caught back in a simple clip...nor how effortlessly lovely she looked in a lightweight sweater and jeans.

Was her blonde loveliness the reason her current visitor was there? Anatole's eyes snapped across to the young man who'd stood up, and was now addressing him.

'Giles Barcourt,' he said in an easy manner, oblivious to what Christine instantly saw was a skewering look from

Anatole. 'I'm a neighbour. Come to show young Nicky Juno's pups.' He grinned, and absently ruffled Nicky's hair.

Christine saw Anatole slowly take Giles's outstretched hand and shake it briefly.

'Giles—this is…' she swallowed '…this is Vasilis's nephew, Anatole Kyrgiakis.'

Immediately Giles's expression changed. 'I'm sorry about your uncle,' he said. 'We all liked him immensely.'

There was a sincerity in his voice that Christine hoped Anatole would respect. She saw him give a tight nod.

'Thank you,' he said.

His glance moved between her and Giles assessingly. She felt her spine stiffen. Then he was speaking again.

'A puppy sounds like a very good idea,' he said.

Was he addressing her or Giles? Whichever it was, it was Giles who answered.

'Absolutely,' he said. 'Take the little guy's mind off… well, you know.' His glance went back to Christine. 'I'll take myself off, then,' he said cheerfully. 'We'll see you on Friday week. Come a bit earlier, so the tinies can have some playtime together and inspect the puppies.'

His glance encompassed Anatole.

'Dinner with my parents,' he explained, adding without prompting, 'You'd be most welcome to join us.' He smiled with his usual unaffected good humour.

Christine waited for Anatole to make some polite but evasive reply. To her shock, he did the exact opposite. 'Thank you—that's very good of you.'

'Great! Well, see you, then. Cheers, you guys!' He loped off, waving at Nicky, and disappeared.

Anatole watched him go. He'd wondered who the muddy-wheeled four by four in the parking area behind the house belonged to, and now he knew.

He turned back to Christine. 'An admirer?' he said silkily. But beneath the silk was another emotion, one he did not care to name.

Anger flashed in her eyes. Raw, vehement. But she did not deign to honour his jibe with a reply. Instead, she said, 'What are you doing here Anatole?'

Nearly a fortnight had passed since that second encounter with him in London, and she had hoped that he'd taken himself off again, abandoned his declared intention to have anything more to do with her. With Nicky.

But his next words only confirmed that intention. He looked at her. 'I told you I wanted to see Nicky again.'

All too conscious of her son's presence, of the fact that he was tugging at Anatole to get his attention, Christine knew she could not do anything other than reply with, 'Did you not think to ring first?'

'To ask *permission* to see Vasilis's son?' His voice was back to being silky. Then he turned his attention back to Nicky. 'OK, so how about showing me your painting, then?' he asked.

'Yes—yes!' Nicky exclaimed.

Christine took a breath. 'I'll take you up. Nanny Ruth is having her break now.'

She led the way indoors. She was trying hard to stay composed, though her heart was hammering. Behind her she could hear Anatole's deep voice, and Nicky's piping one. She felt her heart clench.

Inside, she headed up the wide staircase and then along the landing to where another flight of stairs led to the nursery floor beneath the dormer windows.

Nicky's playroom was lavish—Anatole's glance took in a rocking horse, a train set, a garage and toy cars, plus a large collection of teddy bears and the like. The walls were covered in colourful educational posters, and the plentiful bookshelves were full of books.

A large table was set by the dormer window, and on a nearby wall there was a wide noticeboard which held a painting of a blue train with red wheels. There were some other paintings pinned up too, and in alphabet letters was spelled out the phrase, *Paintings for my pappou*. A lot of kisses followed.

Anatole felt his throat close, a choke rising. This was clearly the nursery of a much-loved child.

'There it is!' Nicky cried out, and ran to the notice-board, climbing up on a chair and pointing to the painting.

Then he pointed to the others—a red car, a house with chimneys and a green door, and a trio of stick people with huge faces. Smiling faces. Underneath each of the stick people was a name, painstakingly written out in thick pen around dotted guidelines: *Pappou*, *Mumma* and *Nicky*. The stick people were surrounded by kisses.

'That's my *pappou*,' Nicky said. 'He lives in heaven. He got sick. We'll see him later.' He cast a quivering look at Christine. 'Won't we, Mumma?'

It was Anatole who answered. 'Yes, we will,' he said decisively. 'We all will. We'll have a big, big party when we see him.'

The quivering look vanished from his little cousin's eyes. Then they widened excitedly. 'A party? With balloons? And cakes?'

'Definitely,' said Anatole. He sat himself down at the table on the other chair. 'Now,' he said to Nicky, 'how about if we do some more painting. Do you know...' he looked at Nicky '...there isn't a picture of me here yet, is there?'

'I'll do one now,' Nicky said immediately, and grabbed at the box of paints and some of the drawing paper piled on the table. He looked at Anatole. 'You do one of *me*,' he instructed, and gave some paper and a brush to his big cousin, who took them smilingly.

'You'll need some water,' Christine said.

She went into the bathroom leading off the playroom, which linked through to Nicky's bedroom next to Nanny Ruth's quarters. As she filled the jar she swallowed, blinking. But she soon went back, set the filled jar down on the table.

'Thank you, Mumma,' said Nicky dutifully.

Nanny Ruth was very keen on manners.

'You have fun, munchkin,' she said.

She left the room. She had to get out of there—had to stop seeing her son and Anatole, poring over their labours, their heads bent together—both so dark-haired, dark-eyed. So alike…

She clattered down the stairs to the main landing. How long would Anatole be here? Did he expect to stay the night?

He can't stay here—he can't!

Panic rose in her throat, then subsided. No, of course he would not want to stay here. It would not be *comme il faut* for her to have such a guest, even if he *was* her late husband's nephew. Even *without* anyone knowing their past relationship.

But if he wasn't heading back to town tonight he'd have to stay at the White Hart in the nearby market town. It was upmarket enough, in this well-heeled part of England, not to repel him, and they should have vacancies this time of year. She realised her mind was rambling, busying itself with practical thoughts so that she didn't have to let in the thought she most desperately wanted to keep at bay.

Anatole and Nicky…heads together…so alike…so very, very alike.

No! Don't go there! Just don't go there! That was a past that never happened. Anatole did not want a child… did not want a child by me…did not want me for a wife…

Emotion rose up inside her in a billowing wave of pain. Pain for the idiot she'd been, her head stuffed full of silly fairytales!

With a cutting breath, she headed downstairs into her sitting room to phone the White Hart, and then let Mrs

Hughes know they might have an unexpected guest for dinner. Her thoughts ran on—hectic, agitated.

She rubbed at her head. If only Anatole would go away. He'd kept away while Vasilis was alive. As if she were poison…contaminated. But if he was set on seeing Nicky—who seemed so thrilled that he'd come, so animated and delighted…

How can I stop Anatole from visiting, from getting to know Nicky? How can I possibly stop him?

She couldn't think about it—not now, not here.

With a smothered cry she made her phone call, put her housekeeper on warning, then got out the file on Vasilis's foundation and busied herself in the paperwork.

It was close on an hour later when the house phone went. It was Nanny Ruth, back on duty for the evening, wanting a decision about Nicky's teatime.

'Well, why not let him stay up this evening?' Christine said. That way, if Anatole was assuming he would dine here, she would have the shield of her son present. Surely that would help, wouldn't it?

Some twenty minutes later her housekeeper put her head round the door.

'Nicky and Mr Kyrgiakis are coming downstairs,' she said, 'and dinner's waiting to be served.'

Christine thanked her and got up. She would not bother to change. Her clothes were fine. Anatole would still be in his jeans and sweater, and Nicky would be in his dressing gown.

She went into the dining room, saw them already there. Anatole was talking to Nicky about one of the pictures on the wall. It was of skaters on a frozen canal.

'Brrr! It looks freezing!' Anatole was shivering exaggeratedly.

'It's Christmas,' explained Nicky. 'That's why it's snowy.'

'Do you have snowy Christmases here?' Anatole asked.

Nicky shook his head, looking cross. 'No,' he said disgustedly.

Anatole looked across at Christine, paused in the doorway. 'Your mother and I had a snowy Christmas together once—long before you were born, Nicky. Do you remember?'

If he'd thrown a brick at her she could not have been more horrified. She was stunned into silence, immobility.

With not a flicker of acknowledgement of her appalled reaction, he went on, addressing her directly. 'Switzerland? That chalet at the ski resort I took you to? We went tobogganing—you couldn't ski—and I did a black run. We took the cable car up, I skied down and you came down by cable car. You told me you were terrified for me.'

She paled, opening her mouth, then closing it again. He was doing it deliberately—he *had* to be. He was referring to that unforgettable Christmas she'd spent with him and the unforgettable months she'd spent with him—

'What's tobogganinning?' Nicky asked, to her abject relief.

Anatole answered him. He was glad to do so. Had he gone *mad*, reminding Tia—reminding himself—of that Christmas they'd spent in Switzerland?

I'm not here to stir up the past—evoke memories. It's the future that is important now—the future of Vasilis's son. Only that.

He answered the little boy cheerfully. 'Like a sledge— you sit on it, and it slides down the hill on the snow. I'll take you one day. And you can learn to ski, too. And skate—like in the picture.'

'I like that picture,' Nicky said.

'It's worth liking,' Anatole said dryly, his eyes flickering to Christine. 'It's a minor Dutch Master.'

'Claes van der Geld,' Christine said, for something to say—something to claw her mind out of the crevasse it had fallen into with the memory of that Christmas with Anatole.

They'd made love on Christmas Eve, on a huge sheep-skin rug, by the blazing log fire…

Anatole's eyes were on her, with that same look of surprise in them, she realised, as when she'd mentioned Vasilis discussing Aeschylus and Pindar with the vicar.

She gave a thin smile, and then turned her attention to Nicky, getting him settled on his chair, then taking her own place at the foot of the table. Anatole's place had been set opposite Nicky. The head of the table was empty.

As she sat down she felt a knifing pang in her heart at Vasilis's absence, and her eyes lingered on the chair her husband had used to sit in.

'Do you miss him?'

The words came from Anatole, and she twisted her head towards him. There was a different expression on his face now. Not sceptical. Not ironic. Not taunting. Almost…quizzical.

Her eyes narrowed. 'What do you think?' she retaliated, snatching at her glass, and then realising it had no water in it.

He reached for the jug of water on the table, filled her glass and then his own. 'I don't know,' he said slowly. His mouth tightened. 'There's a lot I don't know, it seems. For example…' his tone of voice changed again '… I didn't know that you knew about Dutch Old Masters. Or anything about Hellenistic sculpture. Or classical Greece literature. And yet it seems you do.'

She levelled a look at him. There was no emotion in it. 'Your uncle was a good teacher,' she said. 'I had nearly five years of personal tuition from him. He was patient, and kind, infinitely knowledgeable, and—'

She couldn't continue. Her voice was breaking, her throat choking. Her eyes misted and she blinked rapidly.

'Mumma…?'

She heard Nicky's voice, thin and anxious, and shook her unshed tears away, making herself smile and reach for her son, leaning forward to drop a kiss on his little head.

'It's all right, darling, Mumma's fine now.' She made her face brighter. 'Do you think Mrs H has made pasta?' she asked. It was no guess—Mrs Hughes always did pasta for Nicky when he ate downstairs.

'Yes!' he exclaimed. 'I *love* pasta!' he informed his cousin.

Anatole was grinning, all his attention on Nicky too. 'So do I,' he said. 'And so,' he said conspiratorially, 'does your mumma!'

His gaze slid sideways. He was speaking to her again before he could stop himself. Why, he didn't know. He only knew that words were coming from him anyway.

'We always ate it when you cooked. Don't you remember?'

Again, she reeled. Of *course* she remembered!

I remember everything—everything about the time we spent together. It's carved into my memory, each and every day!

She reached for her water, gulping it down. Then the door opened and Mrs Hughes came in, pushing a trolley.

'Pasta!' exclaimed Nicky in glee as Christine got to her feet to help her housekeeper serve up.

Nicky did indeed have pasta, but for herself and Anatole there was more sophisticated fare: a subtly flavoured and exquisitely cooked ragout of lamb, with grilled polenta and French beans.

There was no first course—Nicky wouldn't last through a three-course meal and he was eager to start eating straight away—but, again, Nanny Ruth's training held fast.

Christine put a few French beans on a side plate, arranging them carefully into a tower to make them more palatable.

'How many beans can you eat?' she asked Nicky, and smiled. 'Can you eat ten? Count them while you eat them,' she said, draping his napkin around his neck—she knew Mrs Hughes's pasta came with tomato sauce.

She turned back to put more dishes on the table, only to see Mrs Hughes lift two bottles of red wine and place them in front of Anatole.

'I've taken the liberty,' she announced, 'of bringing these. But of course there is all of Mr K's cellar if you think these won't do—that's why I haven't opened them to breathe. I hope that's all right with you?'

Christine said nothing, but bitter resentment welled up in her. Mrs Hughes was treating Anatole as if he were the man of the house. Taking her husband's place. But she said nothing, not wanting to upset her.

Nor, it seemed, did Anatole. 'Both are splendid,' he said approvingly, examining the labels, 'but I think this one will be perfect.' He selected one, handed back the other. 'Thank you!'

He cast her his familiar dazzling smile, and Christine could see its effect on her housekeeper.

Mrs Hughes beamed. 'Good,' she said. Then she looked at Christine. 'Will Mr Kyrgiakis be staying tonight? I can make up the Blue Room if so—'

Instantly Christine shook her head. 'Thank you, but no. My husband's nephew has a room reserved at the White Hart in Mallow.'

'Very well,' said Mrs Hughes, and took her leave.

Christine felt Anatole's eyes upon her. 'Have I?' he enquired.

'Yes,' she said tightly. 'I reserved it for you. Unless you're driving back to town tonight, of course.'

'The White Hart will do very well, I'm sure,' replied Anatole.

His voice was dry, but there was something in it that disturbed Christine. Disturbed her a lot.

She turned to Nicky. 'Darling, will you say Grace for us?'

Dutifully, Nicky put his hands together in a cherubic pose. 'Thank you, God, for all this lovely food,' he intoned. Then, in a sing-song voice he added, 'And if we're good, God gives us pud.' He beamed at Anatole. 'That's what Giles says.'

Anatole reached for the foil cutter and corkscrew, which Mrs Hughes had set out for him, and busied himself opening the wine, pouring some for Christine and himself. Nicky, he could see, had diluted orange juice.

'Does he, now?' he responded. Wine poured, he reached for his knife and fork, turning towards Christine, who had started eating, as had Nicky—with gusto. 'This dinner party next Friday...tell me more.'

'There isn't much to tell,' she replied, keeping her voice cool.

She hadn't missed the dry note in Anatole's voice. But she didn't care. Let him think what he would about her friendship with Giles Barcourt. He would, anyway, whatever she said. She was condemned in his eyes and always would be.

'Don't expect a gourmet meal—but do expect hospitality. The Barcourts are very much of their type— landed, doggy and horsy. Very good-natured, easy-going. Vasilis liked them, even though they are completely oblivious to the fact that their very fine Gainsborough portraits of a pair of their ancestors need a thorough cleaning. He offered to undertake it for them, but they said that the sitters were an ugly crew and they didn't want to see them any better. Their Stubbs, however,' she finished, deadpan, 'is in superb condition. And they still have hunters in their stable that are descended from the one in the painting.'

Anatole laughed.

It was a sound Christine had not heard for five long years, and it made a wave of emotion go through her. So, too, did catching sight of the way lines indented around his sculpted mouth, the edges of his dark, gold-flecked eyes crinkled.

She felt her stomach clench and her grip on her knife and fork tighten. She felt colour flare out along her cheeks. Memory, like a sudden kaleidoscope of butterflies, soared through her mind. Then sank as if they'd been shot down with machine gun fire.

'I look forward to meeting them.' His eyes rested on Christine. His tone of voice changed. Hardened. 'Giles Barcourt would not do for you,' he said. 'As a second husband.'

She stared. Another jibe—coming hard at her. Dear God, how was she to get through this evening if this was what he was going to do? Take pot-shots at her over everything? Wasn't that what she'd feared? That his blatant animosity towards her would start to poison her son?

'I am well aware of that,' she said tightly. She took a mouthful of wine, needing it. Then she set it back, stared straight at Anatole. 'I am also well aware, Anatole…' she kept her voice low, and was grateful that Nicky was still enthusiastically polishing off his plate of pasta, paying no attention to anything but that '…that I am not fit to be the wife of a man whose family have owned a sizeable chunk of the county since the sixteenth century!'

'That's not what I meant!' Anatole's voice was harsh, as if he were angry.

His expression changed, and Christine saw him take a mouthful of wine, then set the glass down with a click on the mahogany table. 'I meant,' he said, 'that your years with Vasilis have…have *changed* you, Tia—Christine,' he amended. He frowned, then his expression cleared. 'You've changed almost beyond recognition,' he said.

'I've grown up,' she answered. Her voice was quiet, intent. 'And I am a mother.' Her gaze went to Nicky. 'He gives my life meaning. I exist for him.'

She could feel Anatole's eyes resting on her. Feel them like a weight, a pressure. She saw him ready himself to speak.

But then, with an exaggerated sigh of pleasure, Nicky set down his miniature knife and fork and announced, 'I'm finished!' He looked hopefully at his mother. 'Can I have my pudding now? Is it ice cream?'

'*May* I,' corrected Christine automatically, her voice mild. 'And, yes, I expect so. But you'll have to wait a bit, your…your cousin and I are still eating.'

Had she hesitated too much on the word cousin? She hoped not.

'It's odd to think of myself as Nicky's cousin,' Anatole commented. 'When I'm old enough to be his—'

He stopped abruptly. Between them the unspoken word hung like a bullet in mid-air. He reached for his wine, drank deeply, poured himself another glass. Emotion clenched in him, but he would not give it room.

Yet his eyes went back to Vasilis's son.

The son who could have been his if—

No, don't go there. It didn't happen. Accept it. And the fact that it did not was what you wanted.

His mouth tightened, eyes hardening. But by the same token it was what Tia *had* wanted. And because she hadn't been able to get it from him—well, she'd gone and got it from his uncle.

In his head, he heard Christine's words.

You may not have wanted to marry me, to have a child with me—but your uncle did! It was his choice to marry me—

He felt his mind twist. Could it possibly be *true*? Could his lifelong bachelor uncle actually have *wanted* a child? A son?

But even if that *were* true, why take someone like Tia for a wife—of all women! His own nephew's ex-lover—thirty years his junior! If he'd wanted a wife there would have been any number of women in their own social circle, of their own nationality, far closer to him in age, and yet still young enough for child-bearing.

His eyes went to Christine.

She'd trapped him. It was the only explanation. She'd played on his good nature, his kindness—evoked his pity for my spurning of her, of what she wanted from me.

His mind twisted again, coming full circle. What did it matter now how Tia had got his uncle to marry her? All that was important to him now was the little boy sitting there, who was going to have to grow up without a father. Without the father he should have had.

A loving, protective father who would have devoted himself to his son, made him centre stage of his life, the kind of father that every boy deserved...

Thoughts moved in his head, stirred by emotions that welled up from deep within. He lifted his wine glass, slowly swirled the rich, ruby liquid as if he could see something in those depths. Find answers to questions he did not even know he was asking—knew only that he could not answer them. Not yet.

His eyes lifted, went to the woman at the foot of the table. Her attention was not on him, but on her son, and Anatole felt emotion suddenly kick through him. Gone was the strained, stiff expression she always had on her face when he himself was talking to her, as if every moment in his company was an unbearable ordeal. Now, oblivious of him, she was talking to her little boy, and her expression was soft, her eyes alight with tender devotion.

Once, it was me she looked at like that—

His gaze moved over her, registering afresh her beauty, her youthful loveliness now matured. A beauty that would be wasted unless she remarried.

Instantly the thought was anathema to him. Urgently he sought reasons for his overwhelming rejection of Tia remarrying—or even having any future love-life at all. Sought them and found them—the obvious ones.

I won't have Vasilis's fatherless son enduring a stranger for a stepfather. Worse, a succession of 'uncles'—Tia's lovers!—parading in and out of his life. Let alone any who crave to share in the wealthy lifestyle that Nicky will have as he grows up—that a stepfather could have too, courtesy of Tia. And Tia could take up with anyone! Anyone at all!

Even if it was some upper-class sprig like Giles Barcourt—there was no harm in a man like that—he'd never make a good husband for Tia…not for the woman she'd become. And besides—another thought darkened his mind,—any man she married would want children of his own, children who would displace Nicky. Yet it was impossible to think she could live in lonely widowhood for ever. She was not yet thirty!

His eyes went to her again, drawn to rest on her as she talked to her son. *Thee mou*, how beautiful she was! How exquisitely lovely—

Emotion kicked again. Something was forming in his mind, taking shape, taking hold. Yes, she would marry again. It was inevitable. Unavoidable. But no stranger that she married could be the father that Nicky needed. No *man* could be the father that Nicky needed.

Unless…

From deep within, emotion welled. In the flickering synapses of his brain currents flowed, framing the thought that was becoming real, forcing its way into his consciousness. There was only one man who could be the father Nicky needed. One obvious man…

Nicky was all but falling asleep as he polished off his ice cream, and Christine abandoned her slice of *tarte au citron* to go and lift him up, carry him to bed. But Anatole was been there before her, effortlessly hefting Nicky into his arms.

Christine followed them upstairs, her face set. It was hard—*very* hard—to see Anatole carry Nicky so tenderly, so naturally.

Into her head sounded those bleak words he'd spoken to her that final harrowing morning.

'I don't want to marry and I don't want children.'

Her face twisted. Well, maybe a young cousin was different. Maybe that was OK for Anatole.

Something rose in her throat, choking her. An emotion so strong she could not bear it.

As she settled her son into bed, kissed him goodnight, Anatole stepped forward, murmuring something to him in Greek. Christine recognised it as a night-time blessing, and felt her throat tighten with memory. It was what Vasilis had said to bless his son's sleep.

And his son had recognised it too. 'That's what my *pappou* says,' Nicky said drowsily. His little face buckled suddenly. 'I want my *pappou*,' he cried, his voice plaintive.

Instinctively Christine stepped forward, but Anatole was already sitting himself down beside Nicky, taking his hand.

Anatole thought how strange it was to feel the feather-light weight of this cousin of his, to feel the warmth of his little body, to feel so protective of him.

It isn't his fault that he is now bereft, he thought. *Or that his mother inveigled Vasilis into marrying her. None of that is his fault. And if it was truly Vasilis's choice— however bizarre, however unlikely that seems—to marry Tia, then my responsibility to my uncle's child is paramount!*

But *was* it just a case of responsibility? That sounded cold, distant. What he felt for this little boy was not cold or distant at all—it welled up in him…an emotion he'd never felt before. Never known before. Strong and powerful. Insistent.

'How about if you had me instead, Nicky?' he said,

carefully choosing his words, knowing he absolutely must get this right. 'How about,' he went on, 'if your *pappou* had asked *me* to look after you for him? Would that do?'

Dark, wide, long-lashed eyes stared up at Anatole. He felt his heart clench. He didn't know why, but it did. He stroked the little boy's hair, feeling his throat tighten unbearably.

'Yes, please,' Nicky whispered. He gazed up at Anatole. 'Promise?'

'Promise,' Anatole echoed gravely. And it was more than a word. It had come from deep within him.

Yet even as the word echoed he wondered if it could really be true, after his own miserable childhood, that he could make such a promise? All his life he'd resolved never to tread this path—but here he was, dedicating himself to this boy who seemed to be calling to something inside him he had not known he possessed. Had always thought was absent from him.

He watched Nicky's face relax, saw sleep rushing upon him. 'Don't forget…' were his slurring last words.

'No,' Anatole said gravely, stroking the fine silky hair. 'I won't.'

He felt his heart clench once more. What was this emotion coursing through him that he had never known he could feel?

A sharp movement behind him made him turn his head. Christine was turning down the night light so that it would give a soft glow, but not be so bright as to disturb. But her eyes were fixed on Anatole.

Anatole was sitting on Nicky's bed, stroking his hair. And she saw an expression on his face that put barbed wire around her throat.

I can't bear this—I can't… I can't—

She walked out of the room, went downstairs to the hall, pacing restlessly until Anatole drew level with her.

She opened her mouth to tell him that he should go, but he spoke pre-emptively.

'Come back into the dining room—I need to talk to you.' His voice was clipped, yet it had an abstracted tone to it.

'Anatole, I want you to go now—'

He ignored her, striding back into the dining room. Christine could only follow. He sat himself down at his dinner place, indicating that she should sit down too.

As if it's his house, his dining room—

Protest rose in her throat, but she sat down all the same.

'Well?' she demanded. Her heart-rate was up, emotions tearing at her. Anatole was looking at her, his gaze veiled, but there was something in it that made her go completely still.

'You heard Nicky,' Anatole said. His voice was taut, but purposeful. 'You heard his answer to my question about taking over from his *pappou*. You *heard* it, Christine— heard him say, *"Yes, please."* Well…'

He took a breath, and she saw lines of tension around his mouth.

'That is what I am going to do.' His eyes flared suddenly, unveiled. 'I am going to take Vasilis's place in his life. I am going to marry you.'

CHAPTER EIGHT

HAD THE WORLD just tilted on its side? Had an earthquake just happened? Her vision was blurred…her heart seemed to have stopped.

'*What?*'

The word shot from her like a bullet. A bullet that found its target in the blankness of Anatole's face.

'Are you *insane*?' she shot again.

He lifted a hand. It was a jerky movement, as if designed to stop more bullets. As if to silence her.

'Hear me out,' he said. 'It's the obvious solution to the situation!'

Christine's eyes flashed. It felt as if her heart had still not started beating yet. 'What *situation*?' she demanded. 'There *is* no situation! I am Vasilis's widow. He has left me *perfectly* well provided for and even more so his son—a son who will before long no longer be so sad at the loss of his *pappou* and who will grow up adored by me and protected by Vasilis's wealth. What on earth about that needs a *solution*?'

Anatole's expression shifted. Something moved in his eyes. But his words, when he spoke, were stony. 'Nicky needs a father. All children do. With Vasilis gone, irrespective of whether Nicky thought of him as his grandfather, another man must take the role he played in his son's life.'

His eyes rested on Christine, shifting in their regard.

'You are not yet thirty, Tia—Christine—and it is impossible to envisage you not remarrying at some point.' He lifted his hand again. 'I take back what I said,' he said stiffly, 'about your likely dissolute lifestyle as the wealthy widow of a deceased much older husband.'

He felt the fury of Christine's eyes hurling daggers on him, even for saying that, even with his stiff apology, but he kept on speaking. It was vital he do so. Imperative.

'But it *is* inevitable that you will remarry,' he persisted. Something flashed darkly in his eyes. 'That neighbour of yours, Barcourt, would be only too eager—or any other man! And I do not mean that as an insult. I mean it as a compliment, Christine.'

He gritted his teeth.

'I appreciate that you would never marry anyone who would not be a doting stepfather to Nicky. And Barcourt— I give him this freely—is clearly cut out to be an excellent father. But he would not, as I said, make a good husband for you.'

His eyes rested a moment on her, his face taut, his eyes implacable.

'I would,' he said.

He took an incised breath.

'I would make an excellent husband for you. Think about it…'

He leant forward a little, as if to give emphasis to what he was saying—what he had to say to make her hear. Accept what had forced its way into his head and now could not be banished.

Urgently, he forged on. 'I am the closest relative to Nicky on his father's side. I discount my own father. He would be as little interested in Nicky as he was in me,' he said scathingly.

Christine could hear something in his voice that for the first time since he had tilted the world sideways for her with what he had said, stopping the beating of her heart, shifted her to react. There had been dismissal in his voice, but something else too. Something that she recognised.

Recognised because she herself had been possessed by it totally and absolutely five years ago.

Pain—pain at rejection…at not being wanted.

But Anatole was speaking still, making her listen to him.

'Who better to be a father to Nicky than myself—his closest blood kin? And who better to be your husband, Christine…' his voice changed suddenly, grew huskier '…than me?'

His eyes washed over her—she could feel it like a silken brush over her senses.

'Who better than me?' he said again, his voice lower, that brush across her senses coming again.

She felt fatal faintness drumming at her again. She desperately wanted to speak, but she was voiceless. Bereft of everything except the sensation of his gaze washing over her, weakening her, dissolving her.

She tried to fight it—oh, dear God, she tried! Tried to remember all the pain he'd caused her.

But his eyes were washing over her now as they had done so many times, so long ago.

'I *know* you, Tia,' he said now, and the name he'd always called her by came naturally to him…as naturally as the wash of his eyes over her. 'And you know me. And we both know how compatible we are.'

He took another breath.

'And now we're much more so. You have matured into this woman you have become—poised, elegant, able to hold your own in company that would have terrified you five years ago! Five years ago you were young and inexperienced. Oh, I don't just mean sexually…'

He'd said the word casually, but it brought a heat to Christine's cheeks she would have given a million pounds for them not to have, and she beat it back as desperately as she could,

'I mean in all the ways of the world.'

His eyes slipped away, stared out as if into the past, a frown folding his brow.

He spoke again—with difficulty now. 'I didn't want to marry you then, Tia. I didn't want to marry anyone. Not just you—anyone at all. There was no reason for me to marry, and many not to. But now...' His eyes came back to her, sweeping in like a beacon, skewering her helplessly. 'Now there is every reason. To make a stable family for Nicky, a loving family—' He broke off, as if that had been hard for him to say.

For a moment Christine could not answer. Too much was pouring through her head—far, far too much. Then, with a scissoring breath, she said, 'I will not have a husband who despises me.'

It was tersely expressed, vehemently meant.

She saw him shake his head.

'I don't,' he answered. 'I don't despise you—'

Her eyes flashed blue fire. 'Don't lie to me, Anatole! You called me a cheap little adventuress! You thought me a scheming, ruthless gold-digger, who manipulated your hapless uncle into putting a wedding ring on my finger! And you thought I tried exactly the same thing on you—was perfectly prepared to get myself *pregnant*—' her mouth bit out the word as if it was rotten '—to make you marry me!'

His face turned stony. 'Whatever your motives for marrying Vasilis, I accept that you have not profited from his death and that you are devoted to your son.'

His eyes shifted again, and a troubled look drifted across them as a new thought formed—one that he had not had before. Had she wanted a baby so much that she'd been happy to marry a man so much older than her? Could it possibly be that it had not been his wealth that had made her marry his uncle? Had his riches *not* been the driving force behind her desire to marry Vasilis? Otherwise, why would she have insisted on not being the main beneficiary of his will?

He looked at her now—directly, eye to eye.

'Why did you marry my uncle?'

The strained look was instantly back in her face. 'I don't wish to discuss it. Think what you want, Anatole. I don't care.'

There was weariness in her voice, resignation.

With a jerking movement she got to her feet. 'It's time you left,' she said, her voice terse.

He stood also. Seeming to tower over her as Vasilis had never done.

Memory drummed in her, fusing the past with the present, making it impossible to separate them. Ramming home to her just how vulnerable she was to the man who stood there, a man who had always been able to melt her bones with a single glance from his deep, dark eyes. Who quickened her senses, heated the blood in her veins.

He wants to marry me—

The words were in her head—unbelievable, impossible. Yet they were there.

'You haven't given me your answer yet,' Anatole said.

His dark gaze was fixed on her. But this was the present, not the past. The past was over, would never return. *Could* never return.

With a summoning of her strength, she pulled herself together. 'I gave it to you instantly,' she countered. 'What you are proposing is insane, and I will treat it as such. And in the morning, Anatole, if you have any brain cells left in your head, you will agree with me.'

She walked out into the hall, moving to the front door, opening it pointedly.

He followed her out of the dining room. 'Are you really throwing me out of my uncle's house?' he said.

There was an edge in his voice that cut at her.

She pressed her lips together. 'Anatole, my husband was

thirty years older than me. Do you think I haven't learnt to be incredibly careful about my reputation?' Her voice twisted. 'I know that my reputation can mean nothing to you, but for Nicky's sake have the decency to leave.'

He walked towards her. There was something in the way he approached her that made all the nerve fibres in her body quiver. Suddenly the space between them was charged with static electricity, flickering with lightning.

He looked at her speculatively. 'Do I tempt you, Tia?'

There was a caress in his voice, intimacy in the way his eyes washed over her. A caress and an intimacy that had once been as familiar to her as breathing. That she had not experienced for five long years. That was now alive between them again.

She could not breathe, could not move.

His hand reached for her and he drew one finger gently, oh-so-gently, down her cheek, brushing it across her parted lips. It felt like silk and velvet, and faintness drummed in her ears.

So long...it's been so long...

She felt her heart cry out his name, but it was from far away. Oh, so long ago. Echoing down the years to now—to this unbearable moment.

'You are more beautiful now than you ever were,' he said softly.

His eyes were holding hers, dissolving hers.

'How could I forget how beautiful you are? How could I not want you again, so incredibly beautiful, so very lovely...?'

She felt her body sway, had no strength to hold herself upright. It was as if all that was keeping her standing was his eyes, holding hers.

'So beautiful...' he murmured, his voice as soft as feathers.

Slowly, infinitely slowly, his mouth descended and his lips touched hers, grazed hers, moved slowly across her sweet, tender mouth. She made no move, not one—could not…would not. Dared not…

He drew back, his eyes searching hers. 'Once, Tia, you would have melted into my arms.'

He smiled—a warm, embracing smile that crinkled the corners of his eyes, that made her remember all that had once been between them.

With that single, long, casual finger he tilted up her chin. 'So tiny, so petite…' He smiled again. His expression changed. 'You'll melt for me again, sweet Tia.'

He let his finger drop, took a breath, gave another final smile. Of confidence…of certainty.

What he wanted was right—was obvious. It was absolutely what should happen between them. It was an impulse, yes, but it had been impulse that had made him pile her into his car that afternoon all those years ago, drive off with her, take her to his apartment…his bed.

And had he not done so she would not be here now—his uncle's widow, the mother of a fatherless child, a young boy who needed a loving father as every child needed one, as every child needed a loving mother too, who made their child the centre of their universe. That was what he could do for Nicky—his uncle's child. Forge for him a loving family, keep him safe in that love all through his childhood… All his life.

I did not have that. Nicky will.

He smiled again, seeing how everything would resolve itself. Nicky would have himself, Anatole, to raise him, and he would have Tia—recreated now as Christine. Once, marriage had seemed impossible to him—fatherhood out of the question. But now, as emotion swept up in him, he knew that everything had changed for ever.

The future was crystal-clear to him and it was centred on this woman—this woman who was back in his life. It made clear, obvious sense all round. His desire for her was stronger than it had ever been. Her mature beauty drew him now even more than her *ingénue* loveliness had moved him—on that count there could be no doubt.

He spoke again to her, his final words for this evening, his tone a low, sensual husk, his eyes a caress.

'You'll melt, Christine,' he said, with promise in his voice, 'on our wedding night.'

Christine lay in bed, sleepless, her eyes staring up at the ceiling. Thoughts, emotions, confusion—all whirled chaotically around in her head. She could make sense of nothing. Nothing at all. Every now and then she would try and snatch at the whirling maelstrom, to try and capture it, but it always eluded her. Fragments skimmed past her again, just out of range.

He wants to marry me.

He despises me.

He kissed me.

None of it made sense—none of it—yet round and round the fragments whirled.

She tossed and turned, and found no rest at all.

But in the morning, when finally she awoke from the heavy, mentally exhausted slumber into which she'd fallen in the small hours, only one fragment was vivid in her head.

Temptation.

Oh, she could tell herself as much as she liked that it was insane that a man who had thrown the accusations at her that he had, a man who had told her to her face that he never wanted to marry her, should now be offering to do just that. Of his own free will.

It was insane that she should pay even the slightest attention to what he'd said. What he'd done. And yet tendrils of something writhed through her brain, finding soft, vulnerable places to cling to, to penetrate. She could feel it spreading in her mind…something so dangerous it terrified her.

Temptation.

Deadly, fatal temptation.

She had felt it once before—just as strong, just as dangerous. Once before she had been about to do something that with every instinct in her body she had known to be wrong. And the conflict had almost destroyed her. Would have destroyed her had it not been for Vasilis.

She had poured it all out to him that desperate day in Athens, when Anatole had made it so ruthlessly clear how little she meant to him—had set out the only terms under which he was prepared to continue with her, and what the consequences would be if she rejected those terms, broke them.

And Vasilis had listened. Had let her weep and sob and pour out all her misery and desperation. And then kindly, calmly and oh-so-generously, he had put forward another possibility for her.

He saved me. He saved me from the danger I was in of yielding to that overpowering temptation, that nightmare torment, that desperate desolation of realising that Anatole was a million miles away from what I yearned for.

Restlessly now, all these years later, she crossed to the window of her bedroom to look down over the gardens. She loved this house—this quiet, tranquil house that was so redolent of her marriage to Vasilis. He had brought her peace when her life had been in pieces.

Her eyes moved to the door set in the wall that led into a little dressing room, and from there into Vasilis's bedroom. A room that was now empty of him.

I miss him. I miss his kindness, his company, his wisdom.

Yet already, in the long months since she'd stood at his bleak graveside, he was beginning to fade in her head. Or perhaps it was not that he was fading, but that another was forcing himself into her consciousness. Into the space that had once been her husband's.

Just as her husband had once taken the space that had belonged to the man now replacing him.

I worked so hard to free myself of Anatole. Yet now he is back in my head, dominating everything.

And he was offering her now, with supreme, bitter irony, what he had never wanted to offer her before.

'Do I tempt you?'

Anatole had taunted her with those words and she had felt the force of them...the temptation to let herself be tempted. And then she had felt the touch of his mouth on hers...

With a smothered cry of anguish she whirled about, forcing herself to get on with the day—to put aside the insanity that Anatole was proposing, force it out of her head.

But when, mid-morning, she went up to Nicky's nursery to spend some time with him and let Nanny Ruth have a break, the first thing Nicky did was ask where Anatole was. She gave some answer—she knew not what—and was dismayed to see his little face fall. Even more dismayed to discover that he remembered what he'd said so sleepily the night before. What Anatole had said.

His little face quivered. 'He said my *pappou* sent him to look after me. But where *is* he?'

She did her best to divert him, practising his reading and writing with him, until suddenly his eyes brightened and Christine, too, heard a car arriving—crunching along the front drive.

A bare few minutes later, rapid, masculine footsteps sounded outside, the nursery door opened, and there was Anatole.

With a whoop of glee Nicky rushed to him, to be swung up into Anatole's arms. Christine could only gaze at them, emotion scything inside her powerfully at the sight of her son's blazing delight at Anatole's arrival—and Anatole, his face softening, showed in every line of his body his gladness to see Nicky.

He turned to Christine, with Nicky held effortlessly in the crook of his arm, one little hand snaked around his neck, and the pair of them smiled broadly at her.

So like each other...

There was a humming in her ears, blood rushing, and she could only blink helplessly. Then Anatole was speaking...

'Who wants to go on an adventure today?' he asked.

Nicky's eyes lit up. 'Me! Me!' came the excited reply.

Anatole laughed and swung him down on his feet again, his eyes going to Christine.

'It's a glorious day out there—how about an outing? All three of us?'

She opened her mouth to give any number of objections, but in the face of Nicky's joyous response could not voice them. 'Why not?' she said weakly. 'I'll let Nanny know.'

She made her escape, finding Nanny Ruth in her sitting room, watching a programme about antiques on the TV and finishing off a cup of tea.

'What a good idea!' she said, beaming when Christine told her of Anatole's plans. She looked at her employer. 'It will distract Nicky. And, if I might say...' Christine got the impression that she was picking her works carefully '... I am very glad that young Mr Kyrgiakis is finally in touch.' She nodded meaningfully. 'He's clearly very fond of Nicky already. It will be important for Nicky to have him in his life.'

Her eyes never left Christine's and then she took a breath, as if having said enough, and got to her feet.

'Now, where does young Mr K plan on going today? I'll make sure Nicky has the right clothes.'

She headed into the playroom, leaving Christine feeling outmanoeuvred on all fronts. With deep misgiving she went downstairs, fetching a jacket for herself.

A whole day in Anatole's company—with only Nicky to shelter behind.

Tension netted her, and she felt her heart-rate increasing. She knew what was causing it to do so. Knew it and feared it.

CHAPTER NINE

'THIS,' ANNOUNCED NICKY with a happy sigh, 'is the best day *ever*!' He sat back in his chair, a generous smear of chocolate ice cream around his mouth.

Christine laughed—she couldn't help it. Just as she hadn't been able to help herself laughing when she'd realised just where Anatole was taking them.

'*A holiday camp?*' she'd exclaimed disbelievingly as they'd arrived in Anatole's car.

He'd somehow procured a child's booster seat, and Nicky had stared wide-eyed with dawning excitement as they parked.

'Day tickets,' Anatole had replied. He'd looked at Nicky. 'Do you think you'll like it?'

The answer had been evident for over six hours now. From the incredible indoor swimming paradise—towels and swimwear for all three of them having been conveniently purchased from the pool shop—with its myriad slides and fountains and any number of other delights for children, to the outdoor fairground, finishing off the day with a show based on popular TV characters.

Now they were tucking into a high tea of fish and chips and, for Nicky, copious ice cream. Christine leant forward to mop his face. Her mood was strange. It had been impossible not to realise that she was enjoying herself today. Enjoying, overwhelmingly, Nicky's excitement at everything. And Anatole's evident pleasure in Nicky's delight.

His focus had been on her little boy, and yet Christine had caught herself, time and time again, exchanging glances with Anatole over Nicky's expressions of joy at the thrills of the day. Brief glances, smiles, shared amusement—as the day had gone on they had become more frequent, less brief.

The tension that had netted her before they'd set off had evaporated in a way she could not have believed possible, and yet so it was. It was as if, she suddenly realised with a start, the old ease in his company, which had once been the way she was with him until the debacle that had ended their relationship, was awakening as if after a long freezing.

It was disturbing to think of it that way. Dangerous!

As dangerous as it had been when, emerging with Nicky from the changing rooms at the poolside, her eyes had gone immediately to Anatole's honed, leanly muscled form, stripped down to swim shorts. Memory had seared in her and she'd had to drag her eyes away. But not before Anatole had seen her eyes go to him—and she knew that his had gone to her.

Although she'd deliberately chosen, from the range available in the on-site shop, a very sporty swimsuit, not designed in the slightest to allure, consciousness of her body being displayed to him had burned in her as she'd felt his gaze wash over her.

Then, thankfully, Nicky, his armbands inflated, had begun jumping up and down with eagerness to be in the water and the moment had passed.

That consciousness, however, resurfaced now as, tea finished and back in the car for their return journey, she realised that Nicky had fallen asleep, overcome with exhaustion after the day's delights. In the confined intimacy of the car, music playing softly, Anatole's presence so close to her was disturbing her senses.

She felt his eyes glance at her as he drove. Then he spoke. 'What I said last night—has today shown you how good it would be, making a family for Nicky?'

His tone was conversational, as if he'd asked her about the weather and not about the insanity of marrying him.

She was silent for a moment. Though it seemed to her that her heavy heartbeat must be audible to him, as it was to her. She tried to choose her words carefully. One of them had to be sane here—and it had to be her.

'Anatole, think about it rationally. You're running on impulse, I suppose. You've only just discovered about Nicky, and Vasilis is barely in his grave. For you—for *either* of us!—to make any kind of drastic alteration to our lives at such a time would be disastrous.' She looked at him. 'Everything I've read about bereavement urges not to take any major decisions for at least a year.'

Would that sufficiently deter him? She could only hope so. Pray so. Yet in the dimming light of the car she could see a mutinous look on his face. He was closing down—closing out what she'd said.

'It's the right thing to do,' he said.

There was insistence in his voice, and he could hear it himself. How could she not see the obvious sense of what he was proposing? The rightness of it. Yes, he was being impulsive—but that didn't mean he was being irrational. In fact the very opposite! It was so clearly, unarguably right for him to make a family for this fatherless boy by marrying his mother—the very woman who'd once wanted a child by him…the woman he'd desired from the first moment he'd set eyes on her.

And I desire her still! And she desires me too. There is no doubt of that—no doubt at all!

Yet still she was denying it. As her blunt answer proved.

'No,' she answered. 'It isn't.'

Her head dipped, and she stared at her hands, lying in her lap. What more could she say without ripping apart the fragile edifice of her life—plunging herself back into the desperate torment she had once known with Anatole? The torment that had raked her between temptation and desolation?

She felt him glance at her. Felt the pause before he answered, with a tightness in his voice that she could not be deaf to.

'I'm not used to you disagreeing with me,' she heard him say. There was another pause. 'You've changed, Tia—Christine.'

Her head lifted, and she threw him a look. 'Of *course* I've changed,' she said. 'What did you expect?'

She took a breath that was half a sigh, remembering, for all her defiant words, how she'd used to love watching him drive, seeing how his hands curved so strongly over the wheel. How she'd drink in his profile, the keen concentration of his gaze. How she'd always loved gazing at him, all the time, marvelling over and over again at how wonderful, how blissful it was that he wanted her at all, how he had taken her by the hand and led her into the fantasy land where she'd dwelt with him...

He caught her eye now, and there was a glint in it that was achingly familiar.

'You used to gaze at me like that all the time, Tia. I could feel it, know it—sense it.'

His voice had softened, and though there was a trace of amusement in it there was also a hint of something she had not heard from him at all since the moment he'd stalked into her life again.

Tenderness.

She felt her throat catch and she dragged her eyes away, out over the road, watching the cars coming towards them, headlights on now as dusk gathered in the countryside.

'That was then, Anatole,' she said unsteadily. 'A long time ago—'

'I've missed it,' he answered her.

She heard him take a breath—a ragged-sounding one.

'I missed *you,* Tia, when you left me. When you walked out on me to marry my uncle, to become his pampered young bride.' There was an edge in his voice now, like a blade.

Her eyes flew to him, widening. '*I* didn't leave *you*!' she exclaimed. '*You* finished it with *me*! You told me you refused to have a relationship with someone who wanted to marry you, to get pregnant by you!'

She saw a frown furrow his brow, and then he threw a fulminating look at her, his hands tightening on the wheel. 'That didn't mean you had to *go*,' he retaliated. 'It just meant—' He stopped.

'You just meant that I had to give up any idea of meaning anything to you at all—let alone as your wife or the potential mother of your children. Give up any idea of making a future with you!'

Christine's voice was dry, like sandpaper grating on bare skin. She shut her eyes for a moment, her head swirling, then opened them again, taking another weary breath.

'Oh, Anatole,' she said, and her voice was weary, 'it's all right. I get the picture. You were young, in the prime of your carefree life. I was an amusing diversion—a novelty! One that lasted a bit longer than you probably intended at first, when you scooped me off the road. I came from an entirely different walk of life from you—I was pretty, but totally naïve. I was so blatantly smitten by you that you couldn't resist indulging yourself—and indulging *me*. But I know that didn't give me any right to think you might want me long-term. Even if...'

She swallowed painfully, knowing she had to say it.

'Even if there hadn't been that pregnancy...scare...' she said the word with difficulty '...something else would have ended our affair. Because...' Her throat was tight. 'Because an affair was all it was. All it could ever be.'

She knew that now—knew it with the hindsight of her greater years. She had been twenty-three... Anatole had been the first man in her life—and a man such as she had never dreamt of, not even in her girlish fantasies! He'd taken her to fairyland—and even in her youthful inexperience she had feared that it would all be fairy gold and turn to dust.

And so it had. Painfully. Permanently.

'But now I want more,' he replied, and his words and the intensity of his voice made her eyes fly to him again. 'I want much, much more than an affair with you.'

He took a breath, changing gear, accelerating on an open stretch of road as if that would give escape to the emotion building up inside him. Emotion that was frustration at her obstinacy, at her refusal to concede the rightness of what he was proposing.

'Christine, this *works*—you, me and Nicky! You can see it that works. Nicky likes me, trusts me…and, believe me, I meant exactly what I said to him last night. That he can believe that his *pappou* sent me to look after him in his place. To become his father—'

He could have been my son! Had Tia been pregnant then—five years ago—Nicky would be my son. A handful of months older…no more.

Emotion rolled him over. Over and over and over— like a boulder propelled down a mountainside by an overwhelming, unstoppable force. Emotion about what might have been, about what had never been, that silenced him until they arrived at Vasilis's house—now Christine's home.

The home she kept for her son—his uncle's son—just as the legacy of Vasilis's work, his endless endeavours to preserve the treasures of the past, would pass to her guardianship.

And she will guard it well. How strange that I can trust her to do that, that I know now that I can trust her.

Yet it was not strange at all—not now that he had seen her in London, at the exhibition opening, and here as chatelaine of this gracious house. She had grown into it—into a woman who could do these things, *be* these things.

Just as I have grown into what I am doing now. Accepting that I want a wife. A child.

He scooped up the sleeping boy, cradling his weight in his arms as he walked indoors with him. Christine opened the front door, leading the way upstairs in the quiet house—both Mrs Hughes and Nanny Ruth were out for the evening.

In his bedroom, they got Nicky into bed, still fast asleep, exhausted by the day's delights. For a moment, Anatole stood beside her as they gazed down at the sleeping child, illumined only by the soft glow of the night light.

His hand found Christine's. She did not take it away. She stood with him as they looked down at Nicky. As if they were indeed a family indeed…

Was there a little sound from her? Something that might have been a choke? He did not know. Knew only that she'd slipped her hand from his and was walking out of the room. He looked after her, a strange expression on his face, then back at Nicky, reaching almost absently to smooth a lock of dark hair from his forehead, to murmur a blessing on the night for him.

Then he turned and went downstairs.

Christine was waiting in the hall by the front door. Her head was lifted, her expression composed.

'Thank you for a lovely day,' she said.

She spoke calmly, quelling all the emotion welling up inside her. What use to feel what was inside her? It was of no use—it never could be now.

She opened the door, stepped back. He came up to her, feeling that strange, strong emotion in him again. This time he made no attempt to kiss her.

'It's been good,' he said.

His voice was quiet. His eyes steady. Then, with a quick smile, the slightest nod of his head, he was gone, crunching out over the gravel beneath the mild night sky.

As he opened his car door he heard the front door of the house close behind him.

Shut it, if you will—but you cannot shut me out. Not out of Nicky's life—or yours.

Certainty filled him as to the truth of that.

In the week that followed Christine did her best to regain the state of mind she'd had since her marriage to Vasilis. But it had gone—been blown away by the return of Anatole into her life. His invasion of it.

It was an invasion that had been angrily hostile, and he had been scathing in his denunciation of her behaviour. And the searing irony of it was that anger and hostility from him was so much easier for her to cope with. What she couldn't cope with—what she was pathetically, abjectly unable to cope with—was the way he was with her now.

Wooing!

The word stayed in her head, haunting her.

Disturbing her. Confusing her.

Changing her.

And she didn't want to change. She'd made a new life for herself—made it in tears and torment, but she was safe inside it. Safe inside the life Vasilis had given her. *That* was what she wanted to cling to.

Anatole is my past. I can't—I won't—have him as my future!

She dared not. Too much—oh, far too much—was at stake for her to allow that. More than she could bear to pay again.

Her resolve was put to the test yet again the following Friday—the day the Barcourts had invited her and Nicky over. Her hope that Anatole had forgotten proved to be in vain. He arrived in time to drive them over. And at the rambling Elizabethan mansion the Barcourts' welcome to Anatole could not have been friendlier.

'I'm glad you could come this evening, Mr Kyrgiakis. We were all so sorry to hear about your uncle—he was well liked, and very well respected.' Mrs Barcourt smiled kindly at Anatole as she greeted him, then led the way into the oak-panelled drawing room.

Nicky was scooped up by the nursery party, who were rushing off to see the puppies with the nanny, and Giles's sister Isabel, as cheerful as her brother, launched into a panegyric about the beneficial effects a puppy had on childhood, adding that Nicky should also learn to ride— as soon as he could. Giles agreed enthusiastically, volunteering their old pony, Bramble, for the job.

'Don't you agree?' Isabel said to Anatole.

'I'm sure my young cousin would love it,' he answered. 'But it is Christine's decision.'

He glanced at her and she smiled awkwardly. What the Barcourts were making of Anatole, she had no idea— knew only that they were asking no questions about him and seeming to take his presence for granted.

But her relief lasted only until after dinner, when their hostess announced they would leave the menfolk to their port and drew Christine and Isabel off to the drawing room. There, a bottle of very good madeira was produced, and Isabel went off to see her children.

Mrs Barcourt, Christine realised with dismay, was about to start her interrogation.

'My dear, *what* a good-looking young man! *Such* a shame we've seen nothing of him until now!' she exclaimed. She bent to absent-mindedly stroke the ancient, long-haired cat lounging on the hearth rug. 'I take it we'll be seeing a lot more of him now?'

Her smile was nothing but friendly. The question was clearly leading…

Christine clutched her glass. 'He *would* like to get to know Nicky,' she managed to get out.

Her hostess nodded sympathetically. 'Very understandable,' she said. 'And very good for Nicky too.' She paused. 'It's early days, I know, but you *will* need to think of the future, Christine—as I'm sure you realise.'

She stroked the cat again, then looked at her guest, her expression open.

'A stepfather would be excellent for Nicky—but you must choose wisely.' She made a face and spoke frankly, as Christine had known she would. 'Not Giles,' she said, with a little shake of her head. 'Fond though he is of Nicky, you wouldn't suit each other, you know.'

Christine's expression changed. 'No, no... I know that.'

Her hostess nodded. 'I know you do, my dear, and I'm glad of it.' She sat back, picking up her glass. 'You and Anatole seem to get on very well...' She trailed off.

Christine had no idea what to say, but Mrs Barcourt did.

'Well, I shall say no more except that I can see no reason not to look forward to getting to know him better. You must both come over again before long. Ah, Isabel—there you are!' she exclaimed as her daughter breezed in. 'How is little Nicky?'

'Begging for a sleepover, and my brood are egging him on! What do you say, Christine?'

Christine, abjectly grateful for the change of subject, could only nod. 'If you're sure it's no trouble?'

'Not in the least,' Isabel answered cheerfully. 'And tomorrow morning he can try out Bramble, if you're all right with that. Loads of kiddie riding kit here!'

Christine nodded weakly. But belatedly she realised that if Nicky slept here tonight she would be without his protective presence herself.

It was something she felt more strongly at the end of the evening, when she sat beside Anatole in his car, heading home.

He glanced at her. She'd looked enchanting all evening, wearing a soft dark blue velvet dress, calf-length in a bal-

lerina style, with a double strand of very good pearls—
presumably a gift from his uncle—and pearl ear studs.
Her hair was in a low chignon, with pearl clips. Simple,
elegant—and breathtakingly lovely.

Young Giles Barcourt had thought so too, Anatole
thought, with an atavistic male instinct. Was that why
he'd felt the need to make a point of emphasising his family link with Christine? Staking his claim to her?

Re-staking it.

She is mine. She's always been mine!

Certainty streamed through him. Possessiveness.

Remorse and regret.

*Why did I let her go—why did I not rush to her and
claim her from Vasilis before he married her? Instead I
gave in to anger and to my determination not to be forced
into marriage and fatherhood.*

Well, he hadn't been ready then—but he was ready
now. More than ready. All he needed was to persuade
Christine that he was right. And if words could not do so,
then other means might.

He made some anodyne remark to her now—about the
evening, about the pair of Gainsboroughs hanging in the
dining room that Vasilis had itched to see cleaned—and
said that he agreed with their hosts that perhaps they were
best left covered in thick varnish. He had the gratifica-
tion of hearing Christine chuckle, and then she asked if
he'd spotted the very handsome Stubbs in pride of place
over the fireplace.

'Indeed,' he replied. 'Do you think Bramble is one of
the descendants?' It was a humorous remark, and intended
to be so.

'I hope not!' Christine returned. 'That Stubbs stallion
looks very fearsome!'

'Do you mind Nicky learning to ride?' Anatole asked
as he steered the car along the dark country lanes back
to the house.

She shook her head. 'I'm very grateful to Giles and Isabel,' she acknowledged. 'I want Nicky to grow up here, so riding will certainly make him feel at home. And he's very attached to Giles—'

The moment she spoke, she wished she hadn't. Even in the dim interior she could see Anatole's face tighten. She recalled Mrs Barcourt's words to her—not about her son, who was perfectly well understood between them, but about Anatole. Dear God, surely she and Anatole weren't coming across as a couple, were they? Please, *please* not! The very last thing she could bear was any speculation in that direction.

It was bad enough coping with the pressure from Anatole, let alone any expectations from the Barcourts. Consternation filled her about how she was going to handle Anatole's comings and goings—even if they were only to see Nicky. Talk would start—it was inevitable in a small neighbourhood. People would have them married off before she knew it.

Turmoil twisted in her, keeping her silent.

Anatole, too, was silent for the remainder of the short journey.

When they arrived back at her house she got out, preparing to bid him goodnight before he drove back to the White Hart. But instead he said, in a perfectly conversational voice, 'I could do with a nightcap. As the designated driver I got very little of that excellent claret over dinner—and none at all of the port that Barcourt Senior tried to press on me! So I could still have one more.' He glanced expectantly at Christine. 'He mentioned that he gave Vasilis a bottle at Christmas…'

Reluctantly, she let Anatole follow her inside. The house was very quiet—the Hugheses were in their apartment in the converted stables, and Nanny Ruth was away for the weekend. In the drawing room she switched on the table lamps, giving the elegant room a soft warm glow, and extracted the requisite bottle and two port glasses from a lacquered cabinet, setting them down with a slight rattle on a low table by the silk-upholstered sofa.

Anatole strolled across and seated himself, but Christine chose the armchair opposite, spreading her velvet skirts carefully against the pale blue fabric. He poured her a generous measure, and himself as well, then raised his glass to her. His gaze was speaking.

'To us, Christine—to what we can make together.'

His eyes held hers—dark, long-lashed, deep and expressive. She felt their power, their force. The long-ago memories they kindled within her. Emotion swirled, dark and turbid, troubling and disturbing.

It was as disturbing as feeling Anatole's lambent gaze upon her, which did not relinquish her as he took a mouthful of the sweet, strong, rich ruby port. She took a mouthful herself, needing its strength to fortify her.

The bottle had not been opened before—Vasilis's health had worsened steadily, remorselessly after Christmas, and he'd openly prepared her for the coming end. She felt her eyes blur with a mist of tears.

'What is it?' Anatole's voice was quiet, but she could hear the concern in it. 'You're not worrying about Nicky, are you?'

She shook her head. 'No—I'm used to leaving him for a night or two. He never fretted when I went to London with Vasilis.'

Her voice trembled over her late husband's name. Anatole heard the emotion in it and it forced a recognition in him. One he had held back for many years.

'You cared for him didn't you? My uncle?' he said.

His voice was low. Troubled. As if he were facing something he didn't want to face. Something he'd held at bay for five long bitter, angry years.

'Yes—for his kindness,' she said feelingly. 'And his wisdom. His devotion to Nicky—'

She broke off. Thoughts moved within Anatole's mind—thoughts he did not want to think. His uncle—decades older than Tia and yet she'd had a child with him.

His mind blanked. It was impossible, just *impossible*, to envisage Nicky's conception. It was wrong to think of Tia with anyone else in the whole world except himself. Not his uncle, not young Giles Barcourt—no one!

The same surge of possessiveness he'd felt in the car swept over him again as his eyes drank her in, sitting there so close to him, looking so beautiful it made his breath catch.

How did I last this long without her?

It seemed impossible that he had. Oh, he'd not been celibate, but there had been only fleeting liaisons, deliberately selected for their brevity and infrequency. He'd put that down to having had such a narrow escape with Tia, when she'd so nearly trapped him into marriage—into unwanted fatherhood—exacerbating his existing resistance to women continually seeking to marry him. And yet now that he *did* want to marry her—the same woman who'd once dreamt of that very thing—she was refusing him.

Her words to him echoed in his head, giving him a reason for her obduracy that he could not accept. *Would* not.

'But that does not mean you cannot marry again!' he said.

Her gaze shifted away. 'Anatole—please. Please don't.'

Her voice was a thread. It was clearly unbearable to her that he should say such a thing. But he could not stop.

'Did he…care…for *you*?'

He did not like to think of it. It was…*wrong*. As wrong as Tia having feelings for a man who had probably been older than her own father, had he lived.

'He was fond of me,' she said. Her eyes went to him. 'And he adored Nicky.' She took a breath. 'That was what I valued most—that I was able to give him Nicky. He would never otherwise have had a child had he not married me.'

There was defiance in her voice, and Anatole knew the reason for it. Felt the accusation. Knew he had to answer it. That it was time to face what he had said, what he had done.

He took a breath—a difficult one—and looked her in the face, his expression sombre. 'I'm sorry, Christine. Sorry that when we were together I did not want a child. That I welcomed the fact you were not pregnant after all.'

He took a mouthful of port, felt it strong and fiery in his throat.

'I was not ready to be a father.' His eyes met hers. Unflinching. 'But now,' he said, 'I am. I want to be the father to Nicky that Vasilis did not live to be. I feel,' he swallowed 'I feel my uncle would want that. And I want so much for you to want it too.'

There was a choking noise from Christine and immediately Anatole was there, his port glass hastily set down, kneeling on the Aubusson carpet before Christine's chair, taking her hand. The mist of tears in her eyes was spilling into diamond drops on her lashes.

'Don't cry, Tia,' he said softly, lifting a finger to brush away the tears. 'Don't weep.'

His hand lifted the hand he was holding, which was trembling in his grasp, and he lifted it to his lips, smoothing his mouth across her knuckles.

'We can make this work—truly we can. Marry me— make things as right between us as they were wrong before. Make a family for your son with me—for his sake, for my uncle's sake. For my sake. For your sake.'

His eyes were burning into hers and she was gazing down into their depths, tears still shimmering. He took the half-empty glass from her trembling hand, then retained that hand, getting to his feet, drawing her with him. Light from the table lamp illumined her and his breath caught. How lovely she was…how beautiful.

His mouth lowered to hers. He could not stop—could

not prevent himself. Desire streamed within him, and the memory of desire, and both fused together—the past into the present. Her lips were honey to his questing mouth, sweet and soft, and he felt arousal spring within him, strong and instant. His kiss deepened and he heard her make a low noise in her throat, as if she could not bear what was happening. As if she could not bear for him to stop.

His hands slipped from hers, sliding around her slender waist, pulling her gently, strongly, against him. He felt the narrow roundness of her hips against his. Felt his own arousal surge yet more. His blood coursed through him and he deepened his kiss as passion and desire drove him on.

She was quickening in his arms—he could feel it—and he remembered, with a vividness that was like a flash of searing lightning, how she had always responded when he kissed her like this…how her slender body trembled, strained against him…how her eyes grew dazed as they were dazed now, with a film of desire glazing them as her pupils flared with arousal and the sweet peaks of her breasts strained against the wall of his chest.

He felt her nipples cresting, arousing him. She was kissing him back now—ardently, hungrily. As if she had not kissed anyone for a long, long time. As if only he could sate her hunger.

The last of his control broke. He swept her up into his arms. She was as light as a feather, as thistledown, and the soft material of her skirts draped over his thighs as he carried her from the room, up the wide sweep of stairs into the waiting bedroom. He laid her down on the bed, came down beside her.

How his clothes were shed he did not know—he knew only that her hair had been loosened from its pins and was spilling out upon the pillows, that he was parting the long zip of her dress and peeling it from her body so that her pale, engorged and crested breasts, so tender and so tempting, were exposed to him.

Memory knifed through him of all the times he had made love to her—to Tia, his lovely Tia—so soft in his arms, so yielding to his desire. And she was his again! His after so, *so* long. All that was familiar flooded back like a drowning tide, borne aloft by passion and desire, by memory and arousal.

His palm cupped her breast and he heard her moan again, low in her throat. The dazed look in her distended eyes was dim in the shadows of the night. His mouth lowered to her breast, fastening over her crested nipple, and his tongue worked delicately, delectably, around its sensitive contours.

The moan came again, more incoherent, and he felt her hands helpless on his back. Her neck was arched against the pillows, her throat exposed to him, and he drew his fingers down the length of it, stroking softly, holding her for himself as he moved his mouth to her other breast, to lave it with the same ministrations.

But her sweet ripened breasts were not enough. He wanted more. He felt a low, primitive growl, deep in his being.

He drew her dress from her completely, revealing tiny panties, slipping her free of them. Her thighs slackened and the dark vee between was a darker shadow. He propped himself on one elbow, taking her mouth with his again, feasting on it with slow, arousing sensuality, splaying his free hand on her soft pale flank.

He smiled down at her in the darkness. 'Tell me you do not want this. Tell me you do not want *me*,' he said to her. His voice was low. Driven. 'Tell me to go, Tia—tell me now, or do not tell me at all.'

It was impossible for her to give such an order. Her resistance was gone. How could it persist when his mouth, his hands, his tongue, his lips, his body and all his being were taking her where she should not be going, to what she should not be yielding to?

And yet she *was* yielding. Was succumbing hopelessly, helplessly, to what her body was urging her to do. It was taking her over, demolishing, drowning what her head was telling her. Her head was telling her that it was madness, insanity, to do what she was doing. But she could not stop. It was impossible to do so—impossible not to let the muscles of her thighs slacken, not to tighten her fingers over his strong, warm shoulder as delirium possessed her, as her body swept away the long, empty years since Anatole had last made love to her, had last taken her with him to that place only he could take her to. Where he was taking her again…now, oh, *now*!

She moaned again, her head starting to thresh, her spine arching, the muscles in her legs tautening. Her body ripened, strained as he readied her for his possession. The possession she yearned for, craved, was desperate for.

She heard her voice call his name, as if pleading with him. Pleading with him to complete what he had begun, to lift her to that plane of existence where fire and sweetness and unbearable light would fill her, where the rapture that only he could release in her would be.

He answered her, but she knew not what he said— knew only that his body was moving over hers, the strong, heavy weight of it as familiar as it had ever been, and her arms were snaking around him, enclosing him as her hips lifted to him, yearning for him, craving him, wanting only him, only this.

He thrust into her, a word breaking from him that she did not know but remembered well. The past and present fused, melded, became one. As if no years separated them. As if there had been no parting.

His possession filled her and her body enclosed his, embracing his even as her arms wrapped him to her. The strength of his lean, muscled form, the weight of it upon her, was crushing and yet arousing, even as his slow, rhythmic movements were arousing, and her legs wound about his as each thrust of his body pulsed the blood through her heated, straining body.

She wanted him—oh, dear God, how she wanted him—wanted this—wanted everything—everything he could give her.

He cried out—a straining roar—and as if it were a match to tinder she felt her body flood with him, with her, and she was lifted up, up, soaring into that other world that existed only at such times, forced through a barrier that was invisible, intangible in mortal life, but which now, in Anatole's arms, in his passion and embrace and the utter fusion of their bodies, was their sole existence. On and on she soared, crying into the wind as the heat of the sun in that other world burned down upon her.

Then, like the wind subsiding, she was drawn back down, panting, exhausted. *Sated.* Her whole body purged and cleansed in that white-hot air. She was shaking, trembling, and he was smoothing her hair, talking to her, withdrawing from her and yet folding her back against him, so that she was not alone, not bereft. She was crushed against him, his limbs enfolding hers, his arms wrapped tight around her, and his breath was warm on her shoulder, his hand curving around her cheek, his voice murmuring. She could feel the shuddering of his chest, the thudding of his heart that was in tune with hers.

He was saying her name, over and over again. The name he'd always called her. 'Tia, my Tia. *Mine.*'

And she *was* his. She was, and she always had been—she always would be. Always.

Sleep rushed over her, as impossible to resist as if it had been slipped into her bloodstream like an overpowering drug. Her eyes fluttered closed. Muscles slackening, her body slumped into the protective cradle of his arms.

They tightened close around her.

CHAPTER TEN

MORNING WAS BREAKING over the gardens, reaching pale fingers of sun across the dew-drenched lawn. Christine stood at the window of her bedroom, a silk *peignoir* wrapping her, gazing blindly out. Her face was sombre, her thoughts far away into the past. The past that had become the present. The present she could not deny. Nor could she deny that she had allowed something to happen that should *never* have happened.

I called it insanity when he said we should marry. But what I've just done is insanity.

How could it be anything else? She turned her head, looking back towards the sleeping figure in her bed, the bedclothes carelessly stretched around his lean, golden-skinned body so that she could see the rise and fall of his chest—the chest she had clung to in that madness, that insanity of last night, as she had clung so often in that long-ago time that should have been *gone* for ever!

It has to be gone—it has to be! It's over!

And she could not, *must* not, allow it to be anything else. Whatever the unbearable temptation to do otherwise—a temptation that Anatole had made a million times more devastatingly powerful after what had happened last night.

I can't be what Anatole is telling me to be. Urging me to be. It's impossible—just impossible!

Impossible for so many reasons.

Impossible for just one overwhelming reason.

The same reason it's always been impossible.

Pain constricted her throat as she stared across at him now, where he lay sleeping in her bed.

There can be no future between us now—none. Just as there could be no future for us then.

She felt the breath tight in her lungs and moved to turn away. But as she did so she heard him stir, saw his hand reaching across the bed, his face registering her absence. His eyes sprang open and he saw her standing there. Emotion speared in his face but it was she who spoke first.

'You have to go! Right now! I can't have Mrs Hughes realising you spent the night here.'

His expression changed. 'But I did—and in your arms.'

He was defying her to deny it, his eyes holding hers. He sat up, reaching for her, catching her hand. Resting his hand on her flank, warm through the cool silk. Looking up at her.

'It's far too late for pretence,' he said softly. 'Didn't last night prove that to you?'

He drew her to him.

'Doesn't this prove it to you?'

His mouth lowered to hers. His kiss was like velvet— the kiss of a man who had taken possession of the woman he desired. She felt honey flow through her, felt her limbs tremble with it.

His eyes poured into hers, rich and lambent. 'It's happened, Tia.' His voice was as intimate, as hushed as if they were the only two people in the world. 'It's happened, and there's no going back now.'

She tried to pull away. Tried to free herself.

'There *has* to be!' she cried. 'I can't do what you want, Anatole. I can't—I *can't*!'

I mustn't! I daren't! What you are offering me is a temptation beyond my endurance. But I must endure it—I must.

She had endured it before—she must do so again. Must find refuge somehow. Find the strength to keep refusing him. Even now, after she had burned in his arms, in his embrace.

Now more than ever. Now that I know how weak I am...

*how helpless to resist you. Now that I know how hope-
lessly vulnerable I am to you. Now that I know the danger
that stands before me.*

Raggedly, she pulled free of him. 'I won't marry you,
Anatole,' she said doggedly, each word tugged from her.
'I will not. Whatever you say to me—I will *not*.'

Who was she speaking to? Him or herself? She knew
the answer. And she knew what that answer told her—
knew the danger it proved her to be in.

Frustration flared in his eyes. 'Why? I don't understand? *Why*, Tia? How can you possibly deny what there
is between us?'

She would not reply—could not. All she could do, with
a desperate expression on her face, was beg him yet again
to go. For an instant longer Anatole just stood there, then
abruptly he stood up, seized up his discarded clothes, and
disappeared into the en suite bathroom.

Rapidly, Christine got dressed too—pulling on a pair of
jeans and a lightweight sweater, roughly brushing out the
tangled hair that waved so wantonly around her shoulders,
echoing her bee-stung lips in its sensuality…

With a smothered cry she whirled around to see Anatole emerge, wearing his clothes from the night before, but
only the shirt and trousers. He looked…she gulped…he
looked incredibly, devastatingly *sexy*. There was no other
word for it—no other word to describe the slightly raffish
look about him, compounded by the lock of raven hair falling across his forehead, the cuffs of his shirt pushed back
casually, the dark shadow along his jawline.

She could not take her eyes from him—could feel her
pulse quicken, the blood surging in her, colour flushing
across her face, lips parting…

He saw her reaction and smiled. A slow, sensual smile,
full of confidence.

'You see?'

It was all he said. All he needed to say. He walked towards her. *Strolled.*

She backed away, panic suddenly replacing her betraying reaction to his raw sexuality. 'No—Anatole, *no*! I won't let you do this to me—I *won't*!'

She held her hands up as if to ward him off. He halted, his expression changing. When he spoke there was frustration in his voice, and challenge, in equal measure.

'Tia, you cannot ignore what has happened.'

'I am *not* Tia! I am not her any more—and I will *never* be her again!'

The cry of her own voice, its vehemence, shocked her. It seemed to shock Anatole as well. His eyes narrowed, losing that blatantly sexy half-lidded look with which he'd stared at her before. For a moment he did not speak. Just looked at her pale face, the cheekbones etched so starkly. Saw the tremble in her upheld hands.

'No,' he said quietly. 'You're not Tia. I've accepted that. I've accepted that you are Christine Kyrgiakis—Mrs Vasilis Kyrgiakis.'

The use of the description made her start. Made her hear the rest of what he said.

'The widow of my uncle—the mother of his son—the mother of my cousin.' He paused again, as if assessing her, the way she was reacting. 'I have made my case, *Christine*—' deliberately he used the name of the woman she was now, the woman she would always be going forward '—and I have given you the reasons why we should marry. And I believe I have done it in more than words.'

For a second that look was back in his eye—that heavy, half-lidded look that made her tremble as nothing that he could say could make her tremble, making her limbs turn boneless, her heart catch in mid-beat. Then he held up a hand, as if she had tried to interrupt him.

'But for now I'll leave it be. I understand, truly, that you must have time to get used to it. Time to come to terms with it. To see it as being as inevitable as I see it to be.' He took a breath, his tone changing. 'But for now the subject is closed. I accept that.'

He turned away, fetching his jacket, so carelessly thrown on a chair last night, and shrugging it on, tugging his cuffs clear and fastening them, then looking across at Christine again.

'I'll go now—to preserve the appearances that are, I know, so important to you right now.' There was no bite in his words, only acknowledgement. 'But I'll be back later. We have Nicky to collect—and, no, please don't tell me not to come with you. He'll be disappointed if I don't.'

She nodded in dumb acquiescence. It seemed easier than contesting his assertion. All she wanted—desperately—was for him to be out of here, finally to be able to collapse in a state of mental and emotional exhaustion, her body aching and spent.

She sheared her mind away—*no, don't think, not now. Not ever...*

But it was impossible not to think, not to feel, for the rest of the day, and when Anatole returned late in the afternoon—as he'd told her he would—so they could drive over to collect Nicky from the Barcourts, she felt a leap of unbearable emotion as her eyes went to his. And his to hers.

For a moment, as their eyes met, she felt as if she had been transported back in time and was poised to do what she had once done so automatically and spontaneously— run into his arms that would open to her and fold her to him.

Then his eyes were veiled and the moment passed. As he helped her into the car he made some pleasantry about the weather, to which she replied in kind. They chatted in a desultory way during the short journey, and Christine told herself she was thankful.

And she was even more thankful that as they arrived

there was a melee to greet them: Elizabeth Barcourt's grandchildren, their mother and their grandmother, all chattering to them madly.

As for Nicky—he was only too eager to regale them both with the delights of his day.

'I rode a pony! Can I have a pony—*can* I? Can I?' he pleaded, half to Anatole, half to Christine.

A spike drove into her heart as she saw the way her son addressed them both. As if he accepted her and Anatole as a unit. She tensed, and it was noticed by Elizabeth Barcourt, who drew her a little aside as Anatole crouched down to Nicky's level to get the full account of the joys of his day and the thrill of riding a pony for the first time.

'My dear, I'm glad Anatole is able to spend time with you—the more the better.' She cast a look at Christine, and then at Nicky. 'He's a natural with him! One might almost think—'

She broke off, as if conscious she had said too much, then stepped away, quietening her noisy grandchildren and telling them it was time for Nicky to head home.

As they finally set off Nicky's chatter was all of ponies and puppies and the fun he'd had with the other children.

'I'm going to paint a picture of a pony and a puppy,' he announced as they arrived, and then belied his intention by giving a huge yawn, indicating how little actual sleep his exciting sleepover had involved.

'Bath first,' said Christine, and then hesitated.

What she wanted to do was tell Anatole it was time for him to leave, to go away, to leave her alone with her son. But her hesitation was fatal.

'Definitely bath time,' Anatole said, adding with a grin, 'I'll race you upstairs!'

With a cry of excitement Nicky set off up the wide staircase and Anatole followed—as did Christine, much more slowly, her face set.

OK, so the two of them would bath Nicky, and see him

to bed and *then* she'd tell Anatole it was time he left. That was her intention—her absolute resolve. Because no way was he going to spend the night here again.

And not in my bed!

Her face flushed with colour, her features contorting. *He's got to go—he's just got to.*

Close to an hour later, with Nicky tucked up in bed and falling asleep instantly, she walked back downstairs with Anatole. She paused at the foot and turned to him.

'Are you staying at the White Hart tonight or heading straight back to London?' Her voice was doggedly bright, refusing to acknowledge there was any other possibility.

He looked at her. His gaze was half lidded, as if he knew why she was saying what she was.

'Once,' he said, 'you were not so rejecting of me.'

The expression in his eyes, the open caress in his voice, brought colour to stain her cheekbones, and her fingers clenched at her sides.

'Once,' she replied, 'I was a different person.'

He gave a swift shake of his head, negating her denial. 'You're still that person—whether you call yourself Tia or Christine, you're still her. And last night showed me that. It showed *you* that! So why deny it? Why even *try* to deny it? Why try to deny that our marriage would work?'

And now the caress was back in his voice, almost tangible on her skin, which was suddenly flushing with heat.

'Last night showed how alive that flame that was always between us still is. From the moment you saw me, Tia, you wanted me—and I wanted you. I wanted you then and I want you now. And it is the same for you. It blazes from you, your desire for me.'

He reached a hand towards her, long lashes sweeping down over his eyes, a half-smile pulling at his mouth.

'Don't deny it, Tia,' he said softly. 'Don't deny the truth of what we have. We *burn* for each other.' His voice dropped to a sensual husk.

She took a jerky step backwards—an instinctive gesture of self-protection against what he wanted. He didn't like it that she did so, and he stilled. She lifted her chin. Looked straight at him. She must tell him what she needed to say. What he needed to hear.

Her eyes met his unflinchingly, with a bare, stark expression in them. 'I know that, Anatole! Dear God, of *course* I know it! How could I not?'

She shook her head, as if acknowledging a truth she could not deny. Then her eyes reached his, hung on to his, trying to make him hear, understand.

'It was always like that—right from the first. And, yes, it's still there. Last night did prove it, just as you say. But, Anatole, listen—*listen* to me. I can't let myself be blinded by passion! And nor can you! A marriage can't be built on passion alone, and nor can it be based on just wanting to make a family for Nicky. You *have* to see that!'

There was a tremor in her voice, intensity in her face— but in his there was only blank rejection of her rejection of him.

'All my life,' he said slowly, 'women have wanted to marry me. You included, or so I supposed way back then. And yet now, when I *want* to marry, the woman I want to marry is turning me down.' He gave a laugh. There was no humour in it. 'Maybe that's some kind of cosmic karma—I don't know.'

He pressed his lips together, as if to control his words, his emotions. Emotions that were streaming through him in a way he had never known before. A kind of disbelief. Even dismay.

His eyes rested on her. 'So, what *can* a marriage be built on? Tell me what else there needs to be.'

She looked at him, and there was a deep sadness in her voice as she answered. 'Oh, Anatole, the fact that you have to ask tells me how impossible marriage would be between us.'

'Then *tell* me!' he ground out.

She shut her eyes for a moment, shaking her head before she opened them again. She looked at him, her features twisting. 'I can't,' she said. 'But…' She paused, as if profoundly reluctant to speak, yet she did so. 'You would know it—'

She broke off, turned away, walked unevenly towards the front door to open it for him to leave. Marriage between them was as impossible now as it had been when she'd thought she lived in fairyland.

Emotion was pressing upon her—unbearable, agonising—but she would not yield to it. Opening the door, she turned back to him. He hadn't moved. He was just looking at her.

Determinedly, she met his gaze. 'Anatole—please—' She indicated the open doorway.

He walked towards it, pausing beside her. 'We'd make a good couple,' he said. 'We'd have each other and Nicky. Maybe a child of our own one day.'

A smothered cry came from her. '*Go!* Go, Anatole, and leave me alone!'

She closed the door on him, not caring that she'd all but pushed him out. Only when the lock clicked, cutting out the sound of his footsteps on the gravelled drive, muffling the sound of his car door slamming, the engine starting, did she turn, leaning back on the closed front door, shutting him out—out of her house, out of her life.

A child of our own…

That muffled cry came again. That was what she had longed for so long ago—before the glowing fairy dust she'd sprinkled over her life had turned to bitter ashes.

Slowly, bleakly, she headed upstairs to kiss her sleeping son a silent goodnight.

The only person she could love.

Could allow herself to love.

CHAPTER ELEVEN

'MY DEAR, IT'S good to see you again. How are you bearing up?'

It was the vicar's wife, welcoming her into the vicarage where her husband offered her a dry sherry.

'I miss my weekly symposia with Vasilis,' he said, after his wife had asked after Nicky, and how he too was bearing up.

This kind of kind enquiry had continued to come her way, and Christine always answered as best she could. But it was difficult. How could she possibly tell people that Anatole had offered her marriage in order to make a family for Nicky? An offer she could not accept, however overwhelming the temptation.

That temptation still wound itself inside her head even now—despite all she felt, all she told herself, all she had forced herself to feel, not to feel, in the endless month that had passed since Anatole had driven away that last time.

It had been a month filled with anguish and torment over what she had done. A month of missing Anatole.

And that was the worst of it—the most dangerous sign of all—telling her what she so desperately did not want to be told. She longed to be able to put him out of her mind, but it was impossible. And made more so by Nicky's repeated mentions of him, his constant questioning about when Anatole would be back.

'I want him to come!' he would say plaintively, and Christine and Nanny Ruth would be hard pressed to divert him, even though summer was coming and the weather warm enough for them to think of driving to the coast, for a day at the beach.

'But I want Cousin Anatole to come too!' had been Nicky's only response when she'd told him. 'Why can't he come? *Why?*'

Christine had done her best. 'Munchkin, your cousin works very hard—he has lots to do. He has to fly to other countries—'

'He could fly *here*,' Nicky had retaliated. He'd looked across at his mother. 'He could *live* here. He said he was coming to look after me—he *said*. He said my *pappou* told him to!'

His little face had quivered, and Christine's heart had gone out to him. Pangs had pierced her.

If she married Anatole—

No! It was madness to think of yielding. Worse than madness. It would be sentencing herself to a lifetime of anguish.

Instead she had to sentence her beloved son to missing Anatole.

When the first postcard had arrived, she'd been grateful. It had been from Paris, showing the Eiffel Tower and a popular cartoon character. Anatole had written on the back.

> *Will you do me a painting of the Eiffel Tower, with you and me at the top?*

Nicky, thrilled, had rushed off to get his paints.

More postcards had arrived, one every week, from different parts of the globe. And now a month had turned into six weeks. Six endless weeks.

The imminent arrival of his puppy was a source of cheer, and learning to ride, being taught as promised by Giles, helped keep Nicky busy—as did the open day at the pre-prep school he would start at in the autumn.

After meeting some of the other boys there who would be his classmates Christine had arranged some play dates.

She'd even thought about taking Nicky away on holiday for a week somewhere. Perhaps a theme park. Perhaps the seaside in Brittany or Spain.

She didn't know. Couldn't decide. Couldn't think. Couldn't do anything except let one day slip by into another and feel a kind of quiet, drear despair seep over her.

Was this to be her life from now on? It seemed so lonely without Anatole.

I miss him!

The cry came from deep within, piercing in its intensity. She tried to think of Vasilis, to use his calm, comforting memory to insulate herself—but Vasilis was fading. His presence in the house, her life, was only a fragile echo.

She felt him most when she attended to the business of his foundation, but that was intermittent, with the meat of the work being carried out by his hand-picked trustees, who followed the programme her husband had set out for them. She did her bit, played her part, had gone twice to London for meetings, but on her return there was only one man she thought about.

Only one.

The one she could not have.

The one she had sent away.

And the one whom she missed more and more with every passing day.

Anatole was back in Athens again. He'd spent weeks flying from one city to another, relentlessly restless, driven onwards by frustration and a punishing need to keep occupied and keep moving, putting out of his mind all that he had left behind.

The only times he let it intrude was when he paused in airports to buy a postcard for Nicky of wherever he happened to be, scrawling something on it for the boy.

But it did not do to think too much of Nicky. Still less

of Christine. Instead, he made himself focus on what had landed on him here in Athens.

His face set in a grim expression. Both parents had demanded that he visit, and both visits had been hideous. His father intended to get yet another divorce, and wanted a way of getting out of the pre-nup he'd so rashly signed, and his mother wanted him to get back a villa on the Italian lakes she regretted allowing her most recent ex to have.

He was interested in neither demand, nor in the flurry of social invitations that had descended upon him to functions at which women would make a beeline for him, as they always did, his unmarried status a honeypot to them. It had always been like that and he was fed up with it—more fed up than he'd ever been in his life.

I don't want any of this. I don't want to be here. I don't want these people in my life.

Neither the women fawning over him, trying to get his interest, nor his parasitic parents, who only contacted him when they wanted something from him and otherwise ignored his existence, were anything other than repellent to him. And as he headed back to his apartment—alone—he knew with a kind of fierceness that ran like fire in his veins that in all the six punishing weeks he'd spent travelling the world there had been only one place he wanted to get back to. Only one place he wanted to be.

He walked out on to his balcony and the heat of the city's night seemed suffocating. Clogging his lungs. Memory sliced through him, pushing a different balcony high up in the London rooftops into his mental vision. A greenish glow lit the greenery…a soft voice exclaimed at the sight.

A soft voice that had cried out to him again after so many years as they had reached ecstasy together once more. Before that same voice, soft no longer, had banished him.

A vice seemed to close around him, crushing him. He

had lost her once before, through his own blindness. Now he had lost her again and he could not endure it.

I have to see her again. I have to try again—I can't give up on her. I want a family—a family with her, with Nicky.

And why should she not want that too? What impediment could there be?

Across his mind, her words drifted like a ghost intent on haunting him.

'You would know it—'

What had she meant? What did she want that he was not offering her? What was necessary to a good marriage other than what he had set out in plain words, in every caress that he had lavished upon her?

It made no sense.

He shook the thoughts from him, impatient to be gone, to close the yawning space between where he was and where she and Nicky were.

Within hours, those parting miles had vanished, and as he sped out of Heathrow, heading south, gaining open countryside, for the first time since he had left he felt his spirits lighten, his breathing ease.

Elation filled him. And hope renewed. This time—surely this time—he would persuade Christine to finally make her future with him.

This time she won't refuse me.

Hope, strong and powerful, streamed within him.

Christine turned in between the wrought-iron gates, the wheels of her car crunching over the gravel. She'd just collected Nicky from another riding lesson at the Barcourts', and now he was imparting Giles's equine wisdom to his mother.

'You mustn't let ponies eat too much grass,' he informed her. 'It blows them up like a balloon. They might pop!'

'Oh, dear,' said Christine dutifully.

'And you have to groom them after *every* ride. I groom Bramble—but not his tail. Giles does that. Ponies can kick if they get cross.'

'Oh, dear,' Christine said again, thankful that Giles had performed that tricky office.

'I did his mane. I stood on a box to reach,' continued Nicky. 'Bramble is a strawberry roan. He's thirteen hands. That means how high he is. When I'm grown up I'll be too big for him. Now I'm almost just right.'

Murmuring appropriately, Christine rounded the bend in the drive, emerging from the shade into the sunshine that was bathing the gracious frontage of the house, with its pleasing symmetry and the dormer windows in the roofline. The sunshine that was gleaming off the silver-grey saloon car just drawing up ahead of her.

She felt her stomach clench. Her pulse leap. Her breath catch. Anatole was emerging from the car, looking round as he heard her approach, lifting a hand in greeting.

Nicky stopped in mid-word and cried out, ecstatic delight and excitement in his voice, 'He came—he *came*! I wanted him to and he has!'

The next few minutes passed in a blur as, trying urgently to quell the tumult inside her, Christine drew her car up beside Anatole's. Nicky, overjoyed, scrambled out to hurl himself at Anatole, who scooped him in a single sweep up into his arms, clutching him tightly.

Exhilaration streamed through Anatole at the feel of the little lad embracing him. It was good, *so* good to see him again—more than good. Wonderful!

'Oof!' he exclaimed laughingly. 'You're getting heavier and heavier, young man!'

He ruffled the dark hair—as dark as his own, thought Christine, and felt the familiar ache shooting inside her—then lowered Nicky to the ground. He looked across at Christine.

'Hi,' he said casually. Determinedly casually. Determinedly suppressing the urge, the overpowering desire to do to her as he'd done to Nicky—sweep her up into his arms and hug her tightly! But he must not do that. He must be calm, casual. Friendly, nothing but friendly.

For now.

His expression changed slightly. 'Sorry to drop in un-announced. I hope it's OK.' He paused, then said delib-erately, 'I'm booked in at the White Hart.'

He wanted to give her no excuse for sending him away again. To do nothing to scare her off.

Wordlessly, she nodded, feeling relief for that, at least. She was trying to get her composure back, but it was im-possible. Impossible to do anything but feel the rapid surge of her blood, the hectic flare of colour in her cheeks as her eyes hung on him.

He was in casual clothes—designer jeans and a sweater with a designer logo on it, and designer sneakers. He looked totally relaxed and like a million dollars. She felt her heart start to thump.

'I'd better let Mrs Hughes know you'll be here for din-ner,' she said, finally managing to speak.

He tilted an eyebrow at her. 'Not if you have other plans.'

She had no plans—nothing except helping Nanny Ruth with Nicky's tea, bath time and bed. Then her own TV supper in her sitting room.

She made herself smile. 'I'm sure Nicky will want to eat with you.'

'Yes! *Yes!*' Her son tugged at Anatole's jeans. 'Come and play with me. I've been for a ride. And I groomed Bramble. Giles says I'm going to be jumping him soon!'

'Are you, now?' Anatole grinned, letting himself focus on the lad.

He didn't look again at Christine. It would not have been wise.

She was looking...*beautiful*—that was what she was

looking. Beautiful, with her hair pushed off her face by a band, wearing a summery skirt in a blue-printed material, gathered at the waist, and a pale yellow blouse with a short cardigan in a deeper yellow. Her legs were bare, showing golden calves, and her narrow feet were in espadrilles.

He felt desire leap instantly within him. And an emotion that he could not name kicked through him, powerful and unfamiliar. He wanted to go on looking at her. More than look. Wanted to close the distance between them, take her face in his hands and kiss her sweet, tender mouth— as a husband would a wife.

Determination swept through him. *I have to make her mine. I have to persuade her, convince her how right it is for us to marry! Overcome her objections...*

Into his head came her words again—the words he could not understand but needed to understand, about just what it was that she was holding out for.

'You would know it—'

Frustration ground at him again. *What* would he know? What was it she wanted of him that he was not offering her?

I have to find out.

And that was why he had come, wasn't it? To try again—and again.

I'll never give up—never!

The knowledge seared in him, infusing every brain cell with its power. But then Nicky was tugging at him again, chattering away, reclaiming his attention—which he gave with a leap of his emotion to see the boy so eager to be with him. He grinned down fondly at him, and let Nicky drag him off.

Christine watched them go indoors, feeling as if a sledgehammer had just swiped her sideways. Jerkily, she put her car away in the garage, went indoors via the kitchen to seek out Mrs Hughes about revising dinner plans, then she hurried to the sanctuary of her bedroom, her heart hammering, her emotions in tumultuous free fall.

She knew she couldn't keep Anatole out of Nicky's life indefinitely, but how could she possibly bear to keep on seeing him turn up like this…turning her upside down and inside out all over again?

Of their own volition her eyes went to her bed—the bed where she had made love with Anatole in that insane yielding to her own impossible desire for him.

Biting her lip, as if to bite off a memory she must not allow, she headed for her bathroom.

Her cheeks were far too hot. And there was only one cause of that…

As Mrs Hughes wheeled in dinner, it was like *déjà vu* for Christine, as she remembered that first time—so long ago now, it seemed—when Anatole had invited himself.

Nicky, in fine fettle and fresh from bath time, in pyjamas and dressing gown, was exclaiming to Anatole that it would be pasta for dinner. Anatole was saying it would liver and spinach.

'No! No!' cried Nicky, unconvinced. 'That's for *you*!' He gave a peal of laughter.

'Yummy!' retorted Anatole, rubbing his midriff. 'My favourite!'

'Yucky-yuck-yuck!' Nicky rejoined, repeating it for good measure, with another peal of laughter.

Christine calmed him down—getting him over-excited was not sensible. But then, dining here with her son and Anatole was not sensible either, was it? It was the very opposite of sensible. It was little short of criminally stupid.

But how could she deprive her son of what he was clearly enjoying so much? Emotion slid under skin. If she succumbed to Anatole's proposal, this might be their way of life…

For a moment she saw the glitter of fairy dust over the

scene. She and Anatole, Nicky with them, day after day, night after night. A family. A fairytale come true.

Into her head she heard the words that Elizabeth Barcourt had spoken. *'He's a natural with him!'* And the half-sentence that had followed. *'Almost as if—'*

No! The guillotine sliced down again and she busied herself helping Mrs Hughes.

In yet another replay of that first time Anatole had dined here, the housekeeper proffered wine for Anatole's inspection—and this time it did not grate with her, Anatole taking his uncle's role.

Vasilis seemed so very far away now—and she found it hurt her to realise just how long ago their marriage seemed. As if she were leaving him behind.

'You're thinking of my uncle, aren't you?'

Anatole's voice was quiet and his eyes were on her, Christine realised, as Mrs Hughes left the room.

She nodded, blinking. Then she felt a gentle pressure on her arm. Anatole had leant across to press his hand softly on her sleeve. The gesture was simple, and yet it made Christine stare at him, confusion in her gaze. There was something in his eyes she'd never seen before. Something that made her throat tighten.

For a moment their eyes held.

'Mumma, *please* may I start?' Nicky's voice broke the moment.

'Yes—but say Grace first,' said Christine with a smile at her son. A smile that somehow flickered to Anatole as well, and was met with an answering flicker.

In his sing-song voice Nicky recited Grace, with an angelic expression on his face and his hands pressed together in dutiful reverence, rounding off with Giles Barcourt's reminder that puddings came to those who were good.

Anatole laughed and they all tucked in—Nicky to his beloved pasta, Christine and Anatole to a delicious chicken fricassee. As she sipped her wine she felt the difference in atmosphere at this meal from the meal when Anatole had first descended on them.

How much easier it was now.

How much more natural it seemed.

As if it's right for him to be here.

She felt the pull of it like a powerful tide, drawing ever closer. A dangerous tide of overwhelming temptation. But if she indulged—

She tore her mind away, focussing on the moment, on Nicky's chatter, on Anatole's easy replies and her own deliberately neutral contributions when necessary.

As the meal ended, with pudding consumed, Nicky started to yawn copiously. Between them, she and Anatole carried him up to bed, saw him off to sleep, then slowly headed downstairs.

The Greek words of the night-time blessing Anatole had once again murmured over the sleeping child, resonated in Christine's head. And, as if it did in his too, Anatole spoke.

'What arrangements are being made to ensure that Nicky grows up bilingual? I'm sure Vasilis would have wanted that. Obviously I'll do my best, but if I only visit occasionally he may well lose what he has already.'

There was no criticism in his voice, only enquiry.

Christine nodded, acknowledging his reasonable concern. 'Yes, something must be arranged.' She gave a slight smile. 'Our vicar promised Vasilis that he'd teach Nicky classical Greek in a few years, but that won't be enough, I know. I can manage a little modern Greek—enough to teach him the alphabet, but nothing more. Maybe…' she glanced cautiously at Anatole '…maybe you could chat to him regularly over the Internet? And ensure he has contemporary Greek language children's literature to read?'

She started to walk downstairs again. It was not unreasonable to encourage Nicky to keep up his Greek with Anatole—surely it wasn't?

I have to learn to live in harmony with Anatole. Whatever happens, I can't refuse him that.

Her mind skittered away, not wanting to think about the rest of her life with Anatole interacting with Nicky over the years. It was too difficult.

Instead, she went on, 'I could have a word with his headmaster—see if he can recommend a tutor in modern Greek when he starts school in September?'

'School?' Anatole frowned.

'Yes—Vasilis enrolled him at the nearby pre-prep school. It's the same one Giles Barcourt went to. Very traditional, but very well regarded. We both liked it when we visited—and so did Nicky. He's looking forward to starting.'

'Is it a boarding school?' There was a harsh note in Anatole's sharp question.

Christine stared at him. 'Of course it isn't! I wouldn't *dream* of sending him to boarding school! If he actually *wants* to board, when he's a teenager, then fine—but obviously not till then...if at all.'

She saw Anatole's face relax. 'My apologies. It's just that—' He broke off, then resumed as his heavy tread headed downstairs ahead of her. 'I was packed off to boarding school when I was seven. I was a nuisance to my parents, and they wanted shot of me.'

There was harshness in his voice. More than harshness. *Pain.*

She caught up with him as he reached the hall, grabbed his arm. 'Oh, Anatole, that's awful! How could they *bear* to?' There was open shock and sympathy in her voice.

A hollow laugh was her answer. 'I wasn't a priority for them—'

He broke off again, and into Christine's head came a memory from five years ago, when she'd told him how much she missed her father, and he'd told her she was lucky to have any good memories of him at all.

'In a way,' he said, and there was a twist in his voice that was very audible to her, 'Vasilis cared more for me in his abstract manner than either of my parents did. Maybe,' he went on, not looking at her, but looking inwardly, 'that's why I so want Nicky to have me in his life. So I can be to Vasilis's son what he was to me. But...more so.'

His eyes went to her, and there was a veiled expression in them.

'I want you both, Christine. You *and* Nicky. That will not change.'

His eyes held hers, and what she saw in them told her why he had come here.

She made herself hold his gaze. Made herself speak to him. 'And nor will my answer, Anatole.' Her voice was steady, though she felt her emotions bucking wildly inside her. But she must hold steady. She *must*.

Frustration flashed across his features. '*Why?* It makes such *sense* for us to marry!'

Her throat was tight, and her hands were clasping each other as she faced him. 'It made sense for me to marry Vasilis. At least...' she took a painful breath '...it seemed to at the time.' Her eyes were strained, her cheekbones etched. 'I won't—' She swallowed, feeling the tightness in her throat. 'I won't marry again for the same reason.'

And not you, Anatole! Not you over whom I once sprinkled fairy dust only to have it turn to ashes.

She lifted up her hands in that warding off gesture she had made last time. It made him want to step towards her, deny her negation of him. Frustration bit in him, and more than frustration. A stronger emotion he could not name.

But she was speaking again, not letting him counter her, try to argue her down, make her accept what he could see so clearly.

'Anatole, *please*!' There was strain in her voice now, and her face was working. 'Please. I cannot—*will* not—marry you to make a family for Nicky!' She gave a weary sigh. 'Oh, Anatole, we're going round in circles. I don't want what *you* want.'

'Then what *do* you want?' he cried out, with a frustration that shook him in its intensity.

Yet even as he spoke he heard her words, spoken to him the last time they'd stood here, going round in the circles they were caught in, round and round, repeating the impasse of their opposition.

'You would know it—'

The words mocked him, taunted him. He wanted to knock them to the floor, get them out of the way, because they came between him and what he wanted so much— to crush her to him and smother her with kisses, to sweep her up the stairs and into her room, her bed. To make her his own for ever!

But he did not. For yet again they were caught in that endless loop they were trapped in, and she was doing what he had seen her do before.

He saw her walk to the door, open it, to usher him out— out of her life again. As she always did. Always had from the very moment she had left him to marry his uncle.

On heavy tread he did as she bid him, feeling as though gravity were crushing him.

'May I visit tomorrow?' The words sounded abrupt, though he did not mean them to be.

She nodded. Nicky would expect it. Long for it. How could she deprive her son of what gave him such delight?

How can I deprive him of what Anatole is offering?

Like a serpent in her veins, temptation coiled in its dangerous allure. Tightening its fatal grip on her.

'Thank you,' Anatole said quietly.

He paused, looked at her in the doorway. Behind her in the hall he could hear the grandfather clock ticking steadily, measuring out their lives. Their *separate* lives. The thought was anguish to him.

Then he made himself give her a flickering smile, bid

her goodnight. He walked out into the summer's night, heard an owl calling from the woodlands, smelled the scent of honeysuckle wafting at him.

From the doorway she watched him go…watched the car drive off, its headlights sweeping through the dark, cutting a path of light. And then he was gone. Gone yet again.

Was this what her life was to be now? Anatole arriving and departing? Spending time with her only to see Nicky, watching him grow up as year followed year? How could she bear it?

In the quiet hallway she heard the clock ticking past the seconds, the months, the years ahead.

A sudden smothered cry broke from her and she turned away, heading back indoors, shutting the door.

Alone once more.

So alone.

CHAPTER TWELVE

ANATOLE STOOD BY the open window in his bedroom, looking out over the walled garden of the White Hart. Dawn was stealing in, heralding the new day. But not new hope.

His expression was sombre and drawn. His journey here had been in vain. It was pointless to have made it. She had refused him again. Had told him she would always refuse him.

She does not want me.

That was what it came down to. Her rejection of him. She had rejected him when she'd left him to marry Vasilis. She was rejecting him still.

A bitter twist contorted his lips as he stood staring bleakly. He should be used to rejection. Should have got used to it from a young age. He had been rejected by his own parents—who had never wanted him, never loved him.

His mind sheared away from ancient pain. Why was he thinking about that now? He'd always known he wasn't important to them. Had learnt to insulate himself from it. Learnt to ignore it. Discard it. Do without it. He had always lived his life without love. Without wanting love.

He frowned. Why waste his thoughts on his parents? They were not important to him. It was Tia who was important. Tia and her son Nicky.

His expression softened, the twist of his lips relaxing, curving into a fond, reminiscent smile that lit up his eyes as he recalled how wonderful it had been to be greeted by his young cousin so eagerly, to spend the evening with him, absorbed in his world. As Nicky had hurtled towards him, and as he'd caught him up into his arms, an emotion so fierce had swept him, rushing through him like a freight train. Overwhelming him.

What was it, that emotion that had possessed him? A joy so intense, a lifting of his heart that he felt again now, even in recalling it? What *was* that emotion? He'd felt nothing like it before—never in his life.

And it had stayed with him, intensified, curving right through him as his eyes had gone to Christine—so beautiful, so lovely, and so very dear to him.

How can I live without her? Without them both?

He couldn't. It was impossible.

I can't live without them. I need them to breathe, to keep my heart beating!

His expression changed as he rested his gaze on the deep-shadowed garden.

Why? *Why* did he need them to breathe, to keep his heart beating? *Why* did that fierce, protective emotion possess him when he hefted Nicky into his arms? When he gazed at Christine? What *was* it that he felt with such burning intensity?

On the far side of the garden, towards the east, the sky was lightening, tipping the outlines of the ornamental trees and the edges of their silhouetted branches with light. He stood staring at them, feeling inside that same emotion building again, filling him, confusing him, bewildering him.

He heard his own voice calling silently inside his head.

Tia, tell me! Tell me what it is I feel about you. About Nicky.

And in his head he heard her, answering him with the words she'd said that had so confused him, bewildered him.

'*You would know it—*'

He heard the words that completed what she'd said. What she had not said.

If you felt it.

Slowly, oh-so-slowly, as if the whole world had turned about, the two phrases came together—fused.

You would know it if you felt it.

And suddenly, out of nowhere—out of an absence in his being that had been there all his life—he was filled: filled with a rush, a flood of realisation. Of understanding, of knowledge.

That was why he needed her to keep his heart beating! That was why he needed her to breathe!

That was the emotion that he felt—the emotion he knew because he felt it.

It was an emotion he had never known in his life, for no one had ever felt it about *him*—no one had ever taught him how to recognise it.

Accept it.

Feel it.

That was the emotion he felt when he thought about Christine, about Nicky. *That* was what had brought him here to be with them, to beg her to let him stay with her and Nicky all his life. To make a family together.

That was the emotion that filled him now—filled him in every cell in his body—the emotion that was turning his heart over and over and over as realisation poured through him.

He stood there breathless with it, stunned with it. Stood stock-still as he gazed out into the garden which was filling now with gold…with the risen sun.

As he stood there, with the world turning to gold around him, turning to gold within him, he knew there was only one thing to be done right now. To find Christine and tell her.

'You would know it—' she had told him.

Triumph and gratitude, wonder and thankfulness seared him. Well, now he knew—and it was time to tell her. Oh, time to tell her indeed!

Pulling away from the window, he hurried to dress.

* * *

Christine was having breakfast on the little stone-paved terrace beyond her sitting room, with Nicky seated opposite her. Nanny Ruth was upstairs, packing for her weekend away to visit her sister. The morning was warm already, the garden filled with sunshine and birdsong, rich with the scent and colour of flowers.

Nicky was chattering away, talking to her about what they would do when Anatole arrived. 'Can we go to the holiday park again? Can we? Can we?' he asked eagerly.

'I don't know, munchkin—let's wait and see,' she temporised.

Her mood was torn. Hammered down under a barrier as impenetrable as she could make it, battering to be let out, was an emotion she must not feel. The raw, overpowering eagerness to see Anatole again, to let her eyes light upon him, drink him in. But she must not let that emotion break through. If it did—

I might crack, and yield. Give in to what I so long to do, which would bring me nothing but misery and anguish.

No, all she could do was what she was trying so hard to do now—crush down that desperately dangerous longing, suppress it tightly, keep it leashed so that it never broke through.

I've got to be careful! Oh, so careful!

She had to learn how to school herself, how to manage what would from now on be the routine of her life. She had to learn to face seeing Anatole on and off, whenever he visited Nicky through all the years ahead—years that stretched like a torment before her. Wanting so much… yearning for what she could not have. What she had always yearned for but had never had.

She reached for her coffee as Nicky munched his toast, still happily chattering. Lifted her cup to her mouth to take a sip. And stilled in mid-lift.

Anatole was striding across the gardens towards her.

He'd come from the direction of the boundary wall, and the woodland beyond, and a dim part of her mind wondered why. But the rest of her consciousness was leaping into ultra-focus, her gaze fastening on him, that emotion leaping within her that she must not feel but could not suppress as he drew closer. Her clinging gaze took in his ruffled hair, the soft leather jacket he was wearing over a dark blue sweater, his long, lithe jeans-clad legs covering the dew damp lawn in seconds.

He came up to them. Nicky, sitting with his back to him, hadn't noticed him.

Anatole's eyes went to her in a sudden, flickering gaze that was only brief, but she felt a tingle of shock go through her. In it had been something she had never seen before—but an instant later it had gone…gone before she could even wonder at it. She only know that as his gaze flicked away she felt a sense of empty desolation in her so strong she almost sobbed.

Then a grin was slicing his face, and his hands were sliding around Nicky's eyes. 'Guess who?' he said.

Nicky squealed in delight, grabbing Anatole's hands and clambering down to rush around the chair to hug his legs and greet him deliriously.

Then he pulled away sharply. 'You're all wet!' he said indignantly.

Anatole hunkered down beside him to hug him. His heart was pounding, and not just from the long walk he'd had. 'I came on foot,' he said, 'and there's a lot of long damp grass in those fields!'

Christine stared weakly. 'But it's five miles!' she exclaimed.

He only shrugged, for a second making that flickering eye contact with her again that left her reeling and then desolate when he broke it, and laughed.

'It's a glorious morning—it was a joy to walk!' He

pulled out one of the ironwork chairs at the table and sat himself down. 'I could murder a coffee,' he said.

Like an echo, piercing and sibilant, memory stabbed into Christine. He'd used those same words five long years ago, when he'd taken her to his London apartment.

Numbly, she got to her feet. 'I'll… I'll go and make some fresh,' she said, her emotions in turmoil at his unexpectedly early arrival.

In the kitchen, she tried to calm herself. What use was it for her heart to leap the way it did when she set eyes on him? What use at all? What use to feel that dreadful, desolate ache inside her?

Forcibly, she took deep breaths, and when she went back out with a fresh cafetière of coffee, plus toast and some warmed croissants, she felt a little less agitated.

But it only took the sight of Anatole sitting with Nicky at the table, laughing and smiling, to make her feel weak again, to know how useless her attempts to cope with this would be.

'We're going to the beach! We're going to the beach!'

Her son's excited piping made her turn her attention to him.

'Beach?' she echoed vaguely, her mind still churning.

'We can make a day of it.' Anatole grinned. Then his expression changed. 'If that's acceptable to you?'

She nodded. Now that the magic word 'beach' had been uttered it would be impossible to withdraw it without tears from Nicky.

'I'll need to get our beach things packed up,' she said.

Getting away from him again would give her respite, allow her to steady her nerves, arm herself against his presence.

But his arm reached out. 'Don't rush off,' he said.

He took a breath. Met her eyes. That same strange, unreadable flicker was in them that had caught at her so powerfully. She felt herself tense. Something had changed about him, but she didn't know what.

Then he was turning to Nicky. 'Why don't you run upstairs and tell Nanny Ruth we're going to go to the beach?' he said, making his voice encouraging.

Excited, Nicky hared off.

Anatole turned back to Christine. For a second—less than a second—there was complete silence. It seemed to fill the space, the world between them. Then he spoke.

'I need to talk to you,' he said.

There was an intensity in his voice, in his expression, that stilled her completely.

'What is it?' she asked, alarm in her words.

There was something in his eyes that was making her heart suddenly beat faster—something she'd seen in that brief second when he'd arrived.

'Can we walk across the garden?' he asked.

Numbly, she nodded, and Anatole fell into place beside her.

An intense nervous energy filled him. So much depended on the next few minutes.

Everything depends on it—my whole life—

'Anatole, what's wrong?'

Christine's voice penetrated his hectic thoughts. There was a thread of anxiety audible in her tone.

He didn't answer until they'd crossed the lawn into a little dell of beech trees dappled with sunlight, where there was a rustic wooden bench. She sat down, and so did he, wanting to take her hand, but not daring to. His heart was slugging in his chest.

Christine's eyes were on him, wide with alarm. 'Anatole…' she said again, faintly.

Something was wrong—the same dread that had assailed her that nightmare morning when she'd had to tell him she thought she was pregnant was rising up to bite in her lungs.

'Christine…' He took a breath, a ragged one, wanting to look at her, but not wanting to, instead fixing his gaze on the beech mast littering the ground. 'Last night…' He paused, then forced himself on. 'Last night you said you would never marry me just because it made sense to do so, just to make a family for Nicky. And the time before—that morning after,' he said, daring, finally, to steal a glance at her, seeing in a brief instant how still her face was, how taut with tension—how beautiful.

Emotion sliced through him, but he had to blank it. Had to get the words out he needed to say.

'You said you would never marry me just because… because of how good we are together.'

He did not spell it out further—the flush in her cheeks showed him he did not need to.

'You told me…' He drew another breath, 'You told me that there was only one reason you would marry again. And that I would know it…'

He paused again, hearing birdsong in the trees, rustling in the undergrowth. The sounds of life were going on all around him and the world was stretching from here to eternity, all in absolute focus—while he was putting to the test the single thing that would mean everything to him for the rest of his life.

'I know it,' he said quietly.

At his side he felt her still—still completely, as if her very breathing had ceased.

'I know it,' he said again.

And now his eyes went to her, his head turning. Her face was a mask, the pallor in it draining all the blood from her skin. Her eyes were huge. Distended in her face. And in them was something he had never seen revealed before. He felt it like a sudden stabbing of his heart.

But it was there, and he knew it for the very first time in his life—because for the very first time in his life it was in his own eyes, in his face, in his very being as well.

'It's love, isn't it, Tia?' He said her old name without conscious thought, only with emotion. An emotion he had never felt before, never recognised, never believed in.

Until now.

'Love,' he said again. 'That's what you said we needed. The only reason to marry.'

He lifted a single finger to her cheek, felt the soft silk of its texture.

'Love,' he said again.

It was strange…the tip of his finger was wet, and he lifted it away. There was the faintest runnel of moisture on her cheek, below her eye. Another came from the other side. He saw her blink, saw another diamond catch the light and spill softly, quietly.

'Tia!' His voice was filled with alarm. 'Oh, Tia—I don't mean to make you weep!'

But it was too late. Far too late. A cry broke from her—a cry that had been five long years in its engendering. A cry that broke the deadly, anguished turmoil of her heart.

His arms swept around her, hugging her to him, holding her close until she wept no more. Then he sat back, catching up her hands and pressing them with his as if he would never let them go.

He would never let *her* go—never again.

'I ask you to forgive me,' he said, his eyes searching hers, fusing with hers. 'For not understanding. For not knowing. For being so hopeless at realising what you meant.'

His hands pressed hers more tightly yet. Entreaty was in his eyes, his face.

'Forgive me, I beg you, but I didn't recognise love because I've never known it till this moment! Never in all my life experienced it.'

His eyes flickered for a moment, old shadows deep within them.

'They say,' he said slowly, 'that we have to be taught to love. And that it is in being loved that we learn to love.'

His gaze broke from her, looking past the trees around them, looking a long way past.

'I never learnt that essential lesson,' he said.

His eyes came back to her and she saw in them a pain that made her heart twist for him.

She pressed his fingers. 'Vasilis told me a little of your parents,' she said carefully, feeling her way. 'It made me understand you better, Anatole. And you yourself sometimes dropped signs about how unloving your parents were. Still are.' She gave a sad smile. 'Vasilis let me see how I'd wanted more from you than you could give me. He helped me to accept that you could not feel for me what I felt for you.'

'Felt?' The word dropped from his lips, fear audible.

She crushed his hands more tightly yet. Emotion was streaming through her, pouring like a storm, a tidal wave, overwhelming her with its power. But she must find her way through it—find the words to tell him.

'Oh, Anatole, I *made* myself fall out of love with you! I had to! I had no choice. You didn't love me. You *could* not love me! And I had to save myself. Save—'

She broke off. Then, with a breath, she spoke again, her eyes clinging to his as she told him what had been in her heart for so long.

'I fell in love with you, Anatole, when I was new to you—when I was Tia. I knew it was unwise—but how could I have stopped myself when you were so wonderful to me, like a prince out of a fairytale?'

She looked away for a moment, her eyes shadowing, her voice changing as she looked back at him knowing she must say this too. However difficult.

'Anatole, I give you my word that I never deliberately sought to get pregnant. But...' She took a sharp breath, made herself say it. 'But when I thought I was, I knew that

I hoped so much that it was true! That I was going to have your baby. Because…' She took another breath. 'Because then surely you would realise you were in love with me too and would want to marry me, make a family with me.'

She felt her hands clenching suddenly, spasming.

'But when you spoke to me—told me to my face that if that was what I was hoping it would never happen, *could* never happen, that the only marriage you could ever make would be an unwilling one, then… Oh, then something died within me.'

A groan of remorse broke from him. 'That gruesome lecture I gave you!'

Anatole's voice was harsh, but only with himself. He held her gaze, his eyes troubled, spoke again.

'Tia—Christine—I make no excuses for myself, but…' He paused, then continued, finding words with difficulty. 'I can only tell you how much I dreaded being made to be a father when the only one I knew—my own—was so totally and absolutely unfit to be one! Fatherhood was something I never wanted because I feared it so much. I feared that I would be as lousy a father as mine had been. But I've changed, Tia! I've changed totally!'

His voice softened.

'Meeting Nicky—feeling that rush whenever I see him, that incredible kick I get when I'm with him—oh, that's shown me just how much I've changed! Shown me how much I want a family of my own.'

She nodded slowly, her face working. 'I know—I *do* know that. Truly I do. But, Anatole, do you understand now why I had to refuse you when that was all you were offering me? I wanted to accept—dear God, how I longed to accept you!—but I did not dare.'

Her hands slipped from his now and she shifted her position, turning her shoulders away, her body language speaking to him of what speared him to the quick.

'I loved you once, Anatole, and lost you. I married Vasilis—not out of love, but... Well, it suited us.'

Did he hear evasion in her voice? She hurried on.

'All I knew was that to marry you simply to make a family for Nicky would have become hell on earth for me. Hell to know that I had fallen in love with you all over again and that all I was to you was a mother for Nicky, and a partner in your bed...' Her voice twisted. 'To be so close to heaven and yet outside the door still...'

He turned her to him, his hands warm on her shoulders. His voice was firm and strong, filled with a strength that came from the heart.

'I will make heaven for you, Tia. My adored Tia. My Christine—my beautiful, beloved Christine. My love for you will make heaven for you—for us both.'

Tears broke from her in a heart-rending sob and she was swept against him again. She clutched him and kissed him, his cheeks, his mouth, long and sweet and filled with all that she'd had to hold back from him. All that she need never hold back again.

He held her tight, returned her embraces, then sat back a little.

'Heaven for us *all*,' he said. 'You and me and Nicky.' His breath choked him suddenly. 'Nicky whom I will love as if he were my own.'

She stilled as if every cell in her body were turning to stone. Keeping her as silent as she had been for five long years. Then, beneath his gaze, she spoke. Said what she had to say.

Slowly, infinitely slowly, she picked each word with care. 'I have to tell you why I married Vasilis.'

She saw his features twist. Heard him make his own admission. So long denied.

'It hurt,' he said. 'I did not realise it, thought myself only angry with you. But that was because you'd left me for him—rejected me when I still wanted you. On my own terms, yes, but I wanted never to let you go.' He swallowed 'You wanted to leave me. And what he could offer you, I now understand, was more than I could offer.'

He took a ragged breath, met her troubled gaze.

'You wanted a child and so did Vasilis. It was that simple.'

She shook her head. A violent, urgent shaking. 'No— no, it was *not* that simple! Oh, God, Anatole, it was not that simple at all!'

Her voice was vehement, stormy with emotion.

'Anatole… That nightmare morning, when I told you I was not pregnant and you lectured me on how I must never let that happen, well…' Her throat closed, but she forced the words through. 'I was so terrified that I… I used the pregnancy test I'd been too scared to use before! I knew I didn't need to—that I had got my period—but I was so distraught that I wanted every proof I could grasp at! So I did the test—'

She stopped. Silenced by the truth she must tell him now. Her heart was like lead within her.

'It showed positive.'

There was silence. Silence all around. Even the birds were silent. Then…

'I don't understand.'

'Neither did I.' Her voice came as if from far away. 'Apparently it's not that unusual, though I had no idea at the time. There can still be a show of blood. Even when you're pregnant.'

His eyes were on her—staring, just staring. She went on—had to—had no choice but to do so.

'I was beside myself with terror. I knew I would have to tell you when you returned. How horrified you would be. And that was how your uncle found me,' she said, and swallowed, 'when he arrived for lunch with us.' Her face worked. 'He was so kind…so incredibly, wonderfully kind! He sat me down, calmed me down, got the whole dreadful tale out of me. How I'd fallen in love with you, but you hadn't with me, how you'd have felt you *had* to marry me, and how that would have condemned me to a lifetime's misery—condemned *you* too, ruining your life! How I loved you and knew I'd be forcing you to have a child you did not want, forcing you to marry me when you did not want to. And then…' she half closed her eyes '…then he made his suggestion.'

Another deep breath racked through her.

'He said that in the circumstances I needed time—time to think, to accept what had happened. Time to come to terms. To make my decision. Whether to tell you or to raise the child myself. So, as you know, he took me back to London, where I had more doctor's appointments to confirm that, yes, I was, indeed pregnant. And then…' She looked at Anatole. 'And then, knowing what I'd told him, and knowing you as he did, he offered me one other possibility.'

From far away she heard Anatole speak.

'To marry him so he could raise my son—the son I did not want. Marry the woman I did not want to marry.'

The accusation in his voice—against himself—was unbearable for her to hear. The pain was like a spear in her heart.

Her eyes flew to him. 'He did it for *you*, Anatole! To give your son a home, a loving and stable family, to provide for him and for me as his mother, in a way that was the very best way to do it!'

Her expression changed, infused with sadness now.

'He knew he would not live to see Nicky grow up, that he could only be a temporary figure in his life. That's why, as I told you, to Nicky he was his *pappou*. And for that very reason…' she swallowed again, making herself look at Anatole, hard though it was '…he knew that one day he would not be here. That one day—' she took a painful, harsh breath '—I would have to tell you. When the time was right.'

She was silent for a moment.

'And now that time has come, hasn't it, Anatole? Please, *please* tell me it has?' Her voice dropped to a whisper. 'Can you forgive me, Anatole, for what I did?'

His eyes were bleak. 'I am to blame,' he said. 'I brought it on myself.'

'You could not help the way you felt—the way you *didn't* feel!' Her negation of his lacerating self-accusation was instant.

He caught her hands. 'You are generous, Tia, but the fault is mine. That you did not even dare to tell me—' He broke off, anguish in his face.

She crushed his fingers in hers. 'Anatole, please! I understand. And maybe I *should* have told you. Maybe I should have had the courage, the resolution to do so. I've deprived you of your son—'

He cut across her. 'I didn't deserve him.'

His eyes clung to hers and she saw them change from self-accusation to something new.

Hope.

She said the words he needed to hear. 'But you deserve him *now*, Anatole,' she said quietly, from her heart. 'You have come to love him, and that is all a child needs. All that *you* were never given. And now,' she said, and her voice was choked with the emotion running through it, 'now Nicky is *yours*. Your son to love as he should be loved. As he *is* loved!'

She got to her feet, drawing him with her though she was so petite against his height. She gazed up at him, never letting go of his hands.

'And you will have a wife to love you too,' she said.

She lifted her mouth to his and his eyes softened, with a tenderness in them that lit her like a lamp.

'And you will have a husband to love you back,' he said gently.

His lips were a brush upon hers. His hands holding hers fast.

'Nicky is my son.' It was a statement—a truth that seemed to him to be opening the sky in a glory of brightest sunlight, blazing down on him. 'Nicky is *my* son!'

He gave a sudden great exclamation of joy, sliding his arms around her waist, lifting her up and twirling her round and round, laughing, exclaiming until he put her down again, breathless with joy.

'Dear God,' he said, 'can such happiness exist? To have discovered my love for you, for Nicky—and now to discover that you love me back, that the boy I've come to love is mine!'

His expression changed. Grew grave.

'But he is my uncle's child too. I will never forget that, Christine. I owe him that. And I will always be thankful to him for what he did for Nicky and for you.'

She felt her eyes fill with tears. 'He was a good man, my dear Vasilis. A *good* man.' And now her gaze was full upon him, 'Though he was never my husband in anything but name—he would not have wanted anything else, nor I.'

He was looking down at her, taking in the implications of what she'd said.

She gave a sad little smile. 'Did you never wonder why your uncle remained a bachelor? He was in love once, you know, when he was a student. But the woman he wanted to marry did not come from your world, and his parents objected. He resolved to get his teaching qualifications and marry her, be independent of the Kyrgiakis wealth. But…' Her voice became sadder. 'But, unbeknownst to him, while he was studying in England she found she was pregnant and developed eclampsia. They both died—she and the baby with her.'

She took a pained breath.

'I think, you know, that is partly why he offered to make me his wife—because he remembered how alone the woman he loved had been.'

Anatole folded her to him. 'Let us hope and pray,' he said quietly, 'that they are all finally together now. He and the woman he loved, and his own child.' He held her back, his eyes pouring into hers. 'As *we* are together, Tia—my beloved, my dearest adored Christine—as we are together now. You and me and our most precious son—together for ever. Nothing can part us now.' His voice seared with emotion. *'Nothing!'*

He kissed her again, sweetly and passionately, warmly and lovingly, and the world around them turned to gold.

It was Christine who drew back first. 'This is all very wonderful…' she said.

And there was a smile in her voice even as tears were in her eyes—tears of the radiant, unbreakable happiness and joy that swelled her heart until it was bursting within her at the miracle that had happened, at the gift she had been given that she had never hoped to have: the love of the man she loved…

'All very wonderful,' she repeated, her eyes starting to dance, 'but I really think we have to get back to the house. We have a trip to the beach to undertake! Or our son, Anatole—' did her voice choke over the word 'our'? She thought it did, and rejoiced in it '—our son will never forgive us!'

He gave a laugh as warm as the fire of happiness blazing within him and laced an arm around her. They walked back to the house—shoulder to shoulder now, and in all the days to come—ready to start their family life together.

EPILOGUE

THE LITTLE CHURCH was filled with flowers. But the guests were few and very select.

The Barcourts—with Giles's mother and sister looking particularly satisfied with events—occupied the front pew, and on the other side the vicar's wife sat with Mr and Mrs Hughes and Nanny Ruth.

As Christine progressed slowly up the nave, her pale lavender gown emphasising her slender beauty, she was followed by Nicky, holding her short train. He was followed by Isabel Barcourt's daughter as flower girl.

At the altar rail stood Anatole, waiting for his bride. As she reached him Christine smiled, turning to beckon Nicky to stand beside her. The vicar, his expression benign, began the service.

In Anatole's head Christine's words echoed. *'You would know it...'*

And now he did. He knew the power of love—the power that had brought him here, to this moment, where the woman he loved and the child he loved would be his for all eternity—as he was theirs.

Gravely he spoke the words that would unite them, heard Christine's clear voice echoing, until his ring was on her finger and hers on his.

'You may kiss the bride.' The vicar smiled.

She lifted her face to Anatole—to her husband, the man she loved. She let their mouths touch, exchanging their love. And then, with a graceful dip of her knees, she lifted Nicky. Anatole took him from her, hefting him effortlessly into the crook of his arm, and they both turned round.

The organ music surged, the bells pealed out, and the

congregation burst into applause as the flower girl threw rose petals over them. Laughing and smiling, the three of them—husband and wife, mother and father and precious son—headed down the aisle and out into the golden sunshine of their lives beyond.

* * * * *

CLAIMED BY HER BILLIONAIRE PROTECTOR

ROBYN DONALD

For Sheila, who patiently waited a long time for this one!
Many thanks for everything.

CHAPTER ONE

NIKO RADCLIFFE HAD expected an unsophisticated band playing unsophisticated country music. After all, this was the northernmost part of New Zealand, a farming region of small villages, ancient volcanoes and stunning coastal scenery. Narrow and sea-bordered, the peninsula thrust north towards the equator, relying on its beauty and its history to attract tourists.

So the strains of mellow jazz drifting across the car park as he walked towards Waipuna Hall came as a pleasant surprise. Either the Far North had an unusually professional musical culture, or—more likely—the committee who'd organised the Waipuna Centennial Ball had hired the band from Auckland.

At the doors a middle-aged man stepped towards him. 'Good evening. Can I see your ticket, please?'

Niko held it out, and after a quick scan the doorman nodded and said, 'Welcome to Waipuna, Mr Radcliffe. I hope you enjoy the evening.'

Niko had his doubts about that, but he said, 'Thank you,' and walked into the hall, stopping just inside the doors to survey the crowd.

The district had done the occasion proud. Garlands of flowers looped around the walls, their faint evocative perfume floating on the warm air. Men in the stark black and white of evening dress steered partners clad in a multitude of colours. Everyone appeared to be having a fine time.

Whoever had done the decorations had talent, and must have denuded quite a few farm and village gardens of flowers. Their soft, fresh perfume hung in the warm air, the blooms competing in colour with the women's bright copies of Twenties' flapper fashions.

Idly, Niko allowed his eyes to follow one of the dancers. Although she had her back to him, she was above average height, and her sleek head of strawberry-blonde hair made her easy to see amongst the dancers. Her grace should have won her a better partner than the middle-aged man steering her somewhat clumsily through the crowd. When they turned Niko recognised him—Bruce Nixon, husband of the woman who headed the Waipuna Centenary Ball committee.

The music stopped, the floor began to empty, and the noise changed to a buzz of chatter and laughter. His gaze still held by that bright crown of hair, Niko realised the woman and her partner were walking towards Mrs Nixon, the only other person in the hall he recognised. In spite of his unexpected arrival in Waipuna several days previously she'd tracked him down and welcomed him to the Far North.

'And as the new owner of Mana Station it would be appreciated if you could come to our Hall Centennial Ball and meet some of the local people,' she'd told him, her tone reminding him of his rather severe first governess.

He'd agreed to endure the possible boredom of a country ball because his purchase of the cattle station had been a matter of comment in the national media, quite a bit of it critical. The new manager he'd appointed had also informed him of discontent caused by yet another foreign absentee owner buying up a large agricultural holding in New Zealand.

Especially an owner with his background. The only child of a European aristocrat who'd fallen crazily in love with a rugged New Zealander, Niko could barely recall his early life on his father's vast tussock-clad hill station in the South Island. He'd been just five years old when his mother had fled with him back to her father's palace in San Mari, a small European principality.

So it was logical enough for him to be considered a foreigner. The fact that he'd forged an empire for himself in commerce wasn't likely to cut much ice—if any—with pragmatic, farming Kiwis.

Given time, they'd discover that he was nothing like the previous owner of Mana Station, who'd not only stripped the station of every available cent for years, eventually bringing what had once been a profitable farming concern so close to ruin that he'd been forced to sell, but had appointed an inefficient, corrupt farm manager.

Doubtless Niko's dismissal of that man would cause more gossip.

Mrs Nixon looked across the hall, saw him, and smiled, beckoning him across. Noting wryly that he was being openly inspected by at least half of the dancers, Niko set off towards her.

The strawberry blonde could be Mrs Nixon's daughter, although that seemed unlikely. Both Mrs Nixon and her husband were short and rather stout, whereas the redhead was slender.

Niko's gaze narrowed as he took in the younger woman's face—fine features and ivory skin, faintly flushed with exertion. Her violet silk shift subtly revealed soft curves and long limbs. She wasn't beautiful, yet something about her stirred his blood. Her hair was pulled back from her face and confined in a knot at the base of her neck. Ivory-skinned, she turned her head slightly as he walked towards them, revealing slightly tilted eyes and a full, sensuous mouth.

'Mr Radcliffe! I'd begun to think you weren't coming!' Mrs Nixon beamed as he arrived.

'I'm sorry I'm late,' he said smoothly. 'Your ball is obviously a huge success.'

Her smile widened even further. 'I hope you enjoy it. You've met my husband, Bruce, of course.'

While the two men shook hands, she went on, 'And this is Elana Grange, who helped us enormously with the organisation for tonight, and also with the decorations. She's a neighbour of yours—right next door at Anchor Bay, in fact.' The smile she directed at her companion was almost mischievous. 'Elana, this is Niko Radcliffe, the new owner of Mana Station.'

'How do you do, Mr Radcliffe.'

Her voice was cool, and so was the hand she extended, allowed to lie in his for a brief moment, and then retrieved.

For the length of a heartbeat, Niko's initial awareness gave way to a sensation infinitely more primal—a swift, uncontrollable physical response that startled him. Elana Grange radiated a subtly provocative allure that roused him in a way he hadn't experienced before.

Yet he sensed contradictions. Slightly tilted eyes of dark green speckled with gold gave her an exotic air, but her level gaze lacked the coquettish awareness he often saw in women's eyes. And although her mouth hinted at passion, something about the lift of her square chin indicated a controlled reserve.

Which could, of course, be deliberate. Several bitter experiences in his youth had led to a sardonic appreciation of the various methods of feminine provocation. If Elana Grange expected him to be intrigued by her aloofness, she'd discover she was wrong. Niko had learned to deal with women who viewed him either as a challenge, or a path to social and material advancement.

Her sophisticated appearance was completely at odds with the dilapidated little shack she lived in, huddled just outside the gates to Mana Station. He'd noticed it from the helicopter as he'd arrived at Mana homestead, and assumed the place was a ruin. Judging by the state of the roof, its owner was going to face a large repair bill some time soon.

Mrs Nixon said enthusiastically, 'I'm so glad you could make it tonight, Mr Radcliffe. Or should I call you Count?'

'No. My name is Niko.'

Another slight smile curved Elana Grange's soft mouth. It gave her a fey look, an air of cool mystery that summoned another swift, startlingly carnal response in Niko.

Mrs Nixon smiled. 'Very well, *Niko*.' She glanced at the woman beside her. 'Elana was just wondering why you'd chosen to buy Mana Station when it's almost derelict.'

A faint colour warmed the face of the woman beside her. Embarrassed she might be, Niko thought cynically, but his answer would almost certainly be circulated through the district. So he told her the truth. 'I spent my early years on a high country station in the South Island, as well as some school holidays, and developed an affection for New Zealand and its stunning countryside. As for Mana—it needs rescuing.'

An interesting and unexpected comment, Elana decided. However, his purchase of the large sheep and cattle station had caused quite a lot of publicity, and he was probably aware that not all of it had been favourable. Pretending to an affection for the country could be a way to alleviate that.

The Count had an interesting voice, if you liked men's voices deep with a hard edge. He'd judged his handshake perfectly—strong enough to be masterful without causing pain. Once he'd released her hand she'd had to stop herself from rubbing her tingling palm surreptitiously against her side.

Her first glance at the arrogant jut of his jaw had set every warning instinct on full alert. And the unsparing assessment of his ice-blue gaze had reinforced her surge of defensiveness. It was highly unlikely she'd ever become friends with the new owner of Mana Station.

However, her foolish body was buzzing with sensual excitement. His lean, charismatic muscularity emphasised by wide shoulders and his height, Count Niko Radcliffe wore his formal evening clothes with an intimidating confidence that was like nothing she'd seen before.

Cool it, Elana commanded her jumping heartbeat. Handsome men were not that uncommon, and she'd seen enough photographs of him in the media to know what to expect.

But photographs failed to convey his effortless air of authority or the powerful aura that was more than physical, backed by a disturbing smile. According to the media he ran his numerous interests with a formidable combination of intelligence, determination and ruthlessness.

An image formed in her mind of some warrior king of long ago, one who ruled by sheer force of character.

Chemistry, she decided, trying to dampen her foolish reaction with irony. Some men had it in spades. And dangerously attractive though he seemed, Niko Radcliffe's magnetism owed nothing to honesty or kindness or—well, any of the virtues.

But then, royal billionaires probably didn't need honesty or kindness to attract some women.

Immediately ashamed of the snide thought, she banished it. According to Mrs Nixon, an avid reader of gossip magazines, he chose lovers noted for their beauty and intelligence, the latest one a gorgeous English aristocrat.

And in farming circles he had a good reputation. Only a few weeks ago she'd read an article about his rescue of the sheep and cattle station he'd inherited from his father. He'd spent much money killing the wilding pines that threatened to turn the land into forest, and clearing the station of goats. Apparently he was determined to clear it of rabbits too, although he'd admitted he might need a miracle for that.

She risked a swift upwards glance, her pulse speeding as her eyes clashed with his. Somehow she just couldn't see this man, completely assured in his perfectly tailored evening clothes, shooting goats or hauling out pine seedlings.

Ah well, no doubt he had minions to do the heavy work.

Fixing a noncommittal smile to her lips, she said lightly, 'Welcome to Northland, Mr Radcliffe.'

Black brows lifted. 'Niko,' he repeated with a crisp intonation that came close to curtness. But then he smiled.

Elana was shocked by a fierce awareness that tightened her nerves and sinews. That smile was *something*!

And no doubt he was aware of its impact.

He added, 'Congratulations on the decorations. They are superb.'

Striving to control a swift surge of adrenalin, she forced herself to concentrate on his accent. He sounded almost English, but his faint foreign intonation no doubt came from his upbringing in a European palace.

Elana steadied her voice enough to say, 'Thank you—we had an excellent committee to work with.'

The band struck an imperative chord, and once the chatter faded the MC—a local farmer—spoke into the microphone, welcoming the crowd. Something far too close to relief gripped Elana when the man beside her turned to listen.

Stop being an idiot, she told herself robustly. OK, so

the new owner of Mana had the kind of presence that attracted eyes and attention.

Definitely an alpha male—uncompromising and intolerant and intimidating.

Like her father. Just the sort of man she despised.

And feared...

The MC announced the next dance, and the Count turned to Mrs Nixon with a request that summoned a slight flush to her cheeks. 'Dear man, that's lovely of you, but I'm not dancing tonight. I managed to twist my ankle yesterday,' she said.

Horrified, Elana realised that Niko had no polite way out of asking her to dance.

Sure enough, he turned to her, hard eyes veiled by lashes too long for any man. 'May I have the pleasure?'

Say no.

But that would be ludicrous. After all, it was only one dance...

Her smile hiding, she fervently hoped, her abrupt and unwarranted reaction, she placed her fingers gingerly on his outstretched arm.

'So you live above Anchor Bay,' he said as the band struck up a tune. His tone indicated that he wasn't particularly interested.

Matching it, she answered, 'Yes.'

'You must be able to see quite a bit of Mana Station from there.'

'Yes.'

'You'll notice quite a few changes soon.'

Strangely, the purposeful note in his voice chilled her. She looked up, and for a couple of seconds their eyes locked. Blinking, she lowered her lashes against the ironic challenge in his cold blue gaze.

Suavely he asked, 'You're surprised?'

He saw too much. Elana struggled for something banal

and conventional to say, but only managed, 'No.' When his brows drew together she added, 'I'm pleased. It's time someone gave Mana back some pride.'

He nodded. 'Exactly what I intend to do. Don't worry, I won't bore you with farming talk. Let's dance.'

A shiver ghosted the length of her spine as she stepped closer. For a foolish moment she felt she'd taken a forbidden step into an alternative world.

A dangerous world, she realised as they began to move together—a world where the rules no longer applied. Jumping heartbeats took her by surprise and her nostrils flared at the faint, exciting, potently male scent of him and the hard strength in the arms that imprisoned her.

Imprisoned her?

What a ridiculous thought!

Yet the heat of Niko Radcliffe's hand at her waist was stirring a blatant response. Her dress seemed suddenly far too revealing, the violet silk slithering over acutely sensitised skin in a sensuous massage.

Of course he danced superbly; she was ready to bet that lean, splendidly physical body would do anything well, from dancing to making love.

'Are you all right?'

His voice startled her. She had to swallow before she could speak and even then, she sounded hesitant. 'Yes, I'm fine.' A swift defiance made her glance up to meet hooded, glinting eyes. 'Why?'

'You seem a little tense,' he responded coolly, blue gaze unreadable. 'I rarely bite, and when I do, it's not to hurt.'

Heat zinged from her scalp to her toes, lighting fires all the way. That instinctive awareness strengthened into a sensation much more intense, so fiercely tantalising it shocked her.

Was he coming on to her?

No sooner had the thought flashed across her mind than

she dismissed it. Of course he wasn't flirting! It was impossible to imagine Count Niko Radcliffe doing anything so frivolous. So was he testing her?

If so, it was unkind. He was as out of place in Waipuna as she'd be in the rarefied social circles that were his natural habitat. According to Mrs Nixon, gorgeous film stars fell in love with him...

And probably the occasional princess. Gorgeous too, no doubt.

She couldn't care less, she thought sturdily, trying to corral her rampaging senses.

'So you're quite safe,' he drawled.

The note of mockery in his voice stiffened her spine. 'I'm always glad to have that assurance,' she retorted.

'Even when you don't necessarily believe it?'

Elana tried to come up with some innocuous answer, but before anything came to mind he continued curtly, 'Whatever you might have heard about me, I don't attack women.'

As soon as the words left his mouth Niko wondered why he'd said them. He spent more time fending off women than reassuring them of his integrity.

He had no illusions about the reason behind that sort of feminine interest. Money and power talked, and for a certain type of woman it was enough to seduce. Yet for some reason the note in Elana Grange's voice had struck a nerve.

Actually, *she* struck a nerve.

When they'd been introduced he'd noticed her fingers, long and slender and bare of rings, and for a moment he'd wondered what they'd feel like on his skin. And as she'd stepped into his arms, his whole body had tightened in swift, primitive response.

However, elegant though she appeared, he suspected Elana Grange wasn't sophisticated enough for the sort of relationships he chose. His affairs—nowhere near as many as suggested in gossip columns—had always been between two people who both liked and wanted each other, whose minds meshed. He valued intelligence as much as he did sex appeal.

And because he drew the line at breaking hearts, his lovers had always understood that he wasn't offering marriage.

Whatever sort of mind Elana Grange had, she looked like a dream—and danced like one too, her grace fulfilling the promise of her sinuous body.

Elana broke the silence between them. 'Mr Radcliffe, there have been rumours that you plan to develop Mana Station. Is that true?'

'What do you mean by *develop*?'

Wishing she'd stayed silent, she told him. 'Cut it into blocks, sell them off and make a gated community of it—'

'No,' he interrupted curtly. 'I'm planning to bring it back into the vital, productive station it once must have been.'

She couldn't stop herself from asking, 'Why?'

Broad shoulders lifting, he said, 'I despise waste. In San Mari every acre of land is precious, cherished and nurtured over the centuries, treated with respect. All agricultural and pastoral land should be viewed like that.' His tone altered as he finished, 'And call me Niko.'

Hoping no sign of her reluctance showed in her tone, she said, 'Then you must call me Elana.'

He laughed. Surprised, she glanced up, meeting his gaze with raised brows.

'Don't look so startled,' he said. 'When I came back to New Zealand it took me a few weeks to understand that although most people here call each other by their first names, it didn't necessarily denote friendship.'

Elana had never previously pondered the intricacies of

New Zealand ways of addressing people. Perhaps he was interested because he'd grown up in a royal household, where such things were important?

Or perhaps not, she thought wryly. Probably he was just filling in a boring experience with smooth small talk.

She considered a moment before replying, 'You're probably right. I think it's a preliminary to a possible friendship—addressing a person by his or her first name is an indication that you feel he or she might be someone you'd like, once you get to know him or her better.'

'So if you decide you don't like me, you'll call me Mr Radcliffe?'

Elana allowed herself a careful smile. 'I'd probably avoid you. That way I wouldn't have to address you at all.'

'So if I notice you fleeing from me, I'll have to accept that I've done something that's displeased you.'

Bemused, Elana looked up. Their eyes met, and another tantalising rush of adrenalin boosted her pulse rate into overdrive. A point in his favour was the dry amusement in his voice.

Not that it mattered what sort of person he was—or only so far as he was a neighbour.

'Actually, I'm not into fleeing,' she told him briskly. 'And we like to believe we're an egalitarian society. But—didn't I read that you're a New Zealander too?'

'I have dual citizenship,' he said levelly.

A swift change of direction startled Elana until she realised she was being skilfully steered around a jitterbugging pair in the centre of the floor.

'Wrong period,' Niko Radcliffe observed dryly. 'They should be doing the Charleston.'

She said, 'But they're good.' The words had barely been spoken when the young man missed a step and stumbled towards them.

* * *

Instantly her partner's arm tightened, forcing Elana against his steely strength so that she was held firmly for a few seconds against the powerful muscles of his thighs. Sensation, so intense and sensuous it drove the breath from her lungs, scorched through her in a delicious, dangerous conflagration.

Concentrate on dancing, blast you, she commanded her wayward body fiercely, pushing a wilful erotic image into the furthest reaches of her brain and trying to lock the door on it.

Suddenly dry-mouthed, she breathed, 'Thanks.'

'It was nothing.' His voice was cool and uninflected.

Clearly he wasn't suffering the same potent response. Indeed, his arm had loosened swiftly as though he found her sudden closeness distasteful.

Chilled, she had to swallow before she could say, 'Perhaps we should tell them that jitterbugging arrived some years after the Twenties.'

'They're enjoying themselves,' he said dismissively, then surprised her by asking, 'Are you the local florist?'

Elana hesitated. He sounded quite interested—which seemed unlikely. Perhaps faking interest when bored out of his mind was another talent developed in that princely court...

OK, concentrate on small talk now, she told herself. *Ignore those pulsating seconds when you were plastered against him, and something weird happened to you.*

Sedately she told him, 'I work part-time in the florist's shop in Waipuna.'

'Was that always your ambition?' he asked, almost as though he were interested.

'No.' After a second's pause she added, 'I'm a librarian and I used to work in Auckland, but a couple of years ago a family situation meant I had to come home to Waipuna.'

The family situation being the accident that had killed her stepfather and confined her mother to a wheelchair.

'So you decided to stay here.'

Elana glanced up and met a narrowed blue gaze. Another of those unnerving shivers chased down her spine. In a tone she didn't recognise, she said, 'Yes.'

'Is there no library in Waipuna?'

'Yes, run by volunteers. There's no need for a professional librarian.'

'Ah, I see. Do you enjoy working in the florist's shop?'

Surely he couldn't be interested in a small-town woman in the wilds of northern New Zealand? He didn't need to hear that, although she loved Waipuna, she missed the stimulation of her career in Auckland.

She evaded, 'I can't remember a time when I wasn't fascinated by flowers. My mother was a fantastic gardener and apparently from the time I could toddle I drove her crazy by picking any blooms—' She stopped abruptly. *Any blooms her mother had been allowed to cultivate.* 'Often before they'd opened out,' she finished.

He gave the big hall a quick survey. 'You clearly have a talent for arranging them. Mrs Nixon also mentioned that you wrote the booklet—a short history—of the hall. I haven't read it yet, but intend to.'

Elana flushed. 'I hope you find it interesting.'

'Are you a historian as well as a librarian?'

'I did a history degree,' she said.

And wasn't surprised when he asked, 'Why?'

'Because I'm interested in history.' She added, 'After that my stepfather insisted I take a business course.'

'Very sensible of your stepfather,' Niko Radcliffe said dryly. 'From your tone, I gather you didn't want to do it. Was he right to insist?'

Elana didn't like the way he emphasised the word *stepfather*. Steve had been as dear to her as any father could be—infinitely dearer than her own father. She said briskly, 'Yes, he was right. It's been very useful.'

Especially over the past couple of years, after a friend had asked her to tape her great-grandmother's reminiscences and transcribe them so they could be bound into a book to mark her hundredth birthday. Elana found the task absorbing, enjoyed the whole experience and had been astounded when her friend's family insisted on paying her for the time she'd spent.

Even more astonishing, word had got around the district, and soon she was repeating the process. Then the editor of the local weekly newspaper commissioned her to write articles on the history of the district. As she was working for only three days a week at the florist's shop, the money came in handy, and she loved the research.

To her relief the music drew to a close. Niko Radcliffe released her and offered an arm. Forcing herself to relax, she took it, trying to ignore the sudden chill aching through her—a bewildering sense of abandonment.

How could a man she'd only just met have that effect on her?

Be sensible, she told herself robustly as they walked across the hall towards Mr and Mrs Nixon. *So you're attracted to him? So what? You're probably not the only one here tonight to be so aware of him...*

Over the centuries women had learned to recognise an alpha male. For probably most of humankind's existence, a strong capable father to one's children gave them a much better chance of survival.

And, tall and good-looking, with that indefinable magnetism—not to mention the fact that he was rich, she thought sardonically—everything about him proclaimed Count Niko Radcliffe a member of that exclusive group.

Which was no reason to fantasise about feeling strangely at home in his arms. When the next dance was announced he'd choose a different woman to partner him, and that woman might well feel the same subliminal excitement, a reckless tug of sexuality both dangerous and compelling.

Together they walked to where the Nixons had just finished chatting to another couple. Acutely aware of sideways glances, Elana was surprised by an odd regret when they arrived.

Mrs Nixon observed, 'Good evasive action, Niko. For a second I thought we might need to call on my first-aid skills, but you saved the day with that sidestep. Young Hamish and his partner are going to have to practise jiving a bit longer before they're safe enough to do it in public.'

His smile held a tinge of irony. 'Fortunately I had an excellent partner.'

The older woman sighed. 'My grandmother was a great dancer—she could still do a mean Charleston when she was eighty, and her tales of balls and parties used to make me deeply envious. Then rock and roll came onto the scene when my parents were young. I always felt I missed out on being wild and rebellious.'

'Surely punk must have been wild and rebellious enough,' Elana teased.

Mrs Nixon chuckled. 'A bit too much for me, I'm afraid,' she confessed. 'And now I find I've turned into my father—when I hear the hit songs today I mutter about their lack of tune and how they don't sing clearly enough for me to understand the words.'

'Possibly a good thing,' Niko observed coolly. 'Tell me, why did the committee choose the Twenties as a theme for tonight? I believe the hall was built in the early twentieth century, so you should have been celebrating its centennial some years ago?'

Mrs Nixon smiled. 'Nobody was interested in running a ball to celebrate the centennial then, but a year ago a group of us decided Waipuna deserved a Centennial Ball. So we called it that. It meant that people who'd give an ordinary dance a miss came for it—some from overseas,' she finished proudly. 'It's been a lovely reunion.'

He laughed, and Elana's heart missed a beat. 'Good thinking. So why the Twenties theme?'

'Comfort.'

Brows lifting, he echoed, 'Comfort?'

'Comfort,' Mrs Nixon repeated firmly. 'In the early twentieth century women were still confined to elaborate clothes and corsets. We decided unanimously that comfort is more sensible than historical accuracy.'

'To every woman's relief,' Elana observed. 'As well, it's a lot easier to sew a Twenties shift than the gowns they wore twenty years previously.'

Niko glanced down, struck by the way the lights shimmered on her gleaming hair. Freed from the neat knot at the back of her neck it would look like silk. Into his mind sprang an image of the soft swathe spread out across a pillow—of her lithe, ivory-skinned body against white sheets, green-gold eyes heavy-lidded and beckoning...

Strange how exotic eyes and a fall of bright hair could lend spice to an occasion...

Irritated by a fierce surge of desire, he suppressed the tantalising thought and concentrated on the conversation.

He'd expected little entertainment from this evening. If his presence at the ball went some way to convincing the district that he intended to return Mana Station to full production again—which would mean jobs for local people—it would make the new manager's position easier.

Above the babble of conversation and laughter he discerned a rapidly approaching roar as some idiot drove past the hall, achieving as much noise as he could from a badly maintained engine.

When the noise had faded Mr Nixon told him laconically, 'One of the local hoons. Like all young kids with an attitude, they like to stir up the district periodically. No harm to them, by and large.'

Niko nodded. The band struck up for the next dance, and some young guy in evening clothes slightly too big for him came up and asked Elana Grange for it. Smiling up at him, she accepted.

Watching them dance, Niko resisted a swift emotion that veered dangerously close towards possessiveness. Startled by its intensity, he secured one of the matrons Mrs Nixon introduced him to, and guided her onto the floor. But although his partner was a brilliant dancer, and had a sharp, somewhat acerbic wit, he had to force himself to concentrate on her and not allow his gaze to follow Elana Grange around the room.

As the evening wore on he noted she was a popular dance partner, but seemed to favour no particular man, apparently enjoying her turns with middle-aged farmers as well as with younger men.

Keeping her eyes firmly away from Niko Radcliffe, Elana chatted with old friends and acquaintances, grateful that he didn't approach her for any more dances.

By the time midnight arrived she was strangely tired, but she managed to hide any yawns until she slid into her car, pulling out to follow his car. It suited him—big enough to be comfortable for a tall man, super-sophisticated yet tough...

Stop this right now, she told herself grimly. *You're being an idiot. OK, so he looks like some romantic fantasy, all strength and good looks and seething with charisma, but that's no reason for you to feel as though you've overdosed on champagne.*

Frowning ferociously, she stifled another yawn and concentrated on the road as it narrowed ahead. Some time during the ball it had rained and the tarseal shone slickly in the headlights. After a few kilometres the road swung towards the coast and the surface turned to gravel as it dived into the darkness of the tall kanuka scrub crowding the verges.

About halfway home, scarlet tail-lights ahead warned her of trouble. Slamming on her own brakes, she gasped as the seatbelt cut across her breasts.

When her stunned gaze discerned the cause of the sudden stop, she gulped, 'Oh, *no*—'

CHAPTER TWO

SHOCKINGLY, THE GLARE of the headlights revealed a stationary vehicle on its side. The driver had failed to take the corner and the car had skidded into the ditch before sliding along the clay bank that bordered the road on the passenger's side.

Hideous memories of another accident, the one that had killed her stepfather, and ultimately her mother, flashed through Elana's mind. Sick apprehension tightened her stomach and froze her thoughts into incoherence until she realised that Niko Radcliffe was already out of his vehicle and running towards the wreck.

Fingers shaking, she released her seatbelt and opened the door. Her first instinct was to join him, but second thoughts saw her haul the first-aid kit from the glove box.

Clutching it, she ran, heartbeats thudding in her ears as Niko wrenched open the driver's door and leaned inside.

'Oh, dear God, *please...*' Elana breathed a silent prayer that jerked to a sudden stop when she realised he was half inside the car, presumably undoing the driver's seatbelt.

Over his shoulder he commanded harshly, 'Get back. Quickly—I can smell petrol.'

So could she now, the acrid stench cutting through the minty perfume from the kanuka trees. At least the force of the collision had stopped the engine.

'*Go,*' Niko Radcliffe ordered, dragging the driver free of the car in one ferociously powerful movement.

'I'll help you—'

He broke in, 'Have you got a cell phone?'

'Yes, but—'

'Then get back to your car and use it to call for help.'

Torn between summoning the emergency services and helping him, Elana wavered.

'Move! And stay there!'

The peremptory command raised her hackles, but sent her running back. Snatching up her cell phone, she tapped out the emergency number, eyes fixed on Niko and his limp burden as he strode past his own vehicle towards her.

'Ambulance, fire engine and police,' she told the emergency operator, and answered the subsequent questions as clearly and concisely as she could, finishing by saying, 'The smell of petrol seems to be getting much stronger. I have to go now.'

She dropped the phone onto the driver's seat and ran towards Niko and his burden.

He had to be immensely strong, because, although the hard angles of his face were slick with sweat, he'd carried the driver of the wrecked car past their vehicles to what she fervently hoped was a safe distance.

Breathing heavily, he laid the unconscious man on the narrow, stony verge before straightening. 'How long will it take them to get here?'

'About fifteen minutes,' Elana told him unevenly, adding, 'I hope that not too many of the volunteers were drinking champagne at the ball.' She dropped to her knees beside the still—*dangerously* still—driver. 'Jordan,' she said urgently, groping for his wrist. 'Jordan, can you hear me? It's Elana Grange. Open your eyes if you can.'

'Who is he?'

'Jordan Cooper.' Tears clogged her eyes. 'He's only a kid—about eighteen.'

'Any pulse?'

Steady, she told herself when her probing fingers found nothing. *Concentrate.* 'No.'

Inwardly shaking, she explored a little further, and to her intense relief recognised the faint flutter of heartbeats against her fingers. 'Yes. He's alive.' *Barely...*

She laid a gentle hand on the driver's chest, some of her panic fading when she felt it rise and fall beneath her palm. 'He's breathing.'

'Keep checking. Tell me at once if his pulse stops or he stops breathing.'

Vowing to take the next first-aid course available, she infused her tone with a confidence she didn't feel. 'Jordan, hang on in there. You're going to be all right. Help is coming and will be here soon. Keep breathing.'

Did he hear her? Probably not, but that faint flutter steadied a little and his breathing became slightly less harsh.

Niko surveyed her, crouched on the stones, her long fingers clasping the unconscious man's wrist.

As though sheer willpower could keep him alive, she urged again, 'Keep breathing, Jordan, keep breathing. It won't be long now before the ambulance gets here.'

Never had time dragged so slowly. Niko hoped to heaven he hadn't made Jordan's injuries—whatever they were—worse by hauling him from the car. The boy had worn a seatbelt so he'd almost certainly have escaped severe injury, although to knock him out the car must have hit the bank heavily.

And the stench of spilt petrol hung in the cool air, a constant threat.

At last the silence, broken only by the regular mournful *morepork* call of a nearby owl and Elana's commands to Jordan to keep breathing, was interrupted by the sound of engines labouring up the hill.

Her head jerked up. Voice trembling with relief, she said, 'Jordan, the ambulance is almost here. I can see its lights flashing through the bush. Keep breathing. You're going to be all right.'

She fell silent as the ambulance arrived, followed closely by a fire engine and a police car.

Gladly handing over to those who knew what they were doing, Niko gave silent thanks for volunteers, and decided to double the donation he gave to each organisation.

Reaching down, he pulled Elana gently to her feet. Although she valiantly straightened her shoulders, she couldn't hide the shivers that wracked her slender body.

He shrugged out of his jacket and draped it across her shoulders. 'All right?'

'Yes.'

The quaver in her voice and the shiver that accompanied it told him she was in mild shock. Understandable, especially as she knew the kid.

He looped an arm around her shoulder. When she flinched he demanded, 'What's the matter? Did your seatbelt hurt you?'

'No.' She held herself stiffly while he urged her onto the side of the road out of the way of the vehicles. 'I'm all right.'

And presumably to prove it, she moved away from him, putting distance between them. For some reason that exasperated him. Eyes narrowed, he kept a close watch on her while the ambulance personnel got to work and what at first seemed chaos soon resolved itself into a well-oiled routine that swiftly transferred the still-unconscious youth to the ambulance.

'Elana?' A young policeman stopped in front of them, frowning. 'You all right?'

'Don't worry, Phil, I'm fine,' she said, and summoned a shaky smile.

'Rotten thing to happen to you—' He stopped, looking profoundly uncomfortable, then asked hastily, 'You sure you're OK?'

Niko glanced down at her. What was going on? Had she been involved in an accident recently?

'I'm fine,' she repeated, her voice a little firmer, and added, 'Truly, Phil, I'm all right.'

The young cop kept his gaze on her face. 'Can you tell me what happened?'

'Neither of us saw it,' Niko informed him. 'It looks as though he took the corner too fast, over-corrected, then hit the bank at speed. I think we got here almost immediately after that.'

Questions had to be asked and answered, Niko knew, but surely not now. The woman beside him was no longer shaking, but she was still in shock. No wonder, if she *had* been involved in an accident.

Apparently the constable agreed, because he said, 'Thanks for being so quick off the mark—the fire chaps say that it must have been touch and go that the engine didn't explode. They'll deal with it until it's no longer a danger and the guys can tow it away.' He looked at the silent woman. 'Elana, I'm sorry—it must be bringing back really bad memories. Right now, you need something hot to drink and someone to look after you. I'd take you home myself—'

'Phil, don't be silly,' she said weakly. Phil's wife was very pregnant. The last thing she'd need would be him arriving home with someone to look after.

His suspicions confirmed, Niko looked down at her white face. Without thinking, he took her arm and said firmly, 'She can stay at Mana. The homestead's not completely repaired yet, but it's liveable.'

He expected some resistance, and it was in a muted voice she said, 'No, that's not necessary. I'm fine.' But it took an obvious effort for her to stiffen her shoulders as she added, 'I just hope Jordan will be too.'

'The ambos think he's been lucky,' the constable reassured her. 'Not too much damage beyond a bad graze and possible cracked ribs. I hope so too, for his parents' sake. They'll be at the hospital to meet him.' He transferred his gaze to Niko. 'I don't think Elana should be driving. If you can drop her off at home I'll make sure her car gets back to her place.'

'Phil, it's not necessary.' Elana's tight voice made it obvious she didn't like being discussed as though she weren't there.

Niko intervened, 'You're mildly shocked. I'll take you home.'

She pulled away from him. 'I'm all right.' But her voice wavered on the final word.

'Be sensible.' He added crisply, 'Let the professionals take over.'

Her chin lifted. 'You're a professional?'

'No, but this man is. Come on, give him your keys.'

The cop was hiding a smile, one that almost escaped him when Elana stared indignantly at Niko for a few seconds, then shrugged. 'The keys are still in my car,' she said bleakly. 'OK, Phil, I won't drive if you think I shouldn't. I'll just collect my bag.'

Niko found himself admiring both her spirit and her common sense. He said, 'I could do with something hot and soothing right now. I'm pretty good at making coffee, but I'm thinking a tot of whisky should go into it.'

The lights of the remaining vehicles revealed both her

disbelieving expression and a swift, narrowed glance. 'I hate whisky.'

Amused by her intransigence, Niko watched her head for her vehicle, and found himself wondering what had given her that sturdy spirit.

Once she was out of earshot the cop turned to him. 'Rotten thing to happen to her,' he said, frowning.

'To anyone,' Niko returned. Especially to the kid behind the wheel…

The young policeman went on, 'But tougher on Elana than most.' He hesitated, watching her as she opened her car door and bent inside it. 'She lost her parents—well, her stepfather—a couple of years or so ago in an accident. He was killed instantly, and her mother was so badly hurt she never walked again.'

Niko said harshly, 'Damn.'

'Yes. Elana was with them—they were hit head-on by an out-of-control truck.' He paused and shook his head. 'She was lucky—not too much in the way of injuries, but she had to leave a good job in Auckland to come home and look after Mrs Simmons—her mother. She died after a stroke about six months ago.' He paused. 'Hell of a shame for Elana to come across young Jordan like that.'

Niko looked towards her car. Elana was still groping around in the front seat, presumably searching the bag she'd carried—a little satin thing that didn't look big enough to hold the keys to any house. Frowning, he watched her straighten up and step back, bag in hand.

He turned to the constable and extended his hand. 'I'm Niko Radcliffe from Mana Station.'

'Yeah, I recognised you from the photos in the local newspaper.'

They shook hands and turned to watch Elana walk back, clutching her bag, her face drawn and taut.

Niko opened the passenger door of his car. When she hesitated he said, 'Get in.'

Lips parting, she gave him a dark look, but clearly thought better of whatever she'd been going to say and obeyed, after thanking Phil Whoever-He-Was.

'I'll go and have a word with the fire brigade,' Niko told her, and closed the car door on her.

Turning away so she couldn't hear, he said quietly to the cop, 'I'll also ring my housekeeper; she'll stay the night and will keep an eye on her.'

The constable nodded. 'Great. She shouldn't be on her own. I'll get in touch with you when I know young Jordan's condition.' He paused, and gave a brief smile. 'But watch out for fireworks. Elana's pretty independent.'

However, when Niko returned to his car after being reassured that the leaking petrol was no longer a danger, Elana Grange looked far from independent. Eyes closed, she was leaning back in the seat, and even in the semi-darkness he could see that the colour hadn't returned to her face, and that her hands were clenched on her bag as though reliving the impact of a crash. A pang of compassion shook him.

At the sound of the opening door Elana forced up her weighted eyelids and took a deep breath. 'Thanks,' she said, adding, 'I didn't realise just how—how affected I'd be by this.'

'Accidents are always difficult to deal with, and for you now, I imagine much more so.'

So Phil had told him. She blinked back shaken tears. 'I thought—hoped—I'd got over it. The shock, I mean.'

Only to fall to pieces… Sometimes she wondered if she'd ever recover from the tragedy of her parents' deaths.

'Give it time,' Niko said as he set the car in motion. 'It's a truism, but time does heal most things—eventually.' He paused before adding, 'And if it doesn't entirely heal, it usually provides the ability to cope.'

Surprised, she looked up. His angular sculpted profile and the tone of his voice made her wonder if he'd discovered this for himself. Immediately she chided herself for her self-absorption. She wasn't the only person in the world to be forced to live with unexpected tragedy. Other people had even worse events in their lives, and managed to overcome their impact.

In a small voice she said, 'I just miss them so much.'

To her astonishment he dropped one hand from the wheel and closed it over hers. Although strong, his grip was warm and strangely comforting.

'That's the worst part,' he told her, releasing her cold fingers. 'But eventually you'll learn to live without them. And to be happy again.'

His pragmatic sympathy warmed some part of her that had been frozen so long she'd come to take it for granted. Had he too suffered a loss? Possibly. However, she wasn't comfortable discussing her grief with a man she didn't know, even though the events of the evening somehow seemed to form a link between them.

Opening her eyes, she gazed ahead as the headlights revealed paddocks and fences and the sweep of a bay.

'Hey!' she exclaimed. 'Stop!'

'Why?' He kept on driving towards Mana homestead.

'You've gone past my gate. Sorry—I should have told you where I—'

'I know where you live.'

After digesting that she fought back bewilderment to demand, 'Then why did you drive past?'

'Because I agree with your policeman friend. You shouldn't be on your own tonight.'

Silenced by a mixture of shock and outrage, she opened

her mouth to speak, only to have her throat close and the words refuse to emerge.

The man beside her went on, 'I called my housekeeper and she's preparing a bed for you.' And without pausing he added on an ironic note, 'I'm sure there will be a lock on the door. If not, you'll still be quite safe.'

Stung, she blurted, 'I didn't—I wasn't...'

Housekeeper? Did he travel with a domestic ménage? Although various tradesmen and decorators had been working on the sadly neglected and almost derelict Mana homestead for some months, local gossip hadn't mentioned a resident housekeeper.

Perhaps Niko Radcliffe guessed her thoughts, because he said calmly, 'I assume you know that the house is still being restored, although fortunately it's almost finished.'

Elana drew in a sharp breath. 'It's been the talk of the district since you bought the station.' Along with the huge amount of money he was spending on the house as well as the land itself. 'But I'm perfectly all right—a bit shaken, that's all. I don't need to be cosseted.'

'Your policeman friend didn't seem to think so.'

His amused tone rubbed her raw. 'Phil's a nice man but he's always had an over-developed protective instinct. There's no need for you to wake up your housekeeper and put her to this trouble.'

'She's another with an over-developed protective instinct,' he said laconically, turning the wheel to swing between low stone walls. For years they'd proudly guarded the entrance to Mana homestead, but now more than a few of the volcanic boulders had tumbled to the ground.

No doubt they'd soon be put back in place.

Above the clatter of the cattle stop, Elana said grittily, 'I—thank you.' In his forceful, domineering way, Niko Radcliffe possibly thought he was being neighbourly.

'It's nothing.'

His tone told her that, indeed, he meant just that. Because, of course, his housekeeper would be the one who did any actual caring—not that it would be necessary.

She opened her mouth to say something astringent, then closed it as he went on, 'It's been an unnerving experience for you—and understandably so.'

'Which doesn't mean I'm not capable of looking after myself.'

'Is it always so difficult for you to accept help?'

Elana couldn't come up with any sensible response. Much as she resisted the idea, her shock at the accident and fear for Jordan weren't the only reasons for her silence. From the moment she'd seen Niko he'd had a potent effect on her.

And she certainly wasn't going to let him know that.

He broke the silence. 'If Mrs Nixon had been with us, I'm sure you'd have let her sweep you off home with her.'

'I—' Elana paused, then said reluctantly, 'Well—yes. But I've known the Nixons almost all my life, and she'd worry.'

Still amused, he said, 'I can't say I'd *worry*, but I'd certainly be concerned if I'd dropped you off by yourself. And if you're concerned now about local gossip, you don't have to be. My housekeeper will be enough of a chaperone.'

His response made her seem like some virgin from Victorian melodrama. Elana stifled a sharp retort. 'I'm not at all worried about my—well, about my safety. Or my reputation. I just want to go home.'

'No,' he said coolly.

Fulminating, she looked across at a profile hewn of stone, all arrogant angles above a chin that proclaimed complete determination.

Sheer frustration made her demand recklessly, 'Why are you doing this? You realise that it's kidnapping?'

His mouth curved. 'Tell me, would anyone in Waipuna accept that—and I'm including your policeman friend?'

He'd called her bluff. Of course they wouldn't, and neither would she accuse him of it. Curtly she retorted, 'I'd have preferred that we talk the matter over before you drove past my gate.'

'Why? We'd have just had exactly the same conversation, only sooner. And I'm assuming that you're sensible enough to accept that you're not only tired, but still traumatised by the tragedy of your parents' accident.'

Elana flinched, averting her face as he stopped the car outside the old homestead. The harsh glare of the headlights highlighted the amazing change huge amounts of money could produce in a few months. Evidence of years of neglect under the previous owner had been erased, and Mana homestead looked as pristine as it must have when it had first been built over a century ago.

Niko turned and inspected her. She was staring at the homestead, her features sharpened. 'I've upset you. I'm sorry,' he said, resisting the impulse to take her hands in his and offer what comfort he could.

Years ago he'd learned a harsh lesson about giving in to a compassionate impulse. A friend's daughter had suffered a setback, and he'd taken her on a short cruise on his yacht, only to realise that she was falling in love with him. He'd felt no more for her than a brotherly affection, and had told her so as gently as he could. For the rest of his life, he'd be grateful that her attempt at suicide had failed, and that she was now happily married.

Since then, he'd been careful not to raise expectations he wasn't able to satisfy, choosing sophisticated lovers who understood that he wasn't interested in matrimony.

Elana Grange shook her head, her tone flat when she answered. 'I'm rather weary of telling people I'm all right.

Thank you. You're being very kind.' She even attempted a smile as she straightened her shoulders and said in what she probably hoped was her normal voice, 'It's shocking what twenty years of neglect did to this place. Those pohutukawa trees on the edge of the beach are over three hundred years old. The previous owners were going to cut them down. They said they blocked the view.'

'Why didn't they fell them?'

'There was a public outcry, and a threat to take it to the environment court. I don't know why they wanted them removed. They almost never came to Mana.' She paused. 'And the oak tree we've just passed was planted by the wife of the very first settler here.'

'I gather from your tone that you're not sure whether or not I'm going to bulldoze trees down,' Niko said dryly.

Elana hesitated, before telling him the truth. 'It hadn't occurred to me, but I hope you're not.'

'I prefer to plant trees rather than kill them.'

Brief and to the point, and, because he'd decided to restore the homestead rather than demolish it, she believed him. 'Except for pine trees, I believe.'

'Except for wilding pines,' he agreed.

He switched off the engine and got out. On a ragged, deep breath, Elana fumbled with the clip of her seatbelt, then wrestled with the unfamiliar door catch. Before she'd fathomed it out, the door swung open.

'Here, take my hand,' Niko commanded.

Scrambling out, she muttered, 'Thanks, but I'm fine.'

Although he said nothing, she realised he was watching her closely as they walked towards the house. A woman opened the door—the housekeeper, of course—probably in her forties, with a smile that held both a welcome and some interest.

Niko said, 'Elana, this is Mrs West. Patty, Elana Grange

lives next door. She's had a shock, so I'd suggest a cup of tea or coffee.' He glanced down at Elana. 'Or something a bit stronger.'

'Tea will be fine, thank you,' Elana said as crisply as she could, and added, 'I'm sorry Mr Radcliffe felt obliged to put you to all this trouble.'

The older woman's smile widened. 'It's no trouble. I've made you up a bed in a room overlooking the beach.'

'Thank you.' Although it had to be very late Elana was no longer tired. Just strung on wires. Tea might help her to think clearly.

Why on earth had she surrendered to Niko's calm abduction?

The answer stared her in the face. Jordan's accident had flung her back into the shock of losing Steve and, later, her mother.

It was too late now to regret her weakness. She was here at Mana, and, thanks to both Phil and Niko Radcliffe's over-developed sense of responsibility, she had no way of getting home.

Five minutes later she was sitting on a comfortable sofa in a room that breathed sophisticated country style, fighting an aching weariness that clouded her mind. Barely able to prop her eyelids up, she covered a prodigious yawn.

Sitting down had not been a good move. Right then she desired nothing more than the blessed oblivion of sleep—in her own bed. Her eyes were full of grit, and somehow her bones had crumbled. The thought of getting to her feet made her want to curl up and collapse, crash out on the sofa for what was left of the night.

Niko's black brows drew together. 'You're exhausted. Do you want to forego the tea?'

'No.' Her voice sounded oddly distant. She set her shoulders and tried for a smile, failing dismally.

'You did well,' he told her, his voice level.

'So did you.'

Always, until she died, she'd remember how he looked as he dragged Jordan free of the car, the sheer brute strength of the man, and the fierce determination in his face as he carried the youth to safety.

Taking a deep breath, she said, 'I'm going to take the next first-aid course the St John's people advertise.'

'An excellent idea, although I hope you never have to deal with a situation like that again.'

The urgent summons of a cell phone startled her. A mixture of adrenalin and concern forced her shakily upwards.

After a moment she realised Niko was holding out a hand to her. A cold fist of dread closing around her heart, she staggered to her feet. His fingers closed around hers, summoning a tingle of primal awareness that sizzled through her, giving her enough energy to stay upright.

He flicked his phone open, was silent a second or two, then said crisply, 'Speaking. How is he?'

CHAPTER THREE

SWALLOWING, ELANA PREPARED herself for bad news.

Time stretched unbearably in the silence before Niko Radcliffe said in a vastly different tone, 'He's regained consciousness? Great. And at his age bruised or cracked ribs should heal quickly. It doesn't sound as though his other injuries will be any problem. He was lucky.'

Elana sagged, grateful for the strength of his arm around her. Despising herself for her weakness, she tried to pull away, only to find she couldn't.

'Yes, I'll make sure she knows,' he finished. 'Thanks very much.'

And released her after he'd snapped the cell phone shut and tossed it onto the nearest chair. 'That was your police-man friend. The ambulance people seem pretty convinced that young Jordan has nothing more than mild concussion, a shallow cut from flying glass, and what will probably be quite severe bruises caused by the seatbelt, but just might be cracked ribs.'

The mixture of relief and her body's fierce, involuntary response to his nearness set Elana's pulses hammering. Startled, she tried to pull back.

'Sit down,' Niko ordered, eyes narrowing as he scanned her face. 'You're just about out on your feet.' He released her, frowning as she sat too quickly onto the sofa. 'You need something stronger than tea.'

She stiffened her backbone, resisting another debilitating wave of tiredness. 'I don't normally go to pieces. Thank heavens Jordan got off so lightly. I'm very glad he was wearing his seatbelt.'

'Only an idiot would drive without one.' His voice was coolly dismissive.

That tone—so dispassionate as to border on contempt—summoned harsh, painful memories of her father. Catapulted back to childhood, she looked up into her host's hard face, then glanced away.

He went on curtly, 'Especially a kid who doesn't know how to drive safely on a back-country road.'

Mrs West came in carrying a tray, and frowned as she set the tray down on a table. 'Goodness, Ms Grange, you're as white as a ghost. I think you could do with some brandy in that tea.'

Bracing herself, Elana managed a smile. 'No, really, the tea will work wonders. Actually, I'm reacting to *good* news.'

And a chilling flashback...

'Young Jordan was very lucky,' Niko explained, and briefly told the housekeeper the extent of Jordan's injuries.

'Oh, that's wonderful!' Mrs West gave a wry smile. 'Well, you know what I mean! Better bruised ribs than a broken back.'

As she left the room her employer moved across to the tray and asked Elana how she drank tea.

'As is,' she said, 'no milk, no sugar.'

Niko poured a cup of tea and brought it across to her. Gratefully lifting it, Elana began to sip, using the action as a kind of shield against that intimidating ice-blue gaze.

Pull yourself together, she told herself. *Stop being so feeble!* To fill the silence she said, 'This has not been the most auspicious introduction to Waipuna for you. I hope any other visits will be much less dramatic.'

'I hope so too, as I plan to visit frequently.' At her surprised glance he added crisply, 'At least until Mana Station is up and running again the way it should be.'

It would do no harm to spread the word that he intended to take a personal interest in the station. He was no micromanager, and he trusted Dave West, the new manager, but he intended to make the important decisions for the station's future.

And, he thought grimly, make sure they were carried out.

It should have been a pleasant extra that Elana Grange lived right next door. Even now, in spite of dark circles beneath her eyes and features sharpened by tiredness, her subtle magnetism stirred his blood. But independent though she clearly was, it was unlikely she'd be sophisticated enough to understand the sort of relationships he preferred.

So he wouldn't be giving in to that primal summons.

'Why the startled look?' he enquired.

'I suppose—well, I thought you'd be an absentee owner,' she admitted. 'Your life must keep you busy.'

He shrugged. 'For most of their history the people of San Mari had to produce all their own food or starve. Sometimes they starved. So tending their cattle and the land that supported them was hugely important. Things have changed now with the advent of communications and tourism, of course. However, vast areas of the world still need food, and along with my other responsibilities I do what I can to supply it.'

Responsibilities? Elana allowed herself a small smile. That was an interesting way to describe the worldwide empire he'd built for himself. And although he might consider himself a farmer, very few men of the land wielded so much influence and power.

His brows lifted. 'I said something amusing?'

'No.' She hesitated, met his narrowed gaze and expanded, 'I made the mistake of assuming you'd be more like the previous owners, who used Mana as a cash cow so they could live the life they enjoyed.'

His expression warned her he didn't like what she'd said. 'Stereotyping is lazy thinking,' he told her coolly.

'True,' she admitted, and sipped more tea, welcoming its comfort and reassurance as a wave of intense weariness washed over her.

Her host asked, 'Is there anything else besides that tea that you need?'

'Thanks, but it's done the trick. You were right—I'm already feeling better.' She smothered a yawn with a hand. 'I'm sorry, I think it's time I went to bed.'

'Patty will be back in a minute or so to show you your room,' he said. 'If you need anything, ask her.'

Sure enough, the housekeeper appeared almost immediately, and, after saying goodnight and being ordered to sleep well, Elana was ushered up the stairs into a bedroom that breathed luxury without being fussy or ostentatious.

When she didn't have to force her eyelids to stay up, Elana knew she'd appreciate it even more.

Mrs West offered her a nightgown, saying with a smile, 'It's mine, so it won't fit you, but it'll cover you.'

Exhaustion weighed Elana down, slowed her brain, dragged through every word. 'That's very kind of you.'

Drat Niko Radcliffe. Why couldn't he have delivered her home?

Her expression must have revealed her thoughts, because Mrs West said, 'The *en suite* for this room isn't functional yet, but there's a bathroom two doors down the hall to the left. I've put toothpaste and some towels there for you.'

Elana thanked her and set off. It took all the concentration she could muster to wash her face and clean her teeth.

Back in the bedroom Mrs West said as she left, 'The light in the hall will be on, so if you need to go to the bathroom later you'll have no trouble finding your way here. Goodnight and sleep well.'

Feeling as though she'd been beaten with cudgels, Elana climbed into a nightgown several sizes too big, and sank into the enormous bed, gratefully allowing unconsciousness to claim her.

But with sleep came dreams—the same nightmares that had tortured her after the accident. Unable to prevent them, she relived again the horror of seeing the huge stock truck hurtle towards them, her mother's scream cut off by the moment of impact, the pain mercifully shortened by a devouring darkness.

And then thank all the gods, she woke up, whimpering, and stumbled up to her feet, her heart thudding so strongly she felt it might jump out of her breast. After switching on the lamp on the bedside table, she drew in several deep breaths before realising she needed to head for the bathroom.

'Two doors down,' she muttered, clutching the overlarge gown around her. 'On the left...'

The hall light was dim, but she could see easily enough to make out the bathroom door. Tiptoeing, she got there, and was halfway back to her bedroom when she heard a noise behind her. Heart jumping, she increased her pace and prayed for it to be the housekeeper.

'Elana.'

No such luck. The deep hard voice belonged to Niko Radcliffe. Hand groping to pull the wide neck of the nightdress up, she swivelled around. He loomed in the semi-darkness, big and tall and far too close, and showing far too much skin.

At first she thought he was naked and took a short step backwards as her stunned gaze took in wide, tanned shoulders and a muscled chest with a scroll of dark hair across it. A swift relief eased some of her shock when she realised he was wearing pyjama trousers.

'What…?' she breathed.

He took two strides towards her, stopping as she backed away. Frowning, he asked, 'Are you properly awake?'

She ran her tongue over dry lips. 'Of course I am,' she said huskily. 'I needed to use the bathroom.'

'You're shaking. I hope you're not afraid of me.'

Something in his tone made her stiffen. 'No, of course not.' Despairingly, she realised her voice was thin and almost wavering. She had to steady it to continue, 'I'm all right. I—I'm—'

She stopped and shook her head, dragging in more air in a quick gasp. 'Sorry,' she whispered.

He waited a few seconds before saying in a milder tone, 'Can you walk?'

'Yes.'

But when she took a step her legs crumpled beneath her. Mortified, she leant against the wall and clamped her eyes shut to stop the walls—and her host—from suddenly spinning.

'I'll carry you,' he said harshly, and before she could protest she was enveloped in his warmth and strength, the faint, potent male scent of him somehow comforting as well as stimulating, so that she had to fight a craving to rest her head on his shoulder.

'I'm too heavy,' she managed as he lifted her.

'You're not. Just keep still and I'll get you back to your bed.'

Wordlessly, her thoughts and emotions a tangled jumble, she obeyed.

When he straightened after lowering her into the bed she shivered again, suddenly cold and bereft. The light of the lamp picked out the strong bone structure of Niko's face, and a sudden, unexpected sensation gripped her, a kind of urgency, of hunger…

Something in the Count's gaze made her realise that the nightdress neckline had dragged down, revealing far too much of her breasts. Scarlet-faced, she hauled the material up, grateful that he'd immediately turned to pull the duvet over her.

Stone-faced, he said, 'I'll get you something to drink.'

'Not whisky,' she managed with a weak smile.

His answering smile heated every cell in her body. 'No, not whisky.'

She watched him stride from the room, his lithe strength quickening her pulse rate. Body tight with a dangerous tension, she dragged in a deep, shuddering breath and hauled herself up against the pillows, pulling up the duvet to cover her breasts.

How stupid—how *idiotic*—to practically faint, like some Victorian debutante confronted by a man in night attire…

Niko returned almost immediately, a glass of water in his hand. Elana was lying back against the pillows, her hair falling in a cloud of rose-gold silk across her shoulders. He dragged in a sharp breath at the memory of ivory breasts cupped by fabric that hugged every curve, of a faint, elusive perfume, of the feel of her warm body against his.

She tantalised every sense. All compassion momentarily swamped by a dangerous hunger, Niko stiffened.

Then he noticed the tears glittering beneath her lashes. She was in no fit state for anything other than sexless comfort.

'Here,' he said, hoping she wasn't aware of the rough note beneath the words, 'drink this.'

Elana reached out, only to have the duvet fall down. Colour staining her skin, she grabbed the material and hauled it up to her shoulders.

Niko put the glass of water—flavoured by about a teaspoonful of brandy—into her hand. It was still shaking, he noted. Controlling his expression, he said austerely, 'This is why your policeman friend was convinced you shouldn't be alone tonight.'

She stiffened. Alone, she'd have dealt with the aftermath of her nightmare. She wouldn't be fighting this—this weird response.

Hastily she lowered her face and began to drink, praying the heat and colour would fade from her face and shoulders. The liquid caught her breath, but she gulped it down, intent on banishing the aftermath of her nightmare.

Go away, she commanded silently. *Leave me alone, for heaven's sake.*

But the Radcliffe man stayed until the last drop was drained.

'Thank you.' She prayed he couldn't realise how much effort it took to control her voice. 'You've been very kind. I'm OK now.'

'Do you want me to sit with you until you get back to sleep? Or get Patty West to stay with you until then?'

She shook her head so vigorously she had to push back a swathe of damp hair from her face. Surely he had to be joking! Besides, it was sleep that summoned the nightmare, not wakefulness. 'I'll be fine,' she repeated.

Eyes hooded, he looked down at her and nodded. 'All right. I'll see you in the morning.'

Once the door closed behind him Elana tried to relax, to breathe slowly and loosen every tense muscle.

Nothing worked; every sinew, every nerve in her body remained taut, and snatches of thought whirled chaotically around her brain. A glance at her watch told her she'd only had a couple of hours' sleep, not nearly long enough to sate the voracious tiredness that had gripped her. Yet it had gone, replaced by a sharp burst of energy.

Once again she lay back against the pillow, closed her eyes and tried to concentrate on easing tension, calling on the defence mechanisms she'd developed when she'd been a child trying to block out the sound of her mother weeping.

But disturbing memories forced their way through— not childhood pain nor the phantoms of the nightmare, but that moment when her host had looked down at her in the bed and hunger had flared in his arctic eyes.

Alarmed, she'd had to force herself to resist an answering need, something much stronger than awareness and infinitely more potent than normal feminine admiration for a good-looking man. Niko Radcliffe was much more than handsome; he projected a compelling masculinity that both unsettled and excited her.

Her father had been just such a man. Yet his smooth sophistication had been a cover for violence.

Three years ago she'd fallen in love, only to discover that she was following a familiar pattern. Behind her closed lids she saw her mother's face, heard her mother's voice when she'd consoled her daughter after that bitter break-up.

'I'm so glad you had the courage to walk out on Roland,' she'd said quietly. 'I was a coward. It took far too long for me to understand what your father was doing to me—and to you. I was the happiest girl in the world when I married him. I believed he loved me, and I was sure I loved him.' Tears had sprung into her eyes. 'But what he felt for me wasn't love, it was possessiveness, a driving need to control.' She hesitated, then said, 'And when he used force to gain that control, he felt it was my fault, not his, that he hit me.'

Elana remembered admitting bleakly, 'I've always vowed I'd never make the same mistake. And at least Roland didn't beat me. But how can you tell the difference between love and possessiveness early enough—early enough to be able to get away before it's too late? Before you fall in love.'

Her mother's face twisted. 'Oh, darling, if I could give you a set of rules I would. I can't. But after I left your father and found Steve, I realised that what I'd believed to be love was actually desire. I'd been flattered that your father wanted me, even though he and I had nothing in common.'

Elana turned her head on the pillow and closed her eyes.

Her mother's words were etched on her brain cells. 'Desire on its own isn't enough. You need to be friends too. When you fall for a man who excites you, if you can't think of him as a friend it's not love. It's just lust, and it's dangerous.'

For her second marriage her mother had chosen her very best friend, and they had all been so happy together...

Steve hadn't been perfect. A cheerful, slapdash man, he'd made no secret of his adoration for her mother, and he'd met Elana's childish suspicion with tenderness and understanding until she too had learned to love him, to feel safe with him.

She blinked and opened her eyes, staring across the elegant room. Moonlight seeped through a narrow crack in the curtains, and through the glass she could hear the soft hush of waves, the sound that sent her to sleep at home.

Her mother had been wrong when she'd said she couldn't give her a set of rules.

...a man you can't call a friend...

Niko Radcliffe was dangerous. She couldn't imagine him being a mere friend to any woman.

Her wildfire, tantalising response to him wasn't—and never would be—anything more than a strong sexual reaction.

Forewarned, she thought sardonically, *is forearmed. A good mantra to keep you safe...*

A soft knock on the door woke her. She blinked at the sunlight through the drapes across the window, and for a second wondered where she was.

'Elana? Can I come in?' Mrs West asked.

'Yes, of course.'

The door opened. 'I thought I'd better wake you now, or you wouldn't be able to get to sleep at all tonight,' the housekeeper said as she approached the bed, a plastic bag dangling from her hand.

'What time is it?'

'Eleven o'clock.'

Dismayed, Elana blinked at her. 'Heavens,' she said faintly. 'I've never slept so late in all my life before. Thank you very much.'

'You clearly needed the rest.' Mrs West gave a cautious smile. 'I'm afraid I broke into your house. The boss suggested it, so I sneaked in here this morning and took your key from your bag, then drove to your place and collected a change of clothes for you. I hope you don't mind.'

She held out the bag and the key.

After a startled moment Elana replied with real gratitude, 'Not at all. Thank you so much.'

'The boss thought it would be better if I did it rather than him. And I was sure you'd feel a lot better in clean clothing. He's out on the farm right now, but he said to tell you he'll drive you home whenever you want to go.'

'Thank you,' Elana said again, and added, 'I'm sorry he dragged you away from home last night to look after me.'

Mrs West shook her head vigorously. 'Oh, he's a good boss—tough but very fair. My husband and I, we feel very lucky to be here.'

Half an hour later, showered and refreshed and in clean clothes, Elana made her way into the parlour and sat down a little limply in a large armchair. Mrs West had chosen well; a pair of jeans and a T-shirt with clean undergarments gave her strength.

Until the sound of an approaching vehicle set her nerves jangling again.

Stiffening her spine, she scrambled up and walked across to the window to look over what had once been a lawn to the beach. Although the house had been almost fully restored to beauty, the garden scrambled down to the beach, wildly unkempt, a jungle of neglected bushes and trees and a roughly mown lawn. The tide was in, and the sun had turned the estuary into a molten sheet of gold. In summer, just in time for the Christmas holidays, the ancient pohutukawa trees marking the boundary between land and sea would set the water on fire with the thread-like bounty of their dropped flowers.

Normally the view would have lifted her heart. But when she heard her name from behind she jumped and whirled around, a hand pressed to her chest.

'What the hell—?' Niko Radcliffe demanded harshly, taking two long strides to grip her shoulders and hold her upright as her knees struggled to support her.

'I'm all right,' she said, the words jumbled together. She swallowed. 'You can let me go.'

He scanned her face with clinical detachment, before releasing her and stepping back, his gaze narrowed and intent.

After a deep breath she stumbled into speech. 'Sorry,

I didn't realise you were so—so nearby. I heard the quad bike but it seemed quite a distance away.'

He shrugged. 'I wasn't on it.'

Another sharp breath gave her the strength to say, 'I'm not normally so neurotic.' She braced herself. 'Thank you for everything you've done—including the idea of collecting some clothes for me.'

His brows rose. 'You surprise me.'

'Why?' she asked, startled.

'I suspected you'd be annoyed at the invasion of your privacy.'

'Not a bit.' He was still standing too close, and those hard eyes were too inquisitorial. Why didn't he back off? Squaring her shoulders, she asked, 'Have you heard anything about Jordan this morning?'

'Yes. He's recovering well, and sent his thanks to us. So did his parents. They were worried about your reaction to the accident.'

'You didn't—'

He read her mind. 'I told them the truth, that you were sound asleep.'

Elana let out a swift breath. 'Thanks. They're nice people and they have enough to worry about right now.' She looked up at him and managed to produce a smile. 'You've been very kind, but if it's not too inconvenient I'd like to go home.'

'Mrs West is making lunch for us.'

'Oh,' she said inadequately.

'You must be hungry.'

As though in answer her stomach rumbled softly. She produced a wry smile, and looked up to meet one that almost rocked her back on her heels.

'Clearly I am,' she admitted, her voice a little rough.

Niko's smile was *something*—a mixture of understanding and genuine amusement that sent a shiver of excitement through every cell in her body. She had a sudden, terrifying insight into her mother's inability to resist her father.

Her thoughts were interrupted as her host said, 'Then come and eat.'

His intonation reminded her that although he'd been born in New Zealand he'd spent much of his life in Europe. And the way he offered his arm emphasised that heritage. Elana placed her hand on it, awareness sizzling through her at the hard flexion of the muscles beneath her fingers as they walked side by side down the hall.

He was no effete aristocrat, this man. Into her mind flashed a memory of him carrying Jordan away from the car, and she shivered.

'What is it?' he demanded.

'I was thinking about last night—what might have happened if Jordan's car had caught fire. I'm so grateful it didn't.'

'Indeed,' he said decisively.

'I hope Jordan's learnt something from it.'

'Especially not to take corners too fast on narrow gravel roads,' Niko returned, his tone verging on unsympathetic. 'You said he's around eighteen years old?'

Elana nodded. 'About that. Certainly not much older.' After a silent moment she added, 'But old enough to know better.'

'A dangerous age—you tend to believe you're bullet-proof.'

She said quietly, 'Yes.' Yet somehow she found it impossible to picture the man beside her flaunting the careless, dangerous arrogance of youth. He was too controlled, so formidably self-contained it was impossible to tell what he was thinking.

Mrs West had set the meal out on a terrace overlooking the beach, the beams overhead festooned in foliage from a vigorous creeper that allowed golden sunlight in shifting patterns on the tiles.

'Oh.' Elana stopped and stared around. 'Oh, this is lovely!'

'Apart from the surroundings,' her host said dryly and pulled a chair out for her. 'I'm looking for a good landscape architect. Do you happen to know of one?'

'I'm sorry, I don't.' Elana sat down. 'Certainly not in Waipuna.'

Niko sent her an ironic glance as he walked around to the other side of the table. 'I didn't think there'd be one here.' He sat down, and in the same tone said, 'You must have been a charming baby with that amazing hair.'

Startled—both by the abrupt change of subject and the sensation sizzling down her spine and heating her cheekbones—Elana was suddenly intensely aware of his lithe economy of movement, of the strength in those broad shoulders.

Searching for a light response, she managed, 'Apparently it's an inheritance from my grandmother, although it skipped a generation. My mother was a true blonde.'

'Genetics are an interesting study.' He glanced around the wild tangle of foliage that bordered the overgrown lawn. 'I've been told this was once a superb garden.'

'It used to be beautiful.' She added, 'But even now it has a wild beauty.'

He nodded. 'It reminds me of a book I had as a child— a book of fairy tales. It had a picture of the garden around Sleeping Beauty's castle. For some reason it intrigued me.'

Elana looked up, met quizzical blue eyes, and experienced another disturbing jolt of electricity. Hoping her voice was steady, she replied, 'Perhaps we had the same book. Mine had flowering vines—blackberry vines, I suspect, judging by the thorns—tangled around a tower.'

Niko asked, 'Do you think that might have had some influence on your decision to work in a florist shop?'

'No.' She'd taken the part-time job because it was the only one available in Waipuna at the time, and she needed the money. Shrugging, she finished, 'Although, who knows? Like genetics, the unconscious works in interesting ways.'

Half an hour later she set down an empty cup of strong black coffee and looked across the table. Her stomach clenched in unnerving anticipation as a ray of sunlight caught Niko's face, outlining his features in gold. Deep inside her, something wild and uncontrollable coalesced into heat and fire.

She had to draw breath to say, 'Thank you, that was just what I needed. I'll thank Mrs West and then I need to go home.'

He got up. 'Of course,' he said calmly. 'I'll take you.'

Clearly she had no choice in the matter. Nevertheless, she tried. 'Thank you, but it's not necessary. Mrs West brought me a pair of flat shoes as well as my clothes, so I'll walk home. It's only a kilometre away.'

And received another ironic smile. 'I'm sure you could walk it, but my mother would be horrified if I let you.'

A little bewildered, she sent him a disbelieving look. 'She'd never know.'

His shoulders lifted in a shrug. 'I'd know.' His tone confirming that she had no option.

Elana fumed in silent frustration. Some women might find a dominant male an intriguing challenge, but there was a difference between dominant and domineering. Bristling, she realised that Niko Radcliffe came too close to being domineering.

Like her father. And Roland...

Not that it mattered. Once she got home she'd probably never see Niko again. 'Thank you,' she repeated sedately.

Five minutes later, after thanking his housekeeper for her help, she was ensconced in his large car, her discarded clothes from the previous night neatly packed in a plastic bag.

Niko glanced sideways, noting that most of the colour had come back into her ivory skin. Apart from looking a little tired she seemed in good shape. Deliberately keeping the conversation impersonal, he soon had her chatting about the district, enjoying her dry wit as she told him about some of the families who lived and farmed along the peninsula.

As they approached the entrance to Mana he asked, 'Are you descended from one of the pioneering families here?'

'Far from it—we first came here on holiday and stayed in a friend's bach.' She smiled. 'A little holiday shack. I believe you South Islanders call them cribs.'

'I believe they do,' he said, amused. 'I've never considered myself to be a South Islander. Or a New Zealander, come to that.'

She sent him a startled look, then nodded. 'That's understandable. But with dual citizenship you have two countries to call home.'

Surprised, Niko realised he called no place home. Although his mother had taken him back to her father's palace, the huge, echoing building with its gilt and crimson furniture had been no home to him. And the boarding school and universities he'd attended had been the same. His grandfather and his uncle, the next Prince of San Mari, had always been busy with affairs of state.

And although he'd enjoyed them, the holidays spent in the old stone house on the steep, tussock slopes of his father's merino sheep station had never been long enough to put down roots.

Perhaps that was why he'd bought Mana Station. For a home base?

He dismissed the idea. 'So your parents fell in love with the area,' he prompted.

A beam of sunlight fired her hair into an aureole as she nodded. 'Exactly. They liked it so much Steve—my step-father—got a job in Waipuna, and they bought the bach. It was just a bunkhouse then, with a primitive kitchen and an outdoor shower. Steve and my mother turned it into a proper home.'

Alerted by a note of reserve in her words, Niko glanced at her again. Her full mouth was held in a straight line, as though talking of the past pained her.

Or made her angry. Had her mother and father divorced?

Hell, he understood how she might feel; the dissolution of a marriage, whether by divorce or death, was hugely bewildering for children. He could just remember his own confusion and anguish when his mother had taken him to San Mari. He'd missed his father immensely. And still regretted that he'd never been able to forge a proper rela-tionship with him before he'd died.

Beside him, Elana said quietly, 'It's the next gate on the left. You can let me off there—it's not very far to the house.'

'I'll take you all the way,' he said calmly.

About a hundred metres down a narrow drive between the slender grey trunks of more kanuka trees, the house and a separate garage appeared. As they drew to a stop Niko realised the house must have been barely larger than a garden shed before Elana's stepfather added to it.

The buildings snuggled into a flowery garden that stretched towards a low bluff. Sprawling pohutukawa trees formed a green edging to the little cove he knew to be Anchor Bay, its amber curve facing a wide stretch of glittering, island-dotted water. On the far side of the estuary a range of rolling green hills met the sky.

As he got out of the car, Niko looked around. Casual, a little untidy, the garden was humming with bees and bright with flowers. A monarch butterfly flitted through a tangle of low shrubs, brightly orange against green leaves.

Rounding the back of the vehicle, he got an excellent view of Elana's long, elegant legs as she climbed out. A swift, savage hunger bit into him, speeding his heart rate, sending an instant message to every cell in his body.

Damn, *damn*, he thought, angered by his lack of control. He hadn't had such a fierce, predatory response like this since adolescence...

He bent to close the door behind her while she took a few steps towards the house. When he straightened she turned to face him and held out her hand.

Gold-flecked green gaze meeting his directly, her skin stained slightly pink, she said in a level stiff voice, 'Thank you very much for your help and support.'

Very formal, he thought sardonically.

'It was little enough,' he said as they shook hands, and added, 'Patty West did any looking after that was necessary. I hope the accident hasn't affected you too much.'

Her gaze didn't waver, but he thought some of the colour faded from her skin. A kind of regret made him moderate his tone. 'If you need anything, let me know.'

'Thank you,' she said politely, her tone making it clear she had no intention of doing any such thing.

For some futile and unnecessary reason her unspoken refusal exasperated him as much as the cool smile she bestowed on him before turning away to walk towards the house.

Niko waited until she'd unlocked the front door and swivelled around to lift her hand in farewell, before inclining his head, getting back into the car and starting the engine.

He put off any speculation about his unexpected, disturbing reaction to her until he reached Mana Station. Once there, instead of going into the homestead he walked over the untended lawn, stopping at the top of the low bank that bordered the beach. Elana Grange was exactly the sort of woman he'd vowed never to become involved with again—young and unsophisticated.

Frowning, he told himself he'd long since got past the stage of bedding—or wanting to bed—every woman he found sexy. Until he'd seen Elana at the ball he'd been coolly in control of his emotions.

This unwanted, reckless response to her had to be more of a chemical reaction than an emotional one, he decided wryly, one that both surprised and exasperated him. And it would pass.

While he was at Mana he'd be a good neighbour to Elana, and that was all.

Turning, he inspected the homestead. The original architect had combined elements of Georgian serenity with the lighter, more informal verandas and terraces of a tropical plantation home. However, over the years clumsy alterations had been made, cluttering the clean, simple lines.

According to the architect who'd surveyed it after he'd bought the station, it would take as much money and time to restore it to its original state as it would to knock it down completely and erect a new building in its place.

Common sense had told Niko to do just that. Although he planned to keep a close eye on Mana Station he wasn't planning to live there permanently, and even if he were, the last thing he needed was a big, old-fashioned mansion built for a Victorian family. A modern beach house would have been a sensible replacement.

Yet growing up in a palace over three hundred years old, in a country where tradition was an important part of life, meant he'd had the homestead restored and renovated.

Now to do the same to the garden.

Elana had described it as once beautiful.

Given time, it would be again.

CHAPTER FOUR

'HAVE YOU ANY idea of what Niko Radcliffe plans to do with Mana homestead now that it's as good as new?' Mrs Nixon asked.

Hiding a smile, Elana looked up from tying a ribbon around a posy. She'd been expecting this. Mrs Nixon couldn't be called an inveterate gossip, but she did like to know what was happening in the district.

Unfortunately for her, one night spent at Mana homestead a week ago didn't give Elana a hot line to the Radcliffe man's plans. 'No idea at all,' she said cheerfully.

'So it's just the way it used to look, like that old print in the library?'

"That old print" was a charming sketch reputed to be drawn by the first woman to live at Mana homestead. 'From what I remember, exactly the same,' Elana told her, ringing up the sale.

'Perhaps he's planning to sell it. Or turn it into a lodge?'

'I suppose that's a possibility,' Elana returned, suppressing an odd reluctance to speculate. She added, 'It would make a fabulous lodge.'

'It would, wouldn't it? And it's not as though he's likely to spend much time—if any—there.'

Elana handed over the posy she'd just assembled. 'Here you are.'

'Thank you, dear.' While Elana dealt with her credit

card Mrs Nixon leaned forward. In a lowered voice, she said, 'I had a call from Margot Percy yesterday. Greg's not ready to retire yet but apparently all his years of managing Mana don't cut any ice when he applies for a position. Margot said he's getting depressed, saying that all the employers seemed to want someone young and active.'

Surprised, Elana said, 'Really? I know he resigned when Niko Radcliffe bought the place, but I assumed he must have had another place to go to.'

'I thought so too.' In an even lower voice Mrs Nixon confided, 'But Margot told me—and I know I don't have to ask you to keep this confidential—that the Count actually sacked Greg.'

Elana's mild curiosity turned into shock. '*Sacked* him? *Why?*'

'He doesn't know. Just a curt interview, apparently, then, *Pow!—you're sacked.*' She drew a deep breath. 'I really feel for them. Greg's in his late fifties now, and it doesn't look good for them at all.'

Elana felt sick. Somehow she'd allowed herself to be lulled into believing that Niko Radcliffe had a softer side, and some human feelings. 'Where are the Percys now?'

'Oh, they've got a rather nice bach over on the West Coast, quite near Dargaville, apparently. Margot plans to see if she can find work there.' She sighed, then said, 'Oh, I almost forgot! Fran's on her way back from that American conference and will be spending next weekend with us. You'll have to come around and have dinner with us on Saturday.'

'That will be lovely.'

But once she'd left Elana found herself wondering why she was so appalled by Niko Radcliffe's careless destruction of a man's—no, a couple's—life. Why?

She retired to the flower room behind the counter and informed a bucket filled with roses, 'Because that's the sort of man Niko Radcliffe is. Hard, arrogant, inflexible—and obviously ruthless.'

But he'd been kind to her—albeit in a very dictatorial way.

Surely he knew that the situation at Mana hadn't been Mr Percy's fault? 'Obviously not,' she said aloud, then grimaced. Anyone coming into the shop and hearing her muttering to herself would think she was crazy.

So she'd stop thinking about Count Niko Radcliffe and get on with her life.

He meant nothing to her. *Nothing*... Although to her shame she'd dreamed of him several times since he'd delivered her home, waking after each turbulent dream with a strange sensation of loss.

Common sense warned her to be sensible. He might look like some romantic adolescent's idea of a heroic figure, and it was completely unfair that he also had charisma enough to melt an iceberg, but, unfortunately, his impact wasn't just based on physical appeal. Clearly he possessed the intelligence and determination to carve a fortune for himself in the cut-throat world of international commerce, so he must always have possessed that compelling—and disturbing—presence.

Allowing herself to drift into romantic fantasies about him would be more than stupid—it would be idiocy. She'd vowed to never again let a man like her father into her life. Although she might not be able to discipline her dreams, she could banish Niko from her mind while she was awake.

On Saturday afternoon Fran called in to catch up before Elana's dinner engagement with the Nixons that evening. 'Because of course I can't ask you all the questions I want to with the parents listening,' she informed Elana as they sat outside with coffee.

Sunlight warmed the bricks of the terrace Steve had

built to catch the afternoon light, shimmered across the estuary below. For once there was no breeze to toss the blooms in the flowerbeds Elana's mother had planted.

Fran sighed. 'Sometimes I dream of this when I'm away, and I wonder why I ever left Waipuna. Now, tell me all about the Count, as Mum insists on calling him.'

She listened intently while Elana sketchily told her of the accident, and said, 'So you spent the night at Mana homestead with him?'

'And the housekeeper,' Elana pointed out crisply.

'I bet she went off to her own quarters as soon as you turned out the lights. What do you think of the man?'

Elana hesitated. But Fran was one of the few people who knew of the abuse she and her mother had suffered until they'd escaped. 'He's an alpha male, so naturally I'm not at all keen on him.'

'Not all alphas are violent like your father.'

'Intellectually I know that,' Elana admitted. 'Has your mother told you he actually sacked Greg Percy?'

'Yes.' Fran shrugged. 'Tough. But nowadays you don't—and can't—just dump workers for no reason. Possibly Mr Percy's not capable of carrying out the plans Niko Radcliffe has for Mana. If the interesting paragraphs Mum's been reading in the dentist's waiting room have any basis at all in truth—'

'Which is highly unlikely,' Elana interjected dryly.

Fran grinned. 'But possible! Whatever, I can't see Radcliffe living here, it's just too isolated. Right now his company's building a new heliport at Auckland for those who can afford to pay a lot of money to get somewhere fast. Like flying up to Mana for a secluded holiday at the homestead.'

'How do you know?'

'I read the papers,' Fran told her cheerfully. 'He's spent megabucks restoring the homestead, so turning it into a lodge makes sense.' She finished her coffee and grinned. 'Of course, you'll be in charge of decorating the house with flowers.'

Laughing, Elana said, 'I'll believe the lodge story when I see hard evidence for it.' She sobered quickly. 'I hope the new manager Niko Radcliffe's chosen doesn't get the same treatment as poor Mr Percy. His wife—Mrs West—is the housekeeper and she's lovely.'

Fran shrugged. 'Surely plutocrats have minions who deal with hiring and firing? Actually, he's got a good reputation as an employer. No migrant workers in slums are slaving away to add to his billions.'

Oddly relieved, Elana drained her coffee mug and set it down. 'Really?'

'Yes.'

'OK, he's gone up a bit in my estimation.'

'You don't think much of men, do you? Not that I blame you.' She directed a sympathetic glance at Elana. 'Your father was a horrible man, and then you had the bad luck to fall for Roland Whatsisname. At least you got away from that affair comparatively unscathed.'

'And learnt my lesson,' Elana told her crisply.

'Do you remember your father much?'

Remember him?

Oh, yes, she remembered—a harsh voice, shouting, followed by the dreadful anguish of her mother's sobbing. He'd never struck her mother while she was present, but, child though she was, she'd known what he was doing, and she was terrified of him. Even their escape had been marred by fear that her father might find them.

Which he had.

'Yes, I remember him,' Elana said quietly.

Fran reached over and gripped her hand for a moment. 'I think that deep inside you there's still that child who's terrified of your father. Understandable, of course. You never had counselling, did you?'

'No. But I saw how Steve was with Mum. She used to groan periodically about his slapdash approach to life, but he made her—and me—really happy. He taught me to trust him.'

Her friend said, 'Good for him. But did he teach you to trust any other man?'

Elana stared at her. 'What do you mean?'

Fran shrugged. 'You might have learned to trust Steve, but has that trust extended to any other man? Your father was not normal; most men aren't brutal tyrants like him.'

'I *know* that—'

'Yes, but have you ever wondered whether perhaps you won't let yourself become attached to anyone because you're terrified they might turn into a monster like your father?'

Elana opened her mouth to protest, then closed it again. Was there any chance she might be right? Her mother had once told her that her father seemed perfectly normal before they'd married—indeed, she'd been flattered by his concern for her...

'No, I haven't,' she said crisply.

Her friend said cheerfully, 'Well, perhaps you should think abut it. Anyway, what *do* you think of Niko Radcliffe? At first Mum thought he was straight out of a fairy tale—he's practically a prince! Prince Niko—it sounds good, doesn't it?'

'Why isn't he a prince? Why is he just a Count?'

Fran sighed. 'In San Mari they stick to keeping the power in male hands. His mother was a princess, but she married a commoner so he's a Count—and in San Mari that's the equivalent of a royal duke. What do you think of him?'

Elana shrugged. 'He responds to an emergency with a

cool head and plenty of orders, and he's also very strong. He dragged Jordan out of the car and carried him to safety, and Jordan's no light weight.' She stopped before adding, 'Also, he's arrogant.'

Fran's brows shot up. 'How?'

'Well, after interfering Phil Jacobs told him about Mum and Steve and the accident, he practically kidnapped me.'

'I'd call that a strong protective instinct.' Fran grinned at the expression on Elana's face. 'I like that in a man. And I like that he organised a chaperone for you.'

Elana snorted. 'I don't like that he sacked poor Greg Percy.'

Fran sobered. 'You don't know the reason. Niko Radcliffe's known to be a tough negotiator, but he's well-respected. He must have a good reason for sacking Mr Percy.'

'The only reason I can think of is that he blamed him for the state of Mana Station.' Elana shrugged. 'Which is totally unfair—Mr Percy did his best even though the owners drained it of money.'

'I wonder why he stayed there, then? Surely he could have got a better job managing a farm somewhere else?'

Surprised, Elana paused. 'Perhaps he just liked living here?'

'Perhaps it was an easy option. And you're very willing to believe the worst of Radcliffe,' Fran pointed out. 'Your mother's experience with your father was dreadful, and your affair with Roland must have only reinforced your fears. But your mother got over it and married Steve. I truly don't think you have.'

'Of course I've got over it,' Elana told her trenchantly.

'Then why are you so wary about any sort of relationship? Apart from Roland Pearson, has any other man made your heart go pitter-patter?'

'Well, there was Craig Brown in high school—'

Fran grinned. 'He revved up everybody's heartbeat, that

one.' Then she assumed a prim face. 'I meant, of course, since you became an adult.'

Actually, yes. Two. One narrow escape, and the other—well, Niko Radcliffe not only set her heart racing, but alerted every cell in her body, a reaction compounded of fiery awareness and a dangerously disturbing adrenalin rush.

Fortunately her experience with Roland had taught her not to fall for macho charisma. Both touched and exasperated, she said quietly, 'A pitter-pattering heart means nothing more than that—for some purely physical reason—you find someone attractive.'

'Do you think you'll ever trust a man enough to allow him to get close to you?'

'Fran, I'm all *right*.' She eyed her best friend with mingled exasperation and affection. 'OK, so physical attraction is an important part of falling in love, but it's not *the* most important thing. I'm not over the hill yet—I'm twenty-four, the same age as you! And it's not as though I'm a blushing virgin.'

'I agree with you, marriage is a serious business.' Fran leaned forward, and touched Elana's arm. 'I know you can have a good life without marrying or falling in love, but it's—well, it's cowardly to let your mother's experience darken your own life.' She paused. 'You're intelligent and sensible—intellectually you must know that most men are not abusers. You just need to give the terrified kid that's still hiding deep inside you a chance to act on that knowledge.'

Elana opened her mouth, only to close it as Fran went on, 'OK, OK, I know when I've said enough. Tell me, how's your work going?' Before Elana could answer she said sternly, 'I don't mean the florist's shop. You did a brilliant job with the book the museum put out for the centenary of the hall. It must have taken ages—I hope they paid you for your work.'

'I got expenses,' Elana said a little defensively.

Fran's brows shot up. 'I should jolly well think so!'

'I'm hoping to be able to give up working in the shop soon. After the first article I did for the local newspaper I was contacted by a couple of people who wanted me to interview their relatives. I really enjoyed it, and they paid well, and I'm getting more requests now, some even from the South Island. I've turned those down because I can't get away for long enough to do it, but it's fascinating to interview people.'

Fran leaned forward. 'If you were based somewhere central—Auckland, Hamilton, perhaps—it would be a lot more convenient for you.'

'So far I'm finding plenty to write about in Northland. Anyway, with Auckland's property market going berserk, I couldn't afford to buy or even rent there now. And I know Mum hoped I'd stay here for a while.'

'Why?'

Elana hesitated, pain gripping her. Steadying her voice, she went on, 'She wanted me to keep the place where she and Steve had been so happy, but—I don't want to leave. Not yet, anyway.'

Fran reached out and squeezed Elana's tightly clenched hand. 'I think I understand. Coming to live here, and for the first time in your life being happy and feeling safe, must make Waipuna mean a lot to you.'

Elana nodded. Selling the house would be like tearing her heart out, bidding an irrevocable farewell to almost everything that was good and worthwhile in her life.

Fran released her hand. 'Then that's all that matters.' She grinned. 'You know, when you meet the next man who sets your heartbeat jumping, I think you need to trust yourself enough to at least get to know him.'

'What if he's fifty?'

When she'd finished laughing, Fran told her, 'I'm not ageist. Mind you, attached men are emphatically not on the menu.'

'Of course.' Elana hesitated, then shrugged. 'OK, I'll try it. Just don't expect miracles.'

'I'm not.' Fran glanced at her watch. 'And if I'm to buy the food Mum wants to cook for dinner tonight, I'd better go now.'

After she'd waved goodbye, Elana looked around her house, the cottage that Steve and her mother had transformed from a basic shack to a home.

She walked out onto the terrace, stopping to gaze across the estuary, its surface unruffled and gleaming, the ancient trees on the hills over the far side glowing in shades ranging from olive to a shimmering golden green in the spring sun.

Did she unconsciously view all men as a threat? If so, no wonder she'd found the few times she'd had sex with Roland to be embarrassing and without pleasure. She'd thought her lack of passion was due to an inherent coldness.

And she did understand that most men were like her stepfather—kind, practical, and capable of making the right woman as happy as her mother had been in her second marriage.

So based on past experience—and once Niko Radcliffe was safely on the other side of the world—it wasn't likely she'd have to monitor her heart rate anxiously for any betraying surges.

CHAPTER FIVE

ELANA WINCED AS the fire station alarm shrieked a summons to the local volunteers. She peered through the shop windows to the street outside. It had rained during the night so it probably wasn't a scrub fire. A car accident? Pray heaven it wasn't a house fire...

Which reminded her that she had to contact her bank. After hearing a suspicious rattle in the roof a couple of days ago she'd called in the local expert, who'd fixed it, then warned her the whole place needed reroofing some time soon.

'How much will that cost?' she'd asked.

The sum the roofer quoted still made her feel queasy. She'd have to borrow the money. Adding to her concern, only that morning Mrs Nixon had informed her with a worried face that she'd heard an out-of-towner was considering setting up another florist's business in Waipuna.

'They'll be silly,' she'd said. 'Waipuna's really not big enough for two florists.'

No, indeed. Competition could mean that Rosalie, the owner of the shop, might have to downsize...which would almost certainly mean that Elana would lose her job.

Frowning, she turned to check the order book.

Yes, the customer *had* specified orange Peruvian lilies for her daughter-in-law's bouquet. Fervently hoping that the recipient liked the colour, Elana went into the back

room to assemble them, only to be immediately interrupted by the warning buzz of the shop bell. Summoning
a welcoming smile, she went out.

And suffered an explosion of heartbeats when her startled gaze met ice-blue eyes in a hard, handsome face. Her
smile froze on her lips.

Niko's black brows lifted. 'Hello, Elana,' he said
smoothly. 'Don't look so startled. If I remember correctly, I
did mention that I intended to visit Mana reasonably often.'

Mouth suddenly dry, she said, 'I'm sure you remember
correctly. How are you?'

'Very well, thank you.' His tone was amused. 'And
you?'

'Oh, fine.' She produced another smile and added,
'Thank you,' before turning. 'I'll just put these flowers
back into water.'

Which gave her a brief ten seconds to get away from
that challenging gaze and control the jumble of impressions flashing through her brain. In the couple of weeks
he'd been away Niko Radcliffe's formidable, controlled
authority seemed to have become even stronger and more
uncompromising than she remembered.

And her stupid heart was going berserk in her chest. It
took an effort of will to quell the urge to press her clenched
fist there in a futile attempt to rein in that remorseless
thudding.

Everything—the sunshine on the street outside, the
fresh perfume of mingled greenery and flowers inside
the shop, the cold blue of Niko Radcliffe's gaze, the ironic
curve to his sinfully sculpted mouth—suddenly sang to
her, the colours more vivid, their impact physical, a joyous assault on her senses. Something sweet and wild burst
into life within her, every muscle tensing in a sharp pang
of anticipation as she stuffed the lilies back into the vase,
took a deep breath, and returned to the shop.

'There, that's done,' she said inanely, hoping her voice sounded prosaic and very normal.

His brows shot up. 'Not a subtle colour, those flowers. Presumably they're for a colour-blind recipient.'

'They're popular because in a hospital ward they glow like sunlight.'

And immediately regretted her crisp tone. She sounded like a schoolmistress cautioning a child. *Stop this right now. Breathe slowly.*

His brows lifted, but he returned calmly, 'I suppose they do. I want to send flowers to England.'

Elana picked up the pen, found the right form, and looked up enquiringly, but before she could ask for details he handed her a piece of paper. 'Everything you need is there.'

It was. No gorgeous film star or princess—these flowers would go to Lady Sophia Double-Barrelled-Name who lived in a manor house somewhere in England.

So *calm down*, she warned her jumping heart. *That heavy thudding—it's just overreaction. Not only is he way, way out of your league, but he's already committed.*

'Any specific date for them to arrive?' she asked.

'No.'

Niko knew that, sophisticated and experienced as she was, Sophia would recognise the flowers for what they were— a civilised farewell after he'd ended their affair.

Elana looked up, her expression guarded. 'I'll get that off straight away.'

For some reason her tone exasperated him. The only time he'd seen her without that armour of self-possession was when they'd met in the hall at Mana after the accident.

Inconveniently, an image of sultry, shadowed eyes of green-gold and sinuous curves clad in an over-sized nightgown that revealed too much silken skin played across his mind.

As it had far too often since he'd last seen Elana Grange...

Ignoring the memory, he handed her his credit card, forcing himself to concentrate on her hands as she processed it. They were slender and deft, the nails clipped and clean. Ignoring a stray and extremely suggestive thought, he asked, 'Before I left Waipuna Mrs Nixon informed me you wrote the centennial publication on Waipuna's history.'

'Yes,' she said as though admitting a minor crime.

'And that you write articles for an historical magazine.'

After a surprised glance she nodded.

'Then you'll probably be interested in the discovery of boxes and crates of what seem to be discarded documents and old newspapers in the attic, and more in what was once the stables at Mana.'

Her face lit up. 'Really? I wish I'd known that when I took on the centennial book.'

'I've had a quick look at some of the accessible stuff, mostly from the late nineteenth century. There are diaries written by various members of the family who owned it then. It looks as though they never threw anything away.'

'Oh, that's amazing,' she breathed, sounding like someone discovering buried treasure. 'I'm surprised—and so glad—the previous owner didn't burn everything, or dump it. I wonder what else has been abandoned there?'

'Plenty,' Niko told her dryly. 'Why didn't the family who sold the place to them remove their own belongings?'

'The family died out—there was no one to inherit. The station was sold as is, and the money went to charity.' Elana gave him a quick smile, not quite meeting his eyes. 'What are you planning to do with the records?'

'Not burn everything in sight,' he said dryly, and watched her relax. 'I'm going to employ someone to go through it and catalogue the lot. I don't know what's important and what's not. I believe you've done quite a bit of that sort of thing.'

'I—yes,' she admitted.

'I'm offering you the job.'

Her eyes widened, their exotic radiance emphasised by the gold speckles lighting the dark green depths.

Seductive as hell. Deep inside Niko something feral tightened into intense hunger.

In a far from seductive tone, she said, 'It would take me quite a while—I can't give up my job here.'

'I believe it's part-time only.'

'Full-time at the moment—Rosalie, who owns the shop, is in Australia.'

'I presume she's not planning to settle there?'

That drew a reluctant smile. 'No, she's there for the birth of her first grandchild.'

'When will she be back?'

'In a fortnight if the baby arrives on time.'

Niko had expected her swift agreement. According to Mrs Nixon, the fount of all knowledge, Elana's parents had left her with nothing but the house, and her part-time position in the shop couldn't pay very well.

So why was she unwilling? He said, 'Mrs Nixon assures me you're very competent, and after reading the history you wrote, I agree with her. I also like your writing.'

This drew a startled glance. 'I enjoyed doing it. It's just—it did take up a lot of time. And the documents I used were already catalogued.'

'You are a librarian, so I presume you know how to catalogue.'

'Well, yes,' she returned, her reluctance obvious.

'I will, of course, pay you.'

She hesitated, her expression freezing a moment as though something had just occurred to her. Whatever it was, it decided her. 'No, I'm afraid it's just not convenient right now.' Again she paused, before saying, 'I can give you the name of a friend who does this sort of thing for a living—he's very good, and much more experienced than I am.'

How good a friend? Startled by the intensity of that primitive reaction, Niko reined in an instant, angry speculation and said, 'But you're right here, and you have background knowledge that will help.'

'Well, yes,' she agreed, frowning. 'But—'

'Also, you have a fervent advocate in Mrs Nixon.' He added dryly, 'She told me all about your skill at interviewing.'

Elana's smile held wry humour. 'That's not really a recommendation. Mrs Nixon has a wide knowledge of the district as well as an excellent memory.'

Her lips tightened momentarily before easing into their normal ripe contours. Memories of her mouth had bothered him…so seductively feminine, a mouth made for sensuous kisses and softly passionate words, lips that contrasted intriguingly with the inner strength he sensed in her, the way she kept her emotions under strict control. In a way, he could blame those lips for sending him back to England to tell Sophia that their affair was over.

Hunger stirred his body, a fierce need that was becoming familiar. He was long past the wilful, almost uncontrollable desire of adolescence, so although Elana's rejection of his offer was irritating, it should be no big deal.

Yet even now, he found himself wondering what it would take to breach the barriers he sensed within her.

Smooth words? Luxury? The promise of passion?

Or money?

Fighting a silent battle, Elana wished he'd go away. Why didn't she agree, just thank fate for sending her this opportunity? She needed money to repair the roof.

Apart from that, it would be a fascinating project.

She was a coward.

No, darn it, she was being sensible!

She deeply mistrusted the heady rush of sensation that had raced through every cell in her body when Niko walked into the shop. Everything about him was vividly, thrillingly familiar, as though she'd carried him in her heart since she'd last seen him.

Seeing too much—no, *anything*—of him was going to cause chaos to her peace of mind.

But then he wasn't likely to be in New Zealand often, or for any length of time. After a few taut moments, and as warily as though she was taking a huge step into unknown danger, she said quietly, 'I can't give you a decision so quickly. I am working full-time here until Rosalie gets back.'

Bracing herself, she met his narrowed gaze steadily, trying to suppress a sudden twist of tantalising, sharp sensation deep inside her.

Niko wasn't a man who'd suffer second best; he'd expect perfection. Could she deliver?

'Think it over,' he said calmly. 'I'll call you when I get back from Auckland in a couple of days and you can give me your answer.'

She watched him stride out of the shop, a formidable figure in jeans and a checked shirt. No doubt, she decided cynically as she turned towards the back room, it helped that those casual clothes had probably been created by some brilliant tailor who knew exactly how to make the most of broad shoulders, lean hips and long, strongly muscled legs.

And clearly he was totally confident that he'd persuade her.

Stop obsessing about the man! Her traitor heart might still be jumping, but she was afraid. Niko Radcliffe affected her in so many ways, he could be disaster central.

* * *

The next evening after a day of showers and her discovery of another ominous stain in the ceiling, she checked her computer and to her dismay found that disaster central actually looked to be the combination of a dodgy roof and a cautious bank that didn't feel it could lend her the money to fix the roof.

Trying to calm her nerves by watching the news, she discovered that she'd been wrong about that too. Disaster could well be lurking in a storm forming far to the north in heated equatorial waters.

Gaze fixed on the ominous whirlpool symbol on the screen, Elana found herself holding her breath, hoping that it wouldn't go near any of the islands that scattered the tropical sea.

And cravenly, that it would stay well away from New Zealand.

She switched off the television and walked across to the window, narrowing her eyes against the westering sun that shone from an almost cloudless sky, sheening the water with silver.

Actually, she had no option. She had to take on the job of organising all those documents. As soon as she'd confirmed that with Niko Radcliffe, she'd ring the roofer.

Her gaze ranged over the opulent amber curves of the beaches on the estuary. Beyond the river mouth a small yacht headed for safe anchorage in the Bay of Islands, and silhouetted on the horizon was a container ship making its way down the coast to Auckland. It was almost impossible to imagine something as dangerous as a tropical storm whipping those calm waters into destructive waves.

However, they happened. Cyclones were rare, but they could cause chaos and devastation even as far south as Northland.

'What next?' she asked forlornly, then frowned at her

foolishness. Why was she whimpering because fate was forcing her in a direction she didn't want to go? Niko's offer couldn't have come at a better time.

It seemed unlikely she'd earn enough to entirely reroof the house, but she hoped she could convince the bank she'd be able to repay the loan.

'And if they don't agree?' she said aloud, hating the sound of the words.

If that happened, she'd have to sell the house. She turned and looked around the room, its furniture shabby but still gracious. Here she'd learned what love between a man and woman could be, learned that a man could be tender with children. She'd discovered what it was like to feel safe.

A lump in her throat threatened to choke her. She swallowed it, and pulled the curtains. If it happened, she'd survive. She turned back into the room, her gaze lingering lovingly on the pictures her mother had painted of the estuary, and made up her mind. When Niko contacted her she'd tell him that she'd catalogue the documents. After all, she'd enjoy doing it.

So why on earth had she been behaving like a drama queen?

Self-preservation, she thought starkly. Every female instinct she possessed was shouting that the more she saw of Niko, the more dangerously he affected her.

She said aloud, 'All I have to do is remind myself that his life and mine might as well be on different planets.'

Immediately, before she could change her mind, she rang the roofer. Ten minutes later she got off the phone, sighing with relief. At last something was going right— he'd be able to do the job within days, airily dismissing her concern about not paying him immediately. 'No problem, Elana. I know you'll get there. You were always a conscientious kid.'

In her fourth year at Waipuna School his wife had

been her teacher. Life in a small community might occasionally seem stifling, but it had good points too, she thought wryly.

That night she wooed slumber with a singular lack of success.

Fortunately the morning sun radiated a summery promise from a cloudless sky. Her spirits lifted as she inhaled the fresh, herbal scent of the costal forest on the road into Waipuna. She had quite a busy day ahead, but no customers disturbed her for just over an hour until the buzz of the shop bell summoned her from the chiller room.

So of course the person who waited for her had to be Niko Radcliffe, and her idiotic heart had to lose control again.

'Oh—hello,' she said inanely.

Blue eyes scanned her with far too much intimidating speculation. 'What's the matter?'

'Nothing,' she returned, straightening her shoulders and lifting her chin.

'You look tired.'

She ignored the comment. 'I'll catalogue those documents.'

Black brows lifted and his mouth hardened. 'I'm sorry to put you through enough trauma to make this such a difficult decision,' he said.

Sarcastic beast!

'I'm worried about this possible cyclone,' she told him stonily. 'Big storms play havoc with flowers. Most of ours come from Auckland, which will be at risk if the wretched cyclone makes it this far south.'

'We're all concerned about that.'

Why should it bother him? If the storm tracked too close to Northland he could just climb into his helicopter and fly off to his huge station in the South Island where he'd be safe...

Trying to sound brisk, Elana said, 'With any luck it will get lost on the way and end up dying a natural death somewhere on the way to Chile.'

'Let's hope so.'

She nodded. 'I sometimes wonder if the emergency organisations tend to overstate the strength of storms so people won't be idiots and push their luck.'

'Only to have some do just that in spite of all the warnings,' he observed dryly.

As Steve had done. His decision not to wear a seatbelt had killed him.

Niko watched her features harden, her mouth tighten. Why? Although she seemed aware of him, she clearly didn't want anything from him. Did she have an inherent distrust of him—or was it all men?

Perhaps she'd been badly hurt by an affair gone wrong.

And why did he find Elana Grange so attractive—OK, dammit, so intensely desirable? All he should want from her was her expertise at dealing with documents. Yet he couldn't overcome or banish this inconvenient, tantalising tug of sensual hunger.

Too abruptly he asked, 'What changed your mind?'

Elana certainly wasn't going to admit to a shortage of money. 'I surrendered to temptation,' she told him, not hiding the irony in her tone. 'All those documents—who knows what fascinating things I might find in them?'

'Possibly little more than boring day-to-day incidents,' he observed cynically. 'Now we talk money.' And named a sum that made her blink.

'That's far too much,' she blurted.

'Nonsense. It's the going rate.'

'Are you sure?' she demanded.

He gave her a look that silenced her. 'You agreed to do

it. I'm holding you to that. You'll have to fit it in around your hours here, which will mean weekend work for you. Naturally you'll earn extra for that.'

'But—'

He interrupted smoothly, 'I suggest you start by spending a couple of days checking out the documents and making notes. I'll see you tomorrow morning.'

Taken aback, Elana said, 'No, it's Saturday, and the shop doesn't close until one.'

He frowned. 'Come directly to Mana after you've closed the shop and I'll show you where most of the documents are.'

It sounded like an order. Stiffly Elana responded, 'Very well, Mr Radcliffe. Or should I say, *Aye, aye, sir*?'

Niko's exasperation warred with wry amusement. He deserved it. 'Neither. I didn't intend to sound officious, and my name is Niko.'

After giving him a startled glance, she half smiled. 'Very well, Niko, I'll be there around two o'clock.'

Whenever she said it, his name sounded different on her lips. What would it sound like if she were in his arms? Would her voice deepen, turn husky, slur...?

Ruthlessly shutting down that train of thought, he said, 'I suggest you spend at least a couple of days—longer if it's necessary—going through the boxes and crates and making notes.' He glanced at his watch. 'Until tomorrow, then.'

Elana watched him turn and leave the shop, relieved at being able to breathe again. But she dragged her gaze away when he stopped outside to greet a woman she didn't recognise—rather glamorous but a little too overdressed for Waipuna.

Startled by that swift snide judgment, Elana strode into the flower room. She'd never before met a man like Niko

Radcliffe—and never would be too soon to meet another one. His potent male magnetism set her foolish heart throbbing, but, more significantly, he was beginning to invade her mind, turning her into someone who'd just unkindly judged a woman she'd never seen before.

That night the television forecaster charted the progress of the weather system far in the north, still not an official cyclone, but already creating havoc in the tropical islands it crossed. Elana tried to read a library book, which failed utterly to capture her attention; every time she turned a page she somehow saw Niko's face superimposed over the print. Disgusted by her foolishness, she gave up and headed for bed.

The next day a radiant sky and the complete lack of wind mocked any fears of the weather. As she negotiated the cattle stop between the stone walls—now as pristine as when they'd first been built—she tried to discipline her jumping heartbeat. Infuriatingly, it began to race when she pulled to a stop outside the gates. She grabbed her bag from the passenger seat beside her and opened the door.

When she straightened up and turned, Niko was striding towards her, the sun striking blue flames from his black hair. Clad in a casual polo shirt and jeans, he moved with a dangerous litheness that sent erotic little shivers scudding down her spine.

Hoping her involuntary, reckless response was well hidden, she forced a smile and said sedately, 'Good afternoon.'

'Good afternoon. Would you like coffee before we start?'

We start? Surely not…

Her reply was crisp. 'No, thank you. I'll get to work.'

'Before you do, come and have a look at something Patty West found in the attic this morning.'

'What is it?'

'Watercolours of the garden. Amateurish—probably painted by family members, and, judging by the clothes, I'd say late nineteenth century.'

The difference between its previous musty disrepair and the elegance that greeted her when she went into the homestead once more took Elana's breath away. It was a joy to see the house resplendently celebrating its many years with pride and grace.

'I'm so glad you brought this place back to life,' she told her host.

He shrugged. 'The architect and the workmen—and the decorator—have done a very good job.'

Not surprising. His ruthless dismissal of Mana's previous manager proved that Count Niko Radcliffe had no time for people who failed to meet his standards. If he didn't think she was earning her wage he'd almost certainly sack her as brutally as he'd ditched Mr Percy.

He went on, 'The house was well-built originally, and the framework is still good. Only the roof had to be replaced—by the same man who tells me he's expecting to do yours soon.'

Startled, and more than a little annoyed, Elana could only say, 'Oh—yes.'

His smile held more irony than amusement. 'Living in a small country area has plenty of advantages, but I'm sure you understand privacy isn't one of them.'

'Indeed I do,' she said briskly, and changed the subject. 'What are your plans for the garden? Some of the trees look pretty dilapidated. I hope none of them are too far gone to be saved.'

'Relax,' he said, smiling. 'I've been advised of a good

arborist and I'll only agree to sacrificing trees that are a danger. The drawings are out on the veranda.'

He'd spread them out on a table, and stood by as Elana perused them carefully, eyes half-closed against the brilliance of the afternoon sun on the waters of the estuary.

'They're charming.' She scanned a border the artist had delineated carefully. 'Whoever did this studied the plants minutely.'

'If you come across more as you go through the documents, I've organised an expert in conservation for them. My PA has given me a sheet of contacts for you.'

Elana's upward glance met cool blue eyes. She forgot what she'd been intending to say as warmth spread through her, quickening her breath, setting her traitor heart pounding in her ears.

Even her voice sounded odd as she said, 'Thank you.'

Here at Mana, Niko Radcliffe beside her, she was suddenly gripped by an overwhelming sense of belonging, as though she'd been lost and was found, as though somehow the scattered parts of her life were reassembling—not as they had been before, but forming a different pattern, making her whole once more.

As though once, long ago, she'd stood here with this man beside her, looking out over the garden towards the estuary...

She felt strangely, dangerously secure. Bewildered, she wrenched her gaze away from his narrowed survey and focused on the watercolours.

Of course nothing momentous had happened. Struggling to summon some practical common sense, she told herself that those few moments of rightness, of belonging, had to be a flash of *déjà vu,* the occasional startling sensation of reliving a forgotten, or never experienced, occasion.

In other words, her brain was playing tricks on her. So she'd ignore it.

Niko startled her by asking abruptly, 'What's happened? Are you all right?'

'I'm fine.' She blinked, keeping her gaze on the faded pictures. 'I wonder what else has been abandoned.' And went on, 'I'm sure you've got other things to do. If you point me in the direction of the stables, I'll have a look around there.'

'I'll take you there,' he said.

Firmly.

When her teeth closed a second on her bottom lip Niko had to prevent himself from telling her to stop ravaging her soft mouth.

And from wondering exactly how it would feel if she ever nipped his skin...

As his whole body responded to the wayward thought, he cursed silently. This was ridiculous. It was just as well he was leaving Waipuna; his body was betraying him with a lack of discretion he hadn't experienced since his adolescence. Yes, Elana was attractive and intelligent, independent and self-possessed—all things he found desirable in a woman. But this hunger, this wild need was nothing he'd experienced before. Why *this* woman?

Elana looked up, met an intent, hard gaze that sent a scary excitement down her spine, mixed with an even scarier anticipation.

Niko said, 'Before we go to the stables, I'll show you where you'll be working.'

He'd organised an office for her in the homestead, a small room off the veranda. 'Check the equipment,' he ordered. 'My personal assistant said you'll need all this, but take a look. If anything else is necessary it will be supplied.'

After a swift survey of the room she said, 'No, your PA knew exactly what I'd need.'

He told her ironically, 'She knows exactly what anyone needs. In some ways she reminds me very much of Mrs Nixon.'

Elana laughed. 'Then she must have a heart of gold.'

Niko found himself warming to that laughter—it was spontaneous and fresh, close to mischievous. This was a different side to Elana—one he hadn't suspected. Until then she'd been guarded, keeping her emotions controlled and corralled beneath that cool composure.

Her spontaneity touched some part of him, summoning a sudden query. What would she be like as a lover?

Would that spontaneity extend to her caresses, to her kisses? Another charge of hunger, of sheer, potent need, shot through him like a jolt of electricity.

Dangerous—and definitely *not* something he wanted to happen.

Frowning, he looked out of the window. 'I'll see that the garden bed out there is tidied up so you have a decent outlook instead of a tangle of creepers and shrubs and weeds.'

'I rather like it,' she told him, touched by his consideration. 'It's very like Sleeping Beauty's garden—oh, and look, there's an early rose.'

'Roses are your favourite flowers?'

A little surprised, she smiled. 'They're just about everyone's, aren't they?'

He sent her a quizzical glance. 'Judging by your tone, not yours?'

'When I was a little girl I loved aquilegias—the flowers my mother called Granny's Bonnets. They were purple and they fitted over the end of my finger like a little cap. The bumblebees loved them. And I have to admit to falling deeply for those great, flaunting crimson blooms on some magnolia trees.'

'How about huge fluffy pink peonies?'

'Love them too,' she said promptly. 'They won't grow here, of course. They need much colder winters.'

Like the ones in the Southern Alps, where he'd been born.

His question brought her back to some sort of equilibrium. He'd gone from a high country station to a palace and a title. She might be acutely, *desperately* aware of him, but when he decided to marry he'd almost certainly choose someone who'd fit into his life.

Marry? Where on earth had that thought come from?

She forced herself to meet his penetrating gaze. 'How do you want me to report to you?'

And held her breath until he said, 'I don't know how long I'll be away. I have a business deal to close in China. Email me periodically with your progress. No, better still, we'll use the computer's communications programme so we can talk. You know how to do that?' He watched as she nodded, and added, 'I'll email you with dates and times. And don't hurry. I don't care how long you take—just do a good job.'

Which sounded simple, but after seeing the cartons of documents, Elana realised just how much time she might need to spend at Mana.

Niko said a formal goodbye when the chopper arrived; equally formally she wished him a safe journey. But the homestead seemed oddly empty and echoing after he'd gone.

Now, coping with this unexpected, bewildering hunger for a man she knew so little about, she had to be grateful for her mother's hard-won wisdom when it came to charismatic men.

Yet, in a way she didn't understand, the very intensity of feelings evoked by Niko's presence had somehow broken through the numbing grief that had shadowed her emotions these past months.

Was it a stage in recovery, a step to reclaiming her life?

She grimaced. Not likely. Her powerful reaction to him

had to be nothing more than lust. A charismatic, compelling man, he just happened to be around while she was going through perhaps the final stage of recovery from grief. And the unexpected and cryptic *déjà vu* moment in the garden must have been brought on by memories of a happy visit as a child to the homestead.

That evening the forecast brought relief. The tropical storm had turned to the right and was heading out across the Pacific, losing intensity as it sank into cooler latitudes, and well away from both New Zealand and the islands of Polynesia to the north.

'But there's a nasty low sneaking up from the South Pole,' the announcer informed her in an appropriately grave tone. 'It will bring winds and heavy rain to the South Island when it arrives in a couple of days. Farmers, you'll need to check the shelter for your stock, and it might pay to make sure you have stores of food, as if it keeps this intensity roads may be closed by snow in the south, or flooding further north.'

'Oh, joy,' Elana muttered caustically, and switched to another channel.

CHAPTER SIX

THE SHRILL SUMMONS of the telephone woke Elana from her first sleep. Blinking, wondering if she'd dreamt it, she peered through the darkness. Another urgent ring convinced her she was awake—and in the middle of the night this had to be an emergency. Alarm knotting her stomach, she staggered out into the sitting room and lifted the receiver. 'Hello,' she croaked.

His voice harsh, Niko said, 'Sorry to wake you but I've just seen your car being driven towards Waipuna.'

'Wha—*what?*' She drew in a dazed breath, convinced she was dreaming. 'Niko? No, you're in China.'

'Not now, I'm back in Waipuna.'

They'd spoken every day since he'd left a fortnight previously, and each time his face on the computer screen had charged her with excitement—futile and foolish excitement. He'd shown interest in her progress with the documents, and he'd spoken briefly of his impressions of Beijing, but she knew better than to build hopeless dreams.

'You didn't hear it being taken?' he asked.

'No. I'll ring the police,' she told him numbly.

'I've already done that. I'll be at your place in a few minutes.'

Heart banging, she put down the receiver. Her car was vital; without it she'd be unable to get to Waipuna to work, unable to go anywhere. Steve's old banger was still in the garage, but it didn't have a warrant of fitness and probably wouldn't get one without quite a lot of money being spent on it.

'Oh, hell!' she muttered. 'Think positively, for heaven's sake. The police will stop them and they'll return the car.'

But the combination of an adrenalin overdose with a sense of violation made her feel sick. She stood staring blindly out across the estuary, until she abruptly realised she was clad in a sketchy pair of pyjamas—and Niko was on his way.

She ran to her bedroom and scrambled into jeans and a shirt, sliding her feet into the nearest footwear—a pair of sandals.

Only just in time. A beam of light swept across the window. Feeling as though she'd been hit by a train, she raced to the door and opened it, letting out a sheet of warm light as Niko got out of the car and strode up the path towards her.

He looked like something out of a dream, tall and lithe and handsome. No prince from a fairy tale, though—his face was set in hard lines of anger.

'Where did you see the car?' she asked baldly, stepping back to let him in.

'About a kilometre down the road, heading towards Waipuna. Don't worry—the police will stop them before they get to the intersection.'

Appalled, she said, 'I hope no one gets hurt.'

'Your old schoolmate should have convinced you that the police know what they're doing in situations like this.'

He examined her keenly, trying to ignore the swift, reckless rush of hunger setting his body alight. She'd obviously scrambled into her clothes without bothering with underwear. Although her green-gold eyes were still heavy-lidded and slumbrous, she held her soft mouth under tight control, managing to look both determined and profoundly sensuous.

As she had every day when he'd contacted her. He should have emailed her instead of testing his ability to resist this sensuous attraction. Emails were safe and emotionless. Seeing her smile at him from the computer screen had only intensified his desire for her, eating away at his self-control.

He'd missed her. Right now he was gripped by an emotion he'd never experienced before—a sense of rightness, of finding his way, of—of homecoming...

Dismissing such a sentimental thought, he said abruptly, 'Whoever took your car abandoned their own vehicle—probably a stolen one—on the corner just before your gate. Either it's broken down, or they ran it out of petrol.'

Elana winced and stood back. 'I heard nothing. Thanks for ringing me.' After a moment's hesitation she said more sturdily, 'I'll let you know what happens.'

It was a definite dismissal.

Tough. Niko had no intention of leaving her. She was trying hard to sound fiercely independent, but her face was white and she needed support. He said, 'I told the police I'd stay here until they contacted you.' Ignoring her startled expression, he turned to scan what he could see of the garden. 'Where do you keep the car?'

'In the carport—up the drive a bit.' She gestured towards a tumbledown shed some distance towards the road.

'So that's why you didn't hear it going.'

Suddenly vulnerable, Elana hid a shiver at the thought of sleeping while someone stole her car. 'You don't have to stay—'

He interrupted, 'We've already had this conversation.'

'What?'

His smile was sardonic. 'The night we met. Let me in.

I'm not leaving here until we know what's happened. Do you have any other vehicles?'

'Yes. My stepfather's car.' She drew a deep breath. 'I need a cup of coffee. What would you like—coffee or tea?' Although her voice was level, he could tell it took an effort.

'Coffee, thank you.' He asked tersely, 'You've got insurance?'

'Comprehensive.'

Clearly she wasn't going to confide in him. Well, why should she? Their computer conversations had been face to face, but they'd both carefully avoided any intimacy. As for this elemental hunger raging through him—hell, any man would respond to the gentle swell of her breasts beneath her loose cotton T-shirt and the curve of her buttocks as she turned into the house.

Every muscle in his body flexed. Startled and chagrined, he told himself to cool down. For some bewildering reason the thought of any other man watching her and feeling this heady, sensual response affected him with a stark possessiveness as primitive as it was unexpected.

Elana had told him her home had started out as a bach, a basic holiday cottage. It showed its origins. The front door opened into a sitting room with a dining area beyond, separated by a counter from the small kitchen towards which she was heading. The sitting-room furniture looked as though it had been reclaimed from a junk shop, and the wooden dining table was an elderly, highly polished relic of Victoriana, the chairs around it a comprehensive collection of cast-offs.

Yet in spite of its near-shabbiness it was warm and cheerful, and radiated comfort. Flowers picked from the garden were arranged casually in vases, several watercolours clearly by a local artist with some talent hung on the walls, and photographs—one of Elana in cap and gown, beaming radiantly—were displayed on shelves.

The splash of water filling a kettle brought his attention back to the kitchen.

Elana turned and opened the door of an elderly refrigerator, groped inside and turned back, a jug of milk in her hand.

'Do sit down,' she said with a strained smile. 'You're too tall for this place. I'm afraid you might hit your head on the beams.'

'I'm not quite two metres tall,' he said, glancing up. 'There's plenty of room between me and the ceiling.'

It wasn't just his height Elana found overpowering—it was the whole essence of the man. And that owed little to his height, or to his wide shoulders and long legs. His strong personality made the Mediterranean good looks he'd inherited from his mother unimportant. When they'd met he'd reminded her of a warrior king, ruling by sheer force of character. Now, standing in her home, that impression was reinforced.

Abruptly she said, 'I believe your mother's country is very mountainous?'

'Yes,' he said calmly, although his eyes had narrowed slightly.

Wondering why on earth she'd blurted such a foolish observation, she turned away to take down a couple of mugs from the cupboard. 'Were the original inhabitants forced into the mountains at some time by war?'

She could hear the shrug in his voice when he answered. 'No, they chose to live there. San Mari is a beautiful place; it's close enough to the sea for the climate to be reasonably moderate, and the soil is fertile. It provided the first settlers with everything they needed, and the surrounding mountains afforded them protection from the ambitions and wars of others.'

Keep talking, she thought feverishly. *Talking means you don't have to think about how amazing he looks and how he affects you...* 'Do you know who they were?'

'They believe they're descended from the first people ever to arrive in Europe.'

Intrigued, she looked up from pouring boiling water over the coffee in the plunger. 'That's interesting.'

He shrugged. 'No. There might be some truth in their belief that they settled San Mari very early. Archaeologists have been digging in various parts of the country for years. They've made some amazing discoveries and the further they dig, the more excited they get.'

'I suppose Kiwis find this sort of thing interesting because we're such a new country.' She gave a small laugh and expanded, 'That sounds silly, as though New Zealand's just popped up from the depths of the ocean! But humans have been here for such a short time. Maori settlers arrived about eight hundred years ago, and nobody else in the world knew the place existed until two or three hundred years ago.'

'Do you think the isolation is why travelling overseas is such a rite of passage for young New Zealanders?'

Relaxing a little, Elana nodded. 'Yes—we try to get our fill of antiquities while we're experiencing the great OE. Overseas Experience,' she elaborated.

'Is that your ambition? To travel?'

'One day, yes.'

He was good at small talk, but his deep voice and penetrating eyes were undermining her composure. Glancing at the clock, Elana realised it wasn't as late as she'd thought. She willed the telephone to ring, for someone to tell her what was happening to her car.

That would break this headlong compulsion to reach out to him, the disturbing desire to connect in the most intense and compelling way. She needed to get him out of the house before she forgot that he was the scion of some ancient family famed for their wealth, and that he'd bedded some of the most beautiful women in the world.

And before she embarrassed herself by revealing, in some way, just how strongly she was affected by his compelling presence.

'Sugar?' she asked, her voice almost breaking on the word. She had to swallow before she could go on. 'And milk?'

'Neither, thanks. Like you with tea, I drink it black.'

His remark brought back memories of the night she'd spent at Mana.

And how it had felt to be in his arms, held against his chest...

Heat burned through her, and with it something akin to recklessness. He'd wanted her then.

And all that was female in her had responded, temporarily blocking out everything but the urge to surrender.

Fortunately, she'd recognised it for what it was—a sexual pull based on the primitive instinct to reproduce. And even more fortunately a spark of common sense had asserted itself before either of them could give in to it.

But desperately, dangerously, she longed to rediscover the sensations she'd felt in his arms for that brief time, that wildly exciting arousal strangely underpinned by a sense of total security.

Carefully she poured the coffee and asked, 'Would you like something to eat?'

Banal and commonplace, the small courtesy went some way to re-establishing her equilibrium.

'No, thank you.' His voice was cool, the dismissive undertone like a shower of freezing water. Her father's tone... Even when he'd been angry enough to hit her mother, he'd never raised his voice.

Elana hated it. But at least it silenced the heady clamour in her body, her tumbling thoughts.

Still tense, she handed Niko the mug and led the way into the sitting area. Once he'd finished his coffee he'd go. In the meantime, she'd stick to small talk.

'Do sit down,' she said, but he stayed standing until she lowered herself into Steve's favourite armchair.

Once there she searched for a sensible topic, anything to take her mind off the fact that Niko was far too close to her. In the end she asked, 'Are you planning a long stay at Mana this time?'

And could have kicked herself. Hardly impersonal…

'Only a couple of weeks,' he told her crisply.

Presumably to make sure the manager he'd installed was doing his job properly. Although the brutal removal of Greg Percy had revealed a ruthlessness she found abhorrent, she had to admit that Mana Station was already looking much more prosperous.

Of course Niko was spending a lot of money to achieve that. Much more traffic—often local tradesmen's vans—went past her gate now, and from the road she could see fences being replaced and young native trees newly planted beside the small creeks that wound their way down into the estuary. Its pastures were already looking better.

Perhaps he could read her mind, because he said, 'You'll have noticed the traffic. Sorry about the dust, but that will continue until the new houses are finished.'

'Houses?' The station already had several houses on it.

Curtly he said, 'The existing houses—except for the one the manager lived in—are shacks that have had no maintenance for years. It's cheaper to knock them down and put new ones there.'

'I see. The previous owner—'

His shoulders lifted. In a voice that could have frozen

Niagara Falls he said, 'The total mismanagement of the place was not entirely due to the previous *owner.*'

Which meant what? Was he blaming Greg Percy? She glanced up, met eyes of glacial blue, and decided she'd chosen the wrong topic for this conversation. 'Actually, the traffic doesn't bother me. The trees between the house and the road keep this place free of most of the dust.'

And was hugely relieved when the telephone rang. 'That must be the police,' she said hastily, scrambling up and grabbing the handset. 'Hello?'

Niko got to his feet, his gaze fixed on her face.

'Oh, hi, Phil,' she said, turning slightly away.

For some reason Niko wasn't prepared to examine, her withdrawal caused a tight stab of anger.

As though she recognised it she stiffened, then shot him a swift glance before turning away even further. 'OK,' she said quietly. 'Are they all right?'

Damn, did that mean that the idiots who'd stolen her car had wrecked it? And why did Phil the policeman keep turning up all the time? Surely there was more than one cop in Waipuna?

Frowning, Niko saw her stance ease a little.

'Phil, I'll manage,' she said quietly. 'I've still got Steve's car. Thanks for letting me know. Say hello to Jenny, won't you?'

Who was Jenny? The cop's wife? And why the hell, Niko thought sardonically, should he care?

Because he wanted Elana.

There, he'd admitted it. He'd wanted her from the moment he'd seen her at the ball, and since that night everything he'd discovered about her—her sturdy independence, her intelligence and sense of humour, her acceptance of more grief than anyone her age should have to cope with—had increased his regard for her.

He waited while she finished her goodbyes and replaced the telephone.

She paused a few seconds as though gathering strength, then turned and said bluntly, 'The car is a mess. The two men who stole it are either drunk or high on drugs.' She paused, as though collecting her thoughts.

'And you have insurance to cover the costs of getting your car fixed.' Niko kept his voice level, refusing to make it a question.

Nodding, she covered a yawn with her hand. He thought she braced herself before she produced a smile with very little humour. 'I'm sorry—I think reaction's settling in. Thanks very much for coming in to tell me what happened.'

Yet another very definite dismissal, Niko realised, assailed again by a stab of something more than irritation. It faded when he noted ivory skin paler than normal, and that sensuous mouth compressed into a tight line. Lowered lashes shielded her eyes, making it impossible for him to read her thoughts.

Shaken by a powerful desire to protect her, he wasn't going to leave her like this. 'It was nothing,' he said calmly. 'Sit down and finish your coffee.'

The glance she directed at him glittered with irritation, but she lowered herself into the chair. 'I'm all right.'

Niko sat down opposite her, and began to ask questions about her work on the documents. She followed his lead, and as she spoke some of the colour seeped back into her skin. After he'd drained his coffee mug he asked, 'How long is it since you used your stepfather's car?'

She gave him a baffled glance. 'A while. Why?'

'Car engines need to be used every so often.'

Elana nodded, her brow wrinkling as she calculated. After a swift glance at a calendar on the kitchen wall, she said, 'It must be about a month since I tried the engine.'

After a moment's pause she added, 'It hiccupped a bit, but it started.'

'How long since it's been on the road?'

'A couple of years.' The gaze directed his way was direct and more than a little challenging. 'Why?'

'We'd better make sure it actually goes. If it doesn't, you'll have to organise transport to work tomorrow.'

She shrugged, but got to her feet. 'OK, I'll try it.'

And wasn't surprised when he stood and said, 'I'll go with you.'

Leading him along the dark path to the shed where Steve's car resided, Elana wryly recalled Fran's observation that she liked the fact that Niko Radcliffe clearly had a strong protective attitude.

Could be, but more probably it was simply that because of his upbringing he was accustomed to telling people what to do.

The wavering light of the torch picked out her mother's herb garden and the citrus trees, each one protected by a trap from marauding possums. The waves on the beach whispered a soft background to the scent of growing things and the salty tang of the estuary, and above them stars blazed against a sky so intensely black the immensity of the universe ached through her.

In an oddly flat voice Elana said, 'Here it is,' and handed the torch over, explaining, 'There's no light in here, so if you hold it I'll try the car.'

And shivered when their fingers collided as he took the torch.

'Go ahead,' he said in the coolly dismissive tone she hated.

It was a warning—a necessary one. Otherwise the forbidden response that scudded through her might have transmuted into something infinitely more dangerous.

Once in the car, she turned the key. Apart from a click, nothing happened. Tensely, she tried again.

Still nothing.

'The battery must be flat,' she said weakly, and twisted the key once more, willing it to work. Instead it clicked and died.

A dark form against the greater darkness of the night, Niko said, 'Possibly, or it could be the starter solenoid. Hold the torch and I'll take a look.'

What on earth was a starter solenoid? Reluctantly Elana climbed out, took the torch from him and held it while he lifted the bonnet.

'Aim it here,' he said. 'Do you have a screwdriver?'

'Screwdriver?' she asked numbly. Where had he become so familiar with the working of car engines? Not in a palace, surely.

'Yes. If it's the solenoid we'll be able to start it with a screwdriver across the points.'

'Oh. Steve kept his tools here,' she said and turned away, directing the torch to where the battered metal box should have been.

Unfortunately there was no sign of it. And for some reason this threw her more than anything else that had happened that night. The beam of light wavering across the rusty corrugated iron wall of the shed, she said in a voice she had to struggle to keep steady, 'It's not here.'

'Leave it,' Niko commanded. 'You're tired. Give me the torch.'

'I'm all *right*,' she told him abruptly.

It wasn't exhaustion that weighed her down. An overdose of adrenalin, made dangerous by a reckless, headstrong hunger, had been building swiftly since the moment she'd opened the door to him.

The conversations they'd shared while he was away had somehow sparked—or reinforced—an emotion she'd never felt before. The realisation terrified her and, in some strange way, exhilarated her too, as though she were poised on the edge of a high precipice, gazing over a beautiful, unknown landscape filled with hidden dangers.

'You're not all right. We need to get back to the house. I gave my cell-phone number to the police, but they may be trying to ring you.'

She snapped, 'I wish you'd stop telling me how I feel. And what to do.' And had to stop herself from finishing petulantly, *I'm the best judge of what I want.*

Only to realise with stunned shock and a surge of blatant anticipation that what she wanted right now was Niko Radcliffe. In every way...

Wanted him so much it actually *hurt*.

She dragged in a deep breath, but no longed-for serenity washed through her; she still throbbed with that hungry, terrifying need.

Niko reached into the car and removed the keys, then straightened to walk to the front of the car and lower the bonnet. And startled her by saying coolly as he straightened, 'I'm sorry.'

For some reason that brought a reluctant smile to her lips. Hastily banishing it, she said, 'You're going to have to produce a little more contrition than that to make me believe you.'

He laughed, and for a poignant second she saw the mischievous boy he must once have been. Her shaky defences crumbled into nothingness, and she took a step towards him, only to realise from the sudden hardening of his face what she was inviting.

'Take care, it's a bit uneven here,' she told him jerkily, and swivelled to direct the warm light of the torch away from him to the path.

By the time they reached the house she'd regained

enough control to say, 'Thanks for that. I'll see if I've got a screwdriver—'

'Don't worry,' he said levelly. 'There's bound to be one in my car.'

She swallowed. 'It doesn't matter—'

'You might as well know what the problem is with that car.' He stopped and held out his hand. 'Give me the torch. You're shivering. Go inside—you don't need to stay out here.'

She opened her mouth to protest, then thought better of it. Away from him she'd have time to regroup, return to her usual equilibrium, scotch this impetuous, crazy longing for something—something *dangerous*, something that might mark her for life if she surrendered to it.

'All right,' she said, carefully avoiding his touch as she handed him the torch. 'Thanks.'

Safe inside the house, she leaned against the breakfast bar and tried to calm her inner turbulence, struggling to reassert the normal even temperament she took for granted. Hoping it might help, she concentrated on listening for the reassuring sound of the engine starting in Steve's car.

In vain. When the tap came on the door her heart leapt in her breast, and she had to force herself to walk sedately across and open it.

'It's not the solenoid,' Niko told her calmly, eyes slightly narrowed. 'It's more likely to be the battery, although judging by the state of the engine it could be a multitude of other things. Whatever, it means you've got no way of getting to work tomorrow.'

She'd already worked this out. 'I'll hire a car until I get the battery fixed,' she told him sturdily.

He frowned. 'But how will you get to Waipuna tomorrow morning? Walk?'

The flick of sarcasm in his tone irritated her into retorting, 'Yet another advantage of living in a small town. If I talk sweetly to Ted at the hire firm, he'll bring a car out to me.' If he had any vehicles to spare. Ted ran a very small concern—more a hobby than a business.

In a voice she didn't recognise Niko said, 'A friend of yours, is he?'

'You could call him a friend,' she said, keeping her tone level and distant. It was no business of his. Actually, Ted had been Steve's fishing companion. Of the same age and with similar tastes, they'd spent many days out in Ted's launch.

The telephone's shrill summon startled her.

Niko said, 'Answer it—it's probably the police.'

Sure enough, she recognised the voice that said, 'Elana, it's Phil. Bad news, I'm sorry. Not official, mind you—you'll need to get the car examined by a mechanic for insurance purposes, but it looks to us as though it's a write-off.'

She closed her eyes. 'Oh—*curses.*'

'Yeah. Listen, how are you going to get to work tomorrow?'

'I'll manage.'

'You realise that it might take some time for you to get the insurance pay-out? And you know how much it costs to hire a car?'

In some ways Phil was like an older brother. He clearly had a pretty good idea of her financial situation, and, although she didn't mind that, she did not want to be conducting this conversation with him while Niko watched with a hard blue gaze and an expression on his handsome face that chilled her.

Turning her head away, she said, 'Yes, I do. Thanks for ringing, Phil.'

'Sure, but if you can't get a lift, ring me.'

She smiled. 'Not going to happen, Phil,' and hung up.

'Your policeman schoolmate, I gather,' Niko said ironically.

'Yes.'

'Not good news, I'm guessing.'

'No.' She shrugged, covering a yawn with her hand. 'His considered opinion—and that of the other cop on duty—is that my car's a write-off.'

'I see. What time do you start work?'

'Eight o'clock,' she said automatically, then stared at him. 'Why?'

'I'll give you a lift in.'

'No, that's not necessary,' Elana returned swiftly, adding rather too vehemently, 'I can deal with this.'

He shrugged. 'Are you always this intransigent when you're offered some neighbourly help?'

Suddenly she wanted him gone. Tension overwhelmed her, fuelled by a surge of dangerously volatile sensation, a yearning to yield, to let him take over.

She bit her lip to stem an impetuous flood of words, and took a deep breath. 'I can cope. *I do not need to be rescued.*' She marched across the room and opened the door onto the night, holding it there. 'Thank you for helping me, and for offering a lift. It's very kind of you but I don't—'

'I'll pick you up at seven-thirty.'

'Niko—don't…' Her voice trailed away.

Gaze darkening, he came towards her. Her breath locked in her lungs. She tried for a defiant stare, only to gasp when he reached out and touched her mouth. Her heart jumped in her breast and, mesmerised, captured by the intensity of his gaze, she couldn't move. Beneath the caress her lips shaped a word—his name—but no sound came from them.

This, she thought dazedly, this was what she'd wanted ever since they'd danced together. This was why she'd looked forward to all those computer chats while he was away. Into her mind came a fleeting reminder of her mother's warning, only to be immediately dismissed. She wasn't planning to marry Niko. She wasn't in love with him. So she'd be perfectly safe…

But she whispered again, 'Don't…'

'Don't?' he asked in a deep voice that revealed he was feeling the same powerful urge. 'Don't what?'

'I don't know,' she whispered against that gentle finger.

'You're shivering. Are you cold?'

'No,' she said. Then in a shaky, dazed voice, 'Yes.'

'Let me warm you.'

He waited for her nod before he pulled her into his embrace. His arms around her were like a bulwark against the world, a safe shield against anything. Delicious, overwhelming anticipation stripped away the last of her defences. Some distant part of her brain ordered her to pull away.

She couldn't.

In a harsh voice he said, 'Elana.'

'Yes,' she breathed.

He bent his head and claimed her mouth as though he'd been longing to kiss her for months, for years…for ever.

And then he lifted his head, and released her. Suddenly cold, she shivered again, and immediately he took her in his arms once more, holding her more gently while he scanned her upturned face. 'What is it? Are you afraid?'

'Yes—no—not really,' she muttered, a powerful pulse of sensation—exquisite, demanding—turning her into a halfwit.

Something—amusement?—glimmered in the steel-blue eyes. 'Which?' he asked in a tone she'd never heard before.

Dazed, in thrall to voluptuous desire, Elana said desperately, 'I'm not afraid of you.'

'Good.' He bent his head and kissed her again, his mouth as urgent and hungry as the fierce need that ricocheted through her.

She could stop him, push him away, prove that she wasn't weak enough to surrender to this wild excitement, but a more reckless, hungry part of her longed for more...

So when he lifted his mouth a fraction above hers, and said in a rigidly controlled voice, 'Unless you want this to go further, stop me now,' she was dismayed.

Without thought, she croaked, 'That's not fair.'

His brows lifted and he stepped back. 'It's your decision.'

Deep in Elana something snapped. She'd fought this potent, compelling attraction because Niko reminded her of her father—but love and passion were two different things. And as she didn't—*couldn't*—love him, there could be no danger. Instinct told her that he would be a good lover...

'Elana?' No impatience in his voice, none in his eyes, he waited while she hesitated.

Every cell in her body longed for him, craved the surcease of passion in his arms with an intensity that crashed through common sense and resistance. He didn't expect anything of her but an affair...one that would end when he went back to whatever palatial mansion he lived in. She'd be safe. And oh, she wanted him with such intensity she had to keep her teeth clenched to stop them from chattering.

He took her in his arms again, holding her more gently while he scanned her upturned face.

'Elana?'

Reassured, she breathed, 'Yes.'

CHAPTER SEVEN

AND NIKO KISSED her again.

All caution forgotten, heady recklessness released the response Elana had been fighting since the night of the Centennial Ball. She was overwhelmed by a clamorous need—voluptuous, compelling, demanding—that banished coherent thought. Responding with a passion she'd never experienced before, she relished the hardening of Niko's lean body against her, mindlessly pressing herself as close as she could.

His arms tightened around her, fuelling the heat that blazed inside her, a yearning to be even closer, a longing for more—for *everything*, a hunger for Niko that claimed her completely.

The realisation hit her like a blow. Unconsciously she stiffened, and instantly he loosened his grip while he scanned her upturned face. 'You are afraid,' he accused harshly.

She swallowed to ease a dry throat, flicked her tongue along dry lips, and managed to croak, 'I told you, I'm not afraid of you.'

As he claimed her lips once more she felt the explosion of need melting her bones, heating her blood in surrender. This time, when he lifted his head, he asked, 'Which door?'

Elana pointed helplessly towards her bedroom then

gasped when he lifted her and strode towards it. She hid her face against his neck, inhaling the subtle skin scent of the man she wanted.

From some distant, barely accessible part of her brain, a voice whispered, *Stop. Stop, before it's too late...*

But another, more primal voice answered, *You want him. Take him...*

Niko nudged the door open with his shoulder, took the three steps across to her bed, its blankets thrown back, and stopped. His arms tightened around her, and he lowered her to her feet, sliding her down the hard length of his body. The heat inside her exploded into a conflagration.

As she grabbed his upper arms to steady herself she registered powerful muscles, his potent male strength and something else—a confidence in herself that vetoed turning back.

He gazed down at her with narrowed, intent eyes. 'You're sure?'

She'd never been *more* sure of anything. Suddenly dumb, she nodded.

'How sure?'

No words would come. Surely he could see how she felt? Why did he demand reassurance? Elana reached out and touched his mouth as he'd touched hers, her finger lingering along the length of his lower lip. 'Kiss me,' she managed.

He laughed deep in his throat and pulled her so close nothing but their clothes separated them, his mouth taking hers with such passion that all fear, all caution died.

When he lifted his head she struggled for a little distance. 'What is it?' he asked, his voice rough.

'You must be too hot.' She began to unbutton his shirt, smoothing the fabric back so she could stroke the skin beneath.

'That's—*you*—are just making me hotter.' But he stood

there until the last button was free, then shrugged off the shirt.

Elana's breath stopped in her throat. He was magnificent, bronzed skin revealing the taut muscles beneath. Tentatively she reached out and spread her palm against his chest, shivering as the heat of his body reached her.

'Fair's fair,' he said, his voice lazy. And lifted the hem of the T-shirt she'd donned when she'd got up.

Colour flamed through her cheeks, heated her brow, sizzled through every nerve, every cell as he slowly pulled the shirt up. She made an instinctive move to step away, then stopped, fists clenching as she fought for control while he pulled the soft cloth past her head and tossed it over his shoulder.

Elana had to stop herself from covering her taut breasts with her hands, from turning her back. She looked up into his handsome face—more angular, harder, than she'd seen him before.

'You're blushing,' he said softly. 'Are you shy?'

'I'm not—'

The words dried on her tongue when he bent his dark head and kissed the spot where her shoulder met her neck. Her skin tightened at the gentle scrape of his teeth on her skin, and the swift sweep of his tongue. Every sense sharpened fiercely. Sensation zinged from the pit of her stomach—powerful, desperately clamouring for satisfaction, for the exquisite torture of his mouth on her skin again. She shivered in the circle of his arms, yet felt strangely safe.

He straightened. 'Is this the first time—?'

'No,' she managed, her skin fiery.

'You're beautiful,' he said quietly.

Chilled, because she knew she wasn't beautiful, Elana shook her head and tried to pull back. It had to be a shallow compliment, something he'd probably said to each of his lovers—who'd all been stunning, according to Mrs Nixon.

He loosened his arms, frowning down into her face. 'I mean it. Not conventionally, but you move like a dancer and your skin is exquisite and your eyes manage to be both seductive and intelligent. As for your mouth—'

He lowered his head, banishing her momentary loss of confidence with the sheer, unsullied eroticism of his kiss as their tongues duelled.

Elana's heartbeat rocketed, and with it a sensual anticipation. Either he was the best liar she'd ever met, or he really meant it. Whatever, she didn't care. Love didn't enter this. They'd come together as equals. When it was time to part she might miss the rapture he promised, but she wouldn't be shattered by his absence.

There was no mistaking the guttural note in his voice when he lifted his head. 'Just looking at you makes me want you.'

She believed him. Her breasts felt heavy and languorous, their rosy centres tight and pleading. She forced her voice into an unnatural steadiness. 'It's mutual.'

But he already knew that. Almost angrily, he said, 'But I have no protection.'

Elana dragged in a sharp breath. Wracked by passion, she muttered, 'It's all right. I'm—I'm safe.'

His gaze sharpened. 'Sure?'

'Absolutely.'

He laughed deep in his throat and kissed her again, saying, 'Good. So am I,' against her eager mouth.

Then, releasing her, he undid his belt. As he stepped out of his trousers she tried to control her quickened, sharp breathing. He was—magnificent. Like some ancient Greek god brought to life, she thought, shuddering with need.

And nothing could slow the hungry sweetness of passion that snaked sinuously through her body, setting her aflame.

After swallowing desperately she managed to mimic

his words of a few seconds ago—seconds that had somehow changed her life. 'Fair's fair.'

Elana pushed her elderly jeans down, dragging in a fierce, hungry breath as his gaze followed her hands, his features hardening into a mask of desire.

He waited until she stepped free and then picked her up and laid her gently, carefully, on the sheet.

She closed her eyes as her fingers fumbled with her narrow briefs. His voice came as a shock.

'Here, let me.'

Desire leapt a boundary, intensifying into something she'd never felt previously while he gently removed her last garment and slid onto the bed beside her.

'Open your eyes,' he said almost beneath his breath.

'Why?'

He laughed softly and kissed each eyelid. Against her lips he said, 'So you know who you're making love to.'

'I know.' Her voice was thick and the words came slowly.

'And because I find your eyes infinitely alluring with those tiny sparkles of gold amidst the green.'

Charmed, she lifted her lashes, and met his gaze, almost wincing as something odd happened to her heart. Heat flooded her skin and she closed her eyes again when he kissed her once more and slid his arm beneath her, holding her against him while he explored her body with his lips and his hand, driving her so wild with an anguished hunger that she couldn't stop the little whimpers that broke through her lips.

And when his mouth found the pleading tip of her breast delight flowed through her at the sensual tug of his lips, his slow, gentle exploration of her body.

Amid the sensuous turmoil, she recognised the alteration in his heartbeat, and rejoiced. Whatever happened afterwards, she would always know that Niko wanted her as recklessly as she wanted him.

Eventually she could no longer bear such erotic torment. She arched against him, stroking, exploring him as he was discovering her. Under her touch his body flexed, muscles coiling, and he slid his hand further down towards the slick, throbbing heat that ached for something she'd never experienced.

When he reached his destination a shuddering groan tore from her throat and she pressed even harder against him, demanding, seeking, so caught up in the carnal magic of his lovemaking that nothing mattered but his touch. Lost in this torrid anticipation, she could no longer think, no longer make excuses, no longer guard what she was doing.

'Now?'

The harsh, driven intensity of his tone boosted her anticipation to unbearable levels. 'Yes.'

It was all she could say. And all he needed to hear. As she arched against him he thrust into her. The jolt of exquisite pleasure shocked her into crying out, and he froze.

'It's all right,' she managed, her voice a mere thread. And when he didn't move, she tightened her arms against his broad back and lifted her face so that he could see it and whispered harshly, 'Please—'

When he still didn't move, she looked up into his hard, angular face, and arched up, pulling him into her, almost sobbing at the intensity of sensation that surged through her.

'Elana,' he said, making a claim she was more than happy to accept.

The passionate delight he summoned from her flung her into a realm of experience completely beyond anything she'd ever imagined, into a sensory rapture where nothing but Niko and she existed, where *nothing* was more important than giving—and taking.

Because as she crested, as fulfilment hurled her into a blazing ecstasy, he followed.

And then he turned and held her against him while their heartbeats slowed together, and Elana realised with bleak foreboding what she'd just done.

Of course she couldn't be in love with him, but the wild ecstasy of their lovemaking had somehow crashed through the barriers she'd set up. Stupidly, she'd put her heart at risk.

An icy chill had her pull away. He let her go and rolled over onto his back, but she knew he was watching her.

'It's all right,' she told him, keeping her voice steady with an effort.

'You're sure?' No warmth in his voice. No emotion at all.

She hated that tone. Loathed it with an intensity that made her shudder.

'You're cold,' he said, and got up from the bed.

Elana hauled up the sheet to cover her nakedness and closed her eyes against him as he dressed, tall and beautifully built, so experienced in making love that he'd taken her to a voluptuous paradise—a paradise so heartbreakingly seductive she'd be crazy to revisit it.

Her eyes flew open as she felt a blanket being spread over her.

Fully dressed, Niko asked, 'Are you all right?'

'Yes, of course,' she said numbly, wishing he'd leave—and longing for him to stay.

'I'll go now. Will you be able to sleep?'

'Yes, of course,' she repeated, with less than her normal assurance. She managed to produce another smile. 'I'm fine. Really.'

To emphasise her control, she reached out and grabbed her light summer dressing gown from its usual position over the back of the chair beside the bed, and without looking at him got into it. 'I'll lock the door after you,' she said, and forced herself to meet his hard gaze without flinching.

Right then she wanted him gone, so she could recover and become the woman she'd always been, not the reckless, foolish one who'd surrendered to such wild ecstasy in his arms.

He nodded, and turned towards the door. Bare-footed, more tense than she'd ever been in her life, she paced across the living room in front of him. At the door she turned to face him with head held high, and said, 'Goodnight.'

It sounded like *goodbye*. Niko looked down at her.

Gone was the woman who'd come alive in his arms, under his touch. She'd retreated into herself as though the flimsy dressing gown were a suit of armour. He had to staunch a fever of desire, an instinct to pull her into his arms and banish that calm control, see her again as she had been in his arms, wild and sensual and recklessly passionate.

Cool air rushed in, carrying with it the salt of the sea and the scent of the gardens and the coastal bush. Recalled to some sort of sanity, he asked, 'Before I go, what's happening to your car?'

'Phil will get a tow truck to take it away. I'll contact my insurance company tomorrow morning.'

Assailed once more by that infuriating, baseless irritation, Niko said more curtly than he intended, 'If there's anything I can do, let me know.'

Her head came up and he caught a flash of fire in her eyes as she returned, 'Thank you, but I'll cope.'

Niko took a couple of steps through the doorway, then turned. Most of the women in his life—including the mother whose one independent act had been her impetuous marriage to his father—relished being looked after, and expected it to include an existence of pampered indulgence...

Somehow he couldn't see Elana living such a life. Her independence was an integral part of her.

'It's just part of being a good neighbour,' he said smoothly, and watched colour heat her cheekbones as her lashes fluttered down a moment, then lifted.

'I—sorry—' She swallowed. Another pause, then more steadily, her tone crisp, 'But I am perfectly capable of running my own life.'

A fierce desire gripped Niko, but this time the strongly sexual hunger was tempered by an emotion he'd never experienced before, a bewildering urge to make the world safe for her. His muscles tensed with the instinct to reach out, pull her into his arms and tell her that from now on nothing would ever cause her grief.

He had to call on every bit of discipline, of the control he prided himself on, before he could step backwards into the safety of the semi-darkness outside and say levelly, 'That's obvious. Am I harassing you?'

Startled, she hesitated, then admitted briefly, 'No—not really.'

'Will it be harassment if I ask Patty West to run you into Waipuna tomorrow morning?' he asked, his voice cool. 'I'm sure she'll have supplies to buy at the supermarket.'

She said, 'I guess—' Then smiled wryly. 'That would be all right, and it would be all right if you drove me in too. I just don't like being out-manoeuvred.'

'Nobody,' he told her crisply, 'enjoys that. All right, if your friend can't get a hire car to you tomorrow morning, ring the homestead and either I or Patty will take you in and collect you after work. Goodnight, Elana, and thank you. Sleep well.'

He turned and strode down the path. Shaken, she held the door open to provide light for him as he walked to his car, then closed it behind him with all the firmness she could muster, although her hand trembled as she locked it.

Why on earth had he thanked her? For the sex?

Had he thanked his other lovers, those elegant, famous creatures he'd taken to bed?

And why on earth had she allowed herself to surrender? When he'd looked at her with that narrowed, unsparing gaze she should have realised how close she was to losing control. Instead, something wild and irresponsible in her had responded with an intensity that now seemed shocking.

Yet even recalling that forbidden hunger made her shiver with remembered ecstasy.

Once the sound of the car engine died away on the cool, sea-scented night air she drew a deep breath and looked around, feeling as though her world had been tipped on its head. At least she could strive for some sort of normality by washing the mugs they'd used for coffee.

She'd been stupid, telling herself she was safe because she didn't love Count Niko Radcliffe. That had been a coward's way of yielding to a hunger she should have scotched when she first felt it.

Whatever sort of man he was, for her he was danger personified.

'Oh, grow up and stop being over-dramatic,' she said aloud. 'He's used to being chased by women—perhaps he was angry that you made it clear you weren't going to—'

She stopped. Going to what? Going to surrender? Going to provide him the sort of interlude he perhaps expected? Going to forget everything her mother had told her about men who wanted to control, not love?

'Stop obsessing about him,' she commanded, washing one of the coffee mugs with so much vigour the handle cracked and fell into her hand. It was her mother's favourite, decorated with painted pansies.

Furious at her carelessness, she stared at it and told

herself to think about organising the insurance tomorrow, work out how she was going to get enough money to reroof the house, to think about—think about—oh, think about *anything* other than her magnetic, dangerous, overbearing neighbour.

She might always regret that she'd surrendered to that mindless hunger, but she'd make sure it never happened again.

And quite possibly Niko could be telling himself exactly the same thing...

At the top of the hill that separated Mana Station from Elana's land, Niko stamped on the brakes and stopped the car just over the cattle stop between the stone pillars. Once out he closed the door and stood frowning over the moon-silvered estuary, trying to draw some peace from it. He'd bought Mana Station because a part of him—perhaps inherited from his father, or from the care that the farmers of San Mari took of their land—made him want to bring it back into life.

Something about farming, about caring for land, about producing food for people, satisfied a deep need in him, as it had for his father. In ten years' time Mana Station would be as it should always have been, green and lush, beautiful and productive.

His gaze swept the moonlit slopes of hills that had once been small volcanoes, lingering on the scars of creeks that were already fenced, and would soon be planted with native trees that would eventually help keep the estuary clear of eroded soil.

Why in hell had he lost control tonight? Dammit, what was it about Elana Grange that stripped him of his usual self-discipline? And why had making love with her seemed so...so what?

The only word that came to mind was *transcendental.*

Shocked, he took a couple of steps away from the car and dragged in a deep breath. Whatever Elana roused in him went far deeper than ordinary sexual desire. It smashed through his willpower. He'd made the decision to keep his distance—the *right* decision—because he didn't want to hurt her. Admittedly, she'd had previous experience, but the sort of relationships he'd indulged in previously now seemed sordid and almost cynical.

Yet he'd capitulated to a need that almost made him afraid. Even now, at the memory of her ardently passionate response the fierce hunger that should have been sated stirred into life.

And he was gripped by that growing need to make sure she was safe, to protect her from everything that might cause her pain.

CHAPTER EIGHT

ONCE SHE'D SHOWERED away every trace of Niko Radcliffe and remade her bed with fresh sheets, Elana crawled into bed and lay for hours gazing through the darkness at the ceiling, bitterly aware that she was never going to be able to sleep in this bed again without remembering the blissful, impassioned time she'd spent in Niko's arms.

He might be accustomed to one-night stands, but she wasn't.

Eventually she did fall asleep, but she dreamt of him, a weird jumble of scenes, the memory of which made her blush with chagrin the next morning while she got ready for work.

And she had to stop this right now. She had other, more vital things to worry about.

Like ringing Ted and hiring one of his cars.

Only to learn that he had no available vehicles. Fate, it seemed, was determined to force her to rely—at least for the day—on Niko. She set the phone down, then picked up her lipstick and glowered at her reflection in the mirror. Her gaze met a subtly different woman from the one she'd seen there yesterday morning. Somehow her lips were fuller, and her expression held a languorous softness she'd never seen before.

'You're imagining things,' she told her reflection severely. 'Making love—no, *sex*—wouldn't change the way you look! It didn't before.'

But her previous experience with the man she'd once believed she loved bore no resemblance to the wildfire storm of sensation she'd experienced in Niko's arms. There, she'd learned what utter ecstasy could do—summon a kind of rebirth, a rediscovery of herself. He'd set her alight, changed her for ever.

At the memory a primitive excitement stirred inside her.

'Cool it,' she ordered beneath her breath, frowning belligerently before she turned away. 'It's not going to happen again.'

Reluctantly she rang Mana homestead, dreading the thought of being answered by Niko.

Fortunately it was the housekeeper, who said immediately, 'I was just about to ring you. The boss said you'd need a ride into Waipuna and back again this evening. What time do you want to leave?'

Elana told her, then finished with, 'I'm sorry to break into your day—I'm hoping to be able to hire a car tomorrow. Thanks very much.'

Mrs West laughed. 'No problem, and you'd better thank Niko.'

Her mood a bit lighter, Elana hung up.

Although glad that neither of the two men who'd stolen her car had been badly hurt, she couldn't help vengefully wishing she could have ten minutes alone with them. It wasn't going to happen, so she had to get Steve's car on the road again. She rang the mechanic, who said he'd be there about five-thirty that afternoon.

'That's fine; I'll be home by then.'

He went over the engine carefully, then straightened up and slammed down the bonnet.

Shaking his head, he told her not unsympathetically,

'Quite frankly, Elana, this heap of rust isn't worth fixing. I'm not even going to try. It will never be roadworthy—and money spent on it would buy you a decent second-hand car. Your best bet is to get the scrap-metal guy to take it away.'

She hesitated before asking, 'Have you had a chance to look at *my* own car? Phil told me it's at your workshop.'

'Yes. It's salvageable.'

Relief flooded through her. 'When do you think it will be ready?'

He shrugged. 'Can't give you a definite date. It's an insurance job so it will take at least several days, possibly more than a week.'

Elana winced, but thanked him and waved him goodbye before ringing Ted at the hire company. To her relief, he'd found a car she could hire for the next couple of days.

'But probably only for a few days,' he warned. 'Things are getting busy right now—school holidays, you know.'

Spirits lifting slightly, she thanked him, hung up and slathered her arms and legs and nose with sunscreen lotion before going outside to weed the vegetable garden.

Hiring a car for any length of time would eat into her savings and right then, with the roof needing attention, she didn't need that.

It would be so simple—so economical—so *sensible* to accept Niko's offer.

Sighing, she noticed that snails had done vicious damage to the lettuce plants she'd put in several weeks ago. On her way to the garden shed to pick up slug bait, she stopped when she heard a car coming down the drive. Niko's large four-wheel-drive vehicle turned the corner.

Blood pounded in her ears as though she'd been running a marathon. The tension gripping her was intensified by the caressing breeze that whispered across her bare arms and legs. Regretting the elderly pair of denim shorts she should have thrown out a couple of years ago, and a faded, even older T-shirt in a colour that didn't suit her, she waited and tried to regulate her breathing.

The big vehicle slowed to a halt in the turning circle. Niko got out and her heart twisted. It took a real effort of will to summon a casual, neighbourly smile.

One glance told her this was not the tenderly passionate lover of the previous night. She braced herself as he got out, and said in her most cheerful tone, 'Hello.'

It sounded false. And lame. And stupid.

He narrowed his eyes and demanded, 'What's the matter?'

'Nothing,' she said automatically.

He stopped—too close—and subjected her to an unsparing scrutiny. 'Liar.'

When Elana stiffened, he said, 'Tell me what's worrying you.'

'Why?' And immediately regretted it. How did he reduce her to a defiant teenager?

'Because I might be able to help.'

Now he sounded like that teenager's out-of-patience parent. When Elana hesitated, he went on coolly, 'Independence is all very well, but refusing help is cutting off your nose to spite your face.'

She drew in a sharp breath and looked up. Drat the man, he was smiling! Something odd—a fiercely exultant twist of sensation—quickened her heart, weakened her knees, and throbbed deep inside her, summoning needs she needed to ignore.

In her best brisk, no-nonsense tone, she said, 'If you must know, I've just found out that Steve's car is not a viable proposition.' She looked up and finished in a voice she tried to keep unconcerned, 'Not worth fixing.'

He frowned. 'So how are you planning to deal with that?'

'I've just been speaking to Ted, and he's managed to organise a car for me for the rest of the week.' She added with a smile that held more wryness than humour, 'And the wreckers will take Steve's old jalopy away.' She added, 'I don't seem to be having much luck with vehicles, but I'm hoping it's just a passing phase.'

And was startled when Niko laughed in genuine amusement. It changed his face entirely. Not exactly softening it—his features were too strong and striking for that—but the warmth increased his powerful male magnetism.

So much so that she found herself almost shivering in the sunlight. *Go back to being the domineering man you really are,* she told him silently.

Like this, he was altogether too much, and her foolish, impressionable heart was softening, melting...

'A passing phase? I imagine everyone you know is hoping that too,' he told her, still smiling. 'Mrs Nixon, for one.'

Elana relaxed a little, but asked suspiciously, 'Have you been talking to her?'

'She's been talking to me,' he told her.

She frowned. 'She's a dear, but she worries too much about me.'

'Possibly she feels that someone has to worry about you.'

'It's not necessary,' she told him.

Her distant tone should have warned him off but he said, 'She told me you have no family.'

Frown deepening, she shrugged. 'Well, none that I know of. My mother grew up in care, and Steve was English. He never said anything about a family.'

'What about your birth father?'

A few seconds of silence preceded her abrupt answer. 'As far as I know, none.' This time, her tone was definitely aloof.

Hard eyes hooded, Niko said, 'It's just as well you have Mrs Nixon, then. I've just had a call from the Prime Minister's office; I have a meeting with him in Wellington. After that I'm flying to the Maldives.'

The Maldives? Meeting someone there, perhaps? Someone gorgeous and blonde from his world...?

A fierce pang that sharpened into an agonising jealousy hit Elana, scrambling her brain.

Was he running away? One glance at his face told her she was being stupid. His inbred arrogance would prevent that. Controlling a stab of pain, she said lightly, 'Have fun.'

The throbbing sound of a helicopter's engines broke into the calm air. He said, 'That's my chopper. Will you drive me back to Mana?'

The question was delivered in a tone that made it sound like an order. She asked, 'Why?' her voice so nakedly bewildered she hastened to add, 'Why is that necessary? Are you all right?'

His smile was brief and mirthless. 'I'm fine, but I'm lending you this car while I'm away.'

'No,' she said automatically. Was this some kind of pay-off for making love with him?

Surely not...

'Yes.' He spoke calmly, blue gaze level and hard. 'I want to make sure you can drive it properly. It's bigger than the cars you're accustomed to.'

Mortified, Elana had to stop herself from wringing her hands. It took all of her self-control to say, 'Why are you doing this?'

Broad shoulders lifting in a shrug, he said dryly, 'I won't be needing it while I'm away.'

Which sounded as though he was going to be gone for some time. She took a deep breath and tried to sound logical and level-headed. 'Niko, this is taking neighbourliness to extremes, and it's not necessary. Thank you,' she added belatedly, her voice trailing away as he tossed the keys to her. Instinctively she caught them, clutching them as he turned away and strode towards the road.

'What on earth are you doing?' she demanded.

'Walking back to Mana,' he said over his shoulder.

She said uncertainly, 'You're—this is ridiculous.'

And prickled at another of those dismissive shrugs.

'Sensible,' he said laconically. 'It doesn't pay to keep politicians waiting when you want something from them. And as you told me not so long ago, it's not very far to Mana from here.'

Torn between anger with him for putting her in this position, and chagrin at the sense of loss that ached through her, Elana glowered at his back. Then she took a deep breath, and surrendered.

After all, once she'd hired a car she wouldn't need to use this one...

'Oh, all right,' she said churlishly. 'Get in, and I'll drive you back.'

If he's smiling when he turns around, he can jolly well walk.

But the threat vanished when he turned. He wasn't smiling. Instead he looked his usual self—totally composed, formidably compelling, and enigmatic.

As though nothing had happened between them.

Niko hid a wry smile as he got into the car. Where had she got that fierce independence? And why on earth did he want to protect her from everything that could upset her, when she was so clearly bent on resisting him?

Until last night. He'd had no intention of making love with her. Yet when she'd looked at him, and touched him, some hidden need he'd never experienced before had made surrender inevitable.

And it had been like nothing before, sweet and fiery and intoxicating.

But going nowhere. Elana's attitude made that more than obvious. So he'd put her from his mind and concentrate on the business ahead, and soon he'd be able to view the situation without this lingering need.

Elana climbed behind the wheel of the vehicle and set her mind to driving it. Fortunately Niko was helpful. Her tension gradually relaxed into something like confidence as they neared the homestead.

'You're a good driver,' he told her as she slowed down. 'I've contacted the police and my insurance company and told them you'll be driving this until you get your own car back.'

She bit back a request to let her know how long he'd be away. One night's passionate lovemaking didn't give her any rights at all.

Besides, he might have every intention of staying away.

Ignoring the acute twinge of anguish caused by that possibility, she eased the vehicle to a stop outside the homestead, and without switching off the engine said, 'Thank you. Travel safely.'

He got out and came around to the driver's door. 'Try to keep out of trouble.'

Elana managed a smile. 'I think you must be a bad omen for me. Trouble arrived with you.'

His expression hardened. 'Rubbish.' He reached in and switched off the engine, holding the key in his hand as she gaped at him.

'Before I leave,' he said, 'I want to ask you something. Do you recognise the calls a kiwi makes?'

Bewildered, she said, 'Yes, I do. I hear them calling sometimes at night. Why?'

'I noticed a dead one on the side of the road last night—

obviously run over. The person I spoke to at the Department of Conservation office said it's not uncommon, and asked if I'd noticed signs of them on Mana.'

Even more surprised, she asked, 'Have you?'

'No.'

'On the road they get dazzled by headlights. On farms, dogs are powerfully attracted to them. It's apparently hard to convince some people that their nice, friendly spaniel or obedient cattle dog will happily kill New Zealand's iconic bird. And until they're almost mature they're unable to protect themselves from stoats.'

He nodded. 'So the DOC ranger told me. I'm considering setting up a kiwi protection zone on the peninsula. Would you be interested in coming on board?'

Her first instinct was to say no. It would mean she saw even more of him, and she didn't dare. But native birds all around New Zealand were in danger from introduced predators. This was a new aspect of Niko, one she admired. After several seconds, she said, 'Yes.'

And wondered bleakly if she'd just made a very bad mistake.

'You know the other landowners here better than I do. What do you think of the possibility of them joining in?'

Frowning, Elana swiftly assessed their neighbours. 'I think they probably would. It's worth a try.'

'Indeed,' he agreed, and glanced at his watch, then held out the car key. 'I'd better be on my way.'

'I—yes. Thank you.'

His brief smile held no humour. 'Elana, it's all right,' he said calmly. 'I can see you're suffering post-coital remorse, but I don't think the less of you, if that's what—'

'I'm not! It's not that big a deal,' she said desperately, hugely embarrassed. Because his opinion of her mattered far too much.

His raised brows brought swift colour to her skin. 'Oh,

darn,' she muttered. 'That sounded awful. I can cope with borrowing your car, but you don't have to feel in any way responsible for me, just because we—well—because we...' Her voice died away and she was blushing like some adolescent after her first grown-up kiss. 'Because we made love,' she blurted.

He gave her an ironic look. 'Was it so hard to say?'

Unable to come up with any answer, Elana bit her lip, and was enormously relieved when he said, 'I'm sorry, that was crass of me. I'll see you again in about a fortnight.'

'Bon voyage,' she managed.

He nodded and turned and walked away.

Blinking, she set her jaw and set the car in motion, concentrating fiercely as she drove it towards Waipuna.

Was this some sort of kiss-off—*Goodbye, thanks for the sex, now forget about it?*

For Niko, had last night just been another episode in a series of one-night stands?

No! Horrified by the fierce pang of desolation that shot through her, she drew in a shaking breath. He had taken her, made her so completely his that she was no longer the woman she'd been before. Fiercely tender, he'd claimed her as though he'd been searching for her all his life and found her at last.

Don't read so much into it, she warned herself. *You're fantasising...*

The following morning she woke to an email from him, informing her that if she needed any help, she was to email him. And he'd contact her in two days at ten a.m. NZ time on the computer using the VOIP tool. Signed, Niko.

Cold, brief and chillingly matter-of-fact.

Well, what had she expected? It was completely stupid to suffer that aching hollowness of loss again, as though he'd meant anything more to her than a casual fling.

Casual? Wrong word.

Very wrong word. A kind of panic gripped her, an ominous understanding that last night had somehow changed her. But—judging by the tone of his farewell, if farewell it could be called—it had had no effect on him.

She should be relieved.

But why did every impersonal word in that email feel like a stab to the heart?

Stop thinking of him. At least she still had the Mana project to keep her busy. Apart from the considerable sum she was being paid for doing it, it would help keep her mind off Niko, and her humiliatingly fervent desire to trust him.

Gritting her teeth, she called the station. She needed to organise a routine that suited them all while Niko was away. 'Or I could bring the documents back home,' she suggested, unwilling to be reminded of Niko every day she went to the homestead.

David West was silent for a moment before saying, 'I don't think the boss would agree to that. They're pretty fragile.'

Bother! After she'd hung up she walked out onto the deck to survey the estuary, narrowing her eyes against the shimmer of early summer sunlight across the water, the wash of gold highlighting the hills on the other side of the water. Each Christmas, the silver buds on the ancient pohutukawa trees burst open into pompons of scarlet and crimson and russet, a vivid contrast to the deep green leaves.

Would Niko be here then?

So much had happened recently...her mother's death, Jordan's accident, the theft of her car, the discovery of the documents...

And meeting Niko Radcliffe.

Relieved by the imperative summons of the telephone, she ran inside. It was the roofer, who gave her a date for his arrival. She hung up, glad yet worried. Even with the income she was earning from her work at Mana, she'd have to stick to a pretty strict budget for the next few months.

Bracingly she told herself she'd coped with everything else, so she'd cope with this, as well as with her stupid heart's yearning after a man she didn't dare allow herself to trust.

As the days slid by she became more and more interested in the documents, especially the diaries. She read accounts of accidents, fatalities, parties and weddings and balls, comments on the news of the day, and one day discovered what she suspected to be a faded bunch of love letters tied up with a blue satin ribbon.

Because it seemed rude to even consider untying that bow to read the outpourings of someone's heart, she put them untouched to one side. Niko was due to contact her in another couple of days, so she'd mention them to him.

And try to rid herself of her desperate, embarrassing anticipation at the thought of seeing him on screen again. Memories of his lovemaking—passionate and tender— vied with memories of his coolness afterwards. Yet the last time he'd contacted her, he seemed—different, more relaxed, as though he enjoyed talking to her.

A knock on the door broke into her thoughts. David West, the manager, apologised for interrupting and said, 'The kids from the high school will arrive here shortly to do some more tree planting. They might get here before I get back from picking the boss up from the airport, but they won't bother you, they know where to go.' He smiled at her startled face.

Niko helping children plant trees? Previously she'd have found it difficult to imagine Niko with a group of young adolescents, but those impassioned minutes in his arms had shown her a different side of him...a side she could trust?

Almost, she thought uncertainly.

David West smiled. 'He's very good with them—treats them like adults, but makes sure they don't get carried away with fooling around. They think he's great. On the first day they came one of the boys was acting the goat, and Niko put a stop to it straight away. Did me good to see the kid settle down to work. Hasn't blotted his copybook since.' As he turned to go, he said, 'By the way, if you're wondering where Patty is, she's at the dentist's—toothache hit her in the middle of the night. Can you take the phone calls if there are any? Just take a message.'

'Yes, of course.'

Elana went back to her office. She'd felt she was learning to understand Niko Radcliffe, but almost every day she learned something about him that turned her preconceptions upside down. Slowly, carefully—almost reluctantly—she was learning to trust him.

Only last night, at dinner with the Nixons, she'd been told of his large donation to the retirement home in Waipuna, and his stipulation that the amount not be circulated. 'He's already making a big difference to Waipuna,' Mrs Nixon had observed, 'and not just financially.'

An hour later, when the telephone summoned her, Elana picked up the receiver and said briskly, 'Mana Station.'

The caller was a woman with a very English accent, clipped and abrupt, who said, 'I want to speak to Niko Radcliffe.'

Startled, Elana told her, 'I'm sorry, he's not here. Can I take a message?'

'No. Who are you? His secretary?'

No reason for her to be so rude. 'No.'

'Oh, his latest girlfriend, I suppose.' Her tone altered.

'If that's so, then take care. He's a brute—and not just verbally. Watch out for his fists if you make him angry.'

Stunned, Elana opened her mouth to speak, but it was too late. The connection had been cut off.

Feeling sick, she put down the receiver and got rather shakily to her feet. A chill iced her stomach and tightened her skin. Shivering, she walked over to the open window and stared unseeingly out.

Who on earth had that been?

She wasn't ever likely to know. A woman who knew Niko well, apparently.

And who seemed to have good reason to hate him. She'd spoken with real venom, spitting out the words as though they were weapons.

Elana took in a great lungful of warm, sea-scented air, and turned away. Questions—hateful questions with no answers—buzzed like wasps through her brain. She winced, feeling as though something rare and precious had been shattered into painful splinters. She'd even allowed herself to believe she could trust him...

Her nausea intensified into pain, so all-encompassing it overcame any physical agony she'd ever experienced. Not again, she thought wearily. In a world with plenty of decent men, was she doomed to run across only those who were abusers?

First her father, who'd beaten her mother, and then Roland, who'd resented anything that took her attention away from him—but mostly her work and her affection for her mother and stepfather and friends.

At least she'd realised what was happening and managed to break their relationship off without bearing too many emotional scars.

She simply couldn't imagine Niko striking a woman.

But then, she'd noticed no warning signs when she'd fallen in love with Roland, either. It had taken her several months to realise that his constant criticism, his demands that she always tell him where she was and whatever she was planning to do, the days of frigid silence when he thought she'd disobeyed him, were all a form of abuse that was stripping her of confidence.

Emotional manipulation was bad enough; physical abuse had to be worse. Love was a much more complicated affair than the basic physical urge to mate. It involved friendship—and trust.

Perhaps, she thought bleakly, she was a very slow learner.

Had it amused Niko to take her to bed? Had she just been a convenient focus for a temporary lust? He certainly hadn't wasted any time in heading off overseas. It seemed more and more likely.

Yet even with the shock of that call numbing her brain, heat from the memory of their passion stirred deep within her body.

She didn't really know Niko at all, so she couldn't— dared not—trust him. Therefore she couldn't be in love with him. Yet a primal sense of loss that had no basis in common sense ached through her.

And wailing about it wasn't going to solve anything. So she'd just make sure she never surrendered to her baser urges again.

In the meantime, she had work to do. She sat down at the desk and tried to absorb the description of preparations for a late Victorian garden party held in the gardens of the homestead, as told by the eighteen-year-old daughter of the house.

Until she was interrupted by a voice behind her, deep and dark and cool, and instantly recognisable. 'That must be a fascinating read.'

Her heart leapt and her fingers froze on the keyboard. She'd been dreading this moment. She slowly turned, bracing herself against a swift, heartfelt delight that terrified her.

'No,' she said, adding foolishly, 'I didn't hear the helicopter.'

'It's having an overhaul. Dave met me at the airport.' Brows almost meeting over ice-blue eyes, Niko demanded, 'What's the matter? You look as though you've seen a ghost.'

'Nothing,' she said automatically.

Thoughts jostled through her brain, none of them making much sense.

She swallowed and babbled, 'I wasn't expecting you. I thought you said you were going to be away for a fortnight, but it's only been a week.' And stopped, mortified, because now he'd know she'd been counting them. Hastily she added, 'I heard the car, but I thought it was Mrs West coming back from the dentist.' *Tell him now, get it over.* 'Someone rang for you a while ago.'

Oh, she was making a total pig's breakfast of this! His brows shot up, and she finished rapidly, 'Judging by her accent she's English. She didn't leave a message.'

Alarmed, she found herself scanning his face, searching, she realised, for some clue as to whether he'd been expecting the call.

His expression gave nothing away. 'If it's important whoever it was will contact me again,' he said indifferently. And came across to look at the old book opened before her on the desk. 'What is this?'

Every sense sharpening, she had to swallow before she could tell him. She prayed for him to leave so she didn't have to endure the faint scent of his skin—musky and very male, something she recalled only too vividly from their lovemaking.

'It's fascinating,' she ended staunchly. 'I'm so glad these documents have been saved. I wonder what the people you bought Mana from would have done with them if they'd known of their existence. Burnt them, probably.'

Niko straightened, looking down at her with slightly narrowed eyes. 'Obviously you didn't like them.'

She shrugged and turned back to the diary, hoping he'd go away. 'I didn't know them. Nobody did. They lived in Auckland, and spent much of the time overseas. The owner was no farmer. He just saw Mana as an investment that he could plunder.'

'Is that how you think I consider it?'

Without needing to think, she shook her head. 'No. I've seen the changes you've made here—the paddocks already look much greener and the fences are in good shape again. And nobody who sees the place as a cash cow would have brought the homestead back to life, or be paying me for transcribing all these documents before they crumble into dust.' She paused, then added, 'Or have organised a group of schoolchildren to come and plant trees to stop sedimentation in the estuary.'

'Yet I detect a certain amount of constraint in your tone,' he observed dryly. 'Why?'

Go away, Elana urged silently.

His nearness affected her like a physical touch, her skin tightening as sensation ran wild through her, quickening her pulse and shortening her breath.

Again she swallowed. 'Sacking Mr Percy was—unfortunate.'

'How did you know he was sacked?'

'His wife told—' Too late, she stopped.

His smile held no humour. 'She told Mrs Nixon,' he finished for her. 'And Mrs Nixon told you.'

'Yes. She knows I can be trusted not to tell anyone else.'

His gaze hardened. 'I'll tell you why he is no longer working here. The previous owner wasn't the only person siphoning money from Mana. The manager did his share of that too.'

Stunned, Elana couldn't think of a word to say. He went on, 'His wife doesn't know about it, and I have no intention of telling her. But I certainly couldn't trust him.'

'No,' she said numbly. 'No, of course not.'

To her immense relief he stepped back.

'I'll leave you to your work,' he said. 'I hope you'll have lunch with me.'

She hesitated, then swivelled around. 'Patty's been to the dentist, she might not feel up to making lunch for you. If that's so, I'll do it.'

His smile was tinged with irony. 'I'm quite capable of making my own, but thank you. We'll eat together out on the veranda.'

And he walked out of the room, draining it—and Elana—of energy. At the click of the closing door she sagged and drew in a long, softly shuddering breath while a mixture of barely controllable emotions fought for supremacy. Mingled with the aftermath of her shock at seeing him again so unexpectedly was pain for lost trust—and a fierce joy that still shocked her.

Had he taken her complete surrender as a signal that their passionate relationship would continue whenever he was at Mana? It didn't seem likely. There had certainly been no sign of desire in his voice, in his expression…

Elana told herself she was glad. She *had* to be glad his emotions hadn't been touched by their lovemaking.

But those maddened hours spent in his arms had fundamentally changed her in some way she didn't feel ready to examine. His tenderness had touched her deeply, bringing with it trust—a trust totally shattered by the telephone call. As well as anger in that unknown voice there had been a note of yearning, as though its owner was still trapped by longing.

That memory would keep her safe, Elana vowed.

After all, Niko wasn't going to be at Mana often, or for long. He had the world at his feet, and several empires to rule...

At midday she got up, picked up her bag with her lunch in it, and headed for the door. She had no idea which veranda he'd be eating on, but she walked to the one she'd been to before, and sure enough, there was a table set for two overlooking the estuary, and Mrs West bustling out into the sunshine with a tray.

Catching sight of Elana, she said, 'Ah, there you are. I thought I might have to knock and let you know the time.'

Elana forced a smile. 'My stomach's better than any clock. How did your appointment with the dentist go?'

'Remarkably well. And really, visiting the dentist nowadays is nothing like it used to be, thank heavens.' She set the tray on the table and smiled past Elana. 'Hello, Niko. Welcome back.'

Elana had to stop herself from clenching a hand across her breast to hide the jumping of her heart. He'd changed clothes, but, even clad in jeans and a casual shirt that revealed the strength of muscular arms, he was still the sophisticated tycoon.

And in spite of the fear that drove her decision not to resume any sort of relationship with him but the most distant, some primitive, unregenerate part of her was deeply, shamelessly glad she'd chosen to greet the summer day by wearing a dress in the soft amber that suited her so well.

The housekeeper gone, Niko said, 'I hope you've got sunscreen on. Five minutes in this sun will probably be enough to burn that creamy skin of yours. I'll move the table into the shade.'

Something in his tone and the swift survey that accompanied it made her acutely conscious of bare arms and a scooped neckline. Her dress was far from revealing, yet her skin was swept by heat. Every time she thought of him, memories intruded, memories she knew she'd never be able to banish.

Thank heavens she'd picked up that phone... If she hadn't, she might be allowing herself to surrender to his overwhelming charisma. Even knowing what sort of man he was, she had to guard against the heady clamour of awareness.

Trying for a brisk, no-nonsense tone, she replied, 'Don't worry. At this time of the year I don't step outside without slathering myself in sunscreen.'

For Niko Mrs West produced a splendid and substantial lunch of fish on a salad of roasted tomatoes. As she opened her lunchbox, Elana wished she'd made easy-to-eat sandwiches instead of a somewhat unwieldy wrap filled with the leftovers of her previous night's dinner.

Normally she enjoyed sitting on the beautifully restored Victorian veranda fringed by white-painted wooden lace around the guttering, while waves hushed gently on the beach through the trees, and seagulls swooped and called and landed on the lawn, watching them with bright eyes as they ate.

But since she had made love—no, no, *had sex*—with Niko, nothing seemed normal.

'If you're going to make a habit of having lunch out here you'll have to post a sign saying *Please do not feed the gulls*,' she observed, hoping her voice showed no signs of her inner turmoil.

He smiled. 'That's a possibility. I enjoy eating al fresco. I noticed you have a table on your terrace, so I presume you do too. Do you find the gulls a nuisance?'

'Sometimes.' It was stupid to allow herself to be so affected by him, but the memories of her temporary madness had her on a knife-edge.

How on earth did people deal with this sort of situation?

With calmness and common sense and willpower. And conversation, no matter how banal. She said, 'There's a description in one of the diaries of the wedding of one of the sons. They were married in Waipuna, but the reception was held out here, and was clearly a huge event.'

'You sound as though you're enjoying delving into their past.'

'I am.'

Relieved to steer the conversation away from personal subjects, she said, 'I didn't know that you have schoolchildren planting trees for you.'

He shrugged. 'The school has a very vigorous eco group. I heard about it, and wondered if they might be interested in helping to plant the creek banks to stop sedimentation of the estuary. When I contacted the school the headmaster put it to the parents and the group, who all agreed it was a good idea. One afternoon a month they come out and do some work.'

'Are you planning to go ahead with a kiwi conservation group?'

'Yes,' he said calmly. 'Interested?'

She hesitated, then said, 'Yes.' And added, 'I don't know much about other similar groups in Northland, but it's going to take quite a bit of organising.' And had to stop herself from offering to help with that. Stumbling a little, she went on, 'Trapping predators is a big part of it.'

'I know that. You sound surprised.'

'I suppose I am,' she admitted.

He shrugged. 'I remember my father telling me of the discovery of the last living takehe not very far from where we lived. Until then they'd been believed to be extinct.'

Impressed, Elana nodded. Years previously, New Zealanders had been delighted and astounded when the tiny group of birds had been discovered. Since then, there had been a successful effort to raise the numbers.

Niko said, 'I see you know about them.'

'I've read about them. One day I hope to actually see some.'

'Our ancestors didn't understand the damage they were doing to New Zealand's unique wildlife when they chopped down so much of the native forest and turned it into farms.' And with an abrupt change of subject, 'What do you think should be done with all these documents once you've finished with them?'

'The local museum would love them,' she told him, 'but it's run by volunteers, and these documents really should be in some place where they can be cared for properly.'

He nodded. 'Once they are digitised the museum can have copies. The earliest records of my father's station were burnt in a fire that destroyed the original homestead some time in the middle of last century.'

'Oh, that's such a pity.'

His smile held a certain amount of irony, yet it warmed her. 'There speaks the historian. I'm sure the original owners of this station would agree with you.'

'I don't know of any other repository like this in Northland. Everything's in surprisingly good condition.'

Later she'd ask herself grimly what magic he'd produced to talk her into researching a safe place to donate them to. Not that he'd had to try very hard—after working with the documents she took an almost proprietorial interest in them.

She was relieved when Mrs West came out with a tray. 'Coffee and tea,' she announced cheerfully, setting it down on the table. 'If you're too hot, I'll bring out a cold drink.'

Niko looked down at Elana, something in his gaze kindling flames inside her. 'Tea, I presume?' he said levelly.

Her initial tension had been smoothed over by a perilous sense of companionship, but it took an effort to give him what she hoped was a cheerful smile. 'Yes, thank you.'

He chose coffee, and once the housekeeper had left began to pour it. Elana watched his lean hands—hands that had given her such exquisite delight—manipulate the coffee pot. Once again she was caught up in a strange, poignant flash of *déjà vu*, as though she should recognise this garden, this house—this man.

As though they were hugely important to her...

Her hands shook. Hoping he hadn't noticed, she took a deep breath, and pretended to look around the garden. Although it was familiar now, she was suddenly filled by an enormous contentment, as though she had come home.

The sunlight sending down a summer benediction onto the tangled growth in what had once been carefully planted beds, the hum of bees foraging in a regiment of lilies below the veranda railings, the estuary flashing blue between the heavy swooping branches of pohutukawa trees—all reminded her of Sleeping Beauty's castle garden in her book of fairy tales. The conversation she'd had with Niko on that was still sharply etched in her brain.

She stole a glance across the table, her cheeks heating when she met Niko's half-closed eyes. Deep inside her, an odd sweet burn of sensation tightened, insistent, demanding.

'Drink your tea,' Niko said, his voice harsh. 'Then I'll take you home.'

Almost she nodded. Just in time, she squelched the urge. She knew instantly what would happen once they got home. Her body craved what he was offering, yearned for it, longed to surrender to the promise in his eyes. And her foolish mind wanted it too—wanted him with a hunger that threatened to overwhelm any weak vestige of common sense, ignore the voice inside her that reminded her she could not trust this man.

She was afraid to trust him—but even more afraid of trusting herself.

Her throat dried, but she managed to say, 'I'm working right now.'

'I think I can arrange to change that.'

Her gaze snared by his, she managed to hold his gaze and shake her head. Twice. 'No.'

CHAPTER NINE

IT WAS MORE a croak than a word, but Niko understood.

Almost certainly, judging by Elana's set shoulders and the defiant lift of her chin, she meant, 'Not again, not ever...'

The fierce anger that gripped him shocked him into silence as he fought for control. What followed was even more disturbing—an emotion so strong it almost overwhelmed him. Dismay? No, infinitely more than that.

He drew in a hard breath and told himself sardonically that he'd fallen into the classic playboy's trap of assuming that money and power would buy him any woman.

Not this one.

A strange kind of relief took him totally by surprise. Another quality to discover in this intriguing, maddening woman—she would not be bought.

After a swift glance that took in the harsh contours of his face, the thin line of his mouth and his hooded eyes, Elana braced herself for his response—anger, scorn, contempt.

But when he spoke his voice was level and without inflexion. 'I notice you've been using the car.'

'Only to come down here when it's wet,' she told him. Like his, her voice lacked colour and expression. 'The wife of one of your workers has found a job in Waipuna, so I go with her on the days I work at the shop. I pay for some of her petrol costs. It's working very well.'

'Feel free to call on me if you need transport,' Niko told her crisply.

'That's very kind of you,' she returned, vowing never to do so.

The rest of the conversation was conducted with impersonal politeness. He showed her the plans drawn up by the landscape architect he'd hired to return the homestead grounds to their former glory. After scanning them, she told him she was glad that he'd insisted on staying close to the Victorian concept of the garden.

Finally back in her office, she could allow herself to collapse into the chair in front of the computer and endeavour to assemble her thoughts into some sort of coherence.

Only to fail entirely. Resisting Niko had taken enormous self-control; every cell in her body had demanded a renewal of the sexual delight she knew he could give her. However, she'd done it and now he understood she wasn't in the market for an affair, she could relax. She was safe.

But she didn't feel safe. She felt desolate. He hadn't told her why he'd returned early, but his cool attitude made it obvious that whatever he felt for her meant little to him.

Her worlds and Niko's had touched, but there could be no connection between a man with a pedigree a mile long who could probably buy any small country he fancied, and a woman working in a tiny town in New Zealand, with a bank account that was practically non-existent until the insurance money for her car was paid into it. At least work had started on the roof thanks to her job at Mana Station, although she still needed a loan to pay off the balance.

And with any luck, Niko would soon leave Mana and head off to an exotic place where beautiful women in designer bikinis would appreciate him far more than she dared.

The sooner the better.

It took concentrated effort to make any progress with the document she was working on, but eventually the time came for her to pack up and go home.

But it was with a knot of something too close to apprehension in her stomach that she switched off the computer and left the room—a sensation that intensified a hundredfold when she went outside. Niko was standing by the car, and as she walked towards him he delivered one of those unsmiling, ice-blue assessments.

Like checking out a car he wanted to buy, she thought, stiffening with resentment.

Niko watched her, wondering how the hell she created such havoc in him. One word from her, delivered with brutal succinctness, had made it quite clear she didn't want to further their relationship—if several hours in bed together could be called a relationship.

Of course it wasn't. It had been an interlude, nothing more, and he'd soon get over this—this unruly clamour of emotions. He glanced at his watch and said coolly, 'I owe you five minutes' overtime.'

She shrugged. 'No, you don't. It took me that to get here from my—*the*—office. It's a huge house.'

'The Victorians usually assumed they were going to have huge families,' he returned, and opened the door for her.

Watching her climb gracefully into the vehicle stirred something intensely potent within him.

Dammit, he wanted her, foolishly, crazily. But she didn't want him.

Regret? Possibly. But she hadn't been a virgin. And in his arms she'd become a creature of fire and spirit, a wild and blazing sensualist.

Stop that line of thought right now, he thought uncompromisingly.

It could be another man, of course. Possibly her policeman friend—who might, or might not, be married.

Chagrined by the flash of fierce resentment that caused, he closed the door behind her before walking around the vehicle. Out of sight, he stopped a moment, fixing his gaze on the house, now as pristine as when it was built over a century ago, before surveying the garden, still to be rescued and restored.

He hadn't been able to prise Elana from his mind while he'd been away, and he'd been looking forward to seeing her again. Dammit, he was in danger of making an idiot of himself over her.

It's called rejection, he thought sardonically, *and it's not the first time it's happened to you.*

As a callow youth he'd had his heart dented a couple of times, but he'd learned to deal with it. His ego was suffering—no, it was far more than just his ego—but whatever had caused Elana to draw back was her business, not his.

Although he needed to make sure of one thing.

As he drove through the stone entrance to Mana, he asked, 'Are you quite sure you're not pregnant?'

He sensed her stiffening beside him. After a moment she said frigidly, 'One hundred per cent positive.'

'Good,' he said, and left it at that.

Silence stretched tautly between them until they'd reached the small building she called home. Without looking at him, one hand on the door handle, she said steadily, 'Thank you for the loan of your car, but I don't need it now. It's a very pleasant walk to Mana as well as being good exercise for me.'

Niko controlled his swift response, a mixture of frustration and anger. 'If it's raining someone will collect you and bring you home.'

Eyes darkening, she frowned at him, then opened the

door and climbed out. 'That won't be necessary. I do have rain gear that I can use.'

It took all of Niko's self-control not to grit his teeth. However, one glance at her standing beside the vehicle, shoulders square, her lush mouth tight and her gaze level and inflexible, convinced him that getting out of the car to tell her she was being foolishly stubborn was not going to make any difference to her decision.

She said, 'Thank you for the offer, though. And the ride home.'

He replied laconically, 'My pleasure,' and put the car in motion, leaving with a wave of his hand through the open window.

Torn anew by conflicting emotions, Elana fought back a regret that threatened to drown her, and turned to go into the house. It should have welcomed her like the refuge it had always been, but it felt alien, lonely, bereft of memories...

No, not bereft. One memory was engraved on her brain, into her skin, in every cell of her body. Whenever she walked inside she'd remember Niko's passionate lovemaking—the voluptuous excitement he'd roused, the heady need that she'd surrendered to without any fear. And the tenderness with which he'd held her afterwards, the sleepy stroke of his hands across her sensitised skin, the safety she'd felt lying against him.

An agony of grief mingled with an abject fear. 'No,' she whispered.

Surely she hadn't been so foolish? This couldn't be love...

She dragged in a shaking breath. 'No,' she said firmly. She was not so stupid. So he was a fantastic lover. How many women had he bedded to be so proficient?

Hundreds, probably. 'Well, scores, anyway,' she told herself harshly.

But he'd understood her rejection, and he hadn't been disappointed by it, even though it might have been a bit of a shock.

The sound of her telephone was a welcome interruption to her tumbling thoughts.

'Oh, hello, Mrs Nixon,' she said, welcoming that familiar, friendly voice.

'Hello, dear, I haven't seen you for ages, apart from a word or two in the shop. Why don't we have lunch together at the café on the river and catch up on things? I'll pick you up and bring you home. How about Saturday and we can go to the market before we have lunch?'

Arrangements completed, Elana hung up, grateful to have something normal and everyday to look forward to. Count Niko Radcliffe had been taking up too much room in her mind. And lunch with Mrs Nixon was always fun. At least she'd catch up with all the local gossip and some international stuff too.

Until then, she'd avoid Niko as much as she could. And she wouldn't think of him.

Easier said than done, unfortunately. Although he spent much of the time she was at Mana out on the land with the farm manager, she couldn't avoid eating lunch with him, and often morning and afternoon tea. Always a stimulating companion, he treated her with a courtesy she found incredibly painful. Unfortunately, each occasion only reinforced her reckless longing for more than he could give her.

Elana despised herself for it. It was not only embarrassing, it was humiliating. She'd thought she'd been heartbroken when Roland had shown his true colours, but relief had overridden that. Now, however, every night when she fell into bed memories of bliss came crowding back, taking over her dreams. More than once she found herself waking, tears on her cheeks as she gulped back sobs.

'Stick it out,' she told herself grimly. 'It's only infatuation. Niko's certainly not pining for *you*.'

But she ached for him...an ever-present hunger that showed no sign of easing, an acute, savage need that refused to go away. The more time she shared with him, the more potent that longing became.

So lunch with Mrs Nixon was a welcome relief. The café overlooked the Falls, a wall of ancient solidified lava at the head of the estuary over which the river fell into a basin lined with mangrove trees. The sun gilded the moored yachts and launches bobbing gently in the current, and a salt tang mingled with the fresh scent of the native vegetation lining the low banks. Above the falls the river had scooped a pool, and from it came the happy shrieks of children swimming.

Without looking at the menu Mrs Nixon announced, 'I'm going to be completely sinful and have their superb fish and chips.'

The café's fish and chips came with salad and home-made mayonnaise, and were, as its publicity announced, world famous in Waipuna.

After they'd both ordered she leaned towards Elana and said, 'And while we're waiting, you can tell me what you think of the Count now you know him.'

Elana hesitated, then made up her mind. 'Decisive, very astute, very self-contained, and with a proper appreciation of both Mana and the treasure trove of documents we've found there.'

And a superb lover...

Her companion nodded. 'Good. What do you think of his ideas for a kiwi conservation group on the peninsula?'

'I think it's excellent.' Elana told her of the impression the discovery of the last colony of takehe birds had made on Niko, and listened to the older woman's praise for his interest in the rapidly reducing kiwi population on the peninsula.

While they were waiting for the meal to arrive, Mrs Nixon said confidentially, 'You've given me your public views of Niko Radcliffe's character; now, for my ears only, what *do* you think of him?'

Elana laughed. 'Basically the same.' And counter-attacked. 'Anyway, you probably know more about him than I do. From information gathered from the gossip magazines in the dentist's surgery,' she elaborated.

Mrs Nixon's startled expression gave way to amusement. 'Oh, I don't believe much more than half of that. Even the paparazzi don't seem to be able to keep tabs on him, but there are hints that he's been seeing some aristocrat in England.'

Pain seared through Elana. Probably the woman he'd sent flowers to.

'Apart from that,' Mrs Nixon went on, 'he's donated a lot of money to a conservation project in the Amazon somewhere.'

Elana wished he didn't have any good points. However, just because he spent largely on conservation projects didn't mean that she could ignore that hissed warning over the telephone.

Although the past few weeks had shown her a different side of Niko, she couldn't let herself believe anything about him that might persuade her to lower her defences. If she allowed herself to do that, she suspected it would be impossible to control her leashed emotions.

And apart from living next door to each other, and a certain sexual attraction, what had she and Niko in common?

Nothing.

'That's a strange look on your face,' Mrs Nixon observed, startling her.

Hastily composing her expression, she conjured up a smile. 'Is it? What sort of look?'

'Wistful, I think. Yes, wistful. And a little bit sad, too?'

'Mum used to love coming here.' Feeling like a coward for making use of her mother's memory, Elana went on briskly, 'And she'd be shocked to think just coming here would make me miserable. One thing she did was live every moment of her life to the full.'

'Yes, she did.' Unexpectedly, her companion patted Elana's hand. 'You've had a really hard time this past year. Fran and I have been worried about you.'

Touched, Elana said, 'You don't need to worry, you know. I'm managing.'

'I know.' She looked past Elana. 'Well, talk of the devil—guess who's coming in the door, and with a very elegant woman too. I wonder if this is the next woman in his life—although she looks a tad too old for him.'

Elana swallowed, the back of her neck prickling. Her companion smiled above Elana's head. 'Hello, Niko.'

'Mrs Nixon, Elana.'

Summoning a smile, Elana turned to meet Niko's bland gaze. With him was the woman she'd seen beside him in the street.

'Let me introduce Petra Curtiss,' Niko said coolly. 'She is going to oversee the rescue of Mana's gardens.'

Mrs Nixon beamed. 'Oh, how wonderful. They used to be so lovely. Do you want to talk business, or would you like to share our table?'

Elana stiffened. Did she *have* to be so kind and hospitable?

But Niko said coolly, 'We've already talked business. Petra's on her way back to Auckland, and she'll probably be interested in any memories you have of the garden.'

Smiling at Mrs Nixon, the woman beside him said, 'I'd love to hear whatever you have to tell me about it.'

Niko nodded. 'Then we'll sit here,' he said smoothly, and held out the chair opposite Elana.

Which meant he'd be next to her. An exquisite tension gripped her, shredding her thoughts into irrational snippets as her heart skittered into overdrive. She had to force herself to smile when he sat down.

Relax, darn it! She focused on the conversation between the landscape architect and Mrs Nixon, who was very ready to discuss her memories of the garden.

Petra took notes, asked questions, apologised for monopolising the conversation, and impressed them all with her knowledge of plants that would flourish in a seaside garden.

'I grew up by the sea,' she explained. 'Just north of Auckland, so I have a good idea of what will grow up here and what won't.' She smiled across at Niko. 'I wouldn't be nearly so useful if you'd wanted me to rescue the garden at your high country station.'

'Fortunately that's in good shape,' he said urbanely. 'My father was a gardener rather than a farmer.'

An odd flatness in his tone caught Elana's attention. She glanced up, saw that he was looking at her, and her heart jumped in her chest, her pulse quickening, and her lips suddenly strangely hot and full.

Battling for control, she looked down at her meal.

'I was talking to young Jordan's mother the other day,' Mrs Nixon said, smiling at Niko. 'She told me you've been very helpful to him.'

'He's a decent kid at heart, and in a way the accident helped him grow up a bit. It certainly convinced him that he isn't bulletproof,' Niko said calmly.

'I believe he's working at Mana on the weekends?'

'He's saving up for a course on safe driving.' Niko sounded a little bored now, a tone that made Elana bristle.

Mrs Nixon smiled. 'In Auckland, I believe. You told him about that?'

'It seemed a logical thing to do,' Niko said dryly. 'I pointed out that if he wanted to drive fast he needed to know how and where to do it without killing himself or anyone else.' Smoothly changing the subject, he asked, 'Is that a dolphin I can see out there?'

'Oh, yes!' Elana scrambled to her feet, closely followed by Petra Curtiss.

The dolphin turned out to be two, a mother and a baby. Elana pointed them out, saying, 'I wonder why they're on their own.'

'I was wondering that too. They're usually in groups, aren't they?'

'Yes, the pods are family groups, so the babies are protected.'

'Do you often see them here?'

'Not here, no. Never, in fact. Ah, here come the rest.'

Entranced, they stood watching, rapidly joined by several other diners at the café, until eventually the pod of dolphins decided to leave.

Back at the table, Elana sensed a change in the atmosphere. Not one she could put her finger on, but both Mrs Nixon and Niko seemed different somehow, and although they finished their meal in pleasant conversation she still registered a coolness—mostly, she realised, from Niko.

When the meal finally finished she stifled a sigh of relief. Only to be shocked into near panic when Niko said smoothly, 'I'll take you home, Elana.'

'Oh, but—'

'It will save Mrs Nixon from going so far out of her way,' he said.

Mrs Nixon hesitated, almost as though she was reluctant to agree to this but unable to think of a polite way to stop it, before nodding. 'Very well. Thank you.'

Elana said, 'Thank you, Niko.' And smiled at Mrs Nixon. 'Thanks so much, it's been great fun.'

Farewells over, Mrs Nixon drove off, immediately followed by Petra Curtiss on her way back to Auckland.

As she and Niko walked towards his car, Elana said, 'It was kind of you to give Jordan something else to think about besides hooning around the back roads.'

Again that swift lift of broad shoulders. 'It's a stage in many young men's lives. He'll be fine. And the roads will be safer.'

She chuckled, then added more soberly, 'I hope so.'

'You should do that more often,' he said, stopping by the car to open the door for her.

Startled, she looked up. 'What?'

'Laugh,' he said succinctly. 'It's a pretty sound.'

Elana flushed. 'Thank you,' she murmured, climbing hastily into the front seat.

He walked around the car and got in, but instead of starting the engine he turned to face her. 'Hasn't anyone told you that before?'

'Not that I recall,' she said abruptly, strangely self-conscious. Relieved when he switched on the engine, she strapped herself into her seatbelt and gazed resolutely ahead as they headed back towards Mana, wondering at Niko's unexpected kindness to Jordan. No wonder the young man respected him.

It was probably naïve of her to be surprised—and warmed—by Niko's determination to introduce conservation to Mana. New Zealand farmers had come to realise just how fragile the ecosystem could be, and many were planting along stream banks. Then there was the kiwi restoration project he was working on with the other local landowners. He was a complex man, hard to read, clearly generous and charitably minded.

And she found it impossible to dismiss the memory of his tenderness during their lovemaking...

Even though, according to the woman who'd made that phone call, he was also capable of violence.

A chill ran down her spine.

'What's the matter?'

Niko's abrupt question startled her. 'Nothing,' she returned after a moment of hesitation. And couldn't stop herself from enquiring, 'Are you watching the road?'

His smile was sardonic. 'I am. I've also allowed myself the occasional glance at your profile. You've looked rather downcast since you got into the car.'

'I was thinking of Jordan,' she said, not entirely truthfully.

Why on earth should he be glancing at her? He'd accepted that she wasn't going to make love with him again. Obviously it didn't upset him.

'He'll be all right,' Niko said, his tone revealing complete conviction.

'I know. But occasionally I wonder what would have happened if we hadn't been driving home that night.'

'That's a waste of time.'

'I suppose it is.'

Niko glanced across at her profile—unreadable now, but she had to be thinking of those she had loved and lost in a car smash.

'How is it that Mrs Nixon seems to know everything that's happened in the district? Is she part of some hidden circle that keeps a close watch on everyone?'

'Ugh!' She shivered at the thought. 'No, there's no secret circle of gossipers in Waipuna. It's just that she was born and grew up here, she knows everybody, and she's so kind-hearted that people confide in her. You may have noticed she hasn't said an unkind word about anyone.'

'Is that why you told her we'd made love?'

She swivelled to stare at him, her expression freezing. 'I did not!' she said unevenly.

'Possibly she knows you so well she could guess.' He spoke in the toneless voice she hated, a voice that made it obvious he didn't believe her. 'While you and Petra were exclaiming at the dolphins in the bay, Mrs Nixon took the time to warn me—without actually coming out and saying it in so many words—that you are in a fragile state emotionally.'

Stunned, Elana stared at him. His face was unreadable, the strong lines and angles of his profile forbidding. 'Oh, for heaven's sake!' she said unevenly. 'So from that you assumed I'd opened my girlish heart to confide in her?'

Niko shrugged. 'She's obviously very fond of you, and you of her. Why?'

'Why am I fond of her? Because—'

Without ceremony he cut in, 'Why did you confide in her?'

She drew in a hard, sharp breath. Between her teeth she stated grittily, 'I did not confide anything. Why on earth would I?'

'How would I know?'

Seething, she said crisply, 'She knows me very well. Possibly she may have noticed a slight difference in my attitude to you, or yours to me, and drawn her own conclusions. I can assure you that I do not announce even to my closest friends who I've gone to bed with—especially when I'm regretting my stupidity.'

CHAPTER TEN

As soon as her angry words had left her lips, Elana regretted them. 'Oh, for crying out loud,' she blurted, 'I don't mean—well, you know how I was—afterwards, I mean.' She stopped, took a deep breath and went on more calmly, 'Niko, I wasn't casting aspersions on your prowess as a lover. I'm just regretting I allowed things to go so far.'

Niko negotiated a right-hand bend, then swung the wheel to avoid a large cattle truck taking up more than its share of the road. Elana gasped as the two vehicles passed each other with inches to spare.

Thanking fate that he was now familiar with the road, Niko eased over onto the narrow verge. Once the car had stopped he glanced sideways, took in Elana's colourless face and tightly clamped eyes, and swore silently.

She was shaking, white-knuckled hands clenched in her lap and her soft mouth trembling. He reined in his temper, furious with himself and whatever benighted coincidence had seen to it that they'd met a truck right then.

Elana bit her lip, trying to regain control over her reaction. Her whole body ached, and she felt sick with the aftermath of a sudden flashback to the accident.

And then she felt a hand on hers, warm and strong. Very strong.

What next? she thought crazily, opening her eyes to stare straight ahead.

Niko said quietly, 'I'm sorry. Are you all right?'

She dragged in a quivering breath. 'I—yes.'

'You're shivering.' His hand tightened around hers. 'Of all the damned times to meet a truck...'

'I'm all right.' Until that truck appeared she'd been fine, buoyed into rudeness by an anger she now regretted. 'I'm sorry too,' she added lamely.

'You don't need to be.'

She let out a silent breath and tried to control her trembling body. Voice tight and controlled, she said, 'And I didn't mean what I said.'

He was silent for several heartbeats—a moment that seemed to drag unbearably. 'I accept that you didn't confide in Mrs Nixon. I made the wrong assumption, and I regret it.'

Startled, she glanced up at him. His face was carved from stone, austere and forceful, and to her surprise she found herself saying awkwardly, 'That's all right.'

His mouth relaxed and his sideways glance shimmered with amusement. 'I gather telling her to mind her own business wouldn't work?'

'I'm afraid not,' she said wryly, settling back into the seat as he set the car in motion again.

'I hope I managed to assuage her fears.'

Desperate to change the subject, Elana asked, 'Do you have lots of relatives?'

'Quite a few,' he told her dryly, slowing as they approached a sharp corner. 'Mostly on my mother's side, but cousins and an aunt on my father's. They live in the South Island.'

'Do you have any official position in San Mari?'

Immediately she wished she hadn't asked it. It was no business of hers.

However he didn't seem to think it an impertinence. 'As my mother's son, and a Count of the princedom, I have obligations. My presence is requested at important official occasions, and I have quarters at the palace when I stay there.'

Her pulse still jumping, Elana sat silently while they drove the last few kilometres. Quite a few relatives, and quite a few lovers, too…and at least one of them filled with vengeful regret.

The thought made her stupid heart ache. When the car drew up outside her house, she summoned all her self-control and said, 'Thanks for bringing me home.'

'I'll see you to the door,' he said brusquely.

Only to the door? Some reckless part of her chilled with desolation. *No,* she told herself angrily, *you do* not *want a repeat of the last time he was here.*

Not now, not ever again. Too dangerous by far. And what had seemed inevitable and *right* that night was, in the unforgiving light of hindsight, a shameful memory of her surrender to an uncontrolled and primitive impulse, a surrender so out of character she longed to push it to the furthest corner of her mind, to wipe it completely.

And knew she'd never be able to do that.

'Niko, you don't need to,' she said in what she hoped was a polite instead of fraught voice.

Without answering, he got out, and by the time she'd freed herself from the seatbelt he was opening her door.

And standing altogether too close.

'Thank you,' she said as she charged past him towards the front door, and sanctuary.

Please, just go, she begged silently as she scrabbled to unlock the door. *Before I lose it entirely and make a total idiot of myself.*

From behind, he said abruptly, 'Give me the key.'

'It's all right. I don't know why it's sticking.'

He reached out, and caught her wrist. 'What's the matter?'

'Let me go.'

Instantly he released her. In a different voice he said quietly, 'It's all right, Elana. Calm down.'

At last she got the key in the lock and twisted it, pushing the door open. She took a step into the house and forced herself to turn. He was frowning, his eyes narrowed and intent, his mouth a hard line.

'You are frightened,' he said quietly, stepping back. 'Why? Do you think I might hurt you?'

'Might you?' she demanded, before she had time to think.

He said frigidly, 'I do not hurt women.'

In spite of the telephone call, the utter disgust in his tone almost convinced her he was telling the truth. Too afraid to rely on it, she said, 'I'm not afraid of you.'

Not of him—she was scared of herself. Terrified, in fact. Because she was falling—falling in love with him...

Not only did she not trust him, she couldn't trust herself.

Still frowning, still with that intent, probing gaze, he said, 'Then what is this all about? Yes, I was irritated when I thought you might have confided to Mrs Nixon, but more *for* you than *with* you. Kind-hearted she may be, but she's a gossip. Small country towns are usually pretty conservative—'

'Her gossip is kind-hearted,' Elana said crisply. 'Even if she does suspect that we—that we—' Her mouth dried and her tongue wouldn't move.

'Made love,' he said curtly. 'That's what we did.'

She hurried on, 'Well, even if she suspects it she's not going to spread it around the district. Your reputation will be safe.'

Niko shrugged, his expression impossible to read. 'I don't care about my reputation. I do happen to care about yours.' He stopped. 'You look surprised.'

She was surprised. And strangely touched. Before she could answer he went on, 'You live here and will bear the brunt of gossip, if there is any. I don't want you to suffer for what happened between us.'

Did he too regret those impassioned hours in her bed?

If so, it wasn't nearly as much as she did, her conviction that she wouldn't fall in love with him echoing through her mind like a forlorn hope.

Yet surely this complex feeling—a mixture of fierce need and something else, something she yearned for—couldn't be love. It was too—too headstrong, too compelling...as though she had no control over it or herself any more.

If this was love, she'd never experienced it before.

It took every ounce of willpower to force her voice into steadiness. 'I won't suffer for it. Waipuna people might be conservative, but they won't throw me on a bonfire for indulging in premarital sex.'

And felt a kind of startled pleasure at the way his brows rose.

'Premarital sex?' he asked, in a tone that sent an erotic shiver the length of her spine. 'I prefer the term *making love* myself.'

And he reached for her, his arms closing around her in a grip that would have allowed her to break free easily.

Except that she didn't want to. She couldn't prevent a fiery hunger that should have added to her fears.

Instead it recharged her, infused her with a boldness that held her still in his embrace when he said softly, 'Tell me to go.'

'Why?'

Yes, that was her voice, low and soft.

And eager...

'Only if you want me to go,' Niko said, his voice husky. 'I don't.'

Somewhere, so far in the back of her mind that it had no power, a little voice whispered, *What are you doing?*

She shivered at the hard strength of his body against her, the way his arms tightened around her, as though she were something precious to him.

And then she recalled the hissed warning about his violence, and stiffened.

Instantly his arms loosened, and he stepped back and surveyed her, eyes darkening as she lifted her head and met his gaze—cold, oh, so *cold*...

He said, 'No?'

It took all of her courage to say, 'I'm *sorry*—'

'You don't need to be,' he said, his voice hard. 'And stop looking so appalled—I'm going.'

Niko swivelled and walked away. *What the hell was going on here?*

She'd been like fire in his arms, her eyes smoky and half closed in invitation, her mouth softening in eager anticipation. And then so quickly it had shocked him, that voluptuous surrender had been replaced by something that looked ominously close to panic.

Why? When they'd made love there had been no fear in her, nothing but an ecstatic surrender that had haunted him since.

The thought that she might be afraid appalled him. Had she read something in the media that made her wonder about him? For the first time he found himself regretting his previous lovers. His emotions were churning in a turmoil of astonishment and anger—and something else, a feeling he'd never experienced before. He needed time to work out what was happening.

Elana watched him leave, something cracking painfully inside her. A fierce longing weakened her as his vehicle disappeared around the corner. Turning, she found her way into the house, tears gathering so thickly she had to stop and wipe them away before she could close the door behind her and relax into the silence and familiarity of her home.

Always before the house had meant comfort and safety, but now it seemed alien, a place that held only memories of a life not of her making.

She made herself a cup of tea and sat down with it on the deck, staring sightlessly over the calm waters of the estuary as she told herself she'd done the right thing.

Making love with Niko had been—beyond wonderful. And intensely dangerous.

Thankfully, she'd been able to summon the strength to stick to her decision not to continue being his New Zealand lover. Painfully she wondered how she'd summoned the courage to do it.

And as she drew on her reserves of courage, she found herself wondering if perhaps the woman who'd told her he could be violent might—just *might*—have been trying to cause mischief.

Because each time she'd said no, Niko had accepted her refusal with cool equanimity and no sign of anger. Either the urge to violence was not in his repertoire of emotions, or he was able to control any impulse to hurt when it suited him.

Which?

Tomorrow she'd have to go to Mana and continue work on the documents. Niko would be there. How would he greet her? And why, oh, *why* was she feeling as though all that was good in her life had come to an end?

She'd never felt like this before. Not even when she'd thought she'd been in love with Roland, when she'd allowed herself to dream of a life with him, only to have those dreams dashed.

Compared to the emotions that gripped her now, her previous affair had been pale and emotionless.

Below on the beach a gull called, the shrill sound cutting through the soft purr of tiny waves. She tried to draw strength from the familiarity—the glorious dazzle of sunlight on the water, its golden swathe covering the hills on the other side of the estuary.

No strength came. But it would, she promised herself as she drained her teacup and walked inside. It was totally unfair of fate to dangle such temptation before her, but at least she'd had the strength to resist.

Not that it improved her mood. In the end she set herself to scouring out a cupboard, and then went out into the garden to pull weeds from amongst the vivid clump of valotta bulbs. They'd been her mother's favourite flowers; she'd loved the luminously scarlet flowers fired by sunlight that bloomed when most summer flowers were fading.

The shrill call of the telephone summoned her inside. She arrived there puffing, only to have the breath stop in her throat when she heard Niko's voice.

'I'm leaving shortly,' he said crisply. 'I don't know how long I'll be away. How far have you actually got with the transcribing of documents?'

Trying to match his businesslike tone, she replied, 'I estimate there's about a month's work left. Possibly six weeks, unless we find any more.'

'I'll be in touch. If you need to contact me about anything, email me, OK? Goodbye, Elana.'

'Goodbye, Niko. Travel safely.'

Heart knotting painfully in her chest, Elana hung up.

So that was it. Goodbye.

He'd been totally cool, his voice emotionless, making sure she understood that he'd accepted her decision not to further their relationship.

It was what she wanted—sensible, safe.

But oh, it *hurt*. She had to blink back an onslaught of weak tears.

Well, she'd been hurt before, and got over it. She'd cope. A few hours with a sexy billionaire meant absolutely nothing in the total scheme of things.

Nothing.

Yet during the following weeks Elana felt she was sleepwalking through her life. Fortunately, apart from Mrs Nixon, who asked her anxiously several times if she was entirely well, nobody seemed to notice. Life plodded on while she worked on the Mana documents, arranged flowers in the shop, wrote articles on historic churches in Northland for a magazine, gardened, and endured the grey weeks as they dragged past.

Each night she promised herself that this would be the night she no longer dreamed of Niko Radcliffe, only to wake in the mornings with tears on her cheeks. She and Niko communicated, but each time she saw him on the screen it twisted her heart.

Fran visited, insisting on staying with her for several nights, and told her she needed to eat more and get out into the sun. 'Pale and ethereal is OK, pale and wan is most definitely *not*,' she'd said firmly. 'And you've lost weight.'

'I have not.'

'Well, you look as though you have. What's the matter? Are you in love? Is it not going well?'

Fran's sensible attitude would probably be helpful, but for once, Elana couldn't confide in her. 'I'm fine,' she said stoutly. 'I've been busy—and being shut inside with a stack of old documents is not conducive to getting a decent tan, which is something I've never managed to achieve in my life, as you well know.'

'No, you just go a lovely soft gold colour,' Fran said enviously. She eyed Elana. 'OK, so you're not talking, but you'd better start looking more cheerful or Mum will take you in hand.'

Both touched and irritated, Elana managed a smile. 'I'm shaking already,' she said.

They both laughed, and to her relief Fran said no more.

Once she'd left, Elana admitted to herself that her heart might be suffering—well, perhaps even cracked. But not broken. A one-night stand, however ecstatic, did not—could not—mean she'd fallen in love with Niko Radcliffe.

Surely the longer he stayed away, the easier it would be to conquer this painful longing.

Nobody had mentioned a date for his return, and she wasn't going to ask. When she'd finished the documents at Mana she'd no longer be constantly reminded of Niko.

On the day the schoolchildren arrived to plant more shrubs and trees on the creek banks, now all fenced off from cattle, Patty West met her at the door of the homestead. Smiling, Elana joined her in waving as the small bus went by with a toot and much waving of hands.

'I'd better get to work too,' Elana said. 'Not much longer for me here, either. I'm nearly finished.'

'We'll miss you.' The older woman looked up at the sound of another engine. 'Good, here comes my man. He's got a doctor's appointment and I've got some shopping to do. We'll be back by lunchtime, though.'

'Do you want me to take any calls?'

'I don't think there'll be any, but if you could, thank you.'

An hour later Elana lifted her head as the telephone rang imperatively. 'Mana Station,' she said into the receiver.

'Elana, it's Rangi Moore—the teacher with the planting group.' He sounded harassed. 'I've got a girl here who's not feeling well—she says she's not feeling sick, but I think she almost fainted, and she's certainly very pale. I can't leave the rest of the group on their own, and I can't contact her parents, so can you ask one of the Wests to come and get her, and—wait a minute. Yes, Sarah?'

Elana waited for a few seconds before he said, 'Her parents had to go to see the accountant in Whangarei today. Sarah doesn't know which firm, and her mother's cell phone is turned off. The heat here is really getting to her. If Mrs West could look after her—'

'The Wests aren't here right now, but it's OK, I'll come and collect Sarah. She can come home with me and you can pick her up from my place on your way back to school.'

'That would be great,' he said, clearly relieved. Then, in a different tone, 'Actually, perhaps you should keep her at the homestead? Her parents know we're here. Do they know you?'

Elana blenched. The prospect of managing a sick child in one of the homestead's gloriously rejuvenated rooms was momentarily terrifying until she recalled the loungers out on the veranda. Tucked into one of those in the shade of the grapevine, the girl would be cool and the rooms would be safe. 'No, I don't know them at all, so, OK, the homestead's probably a better idea.'

'You know where we are?'

She glanced out of the window. 'I can see you from here. You're in the gully by the pump shed. I'll be there shortly.'

By the time she arrived in her car both child and teacher were waiting for her. Tall for her twelve or so years and clutching her school bag as though it were a lifeline, the girl had lost all her colour, the freckles on her face standing out like tiny copper coins.

'Hop in,' Elana said, hoping she made it back to the homestead without any untoward incident. Sarah clambered silently into the front seat and remained silent, her eyes closed, while they drove back to the homestead.

Elana switched off the engine. 'Sarah, stay there,' she said, afraid the girl was going to faint. She opened the door and helped Sarah out, catching her as she staggered.

Straightening up, the girl whispered, 'I want to go home.'

Elana hugged her. 'I'm sorry, but we can't contact your parents. As soon as we can, we'll organise things better for you.' She steered her up the steps onto the veranda and towards the lounger. 'Sit there in the shade. I'll get you a pillow and a glass of water.'

Sarah shuddered. 'I don't want a drink, thank you,' she said in a small voice, and almost fell onto the lounger. She lay back and closed her eyes. 'My head's hurting.'

'I'll see if I can get you something to ease it. Have you had headaches before?'

Sarah nodded. 'Mum gives me an aspirin.'

'I've got aspirin in my bag. I'll be back shortly.'

By the time she arrived back with a glass of water, Sarah had regained some colour. She drank the water and swallowed the aspirin, then opened her eyes. 'I can hear a plane—no—a helicopter.'

A sudden rush of delight took Elana by surprise. 'If it's a helicopter it will be Mr Radcliffe,' she said quietly.

Sarah managed a pale smile. 'I like him. Everyone does. He's nice.'

Nice? If she hadn't been so anxious about the girl Elana could have laughed at that description. Niko could be kind, he was certainly protective, and he was a fantastic lover. But nice...? She steadied her voice and said, 'You're looking a bit better now. How's your head?'

'Still banging.' Sarah closed her eyes, but opened them when the helicopter descended onto the landing pad.

Elana kept her gaze on her as she watched it land. Although she was still pale as a wraith, the landing was giving the girl something other to think of than her misbehaving body.

Once the rotors eased back and the noise began to die away, Sarah asked, 'Does Mr Radcliffe fly it himself?'

'I don't know,' Elana said, adding, 'You can ask him—if it is him.'

Sarah said, 'Yes.' And after a moment in a slightly stronger voice, 'Yes, I will.'

Tension tightened Elana's nerves as the chopper door opened and Niko climbed out, a bag in his hand. He strode towards the house, altering direction when he saw them on the veranda.

A swift rush of adrenalin powered through her, filling her with a forbidden, intense delight. Realisation hit her with immense force.

She loved this man. She would love him for ever. If only she could trust him...

He stopped beneath the balustrade and looked at them. 'What's the matter, Sarah?'

Startled, Elana wondered if he knew all of the children by name.

Sarah managed another half-smile and staggered up from the lounger. 'I feel sick.' After a second adding miserably, 'And my head hurts.'

He nodded and stepped up onto the veranda. 'Close your eyes and see if that makes you feel better while Elana and I go inside so she can tell me about it.'

'I think—' Sarah gagged, clapping her hand over her mouth.

Too late. To Elana's horror the child threw up all over Niko, and then burst into tears, shaking uncontrollably.

Niko reached out and patted her shoulder. In a calm, bracing tone, he soothed, 'It's all right, don't worry about it. Elana will take you to the bathroom.'

Stunned, Elana said, 'Come on, Sarah. You'll feel a lot better once you wash your face.'

'There's a shower room inside the back door,' Niko said.

Elana nodded and took the sobbing girl's hand, steering

her along the veranda. Once in the bathroom she provided her with a warm wet face flannel and a glass.

'Just rinse your mouth out with water,' she told Sarah, who was still crying softly.

That done, she checked the girl's clothes, fortunately unaffected by the bout of nausea, before taking her out and coaxing her to lie on another lounger. Once settled, she asked, 'Do you feel at all better?'

'A b-bit.' Sarah opened her eyes to give Elana a scared look. 'I hope he isn't mad at me,' she whispered.

'He won't be,' Elana said, and realised with some shock that she was certain of it.

Why? Because of his calmness and control? Into her mind there flashed the memory of an incident just after she'd started school. She'd been so proud of being trusted to carry a glass of milk for herself, only to trip and tip it over her father. His reaction was seared into her brain. He'd been icily furious, blaming her mother for being stupid enough to give her a glass of milk in the first place, then stripping Elana of all her pride and her confidence.

She'd actually braced herself for a similar reaction from Niko.

And yet, although his response had startled her, deep inside she'd *known* that he wouldn't react as her father had.

Which meant—*what*? What sort of man *was* Niko Radcliffe? Dared she even consider that he might be a man she could respect? A man she could safely allow herself to love?

Be sensible, she told herself curtly, every word of the unknown woman's warning etched into her brain. Tender and considerate he might have been when they'd made love—and then fiercely and intoxicatingly exciting—but that meant only that he'd had plenty of experience.

She walked across to the balustrade and stood for long

moments staring into the sunburst of colour from a mass of daisies in the garden beneath.

A slight sound behind her made her turn. But it wasn't Sarah. She'd dropped off to sleep and the colour was coming back into her cheeks.

It was Niko, clearly showered and in clean clothes, and carrying a shirt in his hand. He surveyed Sarah and smiled. 'I got this just in case, but I see it's not necessary.'

'No, fortunately her clothes escaped the onslaught.'

'Poor kid.'

Sarah stirred, her lashes fluttering, and opened her eyes to direct a startled, shamed look at Niko.

He said, 'You look much better. How do you feel now?'

'M-much better.' She hesitated then blurted, 'I'm so sorry—I didn't mean to—I—I couldn't—'

Niko interrupted, 'Sarah, it's all right. These things happen, and there's nothing you could do about it. I'm very glad you're feeling much better. Stop worrying, OK?'

She gave him a shy smile. 'OK.'

'Good girl.' He transferred his gaze to Elana. 'Where's Patty?'

Elana glanced at her watch. 'She's in Waipuna, but she should be back pretty soon—before lunch, she said.'

'Any minute then,' he said, and looked down at her, smiling. 'And thanks.'

Strangely touched by his smile, she said unsteadily, 'No need for thanks. Now, I think we should try to get Sarah's mum on her cell phone again.'

But it was still turned off. Elana left another message, and hoped that it wouldn't be too long before the woman called back. Without being coaxed, Sarah swallowed a small amount of water, and then went back to sleep.

She woke when Patty West arrived back—clearly surprised to see Niko—and while the housekeeper and Elana were preparing lunch, she sat talking to Niko as though she'd known him all her life, a talk only interrupted by the arrival of the schoolteacher and his group of tree-planting students.

After a swift inspection of the girl the teacher said, 'Thanks a million, Elana, for taking care of her. And thank you, Mr Radcliffe, for being so forbearing.'

Niko shrugged, smiled and held out his hand. 'It was nothing. And my name is Niko.'

Rangi smiled as they shook hands, then turned to look at his charge. 'She looks good enough to be able to come with us now and stay in the sick bay at school until her parents collect her.' He called her over and asked, 'Do you think you can cope with coming to school with us in the bus?'

Sarah looked torn, then nodded. 'I feel all right now,' she said a little shyly, adding, 'Actually, I feel a bit hungry.'

'Better wait until we get to school before you eat anything,' Rangi advised her. He thanked everyone, rounded up his group and shepherded the children into the bus then gave Elana a hug. 'And thank you, Elana, for taking over. See you around.'

The departure of the bus left Elana feeling oddly ill at ease. Niko remained silent as the sound of the engine died away. She glanced up, met cool blue eyes in a face more angular than usual, and said, 'I'd better be off too, and let you get settled.' And added, 'I didn't know you were coming back today.'

CHAPTER ELEVEN

'I WASN'T.' As though the words were torn from him Niko said, 'I had no intention of coming back so soon, but while I was away I discovered something.'

'What?' Elana asked, wondering. 'What did you discover?'

He paused, blue gaze hooded and unreadable. 'Once— after I told you that I was a citizen of both New Zealand and San Mari—you said that it meant I had two places to call home.'

Heart pounding, she nodded, her gaze fixed onto his hard, handsome face. 'I remember.' *I remember everything you ever said to me...*

'I was amused, because neither of them have ever seemed like home.' He paused, then added, 'In fact, I'd never had a place I thought of as home. The palace was huge and cold and impersonal, and my mother made travelling the globe her hobby. Usually without me. Then, when I was eight I went to boarding school.'

Her heart twisted. He must have understood her shocked response because he shrugged. 'Actually, I enjoyed it, but I certainly didn't call it home—nor did I consider the universities I attended to be homes. I spent some of the holidays with my father, but he lived like a bachelor, and for some time we were both wary of each other. We did find some common ground eventually.'

'I'm glad,' she said quietly, neither her expression nor her voice giving away her emotions.

Niko walked across the veranda and stared out over the much tidier garden for a moment, before turning to face her. He was finding this incredibly difficult, but he needed to tell her what he meant.

Calling on an icy control, he said in a clipped, hard voice, 'While I was away this time I discovered that you— that you mean home to me.'

The words jangled meaninglessly around her brain. She swallowed and croaked, 'What—what are you saying?'

His smile held no humour, and he didn't move. 'I have no idea how it happened, or when—but wherever you are is more home to me than any of the houses I own, either of the two countries I am a citizen of.'

Hope and a fearful happiness burst into flame in her heart. 'Niko, I don't understand.'

'It's quite simple. When I left Mana I finally discovered what love is,' he said, blue gaze fixed on her face. 'It's missing someone so intensely that you dream of them...'

All colour left her skin. Dumbly, eyes more gold than green, she nodded.

He took a step towards her, ready to catch her if she should faint. 'Ah, so you already know that,' he said harshly.

Her lips trembled and he waited, but no words came.

He resumed, 'And it's remembering little unimportant things—the way you lift your chin when you're telling me you don't need looking after, your laughter, refusing to have whisky in your tea after Jordan's accident, the warmth of your skin when we made love, the sound of your voice...'

He paused, but she still didn't speak. 'That's when I re-alised that every time I thought about returning to Mana my spirits lifted enormously.' He stopped, hard blue gaze kindling. 'Because you are here.'

A stunned, disbelieving joy held Elana prisoner. She stared at him, wondering if he meant it, but could find no words to answer. At the back of her mind was fear—a fear she had to deal with.

Still Niko didn't move. Harshly he said, 'Each time we spoke together on the computer, each time I saw you on the screen, I missed you more. I know that missing you every second of every day that I'm away from you is going to be part of my life from now on. I've never felt like that before, and it scares the hell out of me.'

'Scares you?' she whispered, and shook her head. 'I can't believe—'

'Believe it,' he broke in, his voice rough with emotion. 'I want to be with you—wherever you are—because without you my life will lose most of its meaning.'

Elana closed her eyes against the fears rioting through her mind. Did she have the courage to trust the instinct that told her he was no abuser? Memories of him—of his kindness, of consideration, of the times he'd helped her—were they enough?

Quietly he said, 'There's something you're afraid of. What is it, Elana? Do you think I'm like your father? Tell me what it is and we'll work it out together.'

After swallowing to ease her parched throat she said hoarsely, 'My father—how did you know about him?'

His smile was filled with irony. 'Mrs Nixon, who else? Your mother confided in her.'

Shocked and sickened, she felt the heat drain from her face. 'Why—?' Gripped by an intense sensation of betrayal, she couldn't go on.

He shrugged. 'She saw more than I gave her credit for. She thought I should know. And she was right.'

'But *why*?'

He paused, then said roughly, 'I suspect she was worried that I might hurt you. I'm very grateful to her. We might have gone on misunderstanding each other for months if she hadn't warned me. What was your father like?'

She swallowed. 'He hit my mother.'

Niko's shock was followed by disgust and a cold rage that threatened to overwhelm him. 'Did he beat you?'

'No. But I knew what he was doing. I was terrified of him.'

He said something in what must have been the language of San Mari. 'How long did this go on for?'

'My mother ran away with me when I was five. But he found us about a month later, and came after us and hauled me into the car. My mother rang the police but—he rammed the car into a tree. He was killed. I had a broken arm, but I was all right apart from that.' She shivered. 'He was going to kill me. He knew that would be the worst thing he could do to my mother.'

Niko fought back horror. 'His own child,' he said quietly. And before she could answer, he went on, 'I am so sorry that you had to endure such terror.'

Wild thoughts jostled through her mind. She said indistinctly, 'And then I stupidly had a bad experience with a man a couple of years ago.'

'You need to sit down.' He spoke between his teeth, cursed by a jealousy so fierce he couldn't say more, then pulled a chair out and held it while she automatically obeyed. Lowering himself onto the sofa, he asked, 'Do you want to talk about it?'

She sent him an astonished glance. 'No, but at least he wasn't physically abusive. I thought I loved him, but he was—he was a control freak. I got tired of being ordered about and treated like a halfwit. I had to tell him where I was all the time, he expected me to do what I was told.'

Niko shook his head. 'Trusting a man must be very

difficult for you. If I'd known, I'd have been more under-standing.' He got up and walked across to the window, silhouetted against the luminous light outside. Without turning around he said, 'I knew you'd do a good job of working with the Mana documents, but I offered you the job mainly because I couldn't get you out of my head.'

Elana heard the words, but couldn't make sense of them. He turned, and she stared into his face, honed into arro-gant angles as though what he was saying was bitter pun-ishment.

Abruptly he said, 'At first I was certain it was lust—simple, basic, easily controlled.'

He stopped as though expecting her to say something, but no words came to her tongue. She didn't dare believe she'd heard correctly.

Resuming, his voice harsh, he said, 'I assumed that the hunger would go away, that familiarity would breed—oh, not contempt, never that—but boredom. Because that's what's happened before.' His smile held no humour. 'I thought I was like my mother. She fell quickly and easily in love, and out of it just as quickly, just as easily. When I was young I had the misfortune to catch the eye of the sister of one of my friends. It became embarrassing, and in the end I had to tell her that I didn't love her, that we were too young to even think of marrying. She tried to commit suicide.'

Elana braced herself. She didn't want to hear this—hated the thought of it, but she realised it was important to him.

'She didn't succeed, thank the saints, and is now hap-pily married,' he continued, still in that level, emotion-less voice. 'I decided I was too much like my mother to be trusted with the emotions of anyone innocent and un-sophisticated. But the first time I saw you I wanted you.

And every time I saw you it got stronger. And my emotions changed in ways I'd never experienced before.'

Stunned, Elana told him, 'I'm not so young, and I don't consider myself unsophisticated.'

'So if I'd suggested an affair with you—one without marriage—you'd have accepted?'

He waited while she digested this. For the first time in his life he was desperately afraid. Her face was expressionless, and she ran a shaky hand through her bright hair as she met his gaze, her green-gold gaze veiled by long lashes.

When she finally answered her voice was thin. 'No,' she admitted, her painful reluctance obvious. 'I was too afraid. As you said, I don't trust easily.'

He nodded. 'Then we made love. And—it was—it was new and shining and—something I'd never experienced. And I was elated because it was good for you too. Only afterwards you were bluntly clear that you had no intention of furthering our relationship. Yet even then I kept hoping that you'd relent.'

He waited as though expecting an answer, but she couldn't find any words. In the end he said, 'When Mrs Nixon confided in me about your father, I began to understand, but I didn't know how to deal with the situation. And I didn't know exactly what I felt for you. I intended to stay away for at least six months and do some serious thinking. But I missed you.' He paused, then went on harshly, 'Hell, that's such a *stupid* term. *Missed* you—I ached for you, I longed for you, I recalled every word you'd ever said to me, I looked forward to our talks on the VOIP with eagerness, and I dreamed of you when I slept.'

'But you were already with—' She stopped, and drew in a deep breath, then finishing, 'You had a partner when you came here. You sent her flowers—'

'They were a farewell gesture; we'd already broken up.

And I broke it off because I'd met you. I cursed the fact that you were in the shop that day, but in a way I was relieved. I had never felt like that before, and I resented it.' He paused. 'You did too, didn't you?'

'I—well, yes.' And because he was being honest with her, she confessed, 'I suppose I used that, and—something else—as a buffer, a reason not to—'

After several seconds, he said quietly, 'Tell me, Elana. A reason not to do what?'

She realised her hands were twisting together, and stilled them. Although she didn't know what he was offering, and didn't know whether or not she dared accept it, she knew she had to be honest.

'Not to fall for you,' she said harshly. 'Not to trust you.'

'Was it so hard?'

'I—yes.'

He said, 'I can understand your fear. But I don't know how to deal with it. I can promise you that I am no abuser, but how can I expect you to take my word for it?'

'It's not just that,' she said hoarsely.

'Then what?' He paused, then said harshly, 'If you want me to get out of your life, tell me now.'

Her eyes filled with tears. She turned away to hide them, and was instantly enveloped in his arms, held against his strength, his voice reverberating in her ears as he said, 'Tell me, Elana.'

She muttered, 'It—I don't know that I can.' Then drew in a breath. 'All right.'

And told him of the telephone call she'd taken. His arms didn't loosen, and she felt every muscle in his body tighten as she spoke of the woman who'd told her he could be violent.

When her voice died away he was silent for long moments. Tensely she waited.

After what seemed an eon he said quietly, 'I know who

that was. When we broke up she threatened to go to the press with accusations of violence unless I paid her off. I told her I'd sue if she did.'

His arms dropped and he took a step back, eyes hard and a muscle flicking beside his jaw.

Chilled, Elana stared up into a face devoid of expression.

Bleakly he said, 'With your family history I understand why you find it difficult to trust. I can't prove that I'm not a violent man. Just as she can't prove that I am. I can only hope that you know me well enough to trust me.'

'But I don't know you very well at all,' she protested. And then caught her breath. 'And you don't really know me. I—I wouldn't fit into your life.'

'Why do you say that? You fit perfectly into my life.'

'This isn't your real life,' she said on a half-sob.

'Of course it is.' He took a step towards her, then stopped. In a raw voice he said, 'I won't touch you. *You* must make this decision.'

Wrenched by conflicting emotions, she stared at him, her heart in her eyes. 'I don't—I can't believe that you want me.'

'Believe it,' he said tersely. 'I want you, and I love you. I don't know how it happened, or even why, and believe me, I resisted it. But I know now that it's love. I must have fallen in love with you that first night at the ball. You were so brave when we came upon young Jordan, and you gave him every encouragement. I was impressed. And I was jealous of your policeman friend—stupidly.' He paused. 'Elana, if this isn't love, I don't know what is. I do know that it's driving me crazy. If you don't want this from me, tell me now and I'll go and never come back.'

Heart aching, so tense she couldn't formulate any words, she watched him turn away, until his name broke from her lips.

He stopped. For several seconds her future weighed heavily on her, until she gained the courage to say, 'Niko, wait—'

He swung around, and looked at her, nakedly importunate. 'Your decision,' he said.

And in that moment she knew. 'Don't go,' she said, and took a step towards him.

He froze. 'You're sure?'

On another half-sob she whispered, 'I'm not sure of anything, but I'm not a coward either.'

'Far from it,' he said, his voice tender, and reached for her. 'I swore I wouldn't do this, that it wouldn't be fair, but I can't—I don't—' he said roughly, then kissed her, gently at first, followed by kisses of such sweet fierceness that an answering wildness leaped up within her and she responded without fear, with no thought but for this passionate delight.

Finally he lifted his head, and looked down, eyes gleaming, his expression taut, and held her for long moments until her heart eased into a regular beat. When her breathing steadied, he said, 'Elana?'

She said clumsily, 'I love the way you say my name. And I love you.'

'I know that,' he said, and laughed when she lifted her head and fixed him with what she hoped was an indignant glare.

He sobered, and released her, but didn't step away. 'It's a matter of trust for both of us,' he said quietly. 'My parents' marriage wasn't a good model. I think my father loved my mother until he died. There were no other women in his life. But she couldn't cope with his life.'

'That's so sad,' Elana whispered.

'She decided she wasn't suited to marriage, so after she left him she had affairs.' He shrugged. 'And I've spent a fair amount of my adult life fending off women who look at me and see money, with all its benefits. You didn't.'

'How do you know?'

He was silent a moment. Then he said, 'I knew from the first that you were very aware of me. But always there was a barrier, a reserve. You weren't casting any lures. And cynic that I am, I wondered if that was a clever move on your part to whet my appetite. Then we made love.'

Elana drew a sharp breath and held it.

'It blew my mind.' He paused, that humourless smile playing around his lips. 'And then you made it obvious you weren't going to repeat it. You still stayed aloof, and I wondered again if you were just a little more clever than most of my other would-be lovers.' On a steely note he stated, 'Who were not as many as Mrs Nixon's gossip magazine writers suggest.'

'I'm glad,' she muttered, still bewildered by his confession, torn between intense joy and a deep-seated fear.

'I got an indication of the reason you were so distant that day at the restaurant when you and Petra watched the dolphins, and Mrs Nixon warned me off.'

She nodded, but couldn't find the right words to reply, and he continued, 'She clearly felt it was important. So I had your past checked out.'

Elana stiffened, and wrenched herself free, fixing him with a smouldering glare. 'And what,' she enquired starkly, 'did you find out?'

'Basically what you told me. That you and your mother spent time in a refuge after she left him, and that he was killed driving away with you.'

She shivered at the harshness of his tone, and he reached for her. Voice deep and sure, he said, 'I can't promise to be the perfect husband, but—what's the matter?'

'Husband?' Stunned, she closed her eyes. 'I don't—'

Niko made a muffled noise that could have been a laugh

or a groan. Or a combination of both. 'I'm making a total mess of this.' His voice deepened. 'Bear with me, please— it's the first time I've ever proposed to anyone, and it will be the last. I love you, Elana. I want you to be my wife, I want to be your husband. I want to make love with you, make delectable babies with you, quarrel with you, listen to you laugh every day and hear you breathing beside me every night. I want to show you my father's station in the South Island, and as many takehe birds as you want to see. I want us to celebrate anniversaries and buy each other fabulous presents. But more than anything, I hope you want those things too.' He paused a second, before adding, 'If you do happen to want all those things, then please put both of us out of our misery.'

She choked on a laugh mingled with a burst of tears, and whispered, 'Yes.'

'Yes what?'

'Yes to everything.'

And at last he kissed her, and she knew that she trusted him, loved him, would always love him and that she need have no fears for their future together.

EPILOGUE

'PANIA, SWEETHEART, TRY not to make so much noise.' Elana dropped a kiss on her daughter's nose, and was rewarded by a chuckle and a kiss on her own chin.

'But I'm the birthday girl, I'm seven years old today,' Pania said pertly. 'I'm allowed to be happy.'

'Happiness can be quiet, you know, and any more of that yelling is only going to wake the baby, and you know what will happen then.'

'Crying—lots of it,' Pania's brother Kent stated succinctly, ruffling her crown of blonde hair. 'And anyway, you're still a baby, Pania. I'm nearly nine.'

'You're only eight years and a half,' his sister asserted, pulling a face at him. 'When is Daddy coming? Does he know it's my birthday today?'

'Of course he does. He should arrive—' Elana stopped. 'Ah yes, what can I hear?'

Pania gave another squeal of pure joy, and ran to the window with the best view of the landing pad. 'It's the helichopper! Look, look, there it is.'

Both children peered across the garden, watching the helicopter as it landed, then raced from the room and down the stairs. Elana waited a moment, and when no wail emanated from the baby's crib she followed them.

Niko had been busy for the past week at what was now

his head office in Auckland, organising everything so their holiday at Mana would be uninterrupted.

She walked across the lawn towards the gate, noting that Kent grabbed Pania's hand before they reached it so she couldn't speed through into the forbidden landing pad. He was already showing signs of being every bit as protective—and autocratic—as his father.

And Pania, with her head of bright hair and her soft heart, reminded her sometimes of her mother. Their little Cara, five months old, was an unexpected gift. She had Niko's black hair and startlingly blue eyes.

Smiling, Elana watched as he got down from the helicopter and strode towards them.

Ten years previously she'd put all her trust in her instinct and her love for him. And she'd never regretted it. He'd shown her how magnificent a marriage of loving hearts could be.

He came towards her, a child hanging from each hand, his face alight with pleasure. 'Elana, darling girl, it's good to be back home,' he said, and kissed her.

Hand in hand they walked back to the homestead, and into their future, the future they had made together.

* * * * *

MILLS & BOON

Coming next month

IMPRISONED BY THE
GREEK'S RING
Caitlin Crews

Atlas was a primitive man, when all was said and done. And whatever else happened in this dirty game, Lexi was his.

Entirely his, to do with as he wished.

He kissed her and he kissed her. He indulged himself. He toyed with her. He tasted her. He was unapologetic and thorough at once.

And with every taste, every indulgence, Atlas felt.

He felt.

He, who hadn't felt a damned thing in years. He, who had walled himself off to survive. He had become stone. Fury in human form.

But Lexi tasted like hope.

"This doesn't feel like revenge," she whispered in his ear, and she sounded drugged.

"I'm delighted you think so," he replied.

And then he set his mouth to hers again, because it was easier. Or better. Or simply because he had to, or die wanting her.

Lexi thrashed beneath him, and he wasn't sure why until he tilted back his head to get a better look at her face. And the answer slammed through him like some kind of cannonball, shot straight into him.

Need. She was wild with need.

And he couldn't seem to get enough of it. Of her.

The part of him that trusted no one, and her least of all, didn't trust this reaction either.

But the rest of him—especially the hardest part of him—didn't care.

Because she tasted like magic and he had given up on magic long, long time ago.

Because her hands tangled in his hair and tugged his face to hers, and he didn't have it in him to question that.

All Atlas knew was that he wanted more. Needed more.

As if, after surviving things that no man should be forced to bear, it would be little Lexi Haring who took him out. It would be this one shockingly pretty woman who would be the end of him. And not because she'd plotted against him, as he believed some if not all of her family had done, but because of this. Her surrender.

The endless, wondrous glory of her surrender.

Continue reading
**IMPRISONED BY THE
GREEK'S RING**
Caitlin Crews

Available next month
www.millsandboon.co.uk

LET'S TALK
Romance

For exclusive extracts, competitions
and special offers, find us online:

f facebook.com/millsandboon

O @millsandboonuk

Y @millsandboon

Or get in touch on 0844 844 1351*

For all the latest titles coming soon, visit
millsandboon.co.uk/nextmonth